PRAISE FOR LUCINDA BRANT

'Brant has carved a niche for herself in this particular patch of history and she is gifted in weaving both story and history into a compelling read.'
Fiona Ingram, *Readers Favorite*

'Witty prose and well-researched context, skillfully drawn characters you'll be captivated by, are the main features in her style.'
Maria Grazia Spila, *Fly High*

'True talent is when an author creates an in-depth backstory of intricately woven together complicated characters and events and yet the reader starts on page one, right in the middle of the action and is none the wiser to the author's machinations, only having eyes for what is happening on each and every page, eagerly turning to the next.'
Eliza Knight, *History Undressed*

'Brant has a deft palette of historical detail which contributes to a strong backbone for the narrative. The characters are larger than life and its not hard to read with a visual image in mind. Brant's writing is filled with freshness and wit... highly recommended.'
Prudence J. Batten, *Mesmered's Blog*

'Once again I am in awe of Lucinda's originality to go outside of the norm and use historical moments to create an elaborate story.'
Crystal, *For Your Amusement: My Life*

'Grab a glass of wine, a quiet corner and plan to read the night away. The intricate web that Lucinda Brant constructs with a most amazing cast of characters is sure to keep you mesmerized.'
SWurman, *Night Owl Reviews*

Autumn Duchess

A GEORGIAN HISTORICAL ROMANCE

Roxton Series Book 3

LUCINDA BRANT

FOR
MELISSA & AMAYA

One

He saw her from across the ballroom.

A striking beauty was staring straight at him.

Jonathon brought himself up short and stared back.

He couldn't help himself.

He could count on three fingers the occasions he had crossed paths with exquisite feminine beauty that it stopped the breath in his throat; twice on the Indian subcontinent, once in the East Indies, and now here, this very minute, in this ballroom, on this green wet island. So it was only natural he should give himself the leisure to drink her in. His admiring gaze wandered from her honey-blonde hair that fell in heavy ringlets over one bare shoulder, to the porcelain skin of her décolletage glowing flawless against the bottomless black of her gown. He would not have been male had his gaze not lingered on her ample breasts, barely contained in a square cut bodice. He tried to find fault with her heart-shaped face, with the small straight nose and determined chin, and with her unusually oblique eyes, but what was there to fault?

Smiling to himself, he fancied everything he saw, and everything he could not he was sure was just as alluring.

He wondered at her age. Not that it mattered. It was a game he played to pass the time at social functions such as this. Dressed all in black and wearing no jewelry about her slender throat or wrists he supposed she was a widow, and thus not in the first flush of youth.

What was a widow doing here?

His fascination increased tenfold.

For all his limited experience of the London social scene, Jonathon knew well enough that widows did not attend social gatherings of this sort, particularly not such a renowned event at the height of the Season. Perhaps her mourning was almost at an end and she was chaperoning one of the young things here tonight? Surely, she was not old enough to have a daughter of marriageable age? Jonathon pulled a face. For some unfathomable reason he did not like the idea that she may have been a child-bride.

Why was she staring at him?

She stood so still, with her hands clasped in front of her, as if she was a statue carved of alabaster draped in black cloth; as much a fixture of the ballroom as a blazing chandelier or the enormous, richly woven tapestry hanging behind her. And so it seemed when dancers began pairing up and passed her as if she was indeed no more than part of the furniture. Why? Perhaps she was so well known in Society that her incredible beauty was taken for granted? In a ballroom awash with beautiful young things draped in silks of soft creams, pinks, and blues, she was a real head-turner.

Jonathon found it impossible not to stare.

He watched as some of the guests even went so far as to go out of their way not to look at her, passing in a wide arc, eyes fixed forward or down to the polished floorboards. The one or two young ladies who did cast a curious, furtive glance in the beauty's direction were instantly reprimanded in furious undertones by parents and guardians alike and quickly cast their gaze away, heads hung, as if in shame at having committed a grave transgression.

Why was she being deliberately avoided?

Why did no one acknowledge her?

Why did no one stop and talk to her?

Why was she being neglected?

It burned him up to see her alone and forsaken.

It was unlikely the beauty had a sordid past or lived openly as some lucky nobleman's mistress for she wouldn't have been invited amongst this august company. The Duke of Roxton was an incorruptible prude and devoted family man, a rare bird amongst his preening peers. The King couldn't praise the Duke's example highly enough; a compliment that was so much sniggered about in Society drawing rooms that even Jonathon, just six months in the capital, had heard it repeated often enough. Whatever the reason for her social ostracism, it was of supreme indifference to him. He was determined to make her acquaintance, curiosity and allure compelled him.

A burst of wild laughter close by brought him out of his reverie. Tommy would know the beauty's identity and her story. He always had the latest gossip. Collecting social minutiae that families desperately tried to suppress was Tommy Cavendish's favorite pastime, second only to eating. And so with no regard for the two turbaned dowagers who were filling Lord Cavendish's insatiable appetite for scandal with the latest wicked crumbs, Jonathon caught at the stiff skirts of the nobleman's frockcoat and unceremoniously pulled him backwards to stand at his side.

"Tommy! Tommy, attend me!" he demanded without taking his gaze from the beauty. "She's in widow's drapery and she's being ignored. Why? What is she doing here?"

"Good Lord, don't tell me one of the fairer sex has finally piqued your interest? Bravo! Who, old dear?" asked his lordship, a wave of his lace handkerchief to the departing dowagers who flounced off in disgust at being so rudely interrupted by a tanned colossus of undetermined social consequence. He hurriedly plastered his quizzing glass to a watery eye and swept an eager roving stare out across the ballroom, the first minuet of the evening underway, before running his eye down to Jonathon's large feet, then up to his head of thick, shoulder-length hair. "Are you truly six feet *four* inches?"

Jonathon pulled the quizzing glass out of Lord Cavendish's chubby fingers and let it drop loose on its riband. "Have done with that silly affectation, Tommy. And that hideous black patch, if that's what it is, is also beyond enough. A wart at best."

"Brute," Lord Cavendish responded without offence as he touched the corner of his mouth with a fat pinkie to reassure himself the heart-shaped mouche remained in place. "Those of us who can't be Samsons must attract Delilahs in other ways."

"Patch and paint doesn't do it for you, Tommy. Trust me. What would Kitty say?"

Lord Cavendish shrugged and patted his portly belly, very snug in its tight-fitting Chinoiserie silk waistcoat. "*M'wife?* Told me to wear a half-moon rather than a heart, and at the temple not the mouth. But what would dearest Kitty know about patches and paint? And, I'm not the one who needs a wife—"

"Tommy, don't start."

Lord Cavendish pretended ignorance and swept a silken arm out towards the crowd gathered on the edge of the dance floor. "Start? My dear friend, the bridal campaign started in earnest months back, if you hadn't noticed. And where better to find a nice little wife than at this esteemed gathering. Pick of the grapes, this bunch. No one with a relative below the rank of Viscount and it's not as if you have to marry money. There's a few dainty dishes with a pedigree as long as *your* arm and no funds to match. Kitty thinks—"

"No, Tommy! *No.*"

"—that there are at least five delicious puddings for you to choose from; all in their early twenties and in their second Season. Although, I wouldn't discount the Porter-Lewisham pikelet, even if she is eighteen."

"*Eighteen?*" Jonathon was revolted. His daughter was just nineteen years old. He turned his portly friend's shoulder towards the dance floor. "Attend, Tommy! The beauty over there. Who is she?"

Lord Cavendish fumbled for his quizzing glass.

"Where is this vision of loveliness, this delectable éclair that has whet your manly appetite?"

"Not over *there*. Over *here*," Jonathon said impatiently. "To my left. The tapestry. She's staring straight at me."

Lord Cavendish made another sweep of the ballroom with his magnified eye, careful not to linger on any particular pretty face for more than a few seconds, but if there was an eligible beauty amongst the press of silk petticoats and fluttering fans, he could not discover her; pretty, yes, but no female so striking as to cause his tall friend to get steamed up under his cravat, unless... No! His smile remained fixed but his brow furrowed. He glanced up at Jonathon and followed his unblinking gaze... *Oh God. No.* He mentally gulped and let drop the quizzing glass, mouth at half-cock, and mumbled something unintelligible. It was a few moments before he found his voice, long enough for Jonathon to witness two dour faced creatures, both dressed in dove-gray silk and with all the charisma of strong-armed jailers, approach the beauty from behind to stand two paces back on either side of her. They reminded him of a couple of gargoyles. The almost imperceptible way in which the beauty squared her snowy white shoulders told him she was aware of their presence and that they were an unwarranted intrusion. But she did not speak, nor did she look at them.

His assessment of these women was justified when a gentleman carrying two glasses of champagne staggered out of the refreshment room, skirted the dance floor ringed with onlookers, and headed straight for the beauty. He lifted both glasses in the air as he twirled this way and that to avoid spilling a precious drop of bubbly, and came face to face with one of the humorless gargoyles who stepped forward and waylaid him before he could get within ten feet of their mistress. He was quietly taken in hand by two liveried footmen, who appeared from the crowd as if from thin air, and was marched away, champagne soaking the front of his canary-yellow frockcoat.

"Well?" he demanded of Lord Cavendish as the Countess of Strathsay curtsied low before the beauty and then rose up to speak a few words. "Who is she that such a sanctimonious stickler for breeding and rank as the Lady Strathsay curtseys until her long nose scrapes the floorboards?"

Tommy Cavendish's mouth was still forming words but then it fixed itself in a tight smile and he tapped Jonathon's arm with the edge of his quizzing glass. "Strang! You cunning steak and kidney pie. For a moment you had me believing you. You can't bamboozle me that easily."

"I'm not. I've never seen her before tonight and I want to know who she is so I don't make a fool of myself upon first introduction. Your contribution would be much appreciated but I will do without it if I must."

Lord Cavendish's usual bonhomie evaporated. He wished Kitty with him. His wife would know how to explain matters much better than he.

"Ah... Yes... Should've realized. She doesn't go out in society any more. Damn shame, if you ask me. Damn waste of a beautiful woman."

"Well?" Jonathon repeated rudely. He watched Lady Strathsay take her leave, shuffling backwards a few feet before turning and abandoning the beauty to the watchful eye of the two gargoyles. "Come on, Tommy. If she's a recluse she could up and leave this claustrophobic social get-together at any moment. So out with it before I lose patience and take the plunge and ask her to dance without the benefit of your assistance."

Lord Cavendish shook his powdered head.

"No, Strang. You do not want to go over there. It will be very bad for you if you do. Believe me, by going over there you'll certainly make a fool of yourself. You'll be boiled mutton for broth before you can be minced for steak tartar." When Jonathon gave a huff of disbelief, his lordship sighed and dropped his quizzing glass to say without artifice, "Strang. Trust me in this. Deb Roxton has favored your dearest Sarah-Jane with her patronage. The Duchess doesn't favor all her Cavendish relatives. Such noble benefaction is not to be scorned. If your daughter is to bag a baronet at the very least, you want to avoid incurring the Duke's displeasure at all costs. Believe me, you, like the rest of us red-blooded males, must admire that divine beauty from afar."

Jonathon was unimpressed. He stared out across the noble bewigged and powdered heads gathering in the vast ballroom and caught sight of the very nobleman whom they were discussing. He watched the Duke make his way through the crowd to come stand beside the beauty. She reached no higher than His Grace's shoulder and, Jonathon suspected, this in heels. The Duke inclined his head, took out his snuffbox and said a few words to which the beauty did not respond. Finally, she turned and tilted her chin up at him, gave a response, and flicked open her fan of black feathers with a quick agitated movement. After an exchange that lasted a few minutes she dared to turn her bare shoulder on the Duke to look the other way. His Grace remained at her side, watching the dancers with an enigmatic smile, and by the inclination of his head he was continuing to talk to her under his breath despite being deliberately ignored. It was Jonathon's opinion that one would have to be blind not to see the impenetrable wall of ice bricks that separated these two.

"If the man who offers for Sarah-Jane is spineless enough to put his Grace of Roxton's good opinion of him before his love for my daughter, then I do not wish Sarah-Jane to be so favored."

Lord Cavendish threw up a lace-ruffled hand in defeat.

"You always were an unashamed romantic." He sighed. "And the family had to wonder why Emily ran off with a penniless second son of a second son who worked for the India Company. Ha!"

"The name of the beauty at Roxton's elbow, Tommy."

"What about your quest to have the Strang-Leven inheritance returned? Put the Duke offside and you can throw the ancient ancestral pile and Sarah-Jane's marriage prospects out with the stock pot!"

Jonathon gave a grunt, annoyed. He hadn't spent twenty years sweating it out on the subcontinent making a fortune for his plans to slip out of from under him now before he'd had a chance to fully persuade the Duke of his moral obligations to return what rightfully belonged to the Strang-Levens. So he wasn't about to tread lightly on the off chance he might offend the Duke and thus ruin his daughter's chances of marrying into the nobility.

"Sarah-Jane can find herself a titled husband in Edinburgh just as easily as she can scuffing her silk mules on these noble floorboards."

Lord Cavendish was shocked. "Strang! A *Scottish* lord? One might as well say Macbeth to an actor!"

"Do stop the French cook theatrics, Tommy, and tell me the beauty's name."

Lord Cavendish avoided the question. "Kitty is a remarkable woman," he said and touched his eyeglass to his nose knowingly. "Has the ear of the Duchess. But that's between you, me and the saucepan, old dear."

Jonathon cocked an eyebrow. "Well, *old dear*, the saucepan knows more than I, so out with it!"

"It should please you to know that Roxton is rather ambivalent about your long-lost inheritance, particularly the Hanover Square residence. He's bought a larger, more palatial house on the edge of Hyde Park which better suits his growing brood and, so say the cynics, puts more distance between his dukedom and the nefarious past of previous title-holders. As for Crecy Hall... It's said he's in a dilemma about the Elizabethan turreted terror; his words not mine. As you know, the house was let go to ruin and unfit for habitation, that is until five years ago, when the old Duke, breathing his last, decided to restore Crecy to its former glory."

Jonathon was surprised enough to take his gaze from the beauty to look down at Tommy Cavendish. "For God's sake, *why?*"

"Hold on to the cream in your éclair," Lord Cavendish ordered and continued *sotto voce*. "This Duke of Roxton sees himself as a morally upright nobleman and thus once the true nature of the acquisition of the Strang-Leven inheritance was made known to him by your lawyers, holding on to Hanover Square and the Elizabethan manor does not sit well with our Duke's high principles."

Jonathon was surprised. "Is that so? The clouds part yet again and the sun shines through. And? There's more to tell. Your painted lips are twitching."

Lord Cavendish rocked on his heels. "But what the Duke feels and thinks is here-nor-there to your cause, I'm afraid. It is the Duke's French mamma who will be your undoing because it was for her the old Duke restored Crecy, as a dower house in her widowhood. And that is where she took up residence on his death three years ago. And so it is *Antonia*, Duchess of Roxton you must not only persuade Crecy should be returned to the Strang-Levens but also whom you must *evict*."

"Roxton's *mother?*" Jonathon rolled his eyes to the ornate ceiling, muttering, "A cantankerous old widow to contend with, and French into the bargain! *Fabuleux. Un malheur n'arrive jamais seul!* The weather is ever cold in this country and now it turns frigid." He let out a sigh and squared his shoulders, giving Tommy Cavendish a nudge as he returned his gaze to the beauty, who said something to the Duke over a bare shoulder that made the nobleman clench his snuffbox and shut his mouth hard. That they were arguing couldn't be more obvious had they been shouting insults at each other from opposite sides of the ballroom. "So who is she, Tommy, that Roxton dares let off steam in public?"

Lord Cavendish made a noise in his throat that greatly resembled the sound of a startled pheasant. He coughed into his fist politely to find his voice.

"The—um—beauty who has aroused your lust is the Duke's—Lord! I can't *believe* the first female to heat your blood since your return to England is the Duke's—"

"—cousin? Sister, distant third cousin, poor relation—"

"Antonia, Duchess of Roxton. The cantankerous old widow as you so amusingly put it."

Jonathon swallowed hard.

"I'll be damned," he muttered in utter disbelief.

"And so you will be if you go near her."

Jonathon cleared his raw throat.

"She's not old enough, Tommy. Roxton must be my vintage if he's a day."

"We were at Eton together. He's turned thirty. His grizzled locks and the fact his mother is cursed with being absurdly youthful for her years don't help."

Jonathon frowned his distaste. "Child-bride?"

"Do you doubt it? She was snatched from the schoolroom. The fifth Duke was a notorious rake who reformed for her. They were devoted to one another until his death. Enough said." Lord Cavendish waved to a gentleman across the room who was making exaggerated head movements in the direction of the refreshment room. "Time to move on, Strang. Cards, conversation and comfits await us through those archways, and I for one intend to enjoy what's on offer."

Jonathon stayed him, gaze still very much riveted to the Duchess. "Tell me you're hoodwinking me, Tommy. Tell me the truth. Tell me that such an extraordinarily beautiful woman has no blood connection to Roxton. Tell me, Tommy."

Lord Cavendish let out a heavy sigh. "I wish I could. I cannot."

"Then tell me what you do know."

"Will you have done staring openly at her," Lord Cavendish hissed, pulling at Jonathon's velvet cuff. "Roxton's glanced at us twice already, and no wonder with your eyes glued covetously to his mother. He's damned protective of her, and who can blame him? The old Duke's death signaled open season on his much younger wife. Her incredible beauty is matched only by her personal wealth, an inheritance left her by the old Duke to do with as she sees fit; the Strang-Leven inheritance amongst those riches, old dear. Roxton's hands are tied while she is alive. So you see why he keeps her in a gilded cage. Well, that's the line…"

"And the unauthorized version?" When this was met with silence, Jonathon forced himself to look away from the Duchess, down at Lord Cavendish's frowning countenance. "Oh, come on, Tommy! Tell me and then you're free to stuff yourself from the buffet tables with abandon."

His lordship sighed. "You're doggedly persistent."

He again took up his quizzing glass to pretend an interest in the dancing, for not only was the Duke regarding them under heavy brows but those who milled about on the edge of the dance floor were beginning to turn heads in their direction and whisper behind fluttering fans and perfumed lace handkerchiefs.

"The old Duke died almost three years ago. He was three score years and eight and had been ill for a number of years, so his death was not unexpected. Except, that is, by his Duchess, who still mourns his passing as if it was yesterday. She is a divinely beautiful, sweet-natured creature who is to be pitied. Rumor has it sorrow has unhinged her. Sir Titus Foley, a dandified physician who's made a name for himself in the study and treatment of female *melancholia*, has been summonsed to Treat by the Duke, and for the second time in as many years. It begs the question about the balance of Her Grace's mind, does it not? And you didn't hear this from me, old dear, for Kitty would surely have me trussed and spit-roasted."

Jonathon pulled a face of disgust.

"The poor woman has lost her husband, who was the love of her life, her home and her exalted position in society, and her son keeps her under lock and key? Is it any wonder she's suffering from *melancholia*? She has no life at all; bullied and badgered and totally misunderstood is my guess. She don't need the peculiar attentions of a supercilious quack. What she needs is someone to talk to and a sympathetic shoulder to cry on."

Lord Cavendish's burst of high-pitched incredulous laughter was heard across the ballroom.

"*T-T-Talk to*? Oh, *S-S-Strang*! You are my bowl of chicken broth; so necessary to my comfort. Your remedy? So appealingly uncomplicated that you have me almost convinced. I take it you're going to do the manly thing and offer Antonia Roxton your own broad shoulder to cry on?" He wiped his watery eye on the lace ruffles covering the back of a shaking hand. "And for your efforts she'll be eternally grateful and not only sign over the Strang-Leven inheritance to you, but vacate Crecy Hall forthwith, for you to do with as you wish?" He shook his powdered head in disbelief. "May I live to see the day!"

Jonathon grinned. "Just watch me."

Two

The Duke stood beside Antonia, Duchess of Roxton, and drew out his gold snuffbox. He tapped the enameled lid but did not flick it open. It was a deliberate gesture, aimed at giving him a moment to master his frustration and annoyance. He managed to keep his handsome face relaxed and to smile, as if he was enjoying the evening. His guests would never suspect that he had wished the ball over before it had begun when his mother arrived dressed all in black; even her fan and high-heeled shoes were black. Her hair was arranged without adornments, not even a riband; she wore no cosmetics and her wrists and throat were devoid of jewelry. Her stark display not only made her the most arresting woman in the room it proclaimed a willful disregard for her son and daughter-in-law's efforts to host a social occasion at Treat that did not generate unwanted gossip.

He should not have hoped that this time she would heed his advice and leave off her mourning. He wished he knew what he was supposed to do with her. With other members of his immediate and extended family, retainers, tenants and his servants, his word was law and rarely questioned. He liked to believe that he was a benevolent, and rarely dictatorial Head of the Family. But he felt completely ham-fisted when dealing with his mother. He was at a loss to know what else he could possibly do or say that he had not already done or said that would drag her out of the vat of grief and self-pity in which she was slowly drowning.

What had happened to the once animated, happy creature who travelled through life like a brightly-colored spinning-top; a beautiful tiny whirlwind in pretty silk petticoats and soft perfume, with gold and diamond bracelets adorning her wrists, and enough precious stones showered upon her by his father that he hardly ever saw her in the same piece of jewelry twice? She had been the vital ingredient that had kept the family happy, warm and loving. Not even his father's illness had flagged her spirits. She had been brave and good and so strong he had convinced himself that she had come to terms with the inevitability of his father's passing. She would mourn for a time but then, being so much younger than her husband, would get on with her life, accepting of the fact that the old Duke had had a long and eventful life and his time had come.

But when his father died so too it seemed had she.

It was as if he had lost both parents on the same day and it saddened him beyond measure. The resulting fragile mental health of his mother was an unrelenting worry. He wished he could make her happy. He wished he could make her see that life was still worth living. Three years of gentle persuasion had failed. Thus the time had come to try a different approach, one he was loath to employ but one the eminent physician Sir Titus Foley had assured him was the only way to shake his mother to her senses.

He took a deep breath and pretended an interest in the couples assembling for the first of the country dances.

"I thought we had agreed that come Easter you would give up your black?"

He spoke in French; his mother's native tongue.

"No. That is what you wanted, Julian."

"Three years have come and gone, *ma mere*. Isn't it time?"

Antonia shrugged a bare shoulder, gaze remaining fixed on the entrance doors. "Time? What is time? Without Monseigneur time it is unimportant."

The Duke pursed his lips and mentally counted to five.

"Putting off your black won't diminish your grief but it will—"

"—make my son and his wife more comfortable having a maman who does not grieve in public, *hein?*"

"You know that's not what I meant!" he said through his teeth, the gold snuffbox clenched in his fist.

"But it is how you feel, is it not? You would prefer that your maman she keep her grief private. It would be more—*seemly*, yes?"

"I would prefer that you not grieve at all!"

Antonia looked up at the Duke, a flash of anger in her emerald-green eyes.

"*Comment osez-vous suggèrent une telle chose!* Perhaps my son he would prefer that Monseigneur and I had never been in love? You would prefer your maman she rips out her heart so you need not endure the indignity of her grief?"

At that the Duke turned and looked down at her with a mixture of angry embarrassment and indignation. It caused a momentary forgetfulness, that under the blaze of a thousand candles two hundred pairs of eyes watched and waited from behind fluttering fans and quizzing glasses and over the rims of champagne glasses to view the outcome of this frigid conversation between mother and son.

"It offends me, Madam, that you dare suggest such a preposterous notion," he enunciated coldly. "Particularly when you are well-aware that Deborah and I strive to emulate in every way the married life you and Father shared. Such outlandish comments offer further proof that you are in no fit state to make rational decisions." He stretched his neck, as if the elaborately tied cravat of snow-white lace was suddenly uncomfortably bound about his throat, and returned to gazing out across the ballroom. "I have decided to recall Sir Titus—"

"*What?*" she responded, a quick agitated movement of a slender wrist flicking open her fan. She suppressed a shiver of loathing. "You wish to force me into the care of a-a disgusting, fat-fingered quack? *Incroyable.*"

"Then you have ceased spending endless hours up on the hill talking to yourself?"

"I do not talk to myself," Antonia said matter-of-factly, though color flooded her porcelain cheeks at being caught out. "I talk to your father."

The Duke rolled his green eyes to the ornate gilt ceiling and then down to the diamond buckle in the tongue of his left shoe.

"I see… You think it quite acceptable behavior for a duchess to spend her idle hours in the family mausoleum—"

"As acceptable as a duke permitting his servants to spy on his maman!"

"—in conversation with a marble likeness?" the Duke finished flatly.

Antonia turned wide innocent eyes up at the Duke. "Julian, it is absurd of you to believe your maman she talks to statues."

Again, the Duke mentally counted to five but his sigh of impatience was audible. He tried one last time to be reasonable. "Madam, if you agree to put off your black and accept life as it is now and not as you would like it to be again, I will gladly dispense with the services of Sir Titus Foley, despite his assurances that he can cure you of this excessive and unreasonable melancholy."

The Duke's words sent a chill down Antonia's spine and she visibly stiffened. *Cure her?* What was Julian talking about? As if grief at losing the love of one's life was a dose of influenza that merely required plenty of bed rest and a physician's foul-tasting tonic. She stared out across the ballroom, movement and color, laughter and light, all an inconsequential blur. She couldn't stomach another minute in this house that had once been her home.

"Call my carriage, Julian. *Immédiatement!*"

"Put off your black, Maman, and the children may continue to visit you at Crecy."

Antonia caught her breath. "You would stop the children visiting me?"

"Frederick is asking questions about—about his *grandmère's* odd behavior."

When Antonia stared up at him in mute disbelief the Duke cleared his throat, awkward and uncomfortable under her steady gaze. This impromptu interview threatened to turn into a public scene, a circumstance he wanted to avoid at all costs. Again, he stretched his neck, the cravat tighter than ever.

"You know as well as I servants will gossip before children, thinking them not of an age to understand. But Frederick is almost seven… He has an old head on his shoulders… He's taken the gossip to heart. He worries about you. Frets. He's questioned his mother. Thankfully the twins are too young, as is Juliana, but it won't be long before... In short, Maman, if you continue to wear mourning, if you continue your daily visits to the family vault, you leave me no choice but to limit your contact with the children to public occasions."

Slowly, Antonia closed the sticks of her fan and picked up a handful of her diaphanous petticoats. Mustering up all her quarter of a century as a duchess in the public gaze, she mechanically held out her hand to her son in farewell. A glance over her shoulder at her ladies-in-waiting was all that was required to bring them to heel. "My carriage, Julian."

"Is it too much to ask," he cajoled, raising her hand to his lips, "to put off your black and conform?"

Antonia's face remained a mask of indifference. Inside she was falling apart.

Conform? The word wasn't in her vocabulary. When had she ever been required to conform? She had always been just herself. When she had become the Duchess of Roxton two months after her eighteenth birthday, she was never compelled or felt the need to follow society's dictates. Her husband had never expected it of her. Her spontaneity and exuberance were what Monseigneur had treasured most about her. Why did her son expect her now, as a widow, to conform? It was inconceivable. Cures and conformity. Such absurdities put her all at sea.

She withdrew her hand.

"Is this what Deborah wants too?"

The Duke did not meet her eye. He looked over her fair hair. "Deb is four months with child and I will not have her upset."

Antonia felt tears at the back of her eyes. She must not spill them here.

Did her son not realize her grandbabies were everything to her? Their twice-weekly visits to her dower house on the lake were the only sunshine in her otherwise gray lonely days. Without them, she would surely fade away. But perhaps that was for the best; perhaps that would solve everything. She knew she was a great burden on her son and his wife and that Julian was only doing what he considered right; what he thought his father would want him to do as Duke. Antonia could not blame him for that. She was well aware that as Duke of Roxton her son had inherited a heavy burden of responsibility and that he took his position as Head of the Family very seriously; in her opinion, rather too seriously. But that was not for her to comment. He was a loving husband and father and a benevolent master, which was all that truly mattered.

"You have not told her."

The Duke did not answer. He motioned his mother's ladies-in-waiting forward. "Her Grace is returning to Crecy."

Antonia turned to leave with eyes downcast. Her heart was so heavy, her mind and body so listless that it was as if she was wading through treacle. Yet, something, she wasn't precisely sure what, perhaps the crescendo in conversations close to her or the flash of color and movement as the dancers scattered and their audience parted, made her pause and lift her gaze from the polished floorboards. Her emerald-green eyes widened in surprise, for striding purposefully towards her was a loose-limbed giant of a man with a sun-bronzed complexion.

Dressed in an unadorned, close-cuffed, dark velvet frockcoat, low-heeled shoes with plain silver buckles and with his own thick wavy hair bouncing about his shoulders and falling into his eyes in a most untidy fashion, Antonia wondered if he was a cleric; albeit a very tall and handsome cleric. But his one concession to fashion, a brightly colored embroidered waistcoat of rich peacock blue satin with matching covered buttons, made her dismiss this supposition. Clerics did not wear such beautifully tailored and exquisite fabrics. Still, the waistcoat was so incongruous to the starkness of the rest of his attire that she blinked, as if to assure herself she was not witness to an apparition.

Perhaps he was drunk? Excessive alcohol would explain this sinuous stranger's air of easy-going confidence amongst this gathering of society elite. And only a drunkard would dare stare at her so fixedly. He looked neither left nor right as he skirted the dance floor, the contingent of onlookers forced to scamper backwards in his wake. Not that he seemed to care that the resulting disruption caused the orchestra to break off their music playing. In the abrupt silence, dancers and onlookers alike huddled together, all eyes on this copper-skinned stranger who dared to boldly approach Antonia, Duchess of Roxton.

As if to assure herself of the gentleman's destination, she glanced over her bare shoulders, left then right. Apart from her son and the two ladies-in-waiting breathing down her back as always, there was no one else standing near enough to be considered in the stranger's line of sight.

She continued to stare at the unknown gentleman's progress through the crowd, two-inch heels fixed to the floor and plumed fan let drop on its silken cord around her wrist, wondering what he could possibly want. And then her son stepped in front of her and blocked her view.

"Her Grace does not dance," the Duke stated in a flat drawl.

Jonathon was unperturbed by his host's cold reception. He met the Duke's unblinking gaze squarely and with a smile.

"Is that so, Duke?" he said casually, and took a step to the left so that Antonia was again in his line of sight. He was delighted to discover that her slightly oblique eyes were the color of brilliantly cut emeralds. That she was even more exquisitely beautiful at close quarters strengthened his resolve to have her dance with him. "Why don't you let your mother tell me that herself?" he said with a blunt, friendly familiarity that had the Duke been struck across the face he would not have been more shocked.

Those in the crowd close enough to hear this crude declaration were so taken aback to have a pre-eminent member of their order addressed in such a shockingly informal manner, and by one regarded as a parvenu (an East India merchant at that!), that there was a loud hiss of horrified disbelief as everyone collectively drew in breath.

The collective breath held awaiting the Duke's reply.

"Perhaps you did not hear me," Roxton enunciated frigidly, unused to being so rudely addressed that his close-shaven cheeks diffused a dull brick red, as if he had indeed received a reproachful slap. "The Duchess does not dance. She is returning home immediately. Now you will excuse her."

Neither man gave way. They stared at one another in silence, eye to eye. The crowd breathed and again held its breath. Good manners and societal convention demanded that the guest submit to his host's polite demand. But Jonathon was not a man who gave in easily, not without good reason. He certainly wasn't going to concede just because some unwritten collective tenet demanded it. There was no reason for him to back down unless *she* wished it.

Thus he did not do as Society expected. He did not apologize. He was not penitent. He did not bow and scrape and back away to be swallowed up by the crowd. Instead, he committed an unforgiveable social sin; one Society matrons agreed he would never make a recover. He might as well pack his portmanteaux and leave in the middle of the night to return to whatever social backwater from wither he had materialized.

Jonathon ignored the Duke.

He stepped forward, brushing past the Duke's shoulder, as if his illustrious host was a menial not worthy of his notice and addressed Antonia directly.

"Would your Grace do me the honor of taking a turn about the ballroom with a man who has two left feet and as much elegance as a stick insect treading water?"

Everyone awaited the Duchess's response to this little drama being played out above her head between two large handsome men who were at opposite ends of their social order. Everyone expected her to decline. There was the affront done her son, besides which no one had seen her upon a dance floor since the old Duke of Roxton had fallen ill with the complaint of the lung that had eventually taken his life.

Antonia's impulse was to decline, to give a lame excuse about having a megrim, and quickly depart to save any further embarrassment to her son. But she had never given a lame excuse in her life, nor did she suffer from megrims. And she certainly did not want to see this gentleman, who smiled down at her with all the confidence of receiving an acceptance, humiliated by her refusal. He had already incurred the silent wrath of her son whom she knew had a dread of public scenes. He would punish this stranger for his bad manners by undoubtedly snubbing him at every social gathering thereafter. Just as with a flock of sheep, the rest of society would follow the Duke's lead and the stranger would find himself socially ostracized.

She would not be responsible for this gentleman's social exile.

She met the handsome stranger's smile openly and despite the deep lines that radiated from his dark brown eyes and etched his cheeks, and the fact he possessed a swarthy complexion, no doubt the result of years sailing on the high seas or living in sun-drenched colonial climes, she estimated he could not be more than half a dozen years older than her son. What harm could there be then in having one dance with him if it meant he would not be henceforth cast out by her peers?

Mind made up, she stepped past the Duke and held out her small hand in greeting.

"If you can bear with my lack of practice, M'sieur, I will bear with your two left feet."

Jonathon's white smile broadened, but it was not, as the on-lookers supposed, in triumph because Antonia had accepted his audacious invitation in the face of the Duke's opposition. He was pleasantly surprised that she had replied in softly spoken French without regard to the possibility that he himself might not be articulate in the French tongue. That he had a good linguistic ear and spoke several languages fluently could wait for another day. For now, he was just delighted to have her on his arm.

Without a second glance at the Duke, he led her into the middle of the ballroom under the full blaze of three chandeliers with all the confidence of her acceptance being a commonplace thing.

There was universal indecision as to whether other couples should join them to make up the required number for a cotillion, but then Deborah Roxton swept up to her husband and said loudly that he had promised her this dance. The Duke made no objection, though he looked askance at his wife, and several other couples were quick to form and follow their hosts' lead. Within minutes, word swept through to the refreshment room and the gaming tables and these were all but deserted in favor of watching Antonia, Duchess of Roxton dance for the first time in seven years.

Lord Cavendish watched from the sidelines, all admiration for Jonathon's impudence. And by the looks of longing cast at Strang by at least half-a-dozen eligible beauties as he led Antonia in a cotillion, it was his lordship's considered opinion that far from tarnishing his suitability as a prospective mate, this episode had increased his straight-talking brother-in-law's prospects of bagging a titled heiress tenfold. His lordship couldn't wait to confer with his wife.

Jonathon kept up a banter of inconsequential conversation all to distract Antonia from the fact they were being watched by every guest invited to attend the Roxton April Ball. Later he tried to recall what he had blathered on about, but had no idea as to the precise nature of his ramblings, only that he was acutely conscious of wanting to make her feel at ease.

That he was in fact a very good dancer became apparent the moment the music struck up and he guided Antonia through the steps of the cotillion with all the mastery of a dancing instructor. When she looked up at him with a suspicious questioning frown he winked and smiled down at her in a conspiratorial fashion. It caused her to quickly look away. Inexplicably, her throat was hot. When they touched hands again she was once more herself, that is until he had the boldness to squeeze her fingers and say with a sad shake of his head,

"I really wish you would concentrate, Mme la duchesse. It is difficult enough keeping my two left feet pointing in the same direction without my dance partner's thoughts drifting off from the matter in hand."

Antonia gaped at him. "I beg your pardon, M'sieur—"

"It's Strang. Jonathon Strang."

"I beg your pardon, M'sieur Strang—"

"But when we get to know one another better you will call me Strang."

Antonia drew herself up to all of her five feet two inches in height. "M'sieur Strang, I do not believe—"

The sentence was left to hang as he followed the gentlemen into the center before returning to stand beside her again. He leaned his head down, close to her ear, and said conspiratorially, "But I live for the day you call me Jonathon."

Now Antonia was not only annoyed she was affronted. "M'sieur! I find you infinitely *en gras* and never will I call you anything but M'sieur Strang."

He laughed, flashing a white smile. "Very well, that's a start," he said good-naturedly.

For the remainder of the dance he kept silent, much to Antonia's relief, though his gaze was very much trained on her, which was disconcerting. She was not a vain woman but neither was she witless. She was well aware men admired her beauty, but it was always from a respectful distance, never at such close quarters and never so openly as to put her to the blush. Again, she wondered if this stranger was drunk, but when he had stooped to talk in her ear she had not been overpowered by the smell of spirits. So perhaps he suffered from a nervous disorder that made him appear excessively friendly?

Whatever his affliction, she just wished the dance over with. She disliked the attention dancing with this stranger was creating, and that her partner was enjoying his newfound notoriety. Yet, when she chanced to glance up at him, again he winked at her, not in a lewd manner, but in a way that suggested he was very much in control of his faculties. In fact, she received the impression from the intense look in his brown eyes and the set to his mouth when he was not smiling, that underneath his friendly demeanor there was a steely determination, that once he put his mind to a purpose he had the capacity to go doggedly after it until he had gained his object, and count no cost.

Her suspicions were confirmed when, at the cessation of the music and the dancers began to disperse, he did not return her to where her ladies-in-waiting dutifully stood. He wrapped her arm firmly about his velvet sleeve and whisked her off to the refreshment room. Before Antonia could say two words in protest, he pressed a glass of champagne in her hand and maneuvered her to a quiet corner by a long window with its view over the lantern-lit Ornamental Gardens. With his broad back to the gathering crowd, he positioned his tall frame between a marble pillar and the window, effectively shielding Antonia from curious onlookers.

He drank his champagne with relish.

"Don't it amaze you how famously we're getting along, Mme la duchesse? You speaking Louis' French and me replying in the King's English. Well, I can say that now because this George does speak English. The previous two German Georges weren't very good at it, were they? They had to converse with their English Ministers in French because their mastery, or should I say lack of the English tongue was appalling." He smiled down at her. "Those two Georges could have prattled on to you very well. I dare say the second George liked nothing better than to converse with you in French?"

"Yes. Yes, His Majesty he was a great prattler, M'sieur," she answered distractedly, trying to look past him into the crowd surging towards the tables laden with food and wine for any sign of her son, but her dance partner blocked her line of sight so effectively that the only possible place for her to look without being impolite was up into his face. "Monseigneur he says it is just as well the German Georges spoke a civilized tongue and not their native guttural utterances or he would have been forced to throw his support behind the Young Pretender's claim to the throne."

"Is that so?" Jonathon replied with interest. "I'll wager Bonnie Prince Charlie also conversed in French better than he did English."

"That is very true," Antonia agreed and suddenly dimpled at a memory. She sipped unconsciously at the champagne in her glass. "Monseigneur approved of Charles Stuart's impeccable manners and the fact he could tie a cravat to perfection, but his politics he could not tolerate."

"Monseigneur has his priorities right, that's certain," Jonathon said as casually as he could manage, for that dimple had quickened his pulse. He had made her smile, smile at a memory of her precious Monseigneur, but smile nonetheless. Determined to make the most of that small dimple, he stumbled on, surprising and embarrassing himself as to how well he was able to spout drivel like a gauche youth. "A gentleman's appearance says a great deal about him and what he thinks of the world. There's a vast difference between the nonchalantly dressed man and the man who dresses nonchalantly. I would hazard a guess that Monseigneur would caution that no amount of good tailoring can compensate for poor manners."

Antonia's green eyes lit up. "That also is very true, M'sieur," she answered with approval. "Monseigneur will forgive a nobleman a tattered flounce but there is no excuse for a lack of civility, *hein?*"

"Precisely! A gentleman may have fallen on hard times and not have the means to afford the services of a tailor, but if he has a wealth of good manners he is welcome everywhere."

"*Exactement,*" Antonia agreed. "It is preferable is it not, M'sieur, to entertain the village vicar in his battered tricorne who does not snort his snuff all over his lapels than the cardinal in his new cloak who has the manners of a pig and spits in the communal *pot de chambre*. You laugh, but I tell you, M'sieur, Monseigneur he cannot abide cardinals."

"Well I'm pleased Monseigneur and I are in accord," he replied with satisfaction, taking her empty glass without removing his gaze from her upturned face and setting it on the tray held by a hovering footman. "I can't abide nose-in-the-air preachers either, particularly the spitting variety. I've no doubts that there are any number of subjects Monseigneur and I agree upon. What a pity I'll never have the opportunity to meet the great man…"

But as soon as he uttered these words he knew he had made a tactical error. He could have kicked himself for being so unthinking. His innocuous comment wiped the smile from her beautiful mouth and dropped the lashes over her green eyes, fingers convulsing about the stem of her feathered fan.

He should have been more careful. He should have picked up on the fact that M'sieur le Duc de Roxton, her Monseigneur, remained very much alive to her. She continually referred to her dearly departed duke in the first person. But he had been so caught up in his triumph at making this beautiful, refreshingly candid woman smile that a momentary lapse in concentration had made him speak without thinking. And who could blame him for that?

Being in such close proximity confirmed everything about her that he had first admired from a distance, and more. She certainly didn't appear old enough to be Roxton's mother. But she was definitely the most beautiful creature he had ever laid eyes on. From her glowing skin to the deep cleavage of her white breasts, to her pleasing subtle perfume, and her softly spoken French, every inch of the Dowager Duchess of Roxton was delightfully and enticingly feminine.

God, he was an unthinking ass. He had allowed hubris to override judgment. After all, her dimpled smile had not been for him, it had been for Monseigneur.

"You need another drink," he stated.

Neither of them moved.

Antonia stared vacantly at his flowered waistcoat with its

covered buttons. It was an exquisite piece of finery, delicately embroidered with the exotic flowers and fruit vines of the Indian subcontinent upon a background of sapphire blue satin of such intense richness that she was sure there was many a lady who had been unable to resist smoothing a hand over its surface to satisfy a curiosity that it was as silky to the touch as it was to the eye. She wondered if he possessed other just as exquisite waistcoats and how many. Perhaps he had one for every day of the week? The natives of the Indian subcontinent were such excellent weavers and their intricate embroidery was masterful. She had at least two-dozen petticoats of fine Indian cotton in her clothes press. She wondered where they were, if Michelle was taking good care of the gowns and bodices she had worn before...

It was her way of coping, of shutting out the world of the here and now, to focus on something, anything, that would take her mind off the unbearable hollowness in her heart. She must not fall all to pieces in public. Julian would be mortified. He would never forgive her if she caused a scene here, in his own home surrounded by his peers. He frowned on public displays of emotion. But he was not a cold-hearted man. In truth, he was painfully shy. She had made this surprising discovery about her eldest son only upon his marriage to Deborah. Why had she not known this about him before?

She had always been openly demonstrative with his father.

Strange...

Thank God Julian had Deborah: beautiful, good, sensible and loving. That was her daughter-in-law. She made a fine Duchess of Roxton and was just the sort of wife and mother to his children Julian needed. They were the perfect couple and so happy...

Why had she attended tonight's ball? Why had she not stayed at home with her memories, surrounded by *their* books and *their* belongings, so necessary and comforting to her sanity? She prayed her son would come now and escort her to her carriage for the drive that skirted the lake to the sanctuary of her dower house.

Where were her two watchdogs?

She needed to go home, *now*.

With supreme effort of will she brought her concentration back to the present and forced herself to once again focus on her dance partner's intricate waistcoat. The sapphire blue satin was really quite calming. A sea of sapphire… It was enough of a distraction that after only a few moments she was able to breath deeply, knowing she would not fall all to pieces, not here, not openly, not tonight.

"Indian needlepoint," Jonathon stated quietly and smiled to himself when she was startled into blinking up at him. But her green eyes were bright, as if glazed with tears, and her cheeks delicately tinged with color, so that his smile dropped into a look of concern. Still, he couldn't help a cheeky comment he hoped would snap her out of her sad abstraction. "You are welcome to touch, should you feel so inclined," he offered with a lop-sided grin.

"M'sieur, you are absurd!" Antonia said dismissively, but his mischievous comment had its desired effect. She was instantly annoyed and picked up a handful of her petticoats, a sign that he should step aside to allow her to pass. Yet, when he just stood there, blocking her way, she hesitated to know what to do, after all, etiquette dictated he give way, when he did not, she scowled up at him, at a loss to know his motives.

He enlightened her.

"I am fully sensible to the fact it would be bad-mannered of me to call upon you at Crecy Hall uninvited," he remarked casually. "But it would be equally bad-mannered for you to refuse me once I am at your door. I intend to come uninvited tomorrow for afternoon tea, so if you do not wish to be bad mannered I suggest you *physically* not be at home. I won't accept one of those *"Mme la duchesse is not at home to anyone"* brush offs from your nose-in-the-air butler." He stepped back a pace to allow her to pass and bowed. "Until tomorrow."

Antonia was so taken aback by such arrogance that it was she who remained rooted to the spot, angry disbelief keeping her gaze firmly fixed on Jonathon's white smile. It barely registered that her ladies-in-waiting had finally found her.

With a curtsey, the shorter of the two informed her that her carriage had pulled up in the portico.

A couple of bewigged nobles who were standing close by, drinking champagne, downing oysters and sharing a bawdy joke, were nudged into silence by two of their fellows with their wives in tow and became willing spectators to this little drama; they not the only ones who showed interest in the tall dark-skinned gentleman who had had the effrontery to dance with Antonia, Duchess of Roxton.

If Jonathon was not much mistaken, a general hush had descended on the refreshment room, and with the two gargoyles appearing from nowhere, it would not do to hang about to be further grist for the spectator mill. So before Antonia could move her feet or respond to Jonathon's outrageous invitation to afternoon tea, he turned on a heel and sauntered off to be met half way across the crowded refreshment room by his daughter and her two flaxen haired friends, the Aubrey twins. A look over his shoulder, and his smile became smug, knowing he was still being watched.

For a few seconds at least he had managed to divert her thoughts from her dearly departed Duke. He was confident he could stretch those few seconds of diversion to minutes and then to an hour. But capturing her undivided attention for a full day, now that would be a challenge. But he was more than willing to exert himself. He was determined to give Antonia every attention, to help lift her out of her melancholy and provide her with the diversion she needed to overcome her preoccupation with the dead. And when he had gained her confidence, he would persuade her to see the merit and morality in returning to him the inheritance stolen from his ancestor Edmund Strang-Leven over a century ago.

He would spend every minute of every day of his stay at Treat in this single-minded pursuit.

Of course if the perquisite of this endeavor meant enjoying the company of an exceptionally beautiful woman who did not have designs on marrying him or marrying her daughter to him, it was a consequence he was more than willing to accept. Courting the Dowager Duchess of Roxton to the exclusion of every other female who threw themselves in his way would show Kitty and Sarah-Jane and the scheming mammas of Society that he was deadly serious when he said he was not the least interested in marriage.

Suddenly, the Roxton house party was not another dull social event to be endured for the sake of his daughter's marital aspirations; Antonia Roxton had given it purpose and meaning.

Three

Antonia was used to deference bordering on obsequiousness from everyone except her husband and immediate family. Encountering a plainspoken gentleman that was not in awe of her beauty or her nobility (what stranger spoke to a duchess in such an off-hand manner?) completely bewildered her. It would have gratified and greatly surprised Jonathon to know that he occupied the Dowager Duchess of Roxton's thoughts during the carriage ride around the lake to Crecy Hall. Staring at the padded velvet upholstery between the shoulders of her ladies-in-waiting she decided that only a lunatic or a puff adder could muster the courage to ask her to dance, and defy her son's tacit refusal. During the three years the Duke was ill and subsequent three years since his death no gentleman had dared to do either. And then a conceited, sun-bronzed lunatic had had the insolence to invite himself to afternoon tea! His skin wasn't the only thing to have seen too much sun. She had heard it was not uncommon for men to go mad if they spent too many years in colonial climes, where the sun blazed so hot it blistered the skin.

That he had the audacity to invite himself to her house was in itself an overbearing presumption, but to saunter off and allow himself to be captured by three of the loveliest young ladies at the ball then turn and smile smugly at *her*, as if she cared the snap of two fingers that females found him attractive, decided her that Jonathon Strang was not only a lunatic but an arrogant lunatic. She wondered if he had danced with her to win a wager. Just the sort of ridiculous notion arrogant men who put a high price on their own worth engaged in. The three young beauties probably put him up to it.

She congratulated herself that she had the presence of mind to sweep past him with her chin up and without a second glance. Out of the corner of her eye she was gratified that the tittering beauties clinging possessively to the lunatic's arms had the presence of mind to drop into respectful curtseys with the rest of the ladies and gentlemen who bowed as she passed by with her ladies-in-waiting in tow. Jonathon, too, made her a formal bow.

She stepped from the carriage without seeing the liveried footman who put down the steps, or her butler and the porter who held up a flambeau to light her way into the warmth of the paneled hall of her Elizabethan manor.

He should have been grateful she had danced with him at all. She had saved him from social ruin and he had repaid her with a smug smile. Best to keep men of his stamp in their place, she told herself firmly as she was helped out of her petticoats, stays and chemise then wriggled into a fine cotton nightdress by her personal maid. Tomorrow afternoon she would go for a very long walk. If he did dare show his face at her doorstep and waited for hours alone and unwelcome, he would take the hint and not return. At the end of two weeks his white smile and dark brown eyes would be back in London, or whatever hot imperial outpost he was from, and she need never see him again.

She should have known better.

He was as stubborn as he was arrogant.

The next day, when she returned from a very long walk with her two faithful hounds trotting beside the hem of her many-layered petticoats, there he was, the sunbaked lunatic, seated on the top step of her summer pavilion down by the lake. He leaned comfortably against a fat Palladian column, long legs stretched out and crossed at his booted ankles. He was in shirtsleeves and sleeveless waistcoat, frockcoat discarded, and looked very much at home admiring the vista of sweeping green lawn down to a jetty and the still blue waters of the lake. He was smoking a cheroot and sending smoke rings up into a cloudless blue sky.

"Filthy habit," Jonathon commented, removing the cheroot

from between his even teeth when Antonia brought herself up short at the bottom of the pavilion's polished marble steps and stared hard at him.

He balanced the cheroot on the ornately crafted lid of his small personal tinderbox and rose to his feet, languidly unfolding his long, lean legs as if he had been seated on the wide step for quite some time.

He made her a short bow.

"I discovered the marvels of the rolled leaf while employed with the Company in Hyderabad. It keeps flying insects away. I use a hookah when at home, much more relaxing, but out and about I prefer leaf tobacco to snuff taking, which makes me sneeze, and chewing the stuff rots the teeth. It would be a shame to ruin such a brilliant smile. Not too many fellows back here care to smoke; snuff's more the thing. Still, I've invested in a number of tobacco plantations in the Americas on the off chance smoking will catch on."

When Antonia did not move he came lightly down the broad steps and offered her his arm.

"I am not an invalid, M'sieur!"

She ignored his crooked arm and went up the steps into the pavilion where she removed her broad-brimmed straw bonnet and fringed shawl under the cool of the painted high domed ceiling. She then patted her mussed hair back into place, several golden wisps having escaped the multitude of pins and falling across her cheek, flushed from the walk, and then just stood there, at a loss.

She desperately wanted to remove her kid leather walking boots and pour out a glass of lemon water from the crystal jug that was always made ready for her on a silver tray on the low table. She would then rest her stockinged feet on the striped cushions of the chaise longue situated by the ornamental archway with its view of the jetty and which afforded a cool gentle breeze off the lake, and read for an hour or two before dinner. She was rereading her favorite Roman historian Tacitus, and had also started delving into a pamphlet entitled *Common Sense* by an Englishman who supported the American revolutionary cause; given her by Cousin Charles. Both were waiting for her on the low table, as were several unopened letters.

First she had to get rid of this lunatic intruder.

She had walked further than ever before, stopping only to visit the family mausoleum that sat atop the highest hill on the estate where the best views of the county were to be had. Her son owned all the land as far as the eye could see, so wherever she walked, however far she walked, she never left home and could always see the magnificent marble mausoleum, a beacon that proclaimed to the world the family's ancient nobility—last resting place of the Dukes of Roxton and their nearest kin.

But she rarely stopped to admire the view of lush rolling hills, old growth forest and, closer to home, the altered landscape of lake, ornamental gardens and strategically planted trees fashioned by architect-gardeners. She spent her time inside the vast edifice, in the cool stillness of the muted light that penetrated the enormous oculus set in the dome high above her head, surrounded by long dead Roxton ancestors, and the family that had been taken from her: Monseigneur her husband, his sister the Lady Estée and her husband and Monseigneur's best friend, Lucian Lord Vallentine. Within the space of twelve months all three of her closest loved ones had been taken from her.

That groping fat-fingered physician Sir Titus Foley, worse, her son, claimed her visits to the Roxton mausoleum were proof that she had a morbid obsession with death. But it wasn't death that consumed her when she was within those walls it was life. She had lived such a wonderfully happy and fulfilling life when her husband, sister-in-law and brother-in-law were alive. Was it so difficult to understand the simple premise that with their loss she had lost something of herself? She just wished to be left alone to reminisce in peace.

Where was Michelle to untie her bootlaces?

"I'll stub it if you prefer," Jonathon said to end her preoccupation, the cheroot in the side of his mouth. He poured out a glass of lemon water and held it out to her. "Drink up. Fresh tea's on its way and—"

"M'sieur, me I do not care if you smoke or not, but you will not stay here! It is not—it is not..."

"The plates of little cakes and buttered bread were taken away with the teapot," he continued conversationally, watching her closely as her gaze stole to the far end of the pavilion where a long low mahogany table with squat legs surrounded by tapestry covered cushions for seating was set for a tea party. "I guess they went stale…"

But Antonia wasn't listening as she fixed on the pretty porcelain place settings for six and the child-sized silver cutlery to match. She had had the Sevres china specially commissioned to suit her grandchildren, a miniature version of the Roxton plate up at the big house. Twice weekly the children spent a few hours of the late morning with her at the pavilion. She always had the table set with crystal bowls filled with flowers and fruit, some with sweetmeats, and there were small tumblers filled with cordial. The table was exactly as she had left it before going for her walk.

She had waited for over an hour. And when the children did not come, sent a footman to discover what had detained them. Before her servant had set off, a liveried footman from the big house arrived with a note from the Duke. The ducal missive reinforced his decree of the previous evening: his children's visits would resume when she put off her black, and not before. She took the note with her to the mausoleum and angrily showed it to her loved ones and felt better for it. But returning to the pavilion and the untouched table brought back the sense of aching loss of the here and now.

Unconsciously she relieved Jonathon of the glass of lemon water. She was so thirsty. Yet she did not drink.

"Did I miss the festivities?" Jonathon added lightly, though it was glaringly obvious the little tea party had never eventuated. "Shame. I prefer lounging on a couple of cushions when taking tea. Puts one far more at ease than sitting poker-faced on some stiff-backed chair with legs that can hardly hold up a peahen, least of all some turbaned matron. I remember once, at the Resident's house in Hyderabad, a fat dowager by the name of Mrs. Mastive came to take tea. While we all sat on cushions, she insisted on a chair being brought out. *We English are civilized*," he whined in a high-pitched voice, mimicking the turbaned matron's cadence. "*We do not squat like a native*. Well!" he continued in his own deep voice, "we called her Mrs. *Massive* for obvious reasons. Not to her face, of course. But she *was* massive. Backside the size of an elephant and three double chins! You can imagine what happened to the chair. Lackeys used the splintered shards for kindling. Don't worry; Mrs. Massive didn't feel a thing when she hit the tiles. But she did end up squatting after a fashion."

"Do you always run on at the mouth?" Antonia complained, scowling, oblivious to his mimicry, but his prattle forcing her out of her abstraction.

Jonathon laughed and shook his head. "No. A very recent affliction, I assure you, and all your fault, Mme la duchesse."

"Mine?" Antonia was startled. "I do not see at all why the fault it is mine."

Finally, she drank the glass of lemon water, too thirsty to wait any longer and because she hoped it would settle her nerves. The way he steadily regarded her while he quietly puffed on his cheroot was unnerving. She had not been left alone with a stranger, and certainly never a male, in such a very long time that she was awkward and ill at ease, which was ridiculous at her age, particularly with a gentleman who must be a decade younger.

She sat on the farthest end of the chaise, back ramrod straight, black silk petticoats and layers of white under petticoats billowing out around her, and lightly clasped her hands in her lap. Her chin went up and she lifted a shapely eyebrow in haughty disapproval she hoped cloaked her nervousness.

"I do not understand at all why you are here and not up at the big house where you belong with the rest of the guests."

"I'd rather be here with you."

Antonia did not know where to look.

"You are being absurd again, M'sieur."

"Also your fault," Jonathon said candidly and sat uninvited in the archway closest to the chaise. "I thought the asinine behavior of males when confronted with great feminine beauty was restricted to callow youth; something we grew out of with age. How wrong was I!"

"You should not say such things to me," Antonia demanded, nervousness giving way to uneasiness. Her usual response to compliments about her beauty was one of teasing thanks, but that had been when her husband was alive. Now, and with this gentleman, she was strangely incapable of being off-hand. That he was bluntly truthful did not help. His next statement deepened the color in her cheeks.

"Why not? Don't you like compliments?"

"I... I... It is not... It is not..." She threw up her hands and became angry when he started to laugh. "I do not see what there is to amuse you, just because I do not fall all over your admiration for my beauty. Of course I know I am above the ordinary to look at! I am not blind that I do not see this when Michelle brushes my hair before the looking glass each night. Do you think me witless?" She sat a little taller. "But I tell you, M'sieur, that you are to be disappointed if you think I am one of these females who flutter their eyelids and pretend to be coy all because a handsome stranger dares to state the obvious. Now what has made you grin like an idiot?"

"You called me handsome. I've gone all coy."

Antonia's mouth dropped open and then, in spite of herself, she laughed. "You are not blind either, M'sieur."

"No, not blind," he repeated, thinking she had a lovely laugh. "So what has delayed Roxton's brood?" he added casually, back up against the column, long brown fingers to Antonia's two whippets, who had earlier come prancing up the stairs, dehydration from the long walk and the cool water in their porcelain bowls making them totally oblivious to a stranger in their midst. Now, they took a tentative sniff at the buffed white nails. A lick of welcome at his hand and they got for their good manners a scratch behind the ears before they trotted off to their respective cushions by the chaise and lay down, happy and content. "I presume they are the ones for whom the little iced cakes were baked? Not fallen ill, I trust?" he added when Antonia still did not answer.

Antonia shook her head, throat tight and unable to speak, and in a move she was later to wonder at, withdrew the Duke's note from her pocket and thrust it at him.

Jonathon opened out the single sheet of parchment with one hand, skimmed the short paragraph, refolded it and handed it back without so much as a raised eyebrow. Yet his casual tone belied the quickening of his pulse, that she had taken him into her confidence so soon. Yet, he was shrewd enough to realize her actions said more about her deteriorating relationship with her son, than it did her wish to confide in him. As for the Duke's actions: he thought them despicable.

"So what's it to be, Mme la duchesse? Do you capitulate to Roxton's blackmail? Though, if I may add my penny's worth, snow white skin looks most fetching in black silks."

"I do not wear black to set off my skin!" Antonia replied indignantly, annoyed by his off-hand tone and accompanying broad smile, and also for being weak-willed enough to confide her family troubles in a complete stranger. What had come over her? "I really do not know in the least why it is you are here!" she added in a rush of embarrassment when he continued to puff on his cheroot with a lop-sided smile.

"I told you. I'd rather be here with you. You witnessed those three irrepressible chits pounce on me last night, didn't you?" he asked. "Had you stayed a little longer you would've seen them cart me off to the ballroom. Whereupon I was forced to dance with each and every pretty young thing in the room or receive a severe scolding from my daughter for my marked lack of manners." He exhaled on a sigh and smiled crookedly. "The thought of another day of social chit-chat with girls younger than Sarah-Jane was enough to make me head for the lake, find the first tub and take up oars."

Antonia blinked. "You *rowed* over here?"

"Is there any other way? An early morning ride about the parklands with the Duke and his cronies enabled me to take in the lay of the land. This pretty little red brick manse is surrounded by ha-ha barriers on three sides, to keep the sheep in or out, so I'm told. And the road is not only gated but has two wide-eyed sentries who look as if they've come straight from a pugilist's hellhole and enjoyed the experience. Invasion by boat was the only option left me."

Antonia's shoulders relaxed and she leaned in. "Who is Sarah-Jane?"

"My daughter: The pretty strawberry-blonde who grabbed my arm. The other two are the Aubrey twins. Silly goslings, both of them."

"The strawberry blonde one she is your *daughter*?" For some inexplicable reason Antonia was relieved. "She is very pretty."

"Yes. At nineteen years of age she's determined to marry a Baronet at the very least."

"But… You… You do not look old enough to be her papa. You cannot be much older than my son, yes?"

"Eight years his senior," he revealed. "I shall take your astonishment as a compliment. Like you, I became a parent in my teens. The searing heat of the Indian subcontinent has baked my skin to such a healthy brown glow that I am what is generally referred to as *ruggedly handsome*."

Antonia ignored his flippancy. "And your daughter she wants to marry a Baronet? Please, you will explain this to me."

"A Baronet, *at the very least*," Jonathon corrected. He put aside the cheroot, again balancing it on the lid of his tinderbox, contemplating his answer. "Her Cavendish relatives have instilled in her the importance of marrying for the *right* reasons: Connection, title, *and* wealth."

Antonia was puzzled. "I do not understand at all why these reasons are the right reasons."

Jonathon gave a bark of laughter. Her forthright if naïve responses were delightfully refreshing.

"That is easy for you to say, Mme la duchesse. You are a duchess. You were married to one of the wealthiest and most powerful noblemen in the kingdom."

"But that was unimportant," Antonia stated dismissively. "I did not marry Monseigneur for any other reason than love. Our marriage it was fated."

Jonathon cocked a mobile eyebrow at her.

"Fated? Admit it: Monseigneur's nobility and wealth helped you fall in love."

Antonia was outraged.

"I will admit to nothing of the sort! You are insulting and cynical. There were many wealthy noblemen in France and here who wanted to marry me, but I wanted only Monseigneur."

"Yes, I'm sure they were all lined up at your boudoir door, too," he murmured, momentarily forgetting his good manners and allowing his admiring gaze to dip from her flushed face to her full round breasts barely concealed under a gossamer-thin silk fichu. "Monseigneur must've been quite the man to have captured your heart…"

When her fingers stole to the folds of the fichu he quickly looked away, realizing his remiss, and stared out across the sloping manicured lawn to the jetty. He watched a swan glide into view, out from the tall rushes surrounding a small island, and paddle across the still waters of the lake to meet up with its mate.

"Sarah-Jane does not believe in fate," he said conversationally. "For one so young she is hard-headed about her future. She has no need to marry for money. I made my fortune in trade. But early hardships in India and a father with a turn for business taught her the value of money and hard work... The sapskull who proclaimed trade money couldn't open the front doors of noble houses has a melon for a brain! Sarah-Jane will have her titled husband. There are too many beggarly lords out there who require my blunt to prop up their estates for her to be overlooked." He met Antonia's green-eyed gaze with a crooked smile. "Yet, I am reasonably confident that when the time comes, Sarah-Jane will be guided by my opinion of the young man she settles on for a husband, regardless of his titles and estates."

"And your wife? What does she have to say about your daughter's plans to marry a Baronet *at the very least?*"

Jonathon hooked his long legs back over the ornamental balustrade and faced her squarely, elbows on his knees and gaze unblinkingly on her lovely eyes. "My wife Emily died in childbed trying to give me a son. The boy died with her. Sarah-Jane does not remember her mother at all, which is a great shame and very hard for me because she has a great look of her... She was not quite three years old when her mother died."

"You were very young to be left with the care of a mother-less infant."

"Yes. Not quite two and twenty."

"Tell me about your wife."

"Emily was three and twenty and married when we met. I was reading classics at Oxford and she was visiting a cousin who had a living at Magdalene. I literally bumped into her in the street. I had just turned eighteen and in my ninth miserable year—"

"Miserable?"

"I'd not been home to Hyderabad since a boy. When my elder

37

brother James died, relatives back here persuaded my father that as I was now the only living male heir I needed an English gentleman's upbringing. Hence six excruciating years at Harrow—"

"*Pour Quoi?* Excruciating you say? Why?"

He glanced away, to gather his thoughts and Antonia waited.

"When you're young all you want to be is the same as everyone else," he explained, gaze again very much on her eyes. "And when you discover that you are not, that you are different from your fellows, you are mortified because you believe the fault lies with you. And they—the fellows you are thrown together with at school and who are all the same—they are merciless in pointing out that difference at every opportunity."

"Because your skin it is the color of warm toffee?"

That made him laugh. "Warm toffee? I like it! But no," he said with a shake of his head, "I wasn't warm toffee *then*. That came later, when I returned to India."

"Then I do not understand at all why these boys mistreated you," she said dismissively. "As a boy you were no different to them, *hein?*"

"Yes, I was and I am," he stated quietly. "One day you will know why. But not today..."

"And Emily?" Antonia prompted when he paused, thoughts seemingly miles away, no doubt thinking about those lonely years separated from his family. "You said Emily she was *married?*"

"Yes! Yes, married." He pulled a face. "Married off at seventeen to a much older man who thankfully up and died seven years later—"

"*Thankfully?* Why do you say thankfully? Just because her husband he was much older than she does not mean they—"

"*Excusez-moi*, Mme la duchesse, but when I say thankfully, you must trust that I do not use the word lightly. He was not a good husband. He did not marry Emily because he loved her; he married her because she was a Cavendish and an heiress. In just six years of marriage he managed to dissipate her fortune and ruin her good name by dying in the arms of a whore. If you'd had the chance to meet her you would agree that Emily was a gentle shy creature who did not deserve such ill treatment. His age had nothing to do with it."

Antonia was suitably contrite.

"Please, you will excuse me, M'sieur. I—It was wrong of me to presume..."

Jonathon inclined his head and pulled the hair back out of his eyes and continued. "To be brief, we eloped. The consequence of this thoroughly romantic gesture? Her father, friends and relations promptly disowned her. But who can blame the General for that? Emily's husband may have been a brute with a title and a hopeless gambler but he was a Spencer. I was presumed a nobody with nothing."

"But she loved you."

He smiled.

"Yes, she loved me, and I her. We took the first passage to India and were finally married in Hyderabad, at my father's house..." He let out a breath and stubbed the cheroot, saying without looking up, "She survived all those weeks aboard ship, rough seas, bad weather, giving birth to Sarah-Jane in a God-forsaken African port, the tropical heat and the dreaded insects all without complaint. And in less than three years she was taken from me, before I had made my fortune and before—before she had any idea who I was destined to become..." His smile was gone and his lean face taut. Suddenly he looked at Antonia, adding in French, "Mme la duchesse, I am an honorable man. I will never do or say anything to intentionally deceive or-or *hurt* you. I give you my word."

Antonia held his gaze. She believed him. The sincerity in his deep voice told her he had loved his wife very much. That he spoke the last two sentences in impeccable French should not have surprised her, but it did. Why had she not realized that he could speak her native tongue when he was capable of not only under-standing everything she said but replied in English with such quickness of brain that he had to be simultaneously translating the one language into the other.

She noticed then that he wasn't wearing a frockcoat, just a sleeveless waistcoat over his white shirt. It was a different waistcoat from the night before, but just as exquisite. This one was a deep sea green similarly embroidered but with elephants. His billowing shirtsleeves were rolled loosely to the elbow, no doubt as a con-sequence of rowing across the lake to her dower house.

The distance across the man-made lake from the monolith of stone that was the family palace to her quaint Elizabethan manor house with its gargoyle motifs upon the chimney pots was deceptive. It did not look that far, particularly from the west side of the lake where from atop the hill that housed the family mausoleum, both houses were clearly visible. But the lake was misleadingly large and meandering with many islands and bridges that had to be negotiated if one wanted to cross from the monolith to Crecy Hall, with its summer pavilion and small formal garden tucked away in a wide bend; both houses unseen one from the other.

Crecy Hall had sat crumbling and neglected for a hundred years until the fifth Duke, Monseigneur, had remodeled and refurbished it with his wife's future widowhood in mind. To Antonia such painstaking considerations had seemed so distant that she had never permitted herself to dwell on the inevitability of outliving her husband by many years. And now here she was, a widow, living in the Elizabethan house with its fanciful chimney pots, fragrant gardens, a jetty and an icing-cake pavilion on the shores of the lake with its lovely outlook across tranquil blue waters stocked with fish and where families of swans and ducks glided by. And yet to her it was more prison than house.

He must be thirsty after all that rowing.

Antonia went to pour out a second glass of lemon water from the crystal pitcher but he was quick to do this for her. When he handed her the full glass she offered it to him and he took it with a small smile and drank gratefully of the cool tangy liquid.

"I am very sorry about Sarah-Jane's maman," she said quietly, looking up at him. "You still miss her very much."

"Thank you. Yes." He returned the empty glass to the silver tray but remained standing because Antonia had not sat down again. "It doesn't go away, y'know; the sadness. Even after all these years. One just learns to live with it and get on with life. I suspect it is the same for you... But losing Monseigneur, despite it being three years ago, feels like yesterday. You still can't believe it, can you? I knew that last night, watching you," adding with a small shake of his head, "I thought you were looking at me. What a blow to my self-esteem when I realized later that you hadn't been looking at me at all, but at the entrance doors over my shoulder. You were remember—"

Antonia blanched and swallowed hard. "Stop!"

"—remembering all the times Monseigneur had come striding through those doors," he continued in his deep steady voice. "You were trying so hard to believe that perhaps he would do so again. I know. I used to do the same with my Emily. Hoping she would magically appear in the doorway at some party, or in any of the rooms of our house, and then I would know that it was all a bad dream. But she never came. I knew she never would, but I couldn't stop myself wondering, that if I just wished for it hard enough—"

"*Fermer gueule*. Stop I said! No more! No more!" Antonia pleaded. She pressed her hands to her hot cheeks before running shaking fingers up through her hair as she walked to the furthest corner of her quaint pavilion in a rustle of petticoats. "How-how *dare* you come here and-and *disturb* my-my *peace*."

If she could just remove her wretched boots...

If she untied the laces and kicked off her boots and put her stockinged feet upon the chaise she would feel much better. Her feet ached but it was nothing compared to the heaviness that weighed on her shoulders and pressed on her heart.

Where was Michelle? Where could her personal maid be? What was keeping her? She should be here with her now so she need not be here alone with this stranger who was upsetting her peace of mind.

She would not talk about Monseigneur with this gentleman. She could not. It wasn't fitting. It wasn't right. But what he said—all of it—was true. No one, not her sons, not her daughter-in-law, not her extended family, no one knew how desperately she prayed this lonely life she was leading now, a life without Monseigneur, was all but a bad dream. She would soon wake up and he would indeed saunter through a doorway, come straight up to her, kiss her forehead and say her name in his soft-spoken drawl with that smile he kept exclusively for her. But how could this tall, brown gentleman know that? How could he know her deepest desire? A tiny inner voice of calm and reason told her the answer: *He too had lost the love of his life. Of course he knew.* He had lived the nightmare. He had hoped and prayed just as she hoped and prayed but nothing and no one could change the unalterable veracity of death.

But she had lost so much more than he could ever imagine...

No! That was unfair.

He had loved his wife. She had died in childbirth, her young life and their marriage tragically cut short. Monseigneur had lived a long, very full life. She should be grateful for the twenty-seven years they had shared together. So everyone kept telling her, over and over and over. She was grateful, but nothing had prepared her, nothing could change the deep sense of loss, the aching loneliness and despair of being his widow. No man could replace Monseigneur. No man could love her as he had loved her. No man would want her in that way as much as he had wanted her... And no one could tell her what she was supposed to do with her life now, without him.

Unconsciously, she returned to the chaise and stared at Jonathon, mentally castigating herself for feelings of self-pity at his expense. Tall and with a healthy glow that served to make his brown eyes that much more intense and his teeth whiter than white, she wondered why at eight and thirty he remained a widower. He had danced very well and was graceful and leisurely in his movements for a big tall man. She could see why he would be much sought after at balls and routs. Perhaps he had not met the right woman? Perhaps he would find her here at Treat? Her daughter-in-law seemed to have invited every pretty young woman of marriageable age to the house party. He was too ruggedly handsome and virile not to want to remarry and start a second family. And men could marry at any age. Monseigneur had been older than this gentleman when she had become his duchess. She hoped he found a nice woman to marry. Someone young, fresh and alive...

She would do it herself! She did not need her maid to do such a trivial task. She must be turning lazy in her abstraction. She would untie her own boot lacings. With her boots removed she would feel much better. Her feet ached. That must be why she was more miserably self-centered than usual.

Surely the tea things would arrive soon?

Antonia had no idea tears were streaming down her face.

Four

$\mathcal{J}$onathon patiently watched and waited while Antonia paced the pavilion.

He knew she was remonstrating with herself. She looked wretched. When she covered her face with her hands he pressed his clean white handkerchief on her and she took it without being aware of his existence. He wished he could do or say something to comfort her, but he had said more than enough for one day. He suspected her family was oblivious to her secret hope and here he was, a stranger, baldly throwing it in her face. But it needed to be said. He knew the futility of continuing to hope when there was no hope. After Emily's death, he had lived his life like that for a number of years.

When she finally stopped pacing and came back to the chaise longue, put her boot up on the blue striped cushion and bent forward to grasp at the laces, he grabbed at the chance to be of practical help. He offered to remove her boots for her. Antonia brushed him off, saying she was quite capable of looking after herself.

He stepped back and watched her struggle with the knot in the lacings, twice grasping at the bow then bringing her foot to the stone flooring before again putting her boot to the cushion and tugging in vain at the thin leather cords.

When she lowered her boot to the stone floor a third time, cursing her feebleness, he could take no more. He unceremoniously grabbed her about the waist, picked her up, swung her about and dumped her amongst the cushions on the chaise longue as if she was a mere marionette that weighed less than *papier-mâché*.

Antonia was so stunned by such cavalier treatment that it took her several seconds to react, and before she could protest at such high-handedness, her right boot was on his bended knee and he was tugging at the first knot in the laces. She tried to pull her foot free but he grabbed her about the ankle and held her firm.

"Sit still!" he reprimanded.

"I did not ask for your help!" she countered angrily, trying to recover her composure and her dignity by brushing down her disordered petticoats so they at least covered her stockinged legs below the knees. "I have a maid to do such menial tasks and she—"

"—isn't here. So don't be foolish." Only when she was still did he let go of her ankle. And when she did not move, he returned to the task of unlacing her boot. "As if you could bend to untie these ludicrously long laces in stays!" He deftly undid the knot and gently pulled apart the lacings. "I'd wager you've never had to try before today."

"You think me incapable of looking after myself?" she snapped back haughtily, anger dissolving her self-pity.

He paused and glanced up at her with skepticism. "I'm sure your material comforts are well and truly catered for by an army of servants, Mme la duchesse. Although... I am surprised to find you here alone. Where are the gargoyles?"

Antonia, who was patting her face dry with a white handkerchief she was surprised to find crumpled in her hand, paused. She was mystified. "Gargoyles, M'sieur?"

He carefully extracted her white-stockinged foot from the tanned half boot of soft kid leather and set the boot aside.

"The dreary-faced twosome that follow you everywhere."

"Oh!" Antonia smiled, wriggling her toes and feeling more herself. The dimple appeared. She was very pleased with his description. "Spencer and Willis they do look like gargoyles. Very fitting for my house, yes?"

"Very fitting," he agreed, thumb gently rubbing the ball and instep of her small foot. "Why don't you send them back to sit upon the chimney pots where they belong?"

"If only that were possible," Antonia said with a sigh, suddenly more rested yet supremely unaware as to the reason why. "I do not *want* them. I do not *need* them but Julian he thinks he is doing them and me a great service. They have been with me since just before Mon—over three years now, so me I do not have the heart to dismiss them. And if I did, where would they go? They have no home to go to. Treat it is their home now."

"Distant poor relations?"

Antonia nodded. "Sisters. Willis is unmarried and Spencer her husband was a great wastrel. He gambled away their small fortune and then shot himself. It is very sad for them. And so he Julian took them in and gave them to me. *Parbleu!* What am I to do with two sisters unknown to me? And what are they to do with me? I wonder sometimes at the workings of my son's brain. For one who is married to a woman of acute intelligence, he Julian can be a great blockhead when it comes to his mother. Does he think because we three are women we will of course get on famously? As if being female is all that is required to have mutual interests! Willis knows only schoolgirl French and Spencer pretends not to understand some of the things I say so she does not have to repeat it to Willis. I think what I say shocks her. Do not ask me what in particular because me I do not remember! And just because I cannot create one stitch, so am a useless embroiderer, they think I am a sad loss to womankind! Nor do I care to hear about the good works of Mr. Wesley or the latest sermon by our Reverend Beak, which is all they bore on about over endless cups of tea, which is a beverage I abhor." When Jonathon chuckled and shook his head she squared her shoulders and gave a little shudder. "You see the impossibility of the situation my son he has put me in?"

"I do! I do! But I have every confidence you found a satisfactory resolution."

Antonia could not suppress the dimple.

"*Naturellement*," she replied, and ignoring her internal voice that wondered why she was sharing family confidences with a complete stranger, added proudly, "We came to an arrangement that suits us very well and that he Julian does not need to know about. Spencer and Willis now live in the Bridge Gate House—"

"The gate house beside the bridge that crosses to this side of the lake?"

"Yes. Monseigneur had it built to complement Crecy Hall, so it is also a great piece of fanciful architecture, with turrets and buttresses like Strawberry Hill. It is a functioning house nonetheless and it suits the sisters very well. And so they live there very comfortably and me I live here and we do not bother each other in the least except—"

"—when you visit the big house, and then they accompany you and that is how they earn their bed and board, playing at being your shadow?"

"*Exactement!* They are very good shadows, I think. Sometimes too good and it puts me out of sorts and I want to be angry with them but I cannot because that would be churlish. Following me about at dinners and balls and the like is their only chance to repay Julian his great kindness for taking on the care of them. It gives them a chance to dress up in their best silks and feel important and to look down their noses with disapproval at the behavior of those more fortunate than themselves. Such occasions give them fuel for weeks of endless discourse! It would be too cruel to take away what little excitement they have in life."

"I'm surprised you haven't introduced them to the Lady Strathsay," he replied flippantly, and when Antonia blinked added with a crooked smile, "Doesn't the Countess own to the same puritanical principles as the Gargoyle Sisters? The three of them could wax lyrical for hours on the excesses, real or imagined, of their noble cousins. Their opinions would also, no doubt, greatly add to her ladyship's self-consequence; not that it needs adding to, mind you. But Willis and Spencer certainly wouldn't look out of place in her stiff-necked company." When Antonia clapped her hands to her cheeks, as if in horror, he added quickly, "The Countess is your aunt, so if I have offended—"

"No! No! It is the perfect ploy, M'sieur! Perfect! I do not know why I did not think of it," Antonia assured him. Her green eyes sparkled mischief. "Charlotte she will take to them too, if only because they belong to me. Perhaps she may even ask that they visit with her, and then I will be able to come and go from here as I please and without shadows! And Julian he will not be able to say no because Charlotte she will hound him to a boredom so great until he agrees to allow them to visit her in Buckinghamshire. She has become very proud and insufferable with age and few people will give her the time of day, and so I pity her a little.

"Her husband he is my uncle and lives openly with his mistress and their two children in the West Indies. It is a situation that enrages Charlotte beyond belief. But who can deny my uncle his happiness? By all accounts, his mistress satisfies him in every way. Not Charlotte. She is of that type who is incapable of physically loving anyone; her temperament it is very cold." She pulled a face. "She shared—No! *Shared* it is not the right word—She *endured* her husband's bed only enough times to give him an heir and a spare and then—" Antonia snapped her fingers. "No more." She leaned forward, as if not wanting to be overheard, her face close to Jonathon's, who was still on bended knee before the chaise, and added confidentially, green eyes wide in disbelief, "Can you imagine it, not enjoying to make love? It is *incroyable*, is it not? But I assure you, Charlotte she is such a one."

Jonathon tried not to smile at her innocent delivery of such plainspoken revelations, thinking her the most entertaining creature he had ever encountered. No wonder the Gargoyle Sisters with their puritanical mindset swooned at her pronouncements. And when she leaned in so close that he could count the long black lashes framing her lovely eyes, she unwittingly presented him with the splendid vista of her magnificent breasts spilling forth from tight bodice and gaping gossamer fichu. He dared not take his gaze from her face.

"Why are you walking and not riding about the countryside?" he asked brusquely to mask a frisson of desire. He signaled for her booted left foot to be placed upon his knee, which she did without argument, his attention wholly focused on the knotted laces. "I thought only village girls and poor squires' daughters walked. Sarah-Jane tells me that females of noble birth gallivant about the countryside on nothing less than a fine stead with a groom or two in tow."

"But me I like to walk," Antonia answered stubbornly. "I have walked about the countryside as you say ever since Monseigneur left—" Again, she could not bring herself to say it, though it was the closest she had come to mentioning her beloved husband's death since Jonathon had entered the pavilion, adding swiftly, "It is not for anyone to care if I walk or ride!"

"I agree. But if there's one thing I've learned about Polite Society since returning to England," he said conversationally, ignoring her slip of the tongue and looking up as he unlaced her boot, "it's that Society cares very much if one of their own, a duchess no less, doesn't conform to their ways. I suspect it's not the done thing for you to be trudging up hill and down dale in your fetching half-boots."

Antonia snapped her fingers. "That is what I care for Society's dictates. Conform? Pshaw! Monseigneur he was above all that nonsense."

Jonathon gave a bark of laughter. "Good for him!" thinking Monseigneur must've been one hell of an arrogant nobleman, and liking him for it. "And bravo to you. You should never stop being yourself, Mme la duchesse," admiring Antonia's spirit and thinking she possessed the most luminescent skin and sparkle to her eyes when she was animated.

"Just because I am a duchess does not mean I too do not have two fine legs to walk about like any village maiden, does it not, M'sieur? This I have told Julian a hundred times, but my son he does not listen."

"Oh, I'm sure your legs would put to shame most village maidens," he murmured, instantly dropping his head to remove the half-boot from her foot which still rested on his bended knee. "You must tell your personal maid not to lace your boots so tightly in future," he lectured. "No doubt she's done the same with your stays. If the indentations on the bridge of your foot are anything to go by I'm surprised you can breath at all."

"And what makes you an expert on female corsetry, M'sieur?" Antonia asked haughtily as she sat back and unconsciously wriggled her toes before tucking her stockinged right foot up under her flowing petticoats. Her left foot remained in his warm hand. "No, do not answer me!" she added quickly when he grinned and looked away, adding with unguarded frankness, "I do not like wearing stiffened stays and Monseigneur agreed that I avoid wearing them when we were at home. Whalebone and buckram, they are too confining. At home I wear *jumps*, always."

"*Jumps?* Jumps, Mme la duchesse? Never heard of such an article of female underclothing. Then again, female fashion from the west takes its time reaching the Indian subcontinent. Please to enlighten me."

"I do not know if women here in England they wear jumps but in France they are very much the rage for *déshabillé*. Mine are made for me in Paris by an expert corsetiere. They are similar to stays to look at but the construction it is very different. There is no stiffening of any kind only layers upon layers of fine cotton padding and as such they are very comfortable. It is as if I am not wearing an undergarment at all. They open here, at the front. Look, I will show you," she said matter-of-factly, as if discussing any mundane object and not one intimately connected with her person.

When he glanced up she had let the fichu fall from about her bare shoulders and had dropped her chin to examine her bosom.

"You see these ribbons tied up as bows, they are what close up the front," she lectured, pointing out a row of neatly tied satin bows that ran the length of a soft silk embroidered bodice that covered her breasts. "And because the ribbons are here in the front and not in the back as are the lacings of stays, me I can easily undo them and remove this bodice. Observe," she added in the same studied tone as she tugged on the end of the satin bow closest her décolletage, oblivious to the effect this demonstration would have on her male audience of one. The bow unraveled and the jumps gaped open displaying to superb advantage a deep cleavage barely contained within a thin white chemise with a pretty lace border. She glanced up with a smile of satisfaction. "So you see not always do I need Michelle to help me undress. Jumps are most convenient, yes?"

Jonathon nodded mutely. Convenient? Dear God, no wonder Monseigneur had preferred her in *jumps*. What man wouldn't enjoy tugging at those bows? He'd lay down good money the Duke had been expert at getting her out of her jumps in record time. He was as giddy as a schoolboy and went dry in the mouth thinking about it, astonished that she was devoid of wiles and genuinely oblivious to her powers of attraction. It was no small surprise then that the present Duke had two gargoyles posted as her shadow!

Finally, he tore his gaze from the mesmerizing sight as Antonia retied the satin ribbons into a bow then gathered the fichu about her shoulders and across her breasts. Clearing his throat, he said in a voice he hoped wasn't thinned by desire,

"And here was I thinking, incorrectly as it turns out, you would need to wear buckram or whalebone to keep everything in its proper place."

"I beg your pardon, M'sieur? What is this proper place?"

"Well, er, don't most well-endowed women employ whale-bone to keep their breasts up?"

Antonia gaped at him, green eyes wide in disbelief that he had the temerity to make such a suggestion. "You think *I* need to wear whalebone to keep my breasts *up*?"

He smiled sheepishly but it was not lost on him that she was shocked more at the suggestion than at the question itself. So grief had not stripped her of vanity. Good.

"In my experience, Mme la duchesse, full breasts droop if—"

"*Pour quoi?* Droop? *Droop?* What is this-this *droop?*" Antonia was aghast. Angry pride spurred her to give an outrageously candid and thus indiscreet response. But she had always spoken her mind; it was second nature to her. "Monseigneur he says I have the most perfect breasts imaginable because they are *firm* and *full*, and *suspend* like ripened fruit still on the tree. That is not *droop.*"

Jonathon kept his lips shut tight and his head bent to the task of gently rubbing her aching instep. He could never imagine his Emily, or any other English female of gentle birth, being so frank and openly conceited, and definitely not about such an intimate subject as female breasts, their own or anyone else's. The Dowager Duchess was so delectably frank. Yet it occurred to him that it might be a matter of interpretation, because she spoke exclusively in French; that perhaps she would not be so forthright if she spoke in English. Somehow he suspected that it had little to do with translation and everything to do with the person she was. He liked it. He liked it very much.

"Ripened fruit, Mme la duchesse," he managed to say in a level voice as he again cleared his throat. "Monseigneur certainly has a good turn of phrase. I shall take his word for it."

"Yes, you must. Now please you will let go of my foot because our afternoon tea it is here."

Through one of the ornamental archways Antonia had spied her butler coming down the winding path that connected the pavilion to the dower house, carrying the heavy silver teapot, a small army of liveried footmen snaking behind with the rest of the tea things.

Our afternoon tea. Jonathon liked that too.

"Thank you," she added in a small voice, which brought his gaze up from her stockinged foot to her face. He wondered why she hesitated to look him in the eye. "My feet they feel much better for your attention."

"It was my pleasure, Mme la duchesse."

He was about to rise when a young voice of indeterminate gender spoke at his back, asking anxiously in French,

"Mema? Mema! Your ankle it is not twisted? You've not hurt yourself, have you, Mema?"

And then another, deeper, and most definitely male, voice added with the same concern, "Shall I have the footman fetch your maid, Mme la duchesse?"

Jonathon rose up to all of his six feet and four inches and turned to look down on a thin strip of a boy with a head of tight black curls and inquisitive brown eyes that regarded him with a frown. He looked familiar. Standing at his shoulder was a stocky young man with a shock of red hair and whose eyes were the same color as those possessed by the Duchess and her son the Duke.

"I'm rather large in whatever occupation you care to place me, young man," Jonathon replied placidly to the redhead. "But *footman* I am not." Smiling, he stuck out his hand in greeting to the little boy. "Jonathon Strang Esq. And no, Mema hasn't twisted her ankle."

Five

"*I*t's Frederick, M'sieur," the little boy replied politely as he peered up at the tall man as they shook hands. "Frederick, Lord Alston, but everyone calls me Frederick. You can too. Are you Mema's friend?"

"Yes, I—"

Before Jonathon could say anything further, Antonia flew off the chaise longue in her stockinged feet and sunk to her knees to envelope her eldest grandson in her warm embrace before releasing him and kissing his flushed cheek. She spoke in rapid French.

"You are just in time for afternoon tea, *mon petit chou*. Come sit by me and tell me all about the preparations for your boat race. It is tomorrow, yes? Who is your oarsman? Are Louis and Gus to have their own boat this year like your Papa promised? What does your Mamma say to it?"

With her arm about the little boy's shoulders she smiled warmly at the stocky young man with the shock of red hair and put out her hand to him to have her fingers kissed.

"*Merci*, Charles, for bringing Frederick to me," she said gently.

To Jonathon's surprise the young man blushed and looked bashful. He merely nodded before turning to Jonathon and making him a short bow.

"Apologies for the footman comment, sir. I should have been more observant and noticed your India waistcoat. It's Charles," he added. "Charles Fitzstuart. Lady Strathsay's youngest son."

"But we do not hold that against you," Antonia quipped, as she led her grandson to the chaise. Once comfortably seated together, she proceeded to ask him all sorts of questions about the boat race while Jonathon and Charles Fitzstuart retreated to the archway, Jonathon to put away his tinderbox into a pocket of his discarded frockcoat and Charles to unbutton his riding frockcoat for it was a warm day and the ride over had entailed a long detour to avoid crossing the bridge, which would have alerted the ladies at the Gatehouse Lodge who in turn would have reported his son's trespass to the Duke.

Both men kept out of the way of the butler and the servants, who went about setting up the afternoon tea things on the low table surrounded by cushions. Those delicate porcelain teacups and saucers, small decorative cake plates and silver cutlery no longer required were removed, the remaining four place settings positioned at one end of the squat table. Silverware, sugar bowl, creamer, and a fresh plate of cakes and a bowl of sweetmeats were then arranged amongst the bowls of flowers and fruits to the butler's satisfaction. All but one of the footmen was then waved away, to return to the house. The butler took up his position behind the teapot on its silver stand, the footman ready to offer assistance when required, and waited for a signal from the Duchess to commence pouring out.

But Antonia was not to be distracted from her grandson's chatter. Jonathon admired her skill in teasing information from the boy, so that it was not many minutes before Frederick, who showed a natural reticence for one so young, had lost his shyness in the company of a stranger and was telling her all about the planning that had gone into the building of his sailing craft for the annual Spring race around the largest island on the lake. No detail was too small for Antonia to express immense interest, and she showed such enthusiasm for her grandson's plans that Jonathon marveled at the change in a woman who not half an hour before had been weeping into his handkerchief. Her eyes sparkled, she laughed prettily behind her fan, and she was so full of animation that he knew this was how she was before Monseigneur's death, and how she needed to be again.

He was quite content to remain as spectator, but when Frederick expressed the desire for a glass of lemon water and a slice of cake, Antonia remembered her duty as hostess and signaled for her butler to pour out saying to Jonathon as she led Frederick to the low table,

"You must forgive me my teapot. It is full of coffee. I do not drink tea, do I, Charles? It is insipid. But I have tea up at the house if you prefer?"

"Coffee it is then. Although you would drink tea if I was to make it for you, Mme la duchesse."

"So you think? And why is that, M'sieur?"

"Because I make it the way it is intended to be drunk, mixed with India spices stirred into hot frothing milk and savored. One day you will try my most excellent Chai tea. But today, coffee will do very nicely indeed," he replied, following her to the low table, a heightened color to his cheeks because he realized he had been so preoccupied with watching her in conversation with her grandson that he had been ill mannered enough to ignore the existence of Charles Fitzstuart, who was now regarding him with a suppressed grin. To mask his awkwardness at being so scrutinized, Jonathon picked up off the little table by the chaise the book and pamphlet saying conversationally as he flipped the pages of the dog-eared and well-read copy of Tacitus' *Annals of Imperial Rome*, "Do you drink tea, Fitzstuart?"

"It's Charles, sir. The Duke and Duchess prefer Christian names to be used amongst their younger relatives, particularly in the presence of their children. No titles and definitely no one standing on ceremony. It is all part of the Rousseau educational philosophy," he explained evenly, as if the Frenchman's philosophy on the rearing of children was common knowledge, adding with a glance at Antonia, "I always drink coffee when I visit with Mme la duchesse."

"I presume then that if you *always* drink coffee with Mme la duchesse you speak French like a native?"

"Tolerably well, sir. I have a first in languages from Cambridge."

"Do you indeed?" Jonathon mused, a studied look at the young man, particularly his green eyes, and then a glance at Antonia. "So green eyes are not the only attributes shared by members of this illustrious family. Does your linguistic abilities also extend to an appreciation of the Roman historians?"

"Yes, sir. It was Mme la duchesse who first introduced me to Suetonius, Tacitus and Cicero when I was not much older than Frederick is now. I prefer Cicero's prose, although Mme la duchesse will argue that he is overly self-important."

"Charles, you know he is!" Antonia scolded playfully, patting the tasseled cushions on her left. "Come sit before the coffee it is cold. Marcus Tullius's vanity and pomposity shine through his writings and therefore me I cannot like him, though his letters are beautifully constructed. But Tacitus, he is more perfunctory in his commentary. His observations concerning the domesticity of the Julio-Claudian emperors are vastly more entertaining, particularly because he is biased, especially so towards Augustus's wife. He detests Livia to the point of mania, which is delicious to read but shameful historiography." She smiled at Jonathon over the rim of her porcelain cup watching him struggle to sit at a table designed to accommodate children. "But perhaps we should talk of more general topics, Charles, and not bore M'sieur Strang with our playful arguments about Roman historians?"

"*To plunder, to slaughter, to steal, these things they misname empire; and where they make a wilderness—*"

"*—they call it peace,*" Antonia said, finishing the line in unison with Jonathon, face lighting up with approval. *"Touchè!* So you do know your Tacitus, M'sieur."

"I did not waste all my time when I was at Oxford," Jonathon quipped, his pulse quickening at her smile, and stretched out a hand for the cup of coffee Antonia offered him.

"That is one of your favorite quotes from Tacitus, is it not, Charles? You quoted it just the other day when you asked that I read the Englishman's pamphlet. I am sorry, Charles, but I have not read it yet. But as you see I have it here in my pavilion meaning to do so."

"I have read the pamphlet several times, Mme la duchesse, so am in no hurry to have it returned," Charles replied and attempted to change the subject, "Miss Strang tells me you were born on the Indian subcontinent, sir?"

Jonathon plonked a spoonful of sugar in his cup and stirred slowly, gaze on the young man. He glanced at the pamphlet beside his plate and said blandly, "I can only surmise that by offering Mme la duchesse the treasonous writings of this unknown Englishman, you hope to make a republican of her?"

"You have read *Common Sense*, sir?" Charles asked earnestly, all reticence extinguished in his admiration for Jonathon's choice of reading matter. "What do you make of the-the *treasonous* sentiments expressed, if I may be so bold?"

Jonathon did not get the opportunity to offer his opinion one way or the other because Frederick, who had finally finished off a second slice of seedy cake and drunk all the lemon water in his tumbler interrupted the conversation by blurting out, "Mema! Mema! They are speaking in the English tongue at your table and it is not permitted! Tell them, Mema!"

Antonia opened her eyes very wide at her grandson and turned an astonished expression on her two gentlemen guests. "So they are, *mon petite chou*. Thank you for bringing this social lapse to my attention. How impolite they are. I did wonder what they were gibbering on about but me I was too polite to ask."

Charles Fitzstuart went very red about the ears, baulked and began to stammer a reply before Jonathon, who had cocked an eyebrow at Antonia's theatrical performance while sipping his coffee, cut in saying in French, "*Excuse moi*, Mme la duchesse, a momentary linguistic lapse on our part. We promise it won't happen again."

"Now you must run to the jetty and back! That's the rules," Frederick announced and grinned cheekily, all shyness evaporated at thinking himself very clever at catching out these two grown men and excited at the prospect of watching them run to the lake. "Mema! Tell Charles and M'sieur they have broken your rules, Mema! Tell them they must run to the jetty and back!"

"But who would know the rules if they were not broken from time to time, *mon chou*? It is hardly fair when this is M'sieur Strang's first visit to Crecy Hall. So, he is unaware of my rules. And Charles, he was merely being polite to our guest. Perhaps we should be charitable and give them a reprieve this one time? But not a second time, yes, Frederick?"

There was a long moment of silence while the little boy considered the matter before he nodded his agreement.

"Just this once," he said, exchanging a smile with Antonia. He looked at Jonathon, who was comfortably sprawled out on a number of cushions at the end of the table and feeding cake to the two whippets, and said in all seriousness, which had his listeners suppressing indulgent grins, "Mema is from France so she only understands French. So we speak only French at her house, *always*. Sometimes, if Louis and Gus fight, they forget their French and then it's a run to the jetty for them. Mema says that if they run about by the time they get back to the pavilion they've forgotten why they were tumbling with each other on the lawn! But Julie doesn't run at all because she's just turned three. Her *proper* name is Lady Juliana Antonia and she's a *complete* nuisance."

"Frederick, that is uncharitable."

"But... *Mema*, she is! Julie's *forever* being annoying. Papa he loses patience with her because she babbles on in French *all* the time when we have been *expressly* told to speak English when we're not in the schoolroom on account of the servants being ignorant. Mamma says it's bad mannered not to." He took the glass of lemon water offered him, adding with a grumble to Jonathon, "Mamma says Julie could get away with *mur-murder* because she's going to be the great beauty of the family. Whatever murder is!"

"She must resemble your Mema," Jonathon stated, stretching a long arm up the table for a second slice of almond cake, not a glance at Antonia.

"Yes, yes she does, come to think on it," Charles Fitzstuart agreed placidly.

Frederick rolled his eyes. "*Everyone* says that!"

"Who is to be your oarsman, *mon chou?*" asked Antonia, turning the subject because she was unreasonably annoyed by Jonathon's guarded compliment yet unaffected by her cousin's frank assessment and that bothered her more than she cared to think about. "Is it to be you, Charles?"

Frederick shot Charles a black look. "*Was* to be, but Charles is rowing for the enemy!"

"Enemy?"

"The American colonies, Mme la duchesse," Charles explained evenly.

"That's what I said! *The enemy.*"

"Not all the American colonists are at war with us, Frederick," Antonia said quietly.

"Dair says all Americans are traitorous dogs and the French mean to side with them and then we must hate the French too! But I don't want to hate the French!" Suddenly tears welled up in Frederick's brown eyes and his lip quivered. "Mema," he whispered, "I don't want to hate the French. *I won't.*"

Antonia smiled and beckoned Frederick to her who readily scrambled off his cushion onto her lap. She kissed the top of his curls and held him in a comforting embrace, saying soothingly, "It will not come to that, *mon beau petit-fils.* Your papa he will never let that happen. *Accepté?*"

When Frederick nodded, content to remain cuddled in Antonia's arms, she said to Jonathon by way of explanation, "Alisdair—Dair—he is Charles's elder brother."

"The returned hero of the Long Island campaign?" Jonathon commented with surprise, thinking the two brothers could not be more different, in appearance and temperament. He had had an earful from Sarah-Jane about the recently returned Lieutenant Colonel's adventures in the American colonial war, rather too much of an earful for his liking. In his opinion the man was an egotistical bore, but apparently his lordship was considered swooningly handsome by girls of his daughter's age, and a great matrimonial catch as heir to an earldom and cousin to a ducal house. No doubt his pedigree and good looks cancelled out the man's loutish womanizing; but what would he know? Sarah-Jane had pouted when he had made his opinions known. Not much, so it would seem...

"Charles, please to tell us who it is you row tomorrow."

"Dair offered to row Miss Strang," Charles explained, the color in his freckled cheeks deepening to match his red locks. "But then he had to withdraw his offer because he had earlier promised Her Grace he would row for the Stuarts, with Juliana wearing his burgee, and so was not able to fulfill his obligation to Miss Strang."

"Charles here is rowing my daughter Sarah-Jane," Jonathon stated flatly to Antonia. He raised a mobile eyebrow and bit into a strawberry tartlet. "For the American colonists."

"Yes. Yes. I volunteered my services, sir. It was the right thing to do."

"For Sarah-Jane or the Americans? Never mind! Never mind!" Jonathon said dismissively, not a whisker of sympathy for the ripening color in the young man's cheeks. "I am certain Sarah-Jane is beside herself to have you rowing her boat, regardless of your backing for the traitorous Americans."

Charles's jaw set hard. "You think the American patriots' cause traitorous, sir? That I am a traitor because I believe in free and fair elections; that men should be judged on what they do not who they are?"

Jonathon stared at him as if it was blindingly obvious. "Traitor? It has nothing to do with your political inclinations one way or the other, my boy. Can you row?"

"Well, yes, yes I can."

"So you'll win and that will please her. My daughter loves to win, Charles."

"Does she, sir? Does she indeed?"

When Charles visibly gulped, Antonia stared hard at Jonathon as if to say, *stop teasing the boy!* His response was to wink at her. She decided to ignore him and asked her grandson with practiced innocence, "So who is to row your boat, *mon chou? Mon père?*"

"It is Papa's turn to row Gus and Louis for the Hanoverians."

"What about Gregory or his brother?"

Frederick scrambled off Antonia's lap to resume his place beside her and took another slice of cake.

"Mema?" Frederick responded with revulsion at the idea. "*Gregory?* Gregory doesn't like boats. And his head it is always stuck in a shrub!"

"That is very true." Antonia giggled. "Poor Gregory. He is the eldest son of our head gardener and dreams of being a botanical scientist," Antonia told Jonathon. "He is prone to great abstraction. What of his brother? He rowed the boat of Louis and Augustus in last year's race. He almost beat you and your Papa to the line, did he not? What is his name, Frederick?"

Frederick's face lit up. "You mean Lawrence, Mema! Yes, I wanted him too. But don't you remember? He fell off his horse and broke his arm. The bone it stuck out from—"

"Yes, thank you, Frederick," Antonia cut in, "I remember now."

"Not a nice neat break then?" Jonathon enquired with wide-eyed encouragement; two could play at the Duchess's game.

"No, sir. It was a-a *ferocious* break," Frederick answered with relish. "Lawrence was thrown from his horse and we didn't think anything of it, because Lawrence is a crack jumper of fences. But you'll never guess what happened to him! His arm was all twisted up behind his back. He snapped it in *two* places. And when the sawbones reset the break he let out such a screaming howl that Papa said it was sure to wake the dead. We heard it *from the nursery*."

"Poor Lawrence's broken arm does not solve your problem, Frederick," stated Antonia, unable to resist a sly glance at Jonathon. She had formed a mischievous idea and smiling to herself said seriously to her grandson, "*Mon chou*, did you know, M'sieur Strang he rowed all the way over here to see me today. Yes, from your house… By himself. *Incroyable*, is it not? Such a distance! He is a very good oarsman, I think. Are you not, M'sieur?"

"Did you, sir? *Truly?*" Frederick asked enthusiastically before Jonathon had a chance to reply. "Papa says it's *twice as far* to row from that jetty to this, than to go twice round Swan Nest Island. The race tomorrow is once round Swan Nest on account of Louis and Gus being only five. Papa says next year we can row the whole course." He looked to Antonia, who was smiling encouragingly, and then at Jonathon. "Would you… Would you be my oarsman, sir? I'd be *forever* grateful. I don't want Gregory. He can't swim. Can you swim, sir? Can you?"

"Yes, I swim very well. And I would be honored to be your oarsman, Frederick," Jonathon answered, regarding Antonia with a small smile and a lift of his brows that said he would deal with her later. "But I will do so only on condition that if we win the race Mme la duchesse invites the captains and oarsmen to dine with her here at Crecy Hall."

Frederick looked expectantly at Antonia. "Will you, Mema? Will you invite us?"

"How could I refuse you?" But when Antonia looked at Jonathon it was with an imperious raise of her arched brows. "I give you afternoon tea and now you wish for me to invite you to dinner. Perhaps, M'sieur, you would like also for me to invite you to breakfast so we have covered all the main meals in the day?"

Jonathon gave a bark of laughter. "Oh, I have high hopes that when *that* day arrives I won't require an invitation!"

Antonia's lips parted in astonishment. She was stunned by such brash self-assurance. She was unsure if she should be furious, embarrassed or flattered, for there was no mistaking his inference. She did not know where to cast her gaze and fussed unnecessarily with the tea things. She would certainly ignore such an outrageous suggestion. The sun of the Indian subcontinent had indeed boiled his brain.

Yet the implied suggestion was underscored when Charles, who had been sipping a second cup of coffee, reacted to Jonathon's outrageous remark by breathing in and swallowing at the same time sending him into a fit of coughing and spluttering. He scrambled up from the table, fighting for breath, Jonathon following, clapping him on the back, the butler close behind with a tumbler of lemon water. By the time he returned to the table breathing normally, Antonia had regained her calm. She could not bring herself to look at Jonathon asking her grandson in a light tone,

"Have you named your boat, *mon chou?*"

Frederick nodded but frowned. "She's called the *Emerald Duchess*, after you, Mema."

"What an honor you do me, Frederick! That makes me very happy. But… Something it is troubling you, yes?"

"*I* wanted to name her the *Black Duchess*, but Papa he won't allow it. He says it's tradition for all the race boats to fly a color burgee, but that black is not a color. Nothing and nobody can change his mind. Will it, Charles?"

"I'm afraid that is true, Mme la duchesse. His Grace is adamant."

"And your color, Charles?"

"Blue."

"What luck! That's Sarah-Jane's favorite. She *will* be pleased."

Charles eyed the older man with the suspicion he was being laughed at. "Yes, sir, she was."

When her grandson continued to look glum, Antonia touched his cheek, saying softly, "*Emerald Duchess* is a very good name for your boat. You see my eyes they are the color of emeralds. Monseigneur always said so."

"But if she is called the *Emerald Duchess*, then I must fly a green burgee, and you don't wear colors so I don't want to fly green, I want to fly black. I *tried* to tell Papa that if my boat was the *Black Duchess* then I could fly a black burgee because you *always* dress in black. But *he* said it's not *my* choice to make, it's *yours*."

"Frederick, you must excuse me but I am feeling a little stupid today. I do not understand at all why it is your Papa says it is my choice."

Frederick hung his head of black curls and quickly dashed a hand across his moist eyes. "You can wear black. It doesn't bother *me*. It shouldn't bother Papa. It isn't fair!" he added in a heated rush. "*Papa* isn't playing fair. He's being horridly bad-tempered and—"

"Frederick! That is enough, *petite*," Antonia insisted quietly but firmly. "You are not to speak of your Papa in such a fashion. He is only doing what he believes is the right—"

"But it's *not* right," Frederick persisted. "You *always* wear black. *I* like you dressed in black. Papa shouldn't make you choose."

Antonia privately agreed and she was angry beyond words with her son. But her opinion of the Duke's under-handed methods of persuasion, in ill-using his six-year-old son in this way, in forbidding his children from visiting her in order to get her to bend to his will she would keep to herself until she could confront him. She had decided not to attend the dinner and recital that evening at the big house, but her grandson's distress, and the fact her son had barred his children from visiting the dower house, changed her mind.

"There is no need for anyone to choose, *mon chou*," Antonia managed to say brightly. "As you have done me the honor of naming your boat after me, the least I can do is wear the color of your burgee. Of course I will dress in whatever color you decide, be it emerald-green, sapphire-blue or ruby-red. But I am very pleased you chose emerald-green because it is Monseigneur's favorite precious stone. The emerald ring he wore always it belonged to his grandfather and one day—one day it will belong to you because... because..."

"Because, Mema?" Frederick asked after a long awkward silence that saw Charles drop his gaze, because the Duchess was on the verge of tears, and place a packet of letters tide up with ribbon beside his empty teacup; Jonathon gave the little boy an encouraging smile.

"*Mema*. Because? Because *why?*"

Antonia mentally shook herself out of her abstraction and smiled at her grandson, quickly blinking her wet eyes dry. She had been remembering when M'sieur le Duc had given her his emerald ring for safekeeping. They had been alone in their cavernous bedchamber, a rare circumstance in the last weeks of his life. He propped up on pillows to assist him to breathe without effort, she sitting amongst the bedcovers facing him, a silk banyan thrown over her nightgown. It was early morning and mist hung low in the treetops outside the bedchamber windows with their sweeping views of the Ornamental Gardens. The physicians, their attendants and the retinue of servants required to provide the Duke every comfort in his last days had all been dismissed with a languid wave of the thin white ducal hand; the one with the emerald ring upon it.

They did not speak and were content to hold hands and look at each other. The inevitable was left unspoken. It did not need to be said out loud.

He slipped the large square cut emerald ring from his finger, placed it in the palm of her hand, closed her fingers over the family heirloom and gently kissed her wrist. He had worn the Roxton emerald every day since becoming the fifth Duke of Roxton, when his grandfather had presented it to him at the age of nineteen, just hours before his own death. And now he had removed the ducal ring and given it into her safekeeping. He held her hand and made her repeat the promise out loud. She heard herself speaking the words clearly and reassuringly; inside she was crumbling away for it meant it was only a matter of hours before they would be forever parted on Earth. She had almost fainted with the grief.

"Because? Oh, because Monseigneur he made me promise that his emerald ring I will give to you on your twenty-first birthday," she said gently with forced brightness. "Until then I am to keep it safe. But it is yours, *mon chou*. So if you wish to see it before then, because it is such a very long time before that day arrives, you need only ask me. So, please, you are not to worry any more, yes? For you, I will put off my black for the regatta." When Frederick scrambled off his cushions and threw his arms about her neck, she added with a kiss to his cheek, "And your Papa you must not be angry with. He does what he considers is best for you because he loves you very much. He has a great many worries and we do not want to add to them, do we?"

Frederick shook his head. "Mama says you're Papa's greatest worry."

"*Pour quoi?*"

"Mama said it to Cousin Charlotte. Didn't she, Charles?"

"A throw away comment of no significance, Mme la duchesse."

"It is unlike you to pull the wool with me, Charles. My daughter-in-law is not given to throw away comments."

"Of course not, Mme la duchesse. Forgive me. I was only—"

"Why does Papa worry about you, Mema?" Frederick persisted. "Shouldn't you be worrying about him because you are his mama?"

"Out of the mouth of babes," Antonia murmured. "You are not to worry about your Mema," she added with forced cheerfulness. "Your Papa he does enough worrying for everyone." And she put out a hand for the packet of letters by her cousin's teacup, which he readily gave her. "They are for me to send to the Hôtel Roxton with my next post, yes?" she enquired, making an effort to change the subject and put to the back of her mind her daughter-in-law's observation, which cut her to the quick; if she was fair-minded, because there was some truth in it. But that did not make it any less hurtful. She chanced to glance across the table then and found Jonathon regarding her with an expression that told her he saw through her performance, that he knew very well she was wearing her public face for her cousin Charles and her grandson. And that too bothered her. Why, she had no idea. She looked away, and was about to suggest they take a walk to the jetty to feed the swans with the cake crumbs from their plates when Charles said in his quiet way,

"As we are not pulling the wool, Mme la duchesse, I should tell you that His Grace is in expectation of Sir Titus Foley's arrival on the morrow."

"But when Papa sees Mema is not in black he'll send Sir Titus away again, won't he, Charles?"

"I do not think he will, Frederick," Charles said soberly, and Jonathon could have kicked him for not *pulling the wool,* as the Duchess so quaintly termed being deceitful, as anyone with an ear could hear Frederick's anxiousness.

"Who is this Titus fellow, Frederick?" Jonathon asked in a rallying tone, and shot a glance at Antonia, but she would not meet his gaze. "Not the sawbones who patched up poor Lawrence's arm, is he?"

Frederick shook his head with a pout.

"Sir Titus Foley is a dandified physician who attends on members of the nobility," Charles said with barely disguised derision. "He made a name for himself curing the young Baroness Hartfield and the newly married Lady Fife of *melancholia.*"

"*Melancholia?*" Jonathon huffed his disbelief. "The man sounds like a dandified quack!"

Frederick could barely contain himself and burst out, "He's a— he's a-a big fat *ferret-face.*"

Antonia giggled in spite of herself. "That is very true, *mon chou,* but impolite to say so out loud."

"That's what Porter calls him, Mema. Porter is my tutor," Frederick announced to Jonathon. "And he's in-infactuated with—"

"In*fat*uated," Antonia corrected him gently.

"*Infatuated* with Mema. Whatever *that* means."

"Frederick!" Antonia gasped. "You cannot say such a thing about Porter! He is not here to defend himself and if he were, he would agree that it is quite false to think he—"

"But, Mema, it's not a falsehood. I don't even know what infactuated—um—in*fat*uated means."

This made Jonathon laugh out loud; even Charles could not suppress a grin.

"Porter goes red in the face when you speak to him, Mema," Frederick argued and pulled a face of disgust. "He looks queasy and sick and can't speak—"

"Yes, Frederick, that will do. Thank you."

"Poor Porter!" Jonathon said without sympathy and a sad shake of his head as he followed his hostess's lead and rose from the table. "Queasiness and a ready flush to the face and a stammer. With those symptoms, I'd say the poor fellow has it bad. Wouldn't you, Charles?"

"Yes, sir, I would," Charles agreed and smiled sheepishly when the Duchess glared at him. "*Excusez moi*, Mme la duchesse, but it is you who asked that I not *pull the wool.*"

"Good man!" Jonathon declared with a slap to his back.

Antonia opened her mouth to tell them both what she thought when her personal maid chose that moment to burst into the pavilion, a pair of red Moroccan leather mules in her hand and mouthing apologies for her tardiness as she bobbed a low curtsey and brushed down her petticoats.

"Michelle! Me I do not care in the least to hear your excuses about smoking chimneys and ruined carpets. They are too tiresome," Antonia interrupted imperiously, and stuck out a small stockinged foot for the girl to drop to her knees and slip on her mules. "Now you will return to the house and ready my bath. I have decided to attend Roxton's dinner after all. Yes. I have indeed changed my mind. That is not for you to wonder at. The open robe of black silk with the silver tissue under petticoats will suffice."

"Yes, Mme la duchesse," Michelle replied obediently, up on her feet to again drop a curtsey. She didn't dare take a second glance at the three figures standing by the low table that had upon it the remnants of an afternoon tea. But she did glance at Matthews, the stony-faced butler. Later he would tell her everything. Where she was concerned he could not help himself; were they not secretly engaged? "Should I send a message to Mesdames Willis and Spencer to ready themselves, Mme la duchesse?"

"Naturally. I want them looking their best tonight." When Jonathon cocked an eyebrow at her, Antonia couldn't help throwing him a conspiratorial smile. "They are not to wear gray, tonight, but black."

"Black. Yes, Mme la duchesse."

Antonia thrust the packet of letters at her. "And take M'sieur Fitzstuart's letters. I will write up the direction later and then you can put them on the hall table with the letters I left there yesterday. Not the ones for London, but for Paris, for the Comtesse du Charmond."

"At the Hôtel Roxton, Mme la duchesse?"

"Where else do I have a house in Paris, Michelle? No, do not answer me!"

Michelle was relieved a response was not required of her because she had never been to the Hôtel Roxton, and her mistress had not been there in the five years Michelle had been her personal maid, not since the old Duke had been too ill to travel. But one thing she did know was that the Comtesse du Charmond had not resided at the Hôtel Roxton for at least six months. What letters the Duchess wrote to the Comtesse Matthews was instructed to pass on to the Duke's steward. The Comtesse was a regular correspondent, and Michelle wondered how the Duchess remained none the wiser that her aging cousin no longer kept an apartment in her sprawling Parisian mansion.

"And while I am at dinner, you will find for me the gown of green silk with the vine embroidery and gold-tissue under-petticoats. I think also there is a matching bodice and shoes, and a fan. I will be wearing these tomorrow to the regatta. Do not look at me as if I am drunk! You heard me the first time. Oh, and the emerald choker and matching bracelets. And the green ribbons I will not need for my hair put these in a reticule so I may give them to my grandson tonight." She smiled at Frederick. "They are for his boating waistcoat."

"Merci, Mema."

Antonia held out her hand to Charles in farewell, expecting her maid to obey without comment, but when the girl stood there mouth agape, Antonia raised her eyebrows.

"You do remember where my clothes and jewelry are kept, do you not?"

"Yes, Mme la duchesse. Of course. It's just that you—"

"Good. You will now go away. And, Michelle, you will pretend as one blind, yes? Lord Alston and M'sieurs Fitzstuart and Strang were never at my pavilion. Willis and Spencer are not to find out." She glared at her expressionless butler and footman and then at her maid. "You understand me, *hein?*"

Michelle bobbed another curtsey. The butler inclined his head and the footman did not dare to blink. The trespass of the Duke's son and heir, her mistress's freckled faced red-haired cousin and a tall, handsome, brown skinned stranger were as nothing when compared to the revelation the Dowager Duchess of Roxton was finally putting off her black. Here was news she couldn't wait to throw in the faces of those two stiff-necked matrons, Spencer and Willis. Without another word she bustled away, the butler and footman following up behind with the tea things, also eager to get to the kitchens to spread the news amongst the Duchess's contingent of servants.

Antonia hugged Frederick, kissed his cheek and gently smoothed the mop of black curls from his brow. "Now you must return to the house with Charles before your Papa he finds out and poor Porter he is dismissed for allowing you to come here to see me. I will be at supper and will give you the ribbons in the Gallery, yes? And no more worrying, promise me?"

Frederick beamed. "I promise, Mema." He stepped back and made her a respectful bow then looked eagerly at Jonathon. "And thank you, sir, for agreeing to be my oarsman." He asked his grandmother, "Do you have enough ribbons for M'sieur Strang too?"

"Yes, yes, of course," Antonia replied, as if the idea had not occurred to her.

They watched Frederick tear up the path towards the house ahead of Charles Fitzstuart, the whippets prancing at his boot heels. He turned at the first bend in the path and waited for Charles to catch up and waved to his grandmother.

Antonia and Jonathon waved back.

"He's a very sharp little boy."

"Yes.

"But methinks he thinks too much for one so young."

"Yes. He is his father's son."

"He is very attached to you."

"And I to him..."

Antonia turned away with a small sigh, her grandson and cousin no longer in view. That small sigh made Jonathon frown down at her with concern.

"You don't have to put off your black just because Roxton wishes it."

"I do not do this to please my son but for Frederick because he is a worried little boy," Antonia replied, wondering why he was suddenly gruff. "He should not be worried. He should be enjoying life. There are plenty of years before he needs worry about any matter. Monseigneur he would agree with me. And he would want me to do what is best for Frederick and for all our grandchildren."

"Does Roxton regularly keep his children from visiting to bend you to his will?"

Antonia shook her head. "No… This time it is the first…"

"And Sir Titus Foley? Has Roxton threatened to foist that quack physician's attentions on you?"

"Threatened?" Disconcerted by the word, she looked away, suddenly feeling heavy of heart. "He—my son—he does what is for the best."

Jonathon raised his eyebrows in angry skepticism. "Best? For who? Using his young son to manipulate you to do his will; forbidding his children from visiting; threatening you with quack doctors and their hocus-pocus nonsense; that is in *your* best interests?"

Antonia scowled. "He Julian would never intentionally cause his children distress."

"Not intentionally, no."

"He loves his wife and children very much, and is a good husband and father—"

"—but he could be a more understanding son."

It was a statement Antonia wished she could refute. But she would not lie. Nor would she discuss her family with a gentleman she had met for the first time the night before. It did not matter that he was a willing and sympathetic ear and seemed genuinely concerned for her welfare, or that she was in desperate need of a confidant. To pour out her troubles to a stranger was not only unseemly it was disloyal to her family. She had already shown a marked lack of discretion by sharing Roxton's note with this gentleman. She must not weaken again. As always, she must be strong and disregard her own wants and needs. Her son and his family, Frederick in particular, and what was in the best interests of the Roxton dukedom, they must always come first. She owed it to Monseigneur.

"Why are you here?" she demanded, lifting her chin, cloaking her sadness and deep sense of loneliness in a patronizing façade of noble superiority. "What do you want from me?"

Yesterday, before he had met her, Jonathon could have answered her with ease. He wanted the Strang-Leven inheritance acknowledged by the present Duke of Roxton as misappropriated by his ancestor and he wanted it returned to him, its rightful heir, and he needed Roxton's widowed mother to sign it over to him. Today he had the added complication that the Dowager Duchess of Roxton was in truth the most beguiling woman he had ever met. Watching her with her grandson, he'd caught glimpses of the vibrant, sensual creature that simmered just below the surface of her grief for her beloved duke, and to his astonishment and annoyance he wanted to be the one to reawaken her to the joys of living. But how could he in good conscience take her in his arms, kiss her, and make her laugh when reclaiming his birthright would surely mean taking the house and land her Monseigneur had painstakingly restored for her?

He stared down into her upturned beautiful face, dazed and mute, angry with himself for being so easily ensnared, yet knowing he had walked into her net of his own accord; that she had not enticed him in any way. He wanted to make some flippant remark but found he could not under the steady gaze of her luminous green eyes. He had given his word not to lie to her, and so wondered how best to respond without sounding insincere and trite.

Antonia mistook his silence for cavalier insolence and she straightened her spine, every inch of her small frame a duchess.

"M'sieur, I do not know how persons conduct themselves in good society in India, but here it is not your place to make comment on matters that do not concern you. Most definitely you do not have the right to criticize my son M'sieur le Duc d'Roxton. My family, our affairs, I will not discuss, particularly not with one of M'sieur le Duc's guests. What happens to me, it is not for you to bother about. I do not want your opinion, or your concern. Nor did I ask for your company. Now you will leave me in peace and return to the big house where you belong, and never are you to come here again! That is all I have to say. Good day. You may go away now."

She had every expectation that Jonathon would immediately acquiesce, step aside with a respectful bow and allow her to pass. She was, after all, used to unquestioning obedience. From the day of her marriage her noble pre-eminence amongst servants, retainers, tenants, family, friends and peers had never been in question. So when Jonathon just stood there, silent and unmoved, she sighed her annoyance, muttered something under her breath about him being deaf as well as stubbornly bad mannered, snatched up a handful of her petticoats and brushed past him without a second glance. What he did next was without precedent.

He caught her above the elbow, fingers tight about her silk sleeve, spun her about and yanked her hard up against him. A hand to the small of her back and she could not move, breasts pressed to his chest; petticoats crumpled and concertinaed against his legs. She blinked up at him, astonishment making her mute, blushing furiously, outraged that he dared to touch her without permission, and this the second time. Gone was the even-tempered friendly stranger of first acquaintance. There was an unfathomable intensity to his brown eyes and the thin line to his mouth was unnerving, but what caught the breath in her throat and ripened the color to her cheeks was the sudden rapid beating of her own heart and a sensation, very like pins and needles, that washed over her from throat to toes. From somewhere deep within her something sparked and ignited. It was so thoroughly unexpected that it shocked her beyond belief.

"I am all for laying myself at your feet," he said with suppressed feeling. "But when I prostrate myself before you, it will not be because you are Her Grace the most noble Dowager Duchess of Roxton, but because I have decided that is where I wish to be. You are first and foremost uncommonly interesting, and that alone makes you deserving of my attention. But I am not blind. You are unquestioningly the most beautiful woman I have ever set eyes on. And I am not immune. I find you utterly desirable. So the sooner you see me as a warm-blooded male worthy of your notice and consideration and not a mindless, neutered functionary the better for both of us."

At that he let her go and with a small bow and a curt nod of farewell he strode off across the lawn to the jetty.

He did not look back.

Antonia watched him disappear over the rise of rolling lawn.

$\mathcal{S}$ix

$\mathcal{H}$e was insufferably arrogant. Overbearing. *Dangerous.*

She must keep her distance. Be aloof. Forget he had ever been to her pavilion. Better still, she would ignore him; pretend he had never introduced himself.

Yet, Jonathon's astonishing declaration was still occupying Antonia's thoughts several hours later as she joined upwards of ninety guests dining in the splendid magnificence of Treat's formal banquet room. The rows of polished mahogany tables creaked under the weight of silver, porcelain, large arrangements of flowers and bowls of fruits, and elaborate epergnes of silver and gold. The place settings were Sevres, the knives, forks and spoons highly polished silver. Behind every mahogany ribbon back chair stood a blank-faced liveried footman. Three courses each consisting of twenty to twenty-five dishes were consumed with gusto and much laughter and conversation, the melodic strains of a string orchestra in the upper gallery aiding in digestion. And when the ladies finally adjourned to the Long Gallery for coffee and sweet-meats, the gentlemen remained to unbutton their silk waistcoats, be comfortable, sip liquors and talk politics and horses for an hour or two before rejoining the ladies for conversational whist.

Antonia knew it all, from the place settings to the silver, to the order of the dishes presented. The first course of soups, stews, an assortment of vegetables in sauces, boiled fish and every type of meat, all placed around the table in a precise arrangement that allowed for ease of ladling and serving by the guests themselves.

Next came the remove dishes at each end of the table, tonight wild boars dressed and stuffed and providing a talking point while the second course was on its way. More vegetables, with different sauces, more meat and fish and a plethora of exotic pies with delectable pastry and filled with all manner of game bird, hen and combination thereof. And finally, to the even more elaborate and mouth-watering selection of cakes, jellies, sweetmeats, sugared fruits, ices and creams that made up the twenty-five courses of dessert. With a French pastry chef and a confectioner, the guests were entertained with sugary sculptures and delicate pastries of such sweetness and buttery lightness that the Roxtons were the envy of their noble friends.

And then there was the ritual leave-taking of the ladies with their hostess the Duchess leading the way to the Gallery, where coffee and sweetmeats awaited the ladies who sat about languidly fanning themselves while nibbling on more sweet confections and exchanging the latest gossip.

The vast house and its gilded furnishings, the army of soft-footed servants, the ritualized household customs, the daily routine of every family member, guest, upper and lower servant indoors and out, stable hand, gardener, tenant farmer, tradesman and apprentice, local villagers, parson, shopkeeper and merchant on this large country estate, from just before first light when fires were reset, to the black of a midnight sky twinkling with stars when bedchamber candles were snuffed, everything remained precisely as Antonia had managed it since her marriage to the fifth Duke of Roxton two months after her eighteenth birthday.

Antonia should have been flattered her daughter-in-law, who had taken to her role as the sixth Duchess with all the confidence and aplomb of one born to position and title, had not seen the need to change the practices she had so painstakingly put in place to ensure the smooth running of such a large and complex household. But Antonia wondered if Deborah kept to her routine, not because it was the way she wanted life to be, but because she and the Duke thought it was the way life must be ordered while her mother-in-law remained living on the estate; that any changes, however small and insignificant, would upset the Dowager Duchess of Roxton.

He said she was uncommonly interesting. Monseigneur declared her to be incomparable.

When she had arrived for dinner, Spencer and Willis in tow, it was evident her presence was an awkward surprise. From across the crowded drawing room, her daughter-in-law exchanged a look with the Duke that said *you did not tell me your mother would be attending.* And he had responded with a raise of his eyebrows and a smile he kept exclusively for her that said *I understand your frustration, my love, but I have every confidence you will deal admirably with the situation.*

Antonia liked her daughter-in-law Deborah very much. The young woman had a good heart and she loved the Duke and their children unconditionally. Deborah brought out the best in her husband and fulfilled her duties as his Duchess with aplomb. And she was nobody's fool. She was forthright, opinionated and when required, brutally honest. But Antonia was well aware that Deborah was in awe of her and that this made it difficult for the two women to be as close as Antonia would have liked. Even now, as the sixth Duchess, and having produced four healthy children, three of them boys and thus heirs aplenty for the continuance of the Roxton dukedom, Deborah remained unable to shake off her diffidence and apprehension whenever in Antonia's presence.

...I am not blind. You are unquestioningly the most beautiful woman I have ever set eyes on.

But many men had told her that over the years and she took such verbose compliments with the pinch of salt they deserved. She knew she was beautiful. It was not a vain presumption; it was fact. So why did *his* saying it bother her? She mentally shook herself and resolved to put him out of her mind

With the ladies comfortably ensconced in the Long Gallery, Antonia sipped her coffee and gazed out through the French windows to the tiled terrace and sweep of rolling lawn beyond. A peacock strutted into view, brilliantly colored plumage spread wide for the appreciation of its mate. The peahen did not even bother to raise her head, even when the peacock honked loud and long.

Several of the ladies jumped in fright at the peacock's raucous call. Antonia heard their gasps and the resulting laughter but could not see their startled expressions because she always sat furthest from the tea things, and thus furthest from her daughter-in-law, wingchair turned slightly away from the gathering. She used the excuse that she wished to look out on the view. The truth was more complicated. By sitting in the furthest chair and not involving herself, Antonia hoped her daughter-in-law would be more at ease carrying out her duties as Duchess. After all, it could not be easy for Deborah to play hostess with her mother-in-law, who had had the running of this house for a quarter of a century, witness to her every move.

But Antonia was not one of these women who, having lost her position in society and over a household that had once been hers, tried to find fault with her successor as a means of keeping alive her self-consequence. Antonia's attachment to the trappings of her noble station, to the rituals and responsibilities of being a duchess, and the attendant material comforts that flowed from her marriage to the wealthiest duke in England, were of little consequence if she could not share them with the man she had loved with every fiber of her being.

And so she sat, solitary and silent, an audience of one to the strutting peacock's performance.

I find you utterly desirable... Monseigneur had said she was completely intoxicating...

The breath caught in her throat. She set the fine porcelain cup on its saucer and blinked with dawning realization as to the true meaning of his words. He was attracted to her. Of course that was what he had said but only now had she come to fully appreciate what he meant. But he must be ten years her junior. Never mind she appeared younger than her actual age and was more physically active than many women half her age. But men were only interested in women younger than themselves. Indeed, Monseigneur had been older than Jonathon Strang was now when they had married. No one had raised an eyebrow at the age divide. But a younger man courting an older woman was not only frowned upon it was grist for the scandal mill. Antonia smiled wryly to herself. He's not interested in courting you, you foolish woman! He wants to bed you. The man was not only an outrageous flirt he was also presumptuous.

Surely it could not be many more minutes before the children were filed in by the nursery maids to say good night to their parents and assembled guests? She wondered what explanation, if any, they had been given for not making their usual visit to her pavilion, and if Frederick's truancy had been discovered. She had the green ribands in a pocket ready to give to him.

Without needing to turn or look up, she held out her empty porcelain cup on its saucer, knowing her ladies-in-waiting, who watched her every move, would be there to take it from her and have it refilled. Spencer enquired if she would care for more coffee. Antonia shook her head and continued to fan herself, thoughts seemingly miles away.

Yet she was not so self-absorbed that she had forgotten Spencer had blistered her feet wearing in a new pair of walking boots Antonia had given each of the sisters as an Easter gift; the reason she had hobbled into the carriage like one crippled. Antonia even suggested she remain behind to bathe and wrap her blisters. But Spencer would not be swayed and as Willis agreed with her sister that it was their duty to attend on her, whatever the small inconvenience to them, Antonia gave up the attempt to make them see reason.

"Take your poor feet away, Sally, and find somewhere to sit. Do not *hover*."

"But, Mme la duchesse, I assure you my—"

Antonia turned her head slightly, chin up and looked at her askance. It was enough to silence Spencer and when Willis returned to stand the other side of Antonia's wingchair, a word and a look from Spencer and the sisters retreated to some nether region of the Long Gallery.

Antonia smiled to herself. Her gargoyles. She liked very much Jonathon's moniker. Over the long tedious dinner, she had had ample time and opportunity to set in motion his idea that she bestow on her dour guardians a little holiday with the Countess of Strathsay.

As fortune would have it (though she suspected her son's action to be deliberate) she had been seated beside the Countess of Strathsay, providing her with the perfect opportunity to plant the seed in her aunt's mind that she did indeed need a companion or two for the journey back into Buckinghamshire and then had blithely sought Charlotte's advice on a suitable destination for

Willis and Spencer; the sisters were deserving of a few weeks away from Treat, ideally with like-minded females. Willis had loaned her a most ancient and intriguing tract on pietism, an heirloom handed down in her family. It was by a German by the name of Spener and entitled the *Pia desideria*. Had Charlotte heard of it? No? Perhaps Willis would loan it to her, or better still, the sisters had an English translation of the tract that their German ancestor had studiously translated for his English relatives. Apparently Spener's writings had greatly influenced the Morovians.

And so Antonia had spent an hour listening to Charlotte drone on about her favorite philanthropic pursuit, support of the Morovian missions, and knew her time had not been wasted when the Countess diffidently enquired how Antonia would manage without the services of the sisters? To which Antonia feigned disconsolate resignation and said that she would do as best she could with Michelle and a couple of the upstairs maids for it was only for a matter of weeks, not months that the sisters would be away.

The sooner you see me as a warm-blooded male worthy of your notice and consideration and not a mindless, neutered functionary the better for both of us.

Mindless? Neutered? Functionary? Surely not! Did he think her in her dotage? He had been so angry with her for dismissing him in such a cavalier fashion, and she could excuse him a little for that. He was obviously used to the attentions of fawning, eyelash-batting females who swooned at the sight of such sunbaked virility. Even in her miserable self-absorption, of wishing the impossible appearance of Monseigneur at the ball, she had been sufficiently distracted to wonder why the handsome stranger was staring at her. And when he had confidently asked her for a dance, five minutes in his company told her he was completely self-assured and used to getting what he wanted.

But there was no excuse for manhandling her. He should never have touched her, whatever his anger and annoyance with her high-handed dismissal. She was certain there was a bruise to her arm where he had grabbed her. That he had gone even further and dared to hold her against him in such an intimate way... Was it any wonder she had blushed; that her heart beat rapidly? Both were very natural responses to an upsetting situation. Yet, that did not explain away the totally unexpected and startling third sensation, the throbbing little pulse deep within her that even now, just thinking about the nearness of him, of being in his arms, brought heat up into her throat and pins and needles to her fingertips. She shot up out of her chair, face flushed with mortification, just as two of the guests swept past in a rustle of silks.

With Antonia on her feet, the ladies paused to sink into a curtsey then retreated to huddle together on a horsehair sofa, out of earshot of the main group of ladies chatting comfortably on an arrangement of sofas, yet close enough so as not to be considered bad-mannered. That the Dowager Duchess would hear every word of their *tête-à-tête* was an irrelevance.

No doubt as matriarch of the Roxton family, being deaf, blind and a little senile came with the position, thought Antonia as she sank back onto the wingchair, back ram-rod straight, and took to fanning herself, pretending a loss of hearing. Or, if she was to be charitable, perhaps these two had no idea she understood and spoke English as she spoke exclusively French with her family. It was a common misconception and one she had never sought to correct.

"Lord, no! Whatever gave you that idea? Strang has fleeting *interests*, but never *attachments*, Hettie dearest," Kitty Cavendish was saying. "His is a rather *restrained* sensibility when it comes to women. He's not a monk, but no one could call him a sad rake. *Discernment* is a word that springs to mind. Not any woman will do. But why am I telling you this, my dear? You know this well enough."

"Knew, Kitty. *Knew.*" Lady Hibbert-Baker's sigh of regret was audible. "I had hoped... With him returned to England... Kitty, why has he returned?"

"Business interests; to find Sarah-Jane a husband. Why, any number of reasons," Kitty Cavendish replied airily. "Why wouldn't he want to come home after years on the subcontinent living amongst heathens?"

"But England has never been his home. He was born abroad, a second son of a second son. Kenny says Strang is practically a heathen. Kenny says Strang settling in England is like putting a-a rhinoceros amongst a field of deer, for all he has in common with us. Kenny says there has to be more to it than seeing his daughter married off."

"Rot, Hettie! He went to Harrow and Oxford and his wife was a Cavendish. What could make him more one of us than that? And once he's remarried he'll *be* one of us. In fact, that's what I wanted to talk to you about. Tommy and I have decided we must find Strang a bride. It was all very well for him to remain a widower amongst the natives, but with his inheritance—"

"Inheritance?"

"She doesn't have to be an heiress, Strang has bags of money for everyone, but she must be young, pliable and—"

"—stupid? What inheritance, Kitty? You said inheritance. That's why he's come home to roost, isn't it?"

"No. Not stupid but *persuadable.*"

"Yes. Yes. Yes. A young, stupid bride. That's all very well, but tell me about Strang's *inheritance*, Kitty!"

"Did I mention inheritance? That was foolish of me. Forgive me, but I am unable to tell you. And even if I could, I can't because I don't know. Tommy merely mentioned it to me without further elaboration, which is most frustrating of him."

"You won't take me into your confidence and yet you expect me to help you find Strang a wife?" her companion complained. "You'll have to do better than that, Kitty dearest, if you want my help. Besides, why should I help you when a bride for Strang will surely interfere with my plans to rekindle his interest?"

Kitty Cavendish tried to fob off her friend by saying lightly, "Hettie, you must know how it is with husbands. If Tommy says he can't tell me, he can't, for reasons only known to him. Surely, Kenny has secrets he can't share with you? He is second-in-charge of the Spying-for-England Department."

"It's called the *Secret Service*," Hettie Hibbert-Baker replied loftily. "And Kenny is not only second-in-charge of that, but since our return from New York he is head of something called the *American Colonial War Committee*."

"How *very* impressive of you, Hettie, to remember the name of such an important but quite pointless committee!"

"Is it any wonder when Kenny drones on about it to me until I'm purple! I do try to appear interested because he says it is such an important committee, dealing with those horrid colonials not doing as they're told and wanting something called *independence*. Kenny has the bad manners to bring his committee grumbles to my bed. And I find that if I don't puff up his self-consequence by listening as if I'm *vastly* interested in who's spying for *us* and who's a traitor spying for *them*, and who is providing information to both *us and them*, then nothing else puffs up as well, no matter the efforts I go to on my knees or otherwise, and I'm left so dissatisfied I just want to burst!"

Both ladies fell into a fit of the giggles.

When she could talk, Hettie Hibbert-Baker adjusted her elaborate upswept hairstyle festooned with ribbons and loops of pearls, which her hairdresser had assured her was all the rage in Paris salons, saying, "Is it any wonder, my dearest Kitty, that I prefer hot-blooded men such as Strang who come to a lady's boudoir with nothing more tedious on their minds than my preference for mounting."

More giggles followed by much waving of fans across heaving bosoms and careful dabbing of moist eyes and then Kitty Cavendish said with a little breathless cough, "Do you know, Hettie, I find all this spying deliciously intriguing. Not knowing who is one of *us*, and wondering if your partner at whist might be one of *them*, or if the gentleman with the fascinatingly dark eyes in the next box at the Opera who has his quizzing glass trained on my bosom could be one of them *and* one of us! I should like to meet one of these cloak and dagger men who skulk up backstairs and hide in shadows! Do you think Kenny might oblige me?" She gave a start, as if having a sudden thought and tapped her friend's lace flounce with her fan, saying with practised surprise, "You! Hettie! *You* can tell me if we have a spy in our midst! Kenny must've told you?"

"No, Kitty! Just as you can't tell me about Strang's inheritance because Tommy won't tell you, I couldn't possibly tell you what I don't know that Kenny told me that I don't know!"

Kitty Cavendish pouted and pondered the ivory sticks of her painted lace fan saying with a glance at her friend, "What a shame we must be good and obedient wives and not tell each other the silly little secrets our husbands tell us, particularly when such secrets don't mean a spoonful of jellied eels to us. Of course we are such *dear* friends that I know we could have a conversation that once we left this sofa we would both quite forget we ever had..."

Hettie Hibbert-Baker ummed and aahed and said with a shrug of a bare round shoulder, "I am very forgetful and I really do not know the first thing about what Kenny says to me sometimes that even if I did happen to mention it to you, it wouldn't mean that I had told you anything of any significance whatsoever."

"Precisely!" Kitty Cavendish said with satisfaction. "And I could simply mention in passing what Tommy mentioned in passing to me about Strang so that it would merely be a comment in passing; which is not the same as telling you directly."

"That seems exceedingly fair."

"Yes, it is, isn't it?"

"And not at all disloyal."

"Not at all."

"Shall I tell first?"

"How obliging of you, Hettie dearest. Please do."

"Very well. The reason so many government ministers are staying at Treat with their wives is because there is to be a meeting here of the American Colonial War Committee to deal with the French Question: will the French openly support the American rebels in their war or not? If the French do then it stands to reason that England must declare war on France for siding with the traitorous rebels. But the French want to avoid a war with us at all costs; remember their failure in the French and Indian wars and the territories they lost as a result of that disaster? That's not to say the French aren't already supporting the rebels, but in secret. We, I mean the American Colonial War Committee knows this for a fact because our spies, they are everywhere, particularly in Paris."

"Spies! How marvelous!" cooed Kitty Cavendish.

"Many in the Committee are all for sending a delegation to

Versailles, secret or otherwise, to the French ministers and King Louis to discover for themselves, face-to-face, the French position. Kenny says any overtures to the French should be made in the utmost secrecy, and is in favor of a secret delegation, all to save *our* face should the French double-cross us and choose to side with the rebel colonials regardless of their sincere protestations to the contrary and assurances of their neutrality, a prospect Kenny says is very real given the French loathe us with a passion, which is understandable because we always defeat them. But there is a sticking point and that's the reason we are all here at the Duke's invitation."

There followed a long silence in which Antonia itched to turn her head to stare at the two women for she was certain Kitty Cavendish's jaw, like her own, must be swinging wide in response to the lucid summation given by Hettie Hibbert-Baker, a woman whose penchant for the latest craze in towering hairstyles was considered by Polite Society to be in marked contrast to the walnut size of her intellect.

Kitty Cavendish was indeed stunned, regarding her friend anew, quickly closed her mouth and diverted her gaze to the wide marbled terrace beyond the French windows where some of the ladies were strolling arm in arm, having finished their tea and gossip by the fireplace.

"A-a sticking point, dearest Hettie?" asked Kitty Cavendish, trying to sound light and disinterested.

"Roxton. He's the sticking point. His Grace won't entertain the notion of a secret delegation. The Duke wants open dialogue with the French. Kenny says that's just the sort of stiff-necked attitude he's come to expect from the Duke. And who can entirely trust Roxton's motives when his father the fifth duke was self-styled M'sieur le Duc in the French manner and his mamma is French to her fingertips? Never mind His Grace has taken great strides since inheriting the dukedom to be seen foremost as an Englishman, distancing himself from the French familial connection with an extraordinary *Grand Gesture*. As to what sort of Grand Gesture, I have no idea because Kenny didn't tell me *that* but he did stress it was *extraordinary*. And I am doubly sorry to disappoint you, Kitty. I truly cannot name the spy in our midst. Kenny didn't tell me that either. But then again, he might not know, *yet*. And naturally, it goes without saying that he didn't tell me anything at all, as you and I have agreed. So I have now forgotten the lot!"

"But there is one? A spy. Here? At *Treat?*"

Hettie Hibbert-Baker nodded. "Now it's your turn to tell me what Tommy didn't tell you about Strang. And you must hurry because the whist tables are being settled and I have promised to partner up with Charlotte Strathsay. Oh, look and here comes our hearts delight!"

"All I know," Kitty Cavendish confided, "is that Strang's inheritance has everything to do with a dying distant but titled relative who owns a vast estate in a God-forsaken corner north of the border and who has been breathing his last for a twelve-month. So turn your attention to the task at hand. Getting Strang married. What do you think of the Aubrey twins? I shouldn't think either of them would expect fidelity."

"*Is that it?* Are you truly telling me that's all you know?" Hettie Hibbert-Baker was so incredulous her voice rose on a squeak and attracted the attentions of a few of the ladies coming in off the terrace to join the whist players. "After everything I didn't tell you?

"Yes. Strang needs a bride young enough to give him sons. Martha and Maria Aubrey are the perfect age and the perfect choice, not least because they are my nieces. They are also poor. A needy ignorant niece eternally grateful to Aunt Kitty for bagging her a wealthy husband is just what Tommy and I need to secure our old age... Hettie? Hettie! Do attend to the matter at hand! Give me your opinion of my scheme."

But Hettie Hibbert-Baker was still recovering from her dis-appointment at the unequal exchange of information and replied pettishly, "As Tommy is not as accommodating as Kenny, I pre-sume you expect me to wheedle from Strang everything there is to know about his mysterious inheritance?"

"Will you? That's just what I was hoping, Hettie dearest. Who better than you to discover what needs to be discovered? You would make an excellent spy, and if Kenny had any idea that inside all that padding and fluff atop your pretty little head there resides a working brain, he would employ you on the spot!"

Slightly mollified, Hettie Hibbert-Baker smiled and said archly,

"Are you *asking* me to tumble into bed with Strang? What about your nieces?"

"Oh, I am relying on you to distract Strang long enough to ensure that when this house party is over, my nieces will be the only eligible beauties left worth Strang's consideration. Besides, with Tommy and I championing their cause on one front and you providing hints in their direction between the sheets, Strang will eventually capitulate. He must remarry. Being summonsed home means he can no longer ignore his destiny. It is unavoidable."

"Capitulate. Summonsed. Destiny. These are not words usually associated with Jonathon Strang. An unconventional, free-thinking non-conformist is the Jonathon Strang I knew in Hyderabad. Kenny warned me against him, but..." Hettie Hibbert-Baker sighed on a memory and poised her fan over her almost-bare breasts. "You know me, Kitty, I can never resist a prime piece of beef. I almost broke Kenny's poor little heart. But I just *had* to know him, Kitty. It's not everyday one has the opportunity to sample the divinely exotic. I certainly would never do so here, but in India..." She shrugged. "Must have something to do with the heat."

"Divinely exotic? My dearest Hettie, whatever can you mean?"

There was an extended silence and Antonia unconsciously leaned toward the sofa, the two gossiping friends having dropped their voices behind immobile fans. A sudden burst of raucous laughter that coincided with the peacock's honking and she was up off the wingchair, startled, and brushing down her petticoats, mortified to be eavesdropping on a private conversation, and mentally castigating herself for such banal behavior. She must indeed be declining into her dotage. Overhearing the rest of a conversation punctuated with giggles and gasps was unavoidable.

"Hettie. No! *Really?*"

"You blush beautifully, dearest. Yes! *Really.*"

"I knew Strang's papa for an eccentric," Kitty said in wonder. "Indeed, he spent his entire life on the subcontinent, but I never *dreamed* he would force his young sons to go through with such a heathen practice. It's barbaric!"

"Why when there was every expectation of father and sons remaining in India. The native women won't entertain the idea of fornicating with a man unless he has obliged them in this way."

"Extraordinary! But... Why have a native woman as a mistress? There are Englishwomen on the subcontinent."

Hettie Hibbert-Baker let out a trill of laughter.

"Oh, Kitty! You are *deliciously* naïve. *Firangi* such as Strang don't have a mistress they have a *harem* of native women. It's what's done out there. And believe me, Kitty, Jonathon Strang had no shortage of native women lining his veranda for the chance to ride the length and breadth of his stallion, and I'm not talking Newmarket!"

"Well, my bitter-sweet tartlet, are you and Hettie prepared to share your sure bet for Newmarket?"

"Tom-my!" Kitty Cavendish declared, gasping for breath and wiping dry her eyes with a scrap of lace she called a handkerchief. She stood, a glance over her husband's silken shoulder confirming that the gentlemen had left their port to join the ladies at last. "How very unfair of you to sneak up on us!"

"Then you weren't talking horseflesh at all," Lord Cavendish said silkily, eyeglass trained on Lady Hibbert-Baker whose gray eyes danced behind her fluttering gouache fan. "Did you add the spoonful of *inheritance* and *summonsed home* to your teacup of conversation, my custard cup?" he asked his wife in an under-voice.

"Without a trip of the tongue."

"Excellent."

"Excellent?" Kitty Cavendish pouted into her husband's cravat and pretended to brush lint from his silken shoulder. "You haven't even told me, your dearest wife, the identity of the Scottish relative who had Strang *summonsed home*, and yet I'm expected to sprinkle my conversation with your sugar dust gossip."

"I gave Strang my word, sugar plum," Lord Cavendish apologized in a whisper. "But if you do what I ask, you shall see my soufflé rise to perfection. Strang will then be forced to give up his humble pie arrogance, and the whole world will rejoice, not least of all our dearest niece."

Kitty Cavendish had no idea where her husband's culinary metaphors were leading, but she clung to his last word, saying curiously, "Sarah-Jane doesn't know either what you know about her father?"

"Not a salt crystal. He says his immense wealth is sweetener enough for the drones out there seeking to marry his honeybee daughter." Lord Cavendish glanced again at Hettie Hibbert-Baker. "And she? Was anything forthcoming from between the ears of that spun sugar confection?"

Kitty's smug smile raised her husband's eyebrows. "Never again underestimate her, Tommy. Fair warning."

"Is that so? Interesting. Thank you for the warning, my love. And my postulation about colonial tea parties and spy glasses?"

"Our esteemed friends have indeed gathered for a tea party, to talk French. As to ownership of the spy glass, that is still in question."

Lord Cavendish stepped away from his wife and coughed, as if needing to clear his throat, and put up his quizzing glass, saying over his shoulder to Jonathon who had just sauntered up to him,

"Methinks I've caught my bitter-sweet tartlet and Hettie Cream Puff here, with their hands in the chef's choux pastry. And I've no doubts you're the main course." When no comment was forthcoming he playfully tapped the merchant's velvet sleeve with the rim of his eyeglass. "Oh, do at least humor me about my culinary wit, Strang! Strang?"

But Jonathon wasn't listening. He pushed past Lord Cavendish without comment, ignored Kitty Cavendish and Lady Hibbert-Baker, who was smiling up at him encouragingly, and strode across to an undraped French window to scoop up off the polished floorboards a lady's fan.

Seven

$\mathcal{A}$ntonia had heard more than she cared to know, and not enough to convince her that what she had overheard should be dismissed without consideration. Despite being a devoted wife and mother, she had never been blind to, nor did she pass judgment on, the liberalities and immoralities that surrounded her as Duchess of Roxton. Thus it did not surprise her that Jonathon Strang had, in all probability, kept a harem on the subcontinent, or that he and Henrietta Hibbert-Baker had been lovers. That Lady Hibbert-Baker was keen to rekindle a past affair was also not surprising. Her lover was tall and very handsome in a lean, muscular sort of way and, from what she had overheard, a much sort after lover. Besides which, the woman made no secret of her lax lifestyle and her arranged marriage was no love match as hers had been. But it bothered her that Jonathon would take such a predatory creature as mistress.

As for Henrietta Hibbert-Baker's crude confidences about the man's personal attributes being divinely exotic and considerably above the average, Antonia's cheeks had flamed with embarrassment, like an old maiden aunt unaccustomed to bawdy conversation. She immediately wondered if her widowhood was turning her into one of those sad, pathetically frigid creatures who smothered the reality of a lonely existence by publicly taking the high moral ground in all matters sexual, while privately having a partiality for eavesdropping on tawdry conversations to satisfy a non-existent love life. Something Charlotte Strathsay did with fatiguing regularity.

The thought of turning into the frigidly upright and wholly priggish Charlotte frightened Antonia, bleached the color from her hot cheeks and turned her fingers all to thumbs as she tried to close over the delicate sticks of her carved ivory fan.

The fan fell with a clatter to the floor and unintentionally the point of her damask covered shoe kicked it forward so it skimmed across the polished floorboards and came to rest across the room against an undraped French window. Antonia's ladies-in-waiting, seeing their mistress on her feet, had come to stand behind her wingchair, scrambled to retrieve it, scuttling after it like cats after a mouse. The gentleman who had been occupying Antonia's thoughts got to the fan before them both.

Realizing the Dowager Duchess of Roxton was on her feet and staring at them with tacit disapproval, Lady Hibbert-Baker lost her silly grin, and she and Kitty Cavendish dipped into a curtsey of respectful recognition, gaze remaining to the floor. Lord Cavendish bowed low, showing Antonia the top of his powdered wig as she swept past them without a second glance that had them all wondering if, after all her years living in England, the Dowager Duchess of Roxton did indeed understand enough of their native tongue to eavesdrop.

"Ah. I see I am not forgiven, Mme la duchesse," Jonathon said in French, blocking Antonia's exit.

He held out her fan. It was not immediately taken back.

Antonia kept her eyes level with the covered buttons of his embroidered red silk and gold thread waistcoat. "M'sieur, you have made a habit of getting in my way. You must desist."

"I understand why you are angry with me, and I ask your forgiveness," he said conversationally, tall frame shielding Antonia from the curious glances of his Cavendish relatives, who had crowded in to hear what was being said. "I should never have touched you without permission, and never in the way that I did. My ungentlemanly behavior has been gnawing away at me since I left you." He smiled in spite of himself. "If it's any consolation I ate very little at dinner as a consequence of my shame. And not once did you look at me throughout all seventy-eight courses."

This did bring Antonia's emerald-green gaze up to his dark eyes.

"The puzzlement in your lovely eyes tells me you had no idea I was seated across from you at table. Another chink to my self-esteem! But what I won't do," he added seriously, "is take back what I said to you in the pavilion—"

"M'sieur! No! Stop! I won't listen—"

"After all, good friends should be able to speak their minds without standing on ceremony. I told you I would not lie to you and I won't. Friends tell each other the truth."

"Friends?" she asked curiously, unconsciously taking the fan by its gold threaded tassel from his long, brown fingers and slipping the twisted gold rope over her wrist.

"Good friends, Mme la duchesse," Jonathon replied with a smile, gratified that this tactic had the desired effect of throwing her off-balance. He offered her the crook of his velvet sleeve. "That is, if Mme la duchesse d'Roxton will permit a bronzed East Indian merchant who has not an ounce of social address, and very little to recommend him, to be her friend...?"

"Always you are absurd, M'sieur," Antonia answered briskly, yet felt a huge relief that what he was asking of her was friendship. Still, she was wary of his motives. "Why do you want to be friends with me?"

Jonathon smiled at the small hesitant note in her voice. She was such a refreshing change from the brash over-confident women usual to her elevated station in life. "I would like nothing better than to discuss my reasons with you while taking a stroll down the length of this grand Gallery," he answered, the crook of his velvet sleeve still on offer. "But I should like to do so without an audience..."

Antonia knew immediately he was referring to Spencer and Willis who hovered nearby. A slight turn of her head and two words over her bare left shoulder and they were consigned to wait by her wingchair. Spencer opened her mouth to protest, but one dark look from Antonia and the sisters curtsied and retreated.

"I'm pleased to report that Frederick and I are now fast friends," he announced. "The boy showed me over his skiff. He's very proud of it. And so he should be. He tells me it once belonged to his uncle Henri... He is your younger son, who is up at Oxford...?"

"Yes. The boat it was Henri-Antoine's when he was a boy," Antonia answered, finally laying her fingers lightly in the crook of Jonathon's arm. "Julian he also had his own boat but by the time his younger brother was old enough to enter the boat races, Julian's boat it was too knocked about to be considered sea worthy."

"Did you know that Frederick has also had his oars painted green in your honor?"

"Oh? Superb! I do so want Frederick to win because his heart it is set on it," Antonia answered brightly, strolling the length of the Long Gallery she knew so well, walls crowded with a collection of massive paintings by master painters of Roxton ancestors through the ages. "But I do not know what are his chances with his father rowing against him with his brothers. Julian he is a very fine rower you see, and he won't throw the race just to let Frederick win. My son he believes everyone, his heir included, should win on merit and hard work."

"I applaud the Duke's sentiments. They mirror my own. But he hasn't counted on my great desire for the *Emerald Duchess* to cross the line first. Frederick and I have a dinner and the pleasure of your company awaiting us at Crecy Hall if we do. Enough incentive for the Duke to be beaten this year, and so I announced to one and all over the port."

Antonia gasped, but her eyes shone. She squeezed his arm. "You did no such thing!"

"Most certainly I did. It doesn't hurt to stir the competitive muscle amongst men, Mme la duchesse."

"But my son, what did he say to your challenge?"

Jonathon grinned. "What man worth his salt does not rise to a challenge?"

"He may be fair minded but that does not mean he likes one little bit to be beaten."

"Well said. Naturally, he took the challenge in the spirit in which it was intended. Oh, and several large wagers were made there and then. My odds, I am afraid to say, are not as good as Roxton's."

"But of course not," Antonia declared matter-of-factly. "He Julian is a very good rower."

"That's telling me straight," Jonathon said good-naturedly.

"How do you know I'm not just as good a rower as Roxton, if not better?"

"Me I do not know," she admitted truthfully with a smile. "But I do know my son and you may believe me when I tell you, M'sieur, that you will have to be a very good rower indeed if you hope to beat him."

"Well, I shall beat him because I have a much stronger incentive to win."

He chanced to glance up at the paneled wall then, at a massive canvas in a heavy ornate frame, and the family portrait considerably sobered his mood. The painting had been executed to celebrate the fortieth anniversary of the fifth duke coming into the title. His beautiful duchess was still absurdly youthful and had a ruddy-cheeked child of no more than five years of age on her lap of heavy damask petticoats, and the son and heir was a tall, handsome young man dressed in pale blue watered silk. But it was at the magnificently dressed nobleman Jonathon focused. The Duke was seated on a gilt chair in his ducal robes and coronet, black silk frockcoat and matching breeches and with white stockings that showcased muscular calves. He had a shock of white hair pulled severely off the starkly handsome aging face, a strong nose, thin, sneering lips and black eyes that stared out arrogantly on the world as if he owned every acre of it.

"A man like that can have any woman he wants, and no doubt did… until you came along," he mused, before tearing his gaze from the canvas to look down at Antonia with a crooked smile. "I'll wager he stole you out of the schoolroom for fear some other rogue would snap you up as soon as you were launched into society."

"He did no such thing!" Antonia protested hotly, and added loftily by way of explanation when Jonathon followed his arms across his chest and looked skeptical. "I was never in a schoolroom. My father was an eccentric court physician and having no son brought me up as one, with a broad-minded education, and to speak my mind. And this is what attracted Monseigneur."

"I was just about to say so," Jonathon lectured her, though his dark eyes were full of mirth. "Monseigneur liked the fact you said it to him straight. Not too many men or women, I'll wager, were brave enough to speak plainly with him, were they?" He eyed the portrait again. "I recognize the type well enough. Don't suffer fools; can't stand trencher-flies; and as proud as they come."

Antonia blinked and looked contrite. "Oh. I thought..."

"You thought I was going to give the archetypal male response and mention your incomparable beauty, pretty toes and magnificent breasts."

"M'sieur!"

"He wouldn't have been male had he not lusted after you, but it wasn't the deciding factor in Monseigneur's capitulation."

"M'sieur, you should not make such outrageous comments to me," she replied curtly, but there was no heat in her voice this time.

"You're not offended by my plain speech, so don't pretend, not with me," he responded bluntly. "I like the fact you haven't an ounce of artifice, that we can speak honestly to one another." He smiled into her eyes. "That we can be friends."

Antonia shut her fan with a snap.

"M'sieur, now it is my turn to wager *you*. Fifty guineas you say so to all the beautiful women of your acquaintance."

"Now there you go again, making me grin like a Bedlam inmate." He held up three long fingers. "Mme la duchesse, there are but three women in this palace of a home who don't have an ulterior motive for offering *me* friendship."

Antonia put up her brows but couldn't stop the appearance of the dimple in her left cheek. "These three women, who might they be?"

"My dear daughter, your daughter-in-law the dear duchess, and then there is you. My daughter is young and has her own set of friends, and certainly doesn't want her crusty old papa as her shadow. The Duchess of Roxton is as charming as she is beautiful, but quite reasonably, the Duke would have something to say if I began haunting her for conversation. He is in love with his wife; that is patently obvious. That leaves you, Mme la duchesse. I am confident I may simply enjoy the pleasure of your company and friendship without fear of being seduced into the padlock of wedlock."

"Of that, I promise you, M'sieur, there is not the slightest danger," and turned with a swish of her layered petticoats at the sound of the double doors at the end of the Long Gallery being flung wide by two liveried footmen to admit the four Roxton children and their assortment of nurses and tutors.

⁓⌇⌒⌇⁓

Had the Duke not been waylaid by the Countess of Strathsay, as he set aside his coffee cup on the tea trolley, it had been his intention to confront his mother and request that she return to join the Duchess at the tea trolley; her performance of turning her chair to the view and away from Deborah as hostess never ceased to annoy him. Despite Deborah's assurances that her mother-in-law's practice of ignoring her while she administered the tea things did not bother her in the least and that it was best to leave Antonia alone, Roxton knew the slight done his wife did indeed hurt her feelings.

It had not been an easy transition for Deborah to take over as Duchess of Roxton from a mother-in-law who had been a Duchess all her adult life, and thus had left an indelible stamp on the noble position and everything that entailed. In Roxton's opinion, his mother could have done a great deal to assist her daughter-in-law ease into the role had she not been wallowing in a perpetual state of self-pity; self-pity that had the potential to spiral out of control as it had twelve months ago.

The third anniversary of his father's passing was tomorrow and he wasn't about to have a repeat of his mother's mournful performance of the previous year. It was the Duke's belief that his duchess had miscarried their fifth child on the second anniversary of his father's death as a direct result of his mother's pitiful and quite unnecessary over-dramatic display of grief upon that occasion. With Deborah in the early stages of the second trimester of her sixth pregnancy, Roxton was convinced that to protect his wife and their unborn child the presence of Sir Titus Foley was necessary to manage his mother through another anniversary. The eminent physician was due at Treat any hour, and his arrival couldn't come soon enough.

93

That his mother had not put off her black as requested and was providing entertainment for his guests by being deep in conversation with a man who paraded about society as an East India merchant when he was anything but a simple man of no family only served to irritate the Duke further. For how was it that she barely acknowledged family and friends yet chose to be pleasant to a stranger who had the gross conceit to ask her to dance, and then show his host extreme insolence by visiting Crecy Hall uninvited, when it was universally made known to servants and guests alike that the dower house was off limits to everyone, even members of the Duke's family, without his express permission.

With an eye on his mother and his mind going over what he intended to say to Mr. Jonathon Strang, he heard one word in five of the Lady Strathsay's prattling speech. Something about the Dowager Duchess not needing something that Lady Strathsay could very well do with for a few weeks, perhaps a month, and if it pleased His Grace to release them to her, she would take very good care to ensure they had a wonderful little holiday at her expense of course, so that when they returned to the service of Mme la duchesse, they would be able to provide even better service in the future. And when all was said and done, surely His Grace would concede that they were rather unnecessary to the comfort of Mme la Duchesse. If His Grace would only give his consent…"

"If Mme la Duchesse has agreed to it, then it is not for me to quibble, my lady," Roxton replied curtly, annoyed that his mother had sent their cousin to him, as if he didn't have more important matters to concern himself with than the release of a couple of her horses! As if she needed his permission. "You are most welcome to them, Charlotte," he added and excused himself before Lady Strathsay could detain him further.

He was almost at Antonia's side when the doors at the far end of the Gallery opened to admit his four children. Their little faces never ceased to make him smile and be more in charity with the world. He watched them walk or be carried up the Gallery, all on their best behavior with the room full of guests. That is, until they spied their grandmother.

With her habitual spontaneity, at the sight of the children Antonia rushed to meet them with arms outstretched. The three boys scampered along the polished floor to get to her first, big grins on their little faces and laughter in their eyes, and when Antonia sank to the floor in a billow of petticoats to be at their height, they threw their arms about her neck to receive her hugs and kisses. She took Julie from the arms of her nurse and cuddled her on her lap, while listening to the twins prattle on excitedly about their papa rowing them tomorrow in the boat race.

Soon all four of the Duke's children were trampling over the yards of Antonia's exquisite black silk and silver tissue petticoats, eager to sit close and have their young voices listened to. They laughed and giggled and spoke French all at once. The hours spent in the nursery instilling in them the need to be on their best behavior in front of their parents' guests evaporated in an instant. Gus held up a bandaged finger for his grandmother's grave inspection and glared at his twin. Louis said it wasn't his fault his brother's finger got in the way of the hammer, and Antonia believed them both. Frederick was conspiratorial and quickly shoved deep into his pocket the coil of green ribbon Antonia passed him, to be taken out later and made into a cockade for his naval hat by one of the nursery maids.

Antonia then watched and applauded Julie's impromptu dance as if the little girl was the only being in the room and agreed that she was indeed the most beautiful fairy she had ever seen. And when the little girl then scrambled onto her lap and began fiddling with the tiny silk bows of her bodice, Antonia did not care in the least, nor did she mind when the five-year-old twins tugged hard at the cascading lace at her elbows to get her attention away from their annoyingly coquettish baby sister.

The nurses and tutors dutifully kept their distance, watching on as if it was a commonplace thing for the Dowager Duchess of Roxton to romp with their noble young charges on the bare polished floorboards. The Duke's guests held back also and watched without a murmur, most wore indulgent smiles, for one would have to possess a heart of marble or no heart at all not to be affected by the unconditional love the Dowager Duchess showered on this brood of happy children and vice versa.

Yet there were those of a more jaundice eye whose attention remained focused on the Duke, awaiting his reaction to his mother getting down amongst the dust, her exquisite petticoats ruined by his children's antics. But if Roxton was disturbed that Antonia's spontaneous behavior was causing many an eyebrow to lift, he did not show it. He watched his children with an indulgent smile, and when the Duchess slipped her hand in his, he said something to his wife that had her smiling and nodding in agreement.

But not everyone was silent on the matter. The Lady Strathsay voiced to Kitty Cavendish what the elder turgid members of the nobility were privately thinking.

"Of course they are all spoiled beyond permission," the Countess enunciated coldly, nostrils quivering with envy at the sight of Antonia sitting on the floor with the four most beautiful-looking children she had ever set eyes on. "Mme la Duchesse has always encouraged their willfulness and Roxton does nothing to curb his mother's outrageous behavior because he fears what it will do to her fragile state of mind. None of us ever want a repeat of her emotional collapse in full view of the world of the previous year. So embarrassing for the rest of the family. Naturally, I blame Monseigneur for Antonia's past and present ills. He over-indulged her terribly, as only a besotted older husband can a much younger beautiful wife." She screwed up her mouth in distaste. "Is it any wonder then that she spoils her grandchildren in the same manner?"

Kitty Cavendish went to respond, but realized it was a rhetorical question when Lady Strathsay hardly drew breath before continuing to vent her vitriol.

"Why Roxton thinks he can instill manners in his children when his mother fells his edicts with one visit to the nursery, is beyond me. And of course the good dear Duchess… One can't but be sympathetic to her plight. Deborah does her best, I know, but what hope has she of setting a good example for her children when Roxton keeps her continually pregnant and thus forever in childbed? Thank God Monseigneur was too old to impregnate Antonia more than twice. Her youngest son is an over-indulged, self-important young man and when Roxton was young he was the most spoiled, willful boy; all his mother's fault. Yet, he surprised us all by growing up to be the most stoic and stolid young man; possibly because he was sent away on the Grand Tour when quite a youth. That cut the cord with his mother well and truly and one must applaud Monseigneur for at least seeing the sense where his heir was concerned. Yes, Kitty, I do believe you are correct; one must look to the future. There is hope for the Roxton dukedom yet in Frederick. That's if Antonia's unbridled influence doesn't spoil him beyond saving. But I suppose now that he and his brothers and sister are no longer permitted to visit Crecy Hall, they will finally settle into being good, obedient children."

Kitty again opened her mouth, intent on voicing her one thought: That by her good friend Deborah Roxton's own admission, her mother-in-law was the most sweet-natured creature alive and the best grandmother her children could ever hope to possess. But the words froze on her tongue when she realized that the nobleman looming large at their backs was the Duke, and that his face was taut with suppressed anger.

"Your support of my family is most gratifying, my lady," he said caustically to the Lady Strathsay, a disapproving glance at Kitty, as if her silence put her in accord with the venomous sentiments of the viper in velvet. "So gratifying in fact that I believe we can dispense with your pearls of misguided, and dare I say, *malicious* sentiments for the foreseeable future." When Lady Strathsay opened her mouth to protest, Roxton's silence dared her to defy him. When she dropped into a respectful curtsey of assent he nodded curtly to Kitty then turned his back to greet his children with a welcoming smile.

"Oh, dear," Kitty said when Jonathon strolled over to stand by her side, "I fear I shall have to spend all tomorrow explaining myself to the dear duchess."

"Will you?" Jonathon asked, not hearing a word, his gaze still on the Roxton family gathering. He watched the Duke put an arm about his Duchess as she kissed her sons goodnight, while the little Lady Juliana, the bane of young Frederick's life, tugged on the lace at Antonia's sleeve to make certain her grandmother was indeed watching her flit about like a fairy. "Remarkable resemblance, don't you agree, Kitty; that child and the Dowager Duchess?"

Kitty shut her fluttering fan with a snap and let it dangle on its silken cord about her wrist. "Strang! Tommy told me what you intend with the Duchess and I don't think—"

Jonathon tore his gaze from Antonia. "I beg your pardon, Kitty, but you have no idea as to my intentions."

"There are other ways of obtaining the deeds to the long-lost family clod of earth without the need to flirt with Roxton's mamma."

"Yes. You are right. But I do so like flirting with a beautiful woman."

"Then flirt with any of the dozen or so pretty and much younger women here this week. Martha and Maria Aubrey are two of the prettiest young girls you could ever hope to meet—"

"They are mere children."

"They are nothing of the sort and if you would only spend time in their company you would soon realize they have a good grasp of the realities about modern marriage. As your wife neither one would seek to interfere in your life."

Jonathon's lips twitched. "Dearest Kitty, a one-eyed man with half a brain knows your game. I saw you huddled close with Hettie. Trying to educe your support, was she?"

Kitty cleared her throat and hoped she appeared vague. "I don't know what you can mean. Hettie is a dear friend and—"

"—one hot summer's night in Hyderabad I foolishly dropped my guard and scampered under the mosquito netting with her," he interrupted flatly, the dull look to his normally friendly brown eyes alerting Kitty to the depressing realization that her friend had no chance of rekindling Jonathon's interest. "No offence to Lady Hibbert-Baker, but it is an encounter I don't care to repeat in the cool greenness that is England."

"Hettie aside, if you are in any way concerned that marriage to Martha or Maria would interfere with your female interests I can assure you that they are thoroughly modern girls."

"How gratifying."

"Oh, Strang! Can you not at least *entertain* the notion of re-marrying?"

He shook his head at her persistence. "When will you give up trying to match-make me, Kitty?"

"When you remarry."

"Then we'll be having this conversation when we're stooped and toothless. I intend to remain unshackled to the grave."

She watched his gaze wander back to the Dowager Duchess of Roxton, who was walking with the children to the end of the Gallery, their goodnights completed for the evening, and pursed her lips in disapproval. Flirting with Antonia Roxton was not in Kitty's plans for her brother-in-law. It was one thing to tup Henrietta Hibbert-Baker, that would not raise the collective eyebrow of Society, but pursuing the Duke of Roxton's widowed mother, a decade his senior, would not only raise the collective eyebrow, it would drop the collective jaw and seriously compromise Sarah-Jane's hopes of marrying Dair Fitzstuart, heir to the Strathsay earldom.

Dair Fitzstuart valued his mother's opinion and Charlotte Strathsay valued society's opinion. Poor Sarah-Jane's hopes and dreams of a titled husband would come crashing down like the proverbial house of cards if one whiff of scandal was ever attached to her or her father's name. Before she could stop herself, Kitty said with a half-hearted laugh,

"You're not seriously pursuing Antonia Roxton. It's a ridiculous notion. You're practically the same age as her son, for God's sake!" When Jonathon remained mute, gaze remaining fixed to the Duchess, she hissed at him from behind her fluttering fan, "Don't make an ass of yourself, Strang! Not with Antonia Roxton. There's a veritable battalion of pretty females here this week who—"

"So you have said. If only they were half as desirable."

"She is beyond your reach!"

"But I have such long arms, Kitty."

"Be serious! She was utterly devoted to the old Duke, even when he was ill and dying. She's still in mourning for him. You'll never win her heart."

"It's not her heart I'm after, Kitty."

Kitty's mouth dropped open. "Strang!"

"Only she can sign over the deeds to what was taken from my ancestor and I aim to make her see the merit in its restoration to my family." When Kitty quickly hid her swinging jaw behind her gold paper-leaf fan, he smiled. "Oh, you're not mistaken. I want that too. *Very* much."

Kitty regarded him archly. "Let us delve into the realms of fairy folk for the moment and believe you can seduce Antonia Roxton... Once you've had your fill, what then? You expect she'll melt like candle wax and sign over the deeds just like that?"

"What I expect, Kitty, is to work for my keep. But she'll sign... eventually."

It was Kitty's turn to be dull-eyed. "Why don't you just dispense with the seduction and lay your cards all before her. Such a sweet-natured creature is bound to see the merit in your case and sign over the Strang-Leven inheritance without argument."

"And spoil our fun? I'm not a complete blackguard, my dear. I mean for her to enjoy herself just as much as me. And then... once she's melted... she'll sign." Jonathon bowed and took his leave. "Now you must excuse me. Like a moth to flame, my candle awaits."

But before Jonathon could take more than two strides towards Antonia a footman waylaid him with a summons: He was required elsewhere. It was the Duke and he wanted a private word on the terrace.

Eight

*T*hose guests still lingering in the Gallery playing at cards, or lounging on the arrangement of sofas and chairs discussing tomorrow's boat race and the activities planned on the lawns, watched with veiled interest the Duke and his merchant guest conversing on the terrace. Two footmen at the French doors waylaid anyone wanting to take fresh air so that the conversation remained uninterrupted and not overheard.

Antonia wondered what her son could possibly be discussing with Jonathon Strang. Her daughter-in-law had returned to the tea trolley where the butler and a clutch of footmen were replenishing the tea and coffee urns and cake plates, and called her over to sit awhile with the few ladies who had not retired for a nap before the evening recital. Antonia dutifully sat, but not on the upholstered wing chair turned away from the French windows chosen for her by the Duchess. She went to the horsehair sofa that faced the terrace; her ever-present ladies-in-waiting hovering close by.

The Duchess enquired if her mother-in-law would care for a cup of coffee. Antonia shook her head but said nothing. She dutifully acknowledged the ladies in the circle with a smile and a nod but that was the extent of her interaction. Everyone looked sideways at the Duchess, who did not repeat her offer. She spoke with Kitty Cavendish about an unremarkable incident that had happened at Drury Lane when she and the Duke had last gone to the theater. Kitty took up the thread and the ladies chatted about the latest plays on offer; yet all were acutely aware that the

Dowager Duchess of Roxton sat amongst them mechanically fluttering her fan, her thoughts elsewhere. No one could be comfortable, least of all Deborah, though she kept a brave face and tried to pretend that there was nothing unusual in her mother-in-law's distracted behavior.

But Antonia was too preoccupied with her own thoughts to join in a conversation about a play she had not seen with people who were intimates of her son and his wife, and she knew only in passing. She wanted to speak with her son but as soon as the double doors closed on her grandchildren's backs the Duke had managed to slip away, and was now on the terrace with Jonathon Strang.

Why, she wondered, did Roxton need to be private with Jonathon Strang in such a public place as the terrace? Why not conduct the conversation in the privacy of his library where no one would see them or wonder at the content of their discussion?

She had watched the footman escort Jonathon Strang across the Gallery and smiled when, instead of following the servant out onto the terrace, he crossed to the second fireplace where the younger guests were playing at charades, led by Dair Fitzstuart. His brother Charles and a number of young people were doing their best to guess the scene acted out before them. Antonia knew almost at once. Dair was a good actor, ably assisted by one of the Aubrey twins. She was surprised they had chosen such an old play, but perhaps it had enjoyed another run at the theater as Fielding's plays often did, no matter their age. The scene was from *The Mock Doctor*, with Dair playing the part of Gregory and Martha Aubrey playing Charlotte, the mute girl who is not mute at all.

Antonia loved playing at charades. She had often teased her brother-in-law Vallentine mercilessly and with his wife Estée and Monseigneur laughed when Vallentine beamed with pleasure, thinking he had guessed correctly the charade in progress only to discover his guess was very wide of the mark. Such a happy foursome... She had lost all three of her best friends within twelve months: First Monseigneur; eight months later influenza carried off his sister Estée and then within weeks of Estée's death her husband Vallentine had just faded away. The loss of Monseigneur had so completely numbed her that the death of Estée and Vallentine so soon after his passing had been beyond her comprehension.

Now, thinking back on it, she realized her overwhelming grief at losing the love of her life had overshadowed all else. Perhaps her grief had been too much for them to bear...

There was an outburst of laughter and applause when the charade was won, guessed correctly, not by the younger set, but by Jonathon Strang, who made the company an exaggerated bow in recognition of their applause which elicited further applause and he put up his hand as if to say, no, he would not join them. His pretty strawberry-blonde daughter gave him a swift kiss on the cheek and then Charles Fitzstuart beckoned her over to confer with him before the boisterous group; it was their turn to act out. The charade commenced and Jonathon watched from the fireplace where he put a cheroot between his teeth, pocketed the slim silver case and, taking a faggot from the fire, stooped to light the tip. He applauded his daughter's efforts with a handclap above his head and with the cheroot smoldering to his satisfaction he sauntered off, a cursory gesture at the waiting footman to lead him on to the terrace.

The Duke was standing with his wide back to the Gallery, hands splayed on the balustrade, waiting. When Jonathon came up he turned, snuffbox at the ready. Jonathon declined the pinch, showing the cheroot between his fingers, and when the Duke indicated the terrace the two gentlemen set off for a leisurely stroll. When they came back to stand before the French windows, Antonia sat up a little taller. Her son was smiling.

When Roxton smiled he hardly ever revealed his white teeth; except if he was greatly amused or angrily embarrassed. Antonia knew him too well. She doubted he and Jonathon Strang were exchanging on-dits. But what had Jonathon Strang said to make her son uncomfortable? She inwardly scowled, though her face was devoid of expression.

Now it was Jonathon Strang's turn to smile, and just as broadly, the cheroot in the side of his mouth as he shook his head, an expression of mocking disbelief on his handsome features. He removed the cheroot, blew smoke into the air and laughed out loud as if told a good joke.

The Duke's smile widened and he turned his back on the French windows, handsome profile to Jonathon Strang who perched on the marble lintel, long legs stretched out before him and crossed at the ankles towards the Gallery, yet he was looking at the Duke. He was now the one doing most of the talking.

Antonia glanced at her son's hands resting on the balustrade. They were balled into fists. She knew her son hated to be the center of attention, that he was shy and awkward when the object of singular scrutiny from a crowd. And yet here he was, on display to the occupants of the Gallery whom he must know were watching him intently, however furtively, in heated gentlemanly argument with his merchant guest.

Only one explanation presented itself: Roxton wanted this argument to be seen, for his guests to witness to what amounted to a very public dressing down of Jonathon Strang. He was openly castigating the man; making certain that Society knew his feelings, that he viewed him with disfavor, and without ever having to say a word against him.

Antonia's instinct was to sweep out onto the terrace and confront them. After all, their white-hot discussion in some way involved her; intuition told her so. A glance at her daughter-in-law and her suspicions were confirmed when Deborah returned her questioning look with an odd little smile of embarrassment, attention diverted from her conversation with Kitty Cavendish, and yet she could not hold her gaze.

"I need fresh air," Antonia announced, up on her heels.

"Of course, Maman-Duchess. But let Willis fetch you one of my shawls first. There is a cool breeze."

"*Merci, ma belle-fille*. But me I do not need a shawl."

"Yes, you do, Maman-Duchess," the Duchess said firmly and accompanied this with a nice smile. She glanced about at the group of women and added in English, "Perhaps we could all take a turn about the terrace once the shawl is fetched for Mme la duchesse?" she suggested, an almost imperceptible nod in direction of Antonia's ladies-in-waiting.

Willis curtsied and departed to have the shawl fetched.

Antonia hesitated. Was her daughter-in-law telling her what to do? She could hardly believe her ears. She certainly wasn't going to stand about and be humiliated in her own home by a young woman who had been elevated to duchess for all of five minutes.

She lifted a handful of her petticoats to leave when Deborah shot to her feet.

The women sitting on the arrangement of sofas all stood as one and held their collective breath. Likewise the gentlemen, who straightened from leaning on the backs of wingchairs and pulled at the points of their waistcoats to occupy the awkward moment.

"When Willis returns, Maman-Duchess," stated the Duchess.

Antonia lifted her chin. "Willis can bring the shawl to the terrace."

"No. We will wait."

"No?" Antonia blinked. Heat flushed her throat. "Deborah, I do not need a shawl, I assure you."

"I do not want you catching cold, Maman-Duchess."

You do not want me to go out on the terrace to speak to my son, that is what you are really saying, Antonia grumbled in her head, adding audibly, "It is not cold and I am not an invalid, *n'cest pa?*"

"I do not disagree with you, Maman-Duchess, but I would be failing in my duty if I did not insist you wait for the shawl."

The Duchess's simple statement, said with soft-spoken straightforwardness, was accompanied by a steady gaze that dared Antonia to question her authority.

The heat in Antonia's throat rushed up into her cheeks and it was on the tip of her tongue to remind her daughter-in-law that although she was indeed the present Duchess of Roxton it was not her place to tell the fifth Duchess of Roxton where she may or may not walk in this house that had been her home and she its mistress for almost thirty years. But meeting her daughter-in-law's soft brown eyes, Antonia's indignation vanished as quickly as it had surfaced. The young woman was biting her lower lip, a sure sign of her nervousness. *It has taken all her courage to challenge me*, Antonia thought with a sad smile. *She must be quaking inside.*

Poor Deborah. She had been placed in a most awkward position, one that only served to reinforce to Antonia the uselessness of her own position as Dowager Duchess. Treat was now Deborah's home and she its mistress. She had every right to her insistence. Any other guest would not have hesitated to do as requested. They certainly would not have questioned the right of their hostess to make such a demand.

She should not have come to dinner. Her presence only made her son and his wife uncomfortable. They did not know what to do with her or how to deal with her. She did not blame them. After all, she did not have the answers to those questions any more than they did.

Of course it was her son who had put Deborah to the task of keeping her inside while he had words with Jonathon Strang. For why else was she not permitted the terrace? This made her more than ever suspicious that the discussion beyond the French windows did indeed concern her.

Slowly, Antonia sank back onto the horsehair sofa and resumed fanning herself.

"We will wait for the shawl," she said quietly, a glance through the French windows, at the Duke and Jonathon Strang, wishing herself a bumblebee on the honeysuckle vine hanging heavily in flower over the terrace balustrade.

To anyone observing the two big men, the Duke of Roxton and Jonathon Strang were enjoying a leisurely stroll along the wide black and white checkerboard tiled terrace, conversing on impersonal topics, as gentlemen, host and guest in particular, are want to do after a long, satisfying dinner: Horses, hunting, dogs, farming, nothing too political, certainly nothing religious and definitely nothing to do with money. They smiled and chatted, the Duke took snuff while Jonathon puffed on a cheroot, both taking in the majestic sweep of landscaped acres, wide meandering artificial lake, and beyond, fertile farming land; every blade of grass, sod of earth, animal, plant, tree, building, road and person belonging to the Duke as far as the eye could see.

But when they returned to stand opposite the French windows near the overhanging honeysuckle, the conversation took on a decidedly serious tone and turned to a topic uppermost in the minds of both gentlemen. Roxton kept his back to the Gallery and was looking out on all that he owned, palms flat on the marble balustrade.

"My steward tells me that a thorough search of the archives has uncovered four survey maps of the estate. The first survey was made when Good Queen Bess granted the land to the first duke; two surveys were made in the fourth Duke's lifetime, just before his marriage to Lady Elisabeth Strang-Leven, your ancestress, and another done five years before his death. The fourth map was commissioned by my father around the time of my birth and thus need not concern you. A preliminary perusal of the boundary lines on the maps completed in my Great-Grandfather's time would suggest there is a case to answer." Roxton looked at Jonathon. "Of course I am no surveyor nor am I a lawyer, and the expertise of both are required before I would be prepared to make a formal declaration."

"And what sort of declaration did you have in mind, your Grace?"

"To the effect that upon his marriage to Elisabeth Strang-Leven, the fourth Duke of Roxton subsumed into the dowry the inheritance of the Lady Elisabeth's younger brother and the Duke's ward, Edmund Strang-Leven."

"Illegally subsumed, your Grace."

"Negligently."

"Wrongfully. I won't settle for less."

Roxton turned and leaned his buttocks against the balustrade and took snuff, an eyebrow raised at his guest. "I beg your pardon," he said with icy politeness, "but you cannot know that the Duke intentionally misappropriated Edmund Strang-Leven's estate. In all likelihood it was a surveying error that saw the Strang-Leven land mistakenly flooded to make way for the Duke's lake. What appeared to be an estate boundary line of a mere quarter inch on a document was in fact most of a neighboring estate, and once these lands were flooded there was no going back. That is not an illegality but a simple miscalculation."

Jonathon exhaled smoke into the air and let out a bark of laughter.

"Simple miscalculation? There's nothing simple about it! I'll grant you may have been able to persuade me to swallow such a fairytale, if that was the only piece of his inheritance Edmund lost to your illustrious ancestor. I have no doubt it sits much better on your straight shoulders to accept as true that a misplaced quill stroke made by a negligent surveyor's apprentice put the boundary west, rather than east, of the coordinates written in his master's little leather bound notebook. That the Duke returned from the city one day, none the wiser to the mistake, to find the ornamental lake he had commissioned twice its size. And—"

The Duke blinked in amazement to be addressed so bluntly. And when Jonathon Strang cut him off mid-sentence was so affronted he momentarily lost the facility of speech.

"Mr. Strang, if you will allow me to—"

"Just a minute, your Grace," Jonathon demanded. "You must allow me to do justice to your ancestor's fairytale. So the Duke returns to his estate and to his shock and horror his head surveyor fronts his master cap in hand with profuse apologies that due to a surveying error not only was the designated land carved out and flooded but three quarters of the arable land from the neighboring estate was also flooded. And due to this *miscalculation*, the neighbor's Elizabethan manor house sits perfectly placed on the shores of the new lake, in a bend that affords it seclusion and privacy from this grand pile of stone, and with a charming aspect of an island; well it is charming *now*, planted out with gardenias, wild roses, and the willows grown up. And the waterfall is truly delightful, hiding as it does a bacchanalian grotto painted with frescos that would give a eunuch a hard on. *Miscalculation?* On Saint Geoffrey's Day belike!"

"Are you daring to call me a liar, sir?"

"Liar? If I thought you were lying to me, your Grace, I'd call you a liar to your face," Jonathon said reasonably and smiled to himself when the nobleman's jaw unclenched. "What I do think is that you have convinced yourself the fourth duke was a better man than he truly was. And that's only reasonable wishful thinking. Every man, other than your career criminal, wants to believe the blood that runs in his veins comes from decent stock." He looked the nobleman up and down and fixed on his green eyes, so like his mother's that he had to suppress a smile. "My sources tell me you're a very decent fellow, a bit stolid, but my guess is you don't suffer fools and are rightly reticent amongst anyone who is not of your close circle of friends; which is as it should be for a young man who wears a ducal coronet. I can't abide catch-farts and kiss-mine-arse fellows; men not fit for the contents of a *pikdan*. And just like you I don't suffer fools and foolish tales. So don't try and bamboozle me with some tale told you by a fawning lackey that your ancestor flooded Edmund Strang-Leven's lands by accident, because that's a great pile of fartleberries!"

"Do you always run on at the mouth?"

Jonathon was momentarily taken aback and then let out such a great bark of laughter that it not only startled the Duke into shying away, but also captured the attention of those sitting with the Duchess about the tea trolley.

"That's just what your mother said to me! And with that same blaze of anger in her eyes too!"

"Leave the Dowager Duchess out of this!" Roxton hissed, points of color in his clean-shaven cheeks, and was instantly annoyed for letting down his guard.

The laughter extinguished from Jonathon's dark eyes. He tapped ash from his cheroot over the balustrade. "There is nothing I wish for more than to leave her out of this but, you and I know, that is impossible."

Roxton lifted his chin, an action Jonathon also found reminiscent of Antonia, and took a breath before saying bluntly, "You can't have the dower house; I don't care how valid your claims, how many lawyers you employ, and whether you are in the right." He met Jonathon's implacable stare with one of his own. "My father left her that house and it is hers, right or wrong."

"She can have it... for her lifetime. But I'll have the deeds signed over now. You know it's the right thing to do."

The Duke's hands balled into fists on the balustrade, an action that did not go unnoticed by his guest. "That is not going to happen."

"It's a very generous offer. Your family has had the use of my family's property for nigh on a hundred years and what I get back is but a third of the estate. Granted your father rebuilt what was falling into decay of Crecy Hall and the pavilion is a charming addition, so I'll take the restoration as compensation and rule the line under that and not require any additional monetary reimbursement. Do you want to shake on it like gentlemen or do you require lawyers, ink and a congenial sip of claret over the documents to seal the bargain?"

"What I *require* is for you to *understand* that Crecy Hall is *non-negotiable.*"

Jonathon took a leisurely draw on his cheroot as he surveyed the Duke. Twenty years conducting business on the subcontinent had taught him a great deal about human nature and how to read his fellows. And he knew that to conduct meaningful business one needed a cool heart and a rational mind and that if a man allowed emotion to be involved no amount of reasoning, cool or otherwise, would see a successful fulfillment of the transaction. Such dealings required patience and time; Jonathon had both in abundance. Besides which, as far as Crecy Hall was concerned he need not involve the Duke at all. To have the deeds signed over required the signature of the mother, not the son. So he let drop the Elizabethan manor house saying with a raise of one eyebrow,

"And what of Hanover Square, your Grace? You cannot excuse away your ancestor's sale of such prime London real estate, land that did not belong to him but to Edmund Strang-Leven, by blaming a surveyor's *miscalculation.*"

The Duke gave a huff of embarrassment. "I was not about to do anything of the kind. Nor will I defend the indefensible. What my Great-Grandfather did in that respect was unpardonable."

Such a candid admission surprised Jonathon. He admired the nobleman's honestly if not his obstinacy, and was well aware what prompted the latter and that his propensity for the former stemmed from the same source: Antonia, Dowager Duchess of Roxton. It was a refreshing change from his usual contact with members of the aristocracy, most of whom were so bloated with self-consequence and self-delusion as to their God-given place atop the writhing mass of humanity that Jonathon was certain a prod of a finger would see them pop.

"Why are you here, Strang?" the Duke asked, snapping shut the enameled lid of his gold snuffbox. "And don't insult my intelligence that you came hot foot from the sub-continent to restore a lost inheritance. My lawyers tell me there is a pile of correspondence between your grandfather and my great-grandfather dating back to the first decade of this century, and yet not one member of your family, until you, had ever bothered to stake a claim to Edmund Strang-Leven's legacy. And you are not in need of funds. You've returned with enough wealth to build your own marble palace if that was your desire, and that's not counting the income from sugar plantations and considerable real estate in the states of New York and South Carolina. And let's leave your daughter's need to find a titled mate out of the equation. That's just a ruse best swallowed by gullible matrons and hopeful younger sons."

"And yet you wish to insult my intelligence by claiming you don't know? Come on, your Grace! Play fair!" Jonathon said with a shake of his shoulder length hair. "If you know my worth then your sources certainly ferreted out what compelled me to leave the country of my birth where I had hoped to live out the rest of my days in perfect contentment. Claiming the Strang-Leven inheritance while I wait for a relative who is a stranger to me to drop off this mortal coil and leave me what I don't want in the least, allows me to tidy up unfinished family business; I am not asking for more than I am owed, but I am willing to take less, if the settlement is agreeable." He allowed himself to smile. "So in that spirit, and not because it makes good business sense, I propose you sign over the Hanover Square mansion. I need a town residence and it is perfectly situated for my future needs. But as to the rest," he added with a wave, as if shooing away a bumblebee, "I don't need the blunt or the headache of lawyers bothering me about trifles. What would it amount to anyway? Ten, twenty, maybe thirty thousand?" He shrugged. "Keep it." Adding with a laugh, "You'll be needing it for your ever-expanding nursery which will soon number a cricket team!"

The Duke found no amusement in Jonathon's overconfident humor. He stood up off the terrace balustrade, ignored the generosity in the merchant's offer and said disdainfully. "The Hanover residence was given to the Dowager Duchess for her lifetime. I can't sign it over to you."

Jonathon too stood straight and faced the seething nobleman. He pulled a face. "Is that so? And here am I making you a perfectly reasonable, and most would suggest a very generous, offer to close this deal as expeditiously as possible."

"Deal? This is not a *deal*. It is an *eviction*. Is evicting a widow from her own home generous and reasonable to you?"

"Is it reasonable to you?"

Roxton baulked. "I beg your pardon?"

"Unlike Crecy Hall, which does require her signature to the deed of title, you don't need her signature or her permission to transfer the deed of title of the Hanover Square mansion to me. You need not involve her at all. So what's your sticking point?"

"I won't go behind her back and sell out from under her the town residence she shared with my father all of their married life. If she found out it would... it would..." Roxton threw up a hand. "I don't know what it would do to her!"

"But you've done this sort of thing before," Jonathon shot back bluntly, turning his head to blow smoke into the air. "So why is it different this time?" he asked. "Paris or London. French or English. Both houses were her homes. The Hôtel on the Rue Saint-Honoré must be full of just as many memories as the one in Hanover Square. I would hazard a guess, the Hôtel means a great deal more to her because she's French to the ends of her pretty toes, *and* it was the boyhood home of your father and his sister. And yet you sold it out from under her, and to people she will most certainly consider far beneath Monseigneur's French nobility." He shrugged. "Your excuse for keeping the Hanover Square mansion is rather lame then, isn't it, your Grace? Perhaps I've misjudged you. You're obdurate for its own sake and sold the Parisian mansion with no regard for your mother's feelings?"

"You cold-hearted bastard," the Duke hissed through his teeth.

Jonathon laughed. "I hardly deserve such an appellation when I'm going out of my way to make this righting of wrongs as painless as possible for you, and for her."

"I don't know what grubby means you employed to ferret out my family's business but I'll meet you before I'll allow you to upset her!"

Jonathon's eyebrows shot up. "A duel, your Grace?" He smiled crookedly and shook his head. "That's not how I do business. Facts, paperwork and lawyers are my forté, not dawn, seconds and swords. The merchant in me is too level headed to indulge in such heated and nonsensical actions. I think the gentleman in you agrees." He extinguished the cheroot on the leather sole of his shoe and dropped the remaining half of the hand-rolled cigarillo into the slim silver caddy he carried in a frockcoat pocket. "By the by, if it's grubby you want, then look to your relatives. One cup of coffee after dinner and I was given the facts without the need to ask. I don't know how she discovered what you are so keen to keep from your mother, but Charlotte Strathsay is champing at the bit to fill her little ear with the news. That woman deserves her moniker *the viper in velvet*."

At that revelation the Duke reddened and was genuinely contrite. "Ah. Then I apologize for my hasty accusation."

"It can't be easy being head of a ducal house," Jonathon said with real sympathy. "All those relatives and retainers and hangers-on to keep managed within the family fold. At least in business, if an employee is treacherous you can dismiss him without a second thought or the threat of repercussion for upsetting another employee by your actions."

"I wouldn't wish it on anyone," Roxton stated candidly with a self-deprecating smile that not only surprised Jonathon but put him more in charity with the nobleman; as did the genuine warmth that came into the deep voice at mention of his children. "Frederick is very excited to have you as his oarsman for tomorrow's boat race."

"Is he? Let's hope I can live up to his enthusiasm! Do you mind?"

"That you are his oarsman? Not at all. It was very good of you to offer."

"More a case of being pushed into it. I can't take the credit."

"Frederick tells me his grandmother put you up to it. That I do mind."

"Why should you? It was a capital idea."

"I mind that you visited Crecy Hall without permission and imposed yourself, uninvited and unchaperoned on the Dowager Duchess."

"Imposed? I wouldn't call having a cup of coffee in her pretty little pavilion an imposition. I rather think she enjoyed the company."

"Or was too polite to turn you away?"

"Oh no, she tried to do that. But I'd rowed such a long way to see her that in the end good manners won out and we settled down to a nice cup of coffee and some seedy cake with Fred— with the swans," Jonathon said, trying to correct his slip of the tongue.

The Duke's smile was thin. "Don't fret. You didn't give away my son's truancy. Nothing, and I mean *nothing*, happens on this estate without me finding out about it, whether I want to know or not; another unwanted perquisite of being head of a ducal house. Listen, Strang," he said in an altogether different voice, a frowning glance at the snuffbox in his hand, "it's difficult for me to tell you this, and I am only taking you into my confidence because I see you are a man that is not easily dissuaded from an action once his mind is made up, and that you won't abide a simple no without an explanation attached..." After a moment of internal struggle, the Duke continued, saying flatly, "The Dowager Duchess is not a well woman. That may come as a surprise to you, a complete stranger, seeing her with her grandchildren or chatting with her neighbors throughout dinner. Indeed she even favored you with a dance last evening. But to those who know her well—and I am telling you this in the strictest of confidences— grave fears are held for-for her—*safety*. I want you to understand how it is. And because that's why I want—no, I *order* you to stay away from her."

Jonathon's eyebrows snapped over his long fine nose. He glanced through the French windows and caught the object of their discussion watching them, and by the way she quickly turned her head, had been watching them for some time.

"She tried to take her own life? I don't believe it!"

"My parents were excessively attached. Despite the great gulf in their ages, they were devoted to one another. I don't think my mother ever comprehended the gravity of my father's illness; that he was, in truth, dying. And so when it happened... Her grieving is excessive and morbid and it has made her—*fragile*. On the second anniversary of his passing, her state of mind was such that had Sir Titus not been in attendance, he is of the opinion she would have succeeded." The Duke frowned. "Why do you say you don't believe it?"

"Don't misconstrue me, your Grace. I believe you. I just don't believe she would indulge in such a drastic and quite selfish act. There's too much spirit in her, too much *light*, to easily extinguish such a life." He did not add that her promise to Monseigneur to present Frederick with the ducal emerald ring on his twenty-first birthday was, he believed, a promise she would honor with her last breath.

Jonathon's conviction surprised Roxton. The merchant had known his mother for a day and yet spoke as if he had known her all his life, and had a right to do so. It made the Duke inexplicably uncomfortable and yet he had to grudgingly concede the merchant had a point. He wished with all his being he was in the right.

"I trust you to keep this confidence to yourself."

"You needn't have asked that, your Grace."

The Duke nodded, pocketed his snuffbox and signaled to the footmen to open the French doors. "And you will stay away from the Dowager Duchess?"

"And Hanover Square?"

"A peppercorn lease in the first instance. Take it for what it is: A goodwill gesture of future intent. The legalities will take time to sort through and the rest of this sennight must be devoted to other, more pressing, matters of state. Another perquisite I could do without." When Jonathon stuck out his hand he took it and an understanding was reached. "And the Dowager Duchess. You will keep your distance?"

Jonathon stepped into the Gallery ahead of the Duke, saying over his shoulder, "As to that, your Grace, as I said last night, your mother can tell me that herself."

Nine

$\mathcal{T}$he day of the annual Treat Regatta was unseasonably warm for the middle of April with the sun shining in a cloudless watery blue sky. A moderate breeze stirred the glassy surface of the lake, willows swayed lazily and dipped spidery fingers into the icy water, while bright new leaves opened to the sun on the mature oaks and beeches strewn across acres of manicured parkland.

People had begun to swarm across the wide expanse of rolling lawn that terraced down to the lake in front of the massive colonnaded frontage of the palace. Tenant farmers with their families and laborers had started their journey hours earlier, arriving in carts usually reserved for hay and bringing with them the locals from two villages unable to make the journey on foot. The Duke's army of household servants, stable hands, gardeners and their families, those not absolutely required to be on duty, wore their Sunday best and mingled amongst the crowds, free to join in the festivities.

Small children holding tightly to the hands of their older brothers or sisters ran to giggle at the Punch and Judy show, gape in awe at the fabulous French marionettes resembling old King Louis of France and his French courtiers, try their hand at juggling or walking on stilts with the assistance of gap-toothed circus performers, but most of all they queued to take a ride around the parklands in the French *Oudry* carriage pulled by four white ponies, its gilded outer panels decorated with fanciful pastoral scenes by the French artist Jean-Baptiste Oudry, its interior dark blue velvet and gold leaf with plush tasseled cushions and glass push up windows. The carriage was said to be a replica of Mme la Duchesse's carriage across the water in Paris.

And when stomachs big and small grumbled with hunger there was an over-abundance of foodstuffs to eat and enjoy, all at the Duke's largesse, from stalls that supplied all manner of meats, from roast beef to venison, to platters of cheese, fruit and breads, candied fruits, sweetmeats, cake and pastries, with flavored cordials and fresh milk for the children and cider and punch for the adults.

Everyone, from the titled to the chimney sweep were expected to feast from the stalls shoulder to shoulder and most did with the greatest of ease and goodwill, yet there were those amongst the Duke's noble guests who simply refused to entertain the idea of sharing food with the common folk. These few remained on the top terrace, seated under an arrangement of colorful marquees that provided shelter from the sun and were at a vantage point to watch over the fete activities and the boat race from afar. Scattered with plush rugs to avoid the damp grass, ribbon back chairs and padded velvet footstools provided comfort for these languishing dowagers and portly gentlemen suffering the gout, while liveried footmen attended to their every need and watched on enviously as their fellows, who had not drawn the short straw in the butler's ballot, enjoyed a day free from the whims of others.

Down at the water's edge, the most important event of the day was getting underway. The six skiffs taking part in the race bobbed up and down on their moorings, painted oars drawn up and in and resting on the thwart, colored silk burgees tied half-way up each oar declaring the political proclivities of the skiff's rower and occupant—Hanoverian for the present Monarchy, Stuart for the previous, American Colonial because England was at war with the rebels, French because the Roxton dukedom had its origins and half its blood from the Bourbon Kings, Spanish as a Catholic kingdom the English had beaten in the past, and the Italian State of Florence because Mme la Duchesse spoke Italian almost as well as she did her native French.

The Florentine Ambassador not only sponsored a skiff each year in her honor, he supplied a Florentine from the Embassy to row in the regatta. The Spanish Ambassador hearing of this was not to be outdone by a small Italian state, so he too offered one of his staff from his embassy to row the Spanish skiff and went one better than his Florentine counterpart by offering a purse of Spanish gold to complement the Roxton Silver cup awarded each year to the race winner.

Servants scurried along the wooden planks of the jetty and onto boats making last minute checks of their respective master's skiff, while the gentlemen rowers themselves milled about on the lawn, attentive valets helping them to strip down to their billowing shirtsleeves then shrugging them into sleeveless, colored waistcoats that matched the color of their silk burgees and thus made them recognizable at a distance once out on the open waters of the lake.

The competitors discussed the route the race would take: under the bridge, once around Swan Nest Island—the largest island on the lake, across to the causeway and then returning to the jetty via the bend in the lake that passed between the Elizabethan dower house Crecy Hall and Bacchus Island with its hidden waterfall—a distance of some five miles. Lookouts had been posted along the route, in small boats, and on the islands to ensure the correct route was followed and in case any of the rowers happened to get into difficulty. The latter set off a spate of good natured one-upmanship, disparaging remarks on the manly attributes and abilities of their fellow rowers while widely inflating their athleticism in the hopes of oversetting the confidence of their rivals and impressing the clutch of beauties who had come to wish the gentlemen luck.

Dressed in their best striped silk *Anglaise à la Polonaise* petti-coats, plumed and beribboned straw bonnets over their teased and curled hair and carrying dainty parasols to shade their milky skin from the sun's rays, the beauties joined the gentlemen in their good natured rivalry, the men careful to keep their comments above the ribald with ladies now present. Those ladies honored with an oarsman as champion, Sarah-Jane Strang and Martha Aubrey amongst the select few, wore matching ribands in their hair and around a plump wrist.

Tommy Cavendish, as Keeper of the Regatta Ledger, flittered amongst rowers, ladies and spectators alike, taking last-minute wagers, behind him a servant carrying the all-important ledger while another followed his fellow with quill and ink. The Duke was the odds-on favorite to win the race for a second year in a row; the strappingly handsome Dair Fitzstuart was at three to one, and the bronzed merchant Jonathon Strang a credible five to one to win.

The Duke's five-year-old twin sons ran up and down the jetty with a group of equally boisterous village children making a general nuisance because there was no one to stop them. This was one of the only days in the year when tutors were also given the day free of their noble charges and were able to mingle freely amongst the crowd and, if they so desired, be as far away as possible from the young minds in their charge. This suited the boys and girls but disconcerted some of the noble guests unused to the presence of children whom, if they were seen at all, were definitely never heard. Lords Augustus and Louis made certain everyone saw and heard them!

And yet Lord Alston, the Duke's heir stood quietly between his father and Jonathon Strang in his green silk waistcoat and naval hat with green riband cockade, chin tilted up to the big men, listening intently to the gentlemen rowers' repartee. His grave and adult-like demeanor won him the approval of nobles, tenants and villagers alike but was considered by his mother, who had been watching him carefully for some minutes, as not the behavior usually associated with boys not quite seven years old. He should have been with his over-excited brothers and the village children getting up to mischief; indeed, as the eldest it was usually considered his right to be leader of the merry band of rabble.

The Duchess worried about Frederick. She did not worry about Gus and Louis who were energetic five-year-olds who got themselves into all sorts of scrapes, bruised their knees, broke their toys and often ruined breeches and stockings with grass stains and mud within five minutes of being let out of doors. Having had the rearing of her nephew Jack since he was five years old and who was now a youth almost sixteen years of age, Deborah was used to the unruly and rowdy ways of boys. But Frederick had never been rowdy. He was grave and precise to a pin in his appearance and advanced beyond his years in intelligence, so his tutors had told her and the Duke. While she was pleased he was no dunce, for he would require a good brain to use wisely the vast

inheritance that would solely be his when he inherited the dukedom from his father, superior intelligence carried with it at least
one disadvantage for the very young, such as her son: that of being
interested in the conversation of adults before being truly ready
to comprehend the subtle meanings behind much of what was said.
Even if he did not grasp the nuances in adult dialogue, Frederick
attuned to the topic and was bright enough to understand all too
well the difference between derision and respect.

And there was one person dear to Frederick's heart who was
the subject of constant speculation and gossip amongst family,
servants and Polite Society that Deborah knew made her son fret.
He was fretting now. She saw the anxiousness in his small face
under his smart naval hat, black curls just like his father's falling
across his brow; large brown eyes, just like hers, occasionally
fixing on the upper lawn, searching the row of marquees. His
preoccupation went unnoticed by his father, who was bantering
back and forth with his fellow rowers as to who would make it
round Swan Nest island without overturning their skiff, but not
by her.

The Duchess, her lady-in-waiting with the Lady Juliana in her
arms following up behind, joined the gentlemen rowers to wish
them the best of luck, and to see her sons put safely in their
respective skiffs before taking up her position in the middle of
the third arch of the stone bridge that spanned the lake to signal
the start of the race by waving and then letting drop into the water
below a weight tied up in a bright red silk handkerchief.

"There is still plenty of time, my darling," Deborah Roxton
whispered near Frederick's ear, pretending to straighten the sit of
his hat so as not to draw attention to her remark. She smiled into
his brown eyes. "The race is not due to start for a little while yet.
Mema will come."

Frederick looked into his mother's kind eyes and her understanding smile did much to alleviate his anxiety. He nodded and
smiled. "She is wearing green today, Maman. For me."

"Of course she is. How lovely," the Duchess replied evenly,
keeping the astonishment from her voice. She gently brushed the
dark curls from Frederick's face, hoping with all her heart he was
right. She smiled and straightened, but not before kissing his

cheek. "For luck. But perhaps you will not need luck, Frederick," she said in a clear voice, so the gentlemen could hear, "as I am told by your daughter, Mr. Strang, that you are a very good rower and will soundly beat the Duke." She turned with a raise of her arched eyebrows to look at Sarah-Jane, who was standing close by in the group of ladies come to watch the gentlemen prepare for the race. "They are the words you used, are they not, Sarah-Jane? *Soundly beat?*" But before the blushing Sarah-Jane could reply, she turned with a swish of her silk and gauze petticoats and a cheeky smile to the Duke, placing a hand on his bare forearm. "So, Roxton, you have competition this year and will need to row *like the devil.* Apologies to Dair and Charles, who are excellent rowers, but as Roxton *soundly beat them* last year, I have their measure. But you, Mr. Strang, remain an unknown quantity... Still, I took the gamble, and now you must prove your mettle." She kissed her husband's cheek swiftly. "I apologize, your Grace, but I have a confession to make. I have wagered on Mr. Strang to win."

A hue and cry went up amongst the rowers, who burst into loud laughter at the Duke's expense, several going so far as to give the Duke's wide back an affectionate thump in sympathy for his wife's disloyalty. Jonathon joined in the good-natured banter, making the Duchess a sweeping bow of thanks before kissing her hand and turning to the group of ladies for support, who to a one applauded him with much hand clapping and impromptu curtseys.

The Duke pretended offence, casting a solemn glance at his laughing opposition then raising a disapproving eyebrow at the ladies for daring to prefer another, but such was the mirth in his green eyes that he couldn't suppress a grin and everyone enjoyed a good laugh at his expense. He pulled his wife to him. "The devil take you, you disloyal wretch!" he murmured and stole a kiss. "I shall just have to make more of an effort to row harder and faster to win back your devotion."

"Please don't," she asked quietly looking into his eyes with a tremulous smile before glancing pointedly at their son who was now holding her hand but whose attention was still very much focused on the row of marquees. "He is wearing green—for her. She made him a promise."

The Duke followed her downward glance and his smile faded.

"Damn." He let her go and made a fuss of unrolling and rolling up his sleeve, saying under his breath, "Best to keep him occupied. He'll have too much to think about once the race is underway," and looking about for Tommy Cavendish announced loudly, "Shall we, gentlemen? It must be time." As the competitors made last minute farewells to their gaggle of female admirers and shook hands with each other, he went down on his haunches to speak to his son. "Frederick? It's time to get your naughty brothers into my boat and for you to get into yours. Will you do me the favor of rounding them up? Gus and Louis will listen to you. I need a last word with Maman and then I will come directly. Take Mr. Strang with you."

When Frederick nodded his father smiled and lovingly flicked his cheek.

He straightened and watched his son go up to Jonathon Strang and, in a gesture that almost brought tears to his eyes, take hold of the man's large sun-bronzed hand and smile up at him. The merchant, who had been having a last word with Charles Fitzstuart, looked down, saw who it was and instantly made a fuss of the little boy. Within a few seconds, oarsman and occupant were walking hand in hand down the jetty with Charles Fitzstuart, Frederick in non-stop conversation with his oarsman.

"You must admit he has a way with children," the Duchess commented at her husband's shoulder. "Frederick in particular, and for that alone I like him, and put ten pounds on him to win against you."

The Duke turned, smiled and took his little daughter from a grateful lady-in-waiting who was struggling with the little girl. He lifted Juliana high into the air and settled her, squealing with delight, on his shoulders and the ducal couple walked the length of the jetty to Roxton's skiff which now had two very excited occupants doing their best to behave, although Gus would not sit down and stood, legs akimbo in the middle of the boat pretending to be a cut-throat pirate, the red silk burgee which had been tied carefully around his arm by an attentive nanny now scrunched up and fixed about his red curls and pulled down over his left eye.

"Papa! Papa! Gus is a pirate! Look, Papa!" Louis shouted in support of his twin. "He lost his eye fighting off the filthy frogs!"

"He'll be mincemeat for pies if he doesn't take his seat," his father admonished with a laugh that only encouraged Gus to stick out his chest with pride and wave at his sister who was flapping her arms excitedly at him from the great height of her father's shoulders.

The other skiffs were beginning to be paddled out from the jetty to take up their position. Only the Duke's skiff remained moored.

Roxton offloaded Juliana with a big kiss, the long-suffering lady-in-waiting scurrying away with her precious bundle because her little ladyship's giggles had been replaced with tears of outrage that she was not to join her brothers in the skiff, and she dressed up for the occasion.

"Good luck, darling." Deborah went on tiptoe to whisper teasingly in her husband's ear, "I will still reward you tonight even if the ruggedly handsome merchant wins."

He pulled her to him. "Handsome? *He's* handsome?"

Deborah laughed at his disgruntled frown and kissed his mouth. She moved within his hold and he let her go, aware that she was wanted on the bridge to start the race. "Swooningly so, is the general opinion of the ladies."

"I don't give a damn about them; what do you think?"

The Duchess smiled impishly, brown eyes alight with mischief. She waved to her twin sons who were calling for their father, blew a kiss to Frederick who was also waving from his skiff which was being expertly maneuvered by his oarsman to come along side his fellow competitors, and turned back to her husband who was still staring at her, although she had seen his head snap round in direction of her airy kiss.

"Well?" he demanded.

She came back to him and looked up into his frowning coun-tenance, a hand on his broad chest. "A wife does like to know she can still illicit a jealous response from her husband; that she is still desirable, particularly one in her fifth pregnancy."

"Desirable? My *desire*, you ungrateful witch, is to blame for your continual breeding. Now let me go before our sons fall out of that boat. Ruggedly handsome indeed! Bah! I'll have my reward tonight—win or no win."

"As to that, if rewards are measured thus, then you are amply rewarded every night. And you dare to call me ungrateful!" Deborah blew him a kiss and skipped away, a last wave to her sons before striding off towards the bridge where a crowd had gathered to watch the start of the race.

It took her a good ten minutes to walk the distance between the jetty and the stone bridge, skirting the lake then out across open lawn scattered with wild daisies yielding in the breeze before meeting up with the long drive of raked crushed stone that went up to the house left and right crossed the blue stone bridge that spanned the lake in three arcs, the highest of which allowed sailing craft to pass from one side of the lake to the other. It was from this vantage point on the highest arch that the Duchess was greeted by Tommy Cavendish and a clutch of noble guests surrounded by tenant farmers, servants and children all come to hang over the barrier to shout encouragement to the oarsmen as the skiffs passed under the bridge.

Deborah had the weight tied up in a red silk handkerchief, saw the skiffs were in formation at the allocated starting line and was ready to let drop the handkerchief when Tommy Cavendish stayed her fingers with a word in her ear and a gentle hand on her upper arm. Something was not right with one of the skiffs. She saw it too.

The skiff being rowed by Jonathon Strang and containing her eldest son had moved out of formation and was returning the short distance to the jetty. Frederick was waving vigorously towards the jetty. The other competitors remained bobbing where they were. That the Duke did not move his boat but was also waving, as were the twins, allowed Deborah to breath easy that there was nothing urgently wrong with her son, his oarsman or the boat itself. Following their gaze, and the gaze of every man, woman and child on the bridge, she saw at once the reason for the commotion and her eldest son's unbridled enthusiasm.

"She's here! She's here! Mema's here!"

It was Frederick. Such were his shouts of excitement that the occupants of the other skiffs turned as one to see what had caused the Duke's son and heir to stand up in his boat and point excitedly toward land. He looked at Jonathon expectantly. There was no need for him to utter a word. Jonathon smiled and immediately set to rowing the short distance back to the jetty, Frederick quick to resume his seat at the helm.

The Dowager Duchess of Roxton was making her way across the lawn to the lake with, what seemed to those on the bridge and out in the lake in skiffs, half the crowd come to Treat for the Regatta following at her back.

Several children were skipping in front of her, leading the way, the local village parson was at her left shoulder, talking in her ear, while on her right, the wife of a tenant farmer was showing off her seventh and latest offspring, a ruddy-cheeked boy not quite two years of age. Spencer and Willis were close behind, trying but failing miserably to keep the villagers at a distance. An old villager with a stoop, but as nibble as any man ten years his junior, came out of the crowd as if from nowhere and with a tug of his imaginary forelock offered Antonia a handful of spring daisies that, from the dirt attached to their roots, had, just moments before, been secure in the ground.

At his impromptu offering, Antonia stopped to talk, gladly accepting the bedraggled bouquet, which she dutifully sniffed, and offered her hand in thanks. The crowd surged forward, jostling aside the besieged ladies-in-waiting, eager to hear what the Dowager Duchess had to say to Old Ernest in her heavily accented English. And when Old Ernest gave his best bow over her hand and straightened with a toothy grin, the crowd applauded his efforts, their approval turning into cheers when Antonia playfully bobbed a curtsey in reply. Their cheers muted into murmurings of satisfaction and delight when little Lord Alston scrambled out of the skiff and ran along the jetty to be gathered up in a loving embrace.

"I *told* Maman you would come. I told her you'd be wearing green! Are those real emeralds? I like your hair! Look! I have the same green ribbons on my waistcoat and on my hat. But it's in the boat. Do your shoes have emerald buckles? M'sieur Strang is wearing green too. His waistcoat is the greenest green I have ever seen! You look like a fairy princess, Mema!" Frederick prattled on, little hand tucked in hers and skipping beside her as they walked to the end of the jetty where Jonathon was waiting for them. "See! M'sieur Strang has a green waistcoat too! His is by far the best waistcoat. It is even better than Papa's, which is red, and it shines in the sun! Mema, Maman has bet M'sieur Strang to win against Papa! And we're sure to win now that you are dressed in green, too. Won't we, M'sieur Strang?" he added eagerly, his free hand taking hold of Jonathon's hand as if it was the most natural thing in the world and drawing him closer. "We will win, won't we, now that Mema is here?"

"I do not think M'sieur Strang he believes it is my dress that will see you win, Frederick," Antonia replied with a laugh. "He expects he will have to exert himself on your behalf if he is to have any chance at crossing the line before your Papa."

She extended her hand to Jonathon only realizing then that she still held the handful of daisies given to her by Old Ernest, and turned a bare shoulder, looking for Willis and Spencer. Finding them not at her back, she was unsure what to do with the flowers until a girl nervously stepped forward from the crowd that had stopped at the lawn and not trespassed onto the jetty, and silently offered to take them from her by extending her hand and bobbing a clumsy curtsey.

"*Merci, cherie*," Antonia said kindly. "Put these to good use and make a daisy crown for your pretty hair." She smiled when the girl's gaze shot from the boards to her face, her smile widening when the girl dared to smile back at the compliment, all nervousness forgotten. So much so that she turned without being dismissed and ran back into the crowd to show her sister the daisies given to her by the Duchess. Antonia turned back to Jonathon, offering him her hand and saying teasingly, "Will you need to exert yourself, M'sieur?"

"For you, Mme la Duchesse, Frederick and I would row the Thames for Doggett's coat and badge!" Jonathon declared with a bow and gently pulled her closer. "For you, I'd exert myself in all manner of physical pursuits. But those fetching petticoats have made me go weak at the knees and I can barely remain upright without aid," he teased, smiling down at her, at the fact she was dressed as befitted her rank when Monseigneur was alive, in a many layered, intricately embroidered silk robe *à la française*, honey curls threaded with green ribbons, the weight held in place with innumerable pins and a handful of diamond clasps, a dazzling emerald and diamond choker encircling her slender throat, and half a dozen diamond and gold bracelets tinkling about both wrists. She had even darkened her lashes and colored her full mouth. A great deal of thought and effort had gone into her toilette and yet he was conscious that it was a sparkling veneer masking what she must be truly feeling on this of all days—the third anniversary of the death of her Monseigneur.

"It's as well my arms are still in perfect working order, aye, Frederick?" he added with a laugh and tussled the boy's black curls. "We'd best get back to our skiff or the race will start without us, and that would give your Papa an unfair advantage."

"You will watch us win, Mema, won't you?" Frederick asked, a note of anxiousness creeping into his voice. But when she smiled and nodded and kissed his pale cheek, he threw his arms about her neck before running off to the skiff, calling for Jonathon to come on!

But Jonathon still held firm to Antonia's hand. He looked down into her eyes, pleased she had not pulled free of his hold. "I know why you're late. It's a decent walk up that hill. He understood of course why you put off your black on this of all days, that you did it for Frederick."

Antonia's eyes widened with surprise that he would instinctively know she had spent the morning talking with her loved ones in the mausoleum. She nodded and lowered her lashes and fixed on his sleeveless waistcoat. It was like the others he had worn, very finely embroidered in the most luminous silk threads, this one woven in the deepest greens and blues she had ever seen, the stitching so close and fine that it formed a perfectly smooth, glass-like surface. She had a sudden urge to run her open palm over the silk, to enjoy the silky softness of such beautiful work-manship caressing her skin, and under the silk, feel the hardness of his chest and torso.

She dared to lift her gaze. He wore no cravat, and the white shirt gaped at the throat revealing bare bronzed skin. She saw him hard swallow and wondered if his pulse was beating as rapidly as her own. She knew if she placed her hand over his heart she would feel the thumping against her palm, strong and even and so full of life. So very different from the last time she had placed her hand over the heart of a man, the man she had loved above all others. She, too, swallowed, breathed deeply and mentally forced herself back into the present. This was not the place or time to fall apart, whatever the day, despite the fact he knew how much this day meant to her. She must be strong, strong for Frederick.

"Your—Your waistcoat it is also very fetching. Frederick he is very taken with it. Another embroidery from India?"

"Yes, from India. I have a trunk full of 'em. This one is particularly rich and fine and littered with peacocks." He laughed. "And I feel like one in it!"

"There is nothing sadder than a peacock with his plumage displayed but with no reason to do so. So you must win to do justice to your finery and then you too can strut about like one!"

They both laughed and then fell silent.

"You must go," she said quietly. "Frederick he is calling you and the others—the others are waiting to start the race."

"Don't go home after the regatta without saying good-bye. Promise."

This did bring Antonia's green eyes up to meet his.

"Good-bye? You are leaving? *Pour quoi?*"

"I must. To London."

"London? When?"

"Immediately after the race."

"Why? Excuse me! I should not have—"

"No. I don't mind you asking. Business. I have secured the lease on a new house and must—"

"But surely you have a major-domo to take care of such things from afar and you have just arrived and your daughter—your daughter she will be disappointed to leave so soon."

He smiled to himself at her genuine disappointment. He shrugged, a hand through his hair. "If it was only the house... But there is another, more pressing matter that requires my physical presence. I should have already left but I could not disappoint Frederick... Or miss the opportunity of seeing you in all your sweet green splendor."

Antonia blushed at the compliment and said softly, "Your daughter she is to go with you?"

"No. She is staying with Kitty and Tommy Cavendish."

"They will take her to London to join you at this new house at the end of their stay?"

"No! Ah! No! No! I am not going away for good," he assured her with a grin. "No. I mean to return as soon as possible. Possibly sooner if it turns out to be another false alarm."

"Oh!" She let out a small sigh of relief and quickly masked this by gently clearing her throat and placing her gaze anywhere but up at him because he was grinning.

"Two days and we are already missing each other."

"You are being absurd again!"

"I must return," he said gently. "You will owe me and Frederick a dinner once we win this race." He touched her flushed cheek then lifted her chin with one finger. "I want so much to kiss you. Here. Now. I don't give a fig who's watching and I don't care if you rightly slap my face," and in an impetuous move he raised her hand, turned it over and stooped to press his mouth, first to the soft center of her palm and then to her bare wrist.

Instantly, a frisson of desire ignited her blood, raced up her arm in a thousand pins and needles, stained her throat and washed over her breasts, suffusing the porcelain skin dark pink. Her stays constricted against her ribs, making them unbearably tight, and she could not breathe without effort. She thought she might faint. *Mon Dieu, what is wrong with me?* She quickly tugged her hand free of his lingering kiss and whipped it behind her back. Where his mouth had touched her skin her flesh burned, as if seared by naked flame.

"How-how dare you do that to me!" she breathed, and for want of something to cover the awkward moment, with a snap unfurled her fan of gold paper leaf with its delicately painted scenes of Greek Gods and Goddesses. The cool air fanned across her bosom did little to calm her.

"You blush adorably," he uttered thickly, gaze raking across the rapid rise and fall of her deep cleavage. "And you smell divine. I would ask for the scent by name but you're not wearing any, are you?" He blinked. "Do what?" he asked, staring hard at her. "What do I *do* to you?"

"Stop it! You know perfectly well what it is you do to me! And I do not want to hear talk of blushes and scent when me I do *not* blush. I am hot from standing out here in the sun without a parasol, which is all very well for baked lunatics! And with everything else I had to remember to wear today, because me I was quite used to going without jewelry and wearing black, I forgot to wear scent. Not that I would have had I remembered because I have not worn it in such a long time that it is not worth the wearing. I need a new bottle. So now you must go away and row Frederick and win before I push you into the lake to make you go!"

He laughed at that and made her a short bow. "And you say I run on at the mouth! I think a dip in cold water would do us both good! I should ask you to forgive me but as it is your fault I won't. With you I have no manners. *Au revoir!*"

He turned on a heel and strode to the end of the jetty and climbed down into the skiff to shouts from his fellow competitors, who had all but decided to start the race without him, of "Huzzah!" and "About bloody time, Strang!"

Ten

Antonia watched the start of the race from the end of the jetty. The Duke and the twins waved enthusiastically, and she smiled and waved back, even blowing them a kiss when Gus stood up to show off his pirate bandage. He was still on his feet when the Duchess finally let drop the red silk handkerchief from the bridge. A huge cheer went up in recognition, but louder than usual because the delay had caused children and adults alike to become impatient and there was general relief to finally see some competitive action on the lake.

When the last of the skiffs had passed under the bridge and out of Antonia's line of sight, to the continual roar of those on the bridge, the Duke and his twins were leading, Dair Fitzstuart was a close second, Jonathon with Frederick in the bow a credible third, and Charles Fitzstuart was closing in rapidly on all three. Antonia knew she would now not see the boats until they headed back from the causeway and had navigated Swan Nest Island, so she left the jetty and joined her daughter-in-law and a party of ladies with different colored ribbons in their hair proclaiming their allegiance for a particular oarsman now battling it out on the lake. The bridge afforded the best view and was the only place to watch the battle for the finish line, the winner declared as the first skiff to pass under the middle arch of the stone bridge.

Another roar went up when three skiffs finally came into view from around a bend and entered the last stretch of the race and so close to each other that it was impossible to distinguish which one was in the lead as they rowed stroke for stroke down the straight towards the bridge.

The spectators' cheers became louder as the oarsmen rowed faster knowing the end was in sight. Children and a clutch of youths who had been paddling their bare feet in the icy water ran along the reedy bank waving and jumping, as if their efforts would in someway help the tired oarsmen find the strength to pick up speed. Family groups who had been seated on the sloping lawns enjoying the splendid vista of parkland and lake now made their way to the water's edge to watch the last of the race. A crowd began gathering on the banks of the lake near the festooned pontoon moored on the south side of the bridge where the skiffs would dock at the end of the race.

What was most surprising to Antonia, as the oarsmen and their silk burgees came into clear view, was that Dair Fitzstuart was in the lead—which sent the Aubrey twins into an ecstasy of girlish squeals of delight. The Spanish skiff was just slightly ahead of the Florentine boat for second place, but it was evident that the Spanish and Italian oarsmen were all but spent. Within mere strokes of the bridge these skiffs slowed, and the Stuart boat shot under the middle arch and crossed the line first. Dair Fitzstuart let drop his oars and fell back in the skiff to sprawl out, arms and legs splayed, lungs heaving in air, body exhausted, mop of black hair falling across his wide brow and shirt wet through with perspiration. He was thoroughly exhausted.

More than one female swooned at the sight of such dark and powerful masculinity in repose while the twins swept down to the pontoon dragging Sarah-Jane with them in a rustle of silk petticoats and beaming smiles to congratulate him, never mind Dair's win was a win for the Stuarts and the little Lady Juliana, and not Charles Fitzstuart for the American Colonies, Sarah-Jane's champion; her disloyalty noted by a few of the sticklers for convention as a black mark against her otherwise good character. As to the whereabouts of her own champion and of her father, Sarah-Jane and the rest of the spectators were left to wonder at.

Where her father was concerned she was not overly worried. She had every confidence in his ability to take care of himself. After all, he had spent most of his life surviving the wilds of the subcontinent's jungles, monsoon rains, flooding rivers and the blistering heat of its deserts, so a little race on a still lake in England, which held no fears for her after living in Hyderabad and crossing oceans to this wet island, was as nothing. No doubt Dair Fitzstuart would know his whereabouts once he had breath in his lungs and life into his splendid limbs.

Antonia and Deborah were having the same thought as to the whereabouts of the three remaining skiffs. And while many were caught up in the moment of the race having a winner and were celebrating at the pontoon as the Spaniard and the Italian docked beside the Stuart boat, the look of astonishment on the faces of the Dowager Duchess and Duchess that the Duke had not won his own race for the third year in a row was replaced with furrows of concern that his skiff and the two others remained unaccounted for.

Just as the Duchess picked up a handful of her blue satin petticoats and turned to leave the bridge with the intention of questioning Dair Fitzstuart, Tommy Cavendish caught at her elbow and pointed out to the open water. Two skiffs had rounded the final turn and were now paddling their way towards the bridge, but at a more sedate pace than the frenzied activity of the first three skiffs to race to the finish line. They were staying almost level, as if the oarsmen were deliberately matching each other stroke for stroke.

Charles Fitzstuart's skiff now had passengers. Frederick was no longer with Jonathon Strang but was seated in the bow of Charles's skiff, and huddled up next to him was his brother Louis. All three occupants were bedraggled. Frederick was without his hat, Louis no longer had his red ribbon cockade and Charles was missing his sleeveless waistcoat and his linen shirt was pulled about, as if he had been in a tussle. As if this wasn't alarming enough for Antonia and Deborah, when the skiffs finally passed under the bridge it became evident why the sixth and final skiff was nowhere to be seen.

Devoid of sleeveless waistcoat and shirt, a bare-chested Jonathon Strang was rowing the Duke, and cradled in the Duke's arms and wrapped up in Jonathon's green silk waistcoat was the Duke and Duchess's youngest son Lord Augustus—Gus the

Pirate—little white face surrounded by a mop of drenched red ringlets and bare feet poking out of the makeshift blanket.

The Duchess snatched up her petticoats and ran as fast as her long legs would carry her, kicking off her mules in the grass so her bare stockinged feet could cover the distance to the pontoon in half the time.

A crowd on the bank had surrounded Dair Fitzstuart, who was being congratulated by the Florentine and Spanish oarsmen and heartily applauded by several of his boon companions who had wagered heavily on him to win, and a clutch of ladies that included Sarah-Jane, the Aubrey twins and Kitty Cavendish who wanted to hear every detail of the race. This was in marked contrast to the frenzied activity on the pontoon where the occupants of the two skiffs just come alongside were being helped to alight as quickly as possible.

As the Duchess rushed past the celebratory party and onto the pontoon, orders were barked out at the knot of servants who scurried this way and that to raise the alarm. Up at the big house warm water was to be drawn for baths in the nursery; more warm water for the oarsmen; tell his Grace's valet Frew and the footman attending on Mr. Strang; something hot to drink and to eat for their little lordships. Where was the little Lady Juliana's nanny? Someone fetch Troppe the family physician last seen up on the hill in the third marquee along. No! Stretcher and bearers were unnecessary. The Duke would carry his young son up to the house by cutting across the lawns. Fetch the *Oudry* carriage. It could transport the Duchess and the children to the house.

"He fell into the lake. His lungs took in water. But he'll be all right," the Duke said quickly, holding Gus close to his chest as the Duchess rushed up to him. "He's been stripped and now needs to be kept warm. A hot bath and tucked up in bed with a warm brick and he'll soon be himself in no time. Won't you, Gus?"

"Fell in? *Fell? Into the lake?* Julian? He breathed in *water?* Is he truly all right? Is he breathing?" Deborah asked fretfully, hand to the little lifeless brow. She gently pushed back her son's mop of wet hair and watched his eyes flutter then open. He looked so white. He felt so cold. His lips were tinged blue. Gus was always so full of life and mischief: her little rascal. To see him completely still was as much a shock as knowing he had almost drowned. She began to shiver and shake and looked about her as if she had lost something, before looking back up at the Duke. "Where's Frederick and Louis? Are they all right? Where are they? Where are my *sons*, Julian?"

"Deborah—"

"Roxton, give me the boy and take your wife," Jonathon said quietly at the Duke's ear. When the nobleman hesitated to relinquish his son he added, "She's gone into shock."

"Keep him warm," the Duke repeated unnecessarily to Jonathon as he deposited his little son, wrapped up as tightly as if he was in a cocoon, into Jonathon's arms. "Keep walking; straight across the lawn, east. It's the quickest way to the house. I'll catch you up," then pulled the Duchess into his embrace who promptly burst into tears but was quick to dash a hand across her eyes. "Deborah! Darling!" he cajoled. "Gus will be fine after a good hot bath and a night's sleep. *Truly*. And here come your sons now, none the worse for their adventure."

Frederick came running along the pontoon, Louis on Cousin Charles's shoulders not far behind him; all three waved. Charles had in his free hand Jonathon's wet linen shirt.

Deborah gave a watery laugh of relief to see her sons safe and happy. "I will hate myself in the morning for being such a watering pot when Gus and Louis fly past my window in search of a bug or a beetle, with not a care in the world!" She looked up at the Duke. "It's all your fault. Pregnancy always makes me missish."

"You're always missish," the Duke whispered in her ear, which got him a playful poke in the ribs.

"Frederick! You're soaked through!" she gasped when her son ran into her arms. She looked up at Charles, saw that he was without his shoes and stockings as was Louis. "You're all wet!"

"Reason to get them to the house at once," said the Duke, a nod at Charles to follow, an arm about the Duchess and Frederick holding his mother's hand. "The carriage will take you all. Here it comes now."

"Gus sank like a big rock!" Louis announced proudly, wriggling his bare toes in Cousin Charles's face.

"He disappeared under the water, Maman!" Frederick added,

skipping beside his mother, neither boy the least bit concerned their youngest brother had been in any danger. "Mr. Strang dived in and brought him up. You should have seen him, Maman! He swims like a fish! And we were winning too! Gus spewed up water and everything all over the boat. His guts went *everywhere*."

"Everywhere!" Louis agreed proudly.

"Poor Gus!" said the Duchess, a quick look up at the Duke who rolled his eyes, and then across at Charles, who remained stoically straight-faced, lips pressed together. "Mr. Strang saved Gus?" she asked her husband.

"Strang! Wait up!" the Duke called out just as Jonathon started to head across the lawn. He turned to the Duchess and kissed her forehead. "Yes. He did. Dived in and pulled him out, hauled him up into the skiff, turned him on his side to get the water out of his lungs and had poor Gus coughing and spluttering and back breathing before I could do more than blink! Astonishing."

The Duchess stared anew at the merchant. "Then we owe him a great debt, Julian."

"Yes, an enormous debt." He sighed. "One I have no idea how to repay... Here's the *Oudrey*. You go with the children. Quicker if I take Gus cross-country."

"But I want to come with you."

The Duke took Gus from Jonathon's arms. "Don't be foolish. The baby—"

"I ran from the jetty and I am perfectly fine!" argued the Duchess, but there was no fight in her and she leaned in to have a last look at Gus, who despite his blue little lips and white face blinked up at her from within the folds of the silken green waistcoat with an impish if wan smile that offered her some comfort that her son's life was not in danger. "My poor little pirate," she smiled lovingly. "Papa will take you up to the house and Mama will be with you very soon!"

"Now kiss your pirate son and you'll see him next in a warm bath in the Nursery."

The Duchess watched the Duke stride away across the lawn just as the empty *Oudrey* tumbled into view on the gravel path, being driven at a pace its young regatta occupants had continually urged of its long-suffering driver.

"Louis! Be good enough to stop wriggling so Charles can put you to firm ground. Thank you, Charles."

"Please, your Grace, your thanks should go to Mr. Strang, who is a terrific swimmer. If not for his quick thinking..." Charles Fitzstuart stopped himself and turned to the object of their discussion and held out the wet shirt just as the *Oudrey* drew up alongside. "I gave it a good wringing, sir, so it is damp not soaking."

Jonathon took the shirt with a nod of thanks, and satisfied the Roxton children were now safe and taken in hand, Charles excused himself and followed the Duke's lead and strode off towards the house, eager to get out of his wet clothes and soak in a bath of hot soapy water, but also to remove himself from the depressing sight of his vainglorious and roguishly handsome elder brother being fawned over by every female of marriageable age, not least by Sarah-Jane Strang, with whom he had fallen, quite illogically but irreparably, in love. He hoped his fickle brother was merely toying with the young woman's affections. He prayed with all his heart she was not in love with Dair. He doubted his heart would make a recover if she married his brother and became his sister-in-law.

"Mema! Mema! We're all wet!" Louis announced to Antonia as she finally joined them where the lawn met the pontoon, cheeks flushed, a curl fallen out of its pins and dropped to her bare shoulder.

"Gus spewed *everywhere*, Mema!" Frederick confided to her, adding quickly at her frown, "*Il n'est pas mort.*"

"Gus has no guts left!" Louis confirmed with a grin. "They're still in the boat!"

"Deborah? He is all right? Deborah? Augustus he is all right? Yes?"

"Yes. Yes. Julian says he will be fine," the Duchess replied, distracted. Now the *Oudrey* was here all she wanted to do was get her sons and herself into it as quickly as possible and up to the house before they caught a chill. "Where's Juliana?" she asked, looking about as if she had completely forgotten the existence of her little daughter in her worry for her sons. "Oh! Thank Heavens!" she said on a sigh, seeing her stoic lady-in-waiting not a yard away patiently waiting with the now sleeping little girl in her arms. "Into the carriage, Meg. Quick! The boys are wet through. Frederick?! Louis?! Now if you please."

Louis scampered up onto the velvet cushions beside his mother. Frederick hesitated. He had hold of Antonia's hand and was standing before her, back to the carriage.

"I'm sorry we did not win for you, Mema.

"Oh! Do not think on it, *mon chou*. The race it is unimportant. Your brother he is what is important. And Gus he is safe so that is all that matters, *hein?*"

Frederick nodded and smiled at her smile. Still, he looked worried. "But you wore green for nothing."

Antonia touched his cheek. "For nothing? Not at all! I wore green for you, Frederick. Remember that. Not for the race. For you. So go now, your Maman she has called you twice."

Frederick tugged on her fingers. "Come with us!" Before she could accept or decline he turned and called to his mother, "Mema can come with us; can she, Maman?"

"There isn't room, Frederick!" the Duchess called back impatiently from within the carriage, Juliana now awake and clambering to the window, wanting to see *her Mema*; Louis pulling at his sister's hair and dripping lake water all over the carriage floor. Deborah appeared at the window. "Frederick, do get in! Louis is starting to shiver with cold out of the sun. Oh!" she added, suddenly aware that her mother-in-law was at the carriage steps. "I didn't mean..." She smiled crookedly, biting her lower lip. "There truly isn't room and your petticoats will be ruined. Louis is dripping everywhere and—"

"Deborah, you need not explain yourself to me," Antonia said gently and returned her daughter-in-law's shy smile, stepping back so the footmen could remove the steps and close over the carriage door.

She waved to Frederick, Louis and Juliana, who had pushed herself between her brothers at the window, and waited until the carriage had rounded the bend in the drive before turning away. She came face to face with the arresting sight of Jonathon Strang towel drying his hair, wet and shirtless.

The celebratory party surrounding Dair Fitzstuart had broken up the instant Jonathon Strang strode over to inform them that their carousing was completely inappropriate given the Duke's son had almost drowned and this was the reason the other skiffs had crossed to finish late.

There were murmurings of apology and the group headed off to the marquees behind the crowd of spectators who had been watching the race from the bridge and by the shore of the lake and now drifted across the sweep of lawn to the stalls and entertainments up on the hill. The Aubrey twins went arm and arm in company with the Florentine Ambassador's representative and Dair Fitzstuart, leaving Jonathon Strang talking almost exclusively to his daughter while the Cavendishs stood nearby, Kitty Cavendish pretending an interest in the tabulations in the Regatta Ledger which her husband had open and was perusing, possibly making mental computations in his head, by the frown between his brows.

Antonia was surprised how close she was to the little group. With the *Oudrey* come and gone and the crowd dispersed it was suddenly quiet and so the conversation between father and daughter was clearly audible. Yet they were not conversing in English or French but in a language so foreign to Antonia's excellent linguistic ear that she did not understand a single word. She might be able to speak and read fluently in three languages and comprehend another two with ease, but this was unlike any speech pattern she had ever heard before. She was not one to eavesdrop but she could not help herself because she wanted to make sense of the syllables, the cadence and intonation of this exotic and quite incomprehensible language.

And then she realized her ladies-in-waiting also had their gaze riveted on the small group to which Jonathon Strang was party, and it had nothing to do with aurally deciphering impenetrable linguistics. And as if to reinforce their distraction she too found herself staring openly at the merchant. What language he was talking became secondary as she took full measure of the man, from large bare feet to wet shoulder length hair, and his appearance burned itself into her mind's eye as she finally tore her gaze away, turned and stomped off up the lawn, muttering to herself that the sun must have affected her brain, for why else would the sight of a half-naked man throw her off balance?

What sane man paced about under a watery blue sky wet and shirtless, towel drying his hair? He should have covered his bare chest for the sake of propriety immediately Charles handed him the shirt, regardless of the fact it was wet, and particularly with ladies present, and one of these his daughter! Although Sarah-Jane did not seem at all disconcerted by his appearance but was conversing with him as if she was used to her father parading about in his breeches and nothing more. He wasn't even wearing shoes! Perhaps on the subcontinent that's how men dressed, or went about undressed because of the heat? Going about shirtless would account for his chest and wide back being as sun-bronzed as his face and arms. She had admired pictures, beautifully painted illustrations of Indian men and women with caramel skin in various states of undress, admittedly mostly naked, and in a variety of sexual positions, in a large red leather folio belonging to Monseigneur. It was in their private library at the Hôtel in Paris and she had not even blushed at that; they were most interesting and instructional.

But this was different. Jonathon Strang wasn't a static picture in some ancient text. He was flesh and blood and he was moving about. He was all sinews and muscle. She had never noticed just how broad were his shoulders, as was his back, which tapered to narrow hips...Was that a-a *tattoo*? Surely not. Only pirates and primitives were given to tattooing their bodies. She remembered a most interesting etching of a Maori or was the native warrior from Tahiti? with intricate ink markings all over his face and down his arms. It was in a book—a journal by a certain Captain Cook—also in their library in Paris. Jonathon Strang's indelible ink mark was of a similar intricate pattern just below his hip-bone. Antonia reasoned that his tattoo was not normally on show, even without his shirt, but the waistband of his breeches had drooped, made heavy with water the sodden material clung to buttock and thigh, the breeches with drawers beneath hanging so low that clearly visible was a distinct demarcation where skin bronzed in the hot sun met the smooth white flesh unseen by the light of day. So he wasn't burnt toffee *all over*, well, not under his drawers, not-not *there*.

There was something unexpectedly erotic and inviting about that demarcation line and it intruded without warning into Antonia's thoughts after dinner as she sat in her favorite wingchair in the Gallery sipping coffee; the conversation having descended into inanity and spiteful gossip of which she wanted no part. And then the Countess of Strathsay was heard to extol her eldest son's virtues for a fourth time, basking in the hollow glory of his victory in the regatta. This did penetrate Antonia's subconscious and it was all she could do to stop herself from snapping shut the ivory sticks of her gold leaf fan to draw blood just to have a legitimate excuse to remove herself from her aunt's venomous orbit.

"I was sitting on the hill, which has a commanding view over the entire lake, and it was evident that Dair was so far in the lead that had Lord Augustus not fallen into the lake, Roxton still would not have caught him up," Lady Strathsay announced with a self-satisfied smile. "To point out fact, my dear Lady Cavendish, it was Charles who, at that stage of the race, was second to Dair and may well have finished in that place had the accident not occurred. Thus *my* sons would have finished first *and* second."

"But, my lady," Kitty Cavendish began and was cut off.

"That is a great piece of nonsense, Charlotte," Antonia stated. She handed off her Sevres cup and saucer to her lady-in-waiting. "You cannot say for certain the outcome because in truth the race it should have been abandoned the instant Augustus he fell into the water."

All coiffured heads looked to the Dowager Duchess, surprised she should choose to interrupt, and then turned toward the Countess waiting her response.

"I beg to differ, Mme la duchesse," Lady Strathsay replied with extreme politeness. "Had you been seated where I was, you could not but reach the same conclusion. My one disappointment, that Charles abandoned his chance to come second to his brother."

Antonia's green eyes widened. She could barely contain her astonishment.

"You would have preferred that he Charles row on, and not go to the assistance of M'sieur le Duc to rescue his son who was drowning? *Incroyable.*"

The Countess shrugged, the few ladies who were capable of understanding rapid French now on the edge their collective seats. What the Countess said next had those ladies slack-jawed.

"What is the point of speculating on what might have been, Mme la duchesse, when that boorish merchant proved the hero of the hour, not Charles. So disappointing for a Mamma when her son goes to the rescue and arrives *after* it is all over and is relegated to *valet*. Holding that man's shirt as if *he* was the commoner and not the great-grandson of the Merry Monarch! And then the brash fellow had the effrontery not to put on this article of clothing to cover his nakedness that was then on view to the world, as if he's a prize stallion after a race in need of a good rub down! Outrageous and-and *common*."

"My dear Lady Strathsay, I had no idea you were a connoisseur of the stud," Henrietta Hibbert-Baker interrupted in English before Antonia could reply. She repeated in English some of what the Countess had said about Jonathon Strang to their female audience, adding with a flutter of her blonde lace fan, "I must point out there is nothing common about a prize stallion, particularly Strang, who doesn't town-cry about his considerable assets. Even you must agree, my lady, he does show to advantage in wet breeches and no shirt."

There were murmurings of agreement but the Countess remained suitably blank-faced. She had no idea what the silly woman was talking about and said so, but it was evident everyone else did because they were being childish and giggling behind their fluttering fans. She decided to ignore them all. Besides the creature had the temerity to interrupt in English, thus excluding the Dowager Duchess, which was unforgivably bad mannered. She made a point of explaining in painful detail to Henrietta Hibbert-Baker her social lapse, and in the most patronizing of tones, before turning to Antonia as if their conversation had never been interrupted.

"I despair of Charles attracting a female worthy of his lineage when he goes at the beck and call of others." She sighed her annoyance. "Sometimes I wonder if he is even interested in females *in that way*. He certainly never shows it; unlike Dair who has three females dangling off his arm at any one time, *and* keeps a mistress in Chelsea whose already born him a brat if the gossip is to be believed. Not that I am at all pleased it is common knowledge, but I own to being relieved that he can breed. If only he would now settle down with an heiress worthy of his name and give me a proper grandchild."

"That is very unfair on Charles, Charlotte, and you know it," Antonia said in a low voice. "Possessing a caring disposition is nothing of which to be ashamed. And how do you know he has not attracted any female admirers? I am certain he is interested in females because he regularly corresponds with one in Paris. Perhaps she is the one. Charles has me address letters to our Hôtel and it is from there that the girl's maid she collects Charles's letters. And her replies, they come here to the dower house, and me I send them on to Charles."

"*Charles?* My son Charles, write to a female in-in *Paris?*" The Countess was incredulous. She twisted up her mouth with distaste. "If he does, it's not to anyone you or I would care to know. At least I hope it is not anyone who frequents the Hôtel because they would be highly unsuitable. At best, squalid little merchant princes seeking a rung on the social ladder. If Dair is to be believed, worse. The Hôtel is now inhabited by *tenants*. A Farmer-General has turned half the Hôtel into *leased* apartments and has had the effrontery to lease one to agents of the traitorous rebels fighting us in the American colonies. It is not to be born. But what can one expect from the French. The Duke and his sister must be turning in their graves."

Antonia blinked and sat up very straight. She had no idea what Charlotte was talking about and wondered if the woman's cup of tea had been laced with spirits in a calculated attempt to get her drunk and thus perform some social faux pas. Not that Charlotte needed alcohol to look a fool. She had just maligned the French to a French noblewoman and was oblivious to her rudeness.

"I beg your pardon, Charlotte, but to me you are not making sense. What apartments? What Farmer-General? Who are these traitors? What do the American colonies have to do with Charles and the Hôtel? What do you mean the Hôtel it is *inhabited by tenants?*"

The Countess now sat up very straight. She regarded Antonia with a mixture of incredulity and abject pity. She was also secretly and deliciously triumphant if for no other reason than it was about time the Dowager Duchess of Roxton had her gossamer blindfold removed and saw life as it truly was: disappointing and cruel. Antonia had led a charmed existence, shielded from life's unpleasantness by a devoted husband, a sinister old roué who had kept his duchess cosseted as one does a beautiful fragile butterfly, and now her son, the present duke, was continuing on with his father's preposterous coddling. It was this *coddling* that was to blame for Antonia being oblivious to her preeminent position as a Duchess. At the very least she should show a haughty contempt for those beneath her touch instead of curtseying to a dirty old farmhand for giving her a handful of daisies and allowing that sallow-skinned merchant to kiss her hand in full view of everyone. Such behavior did not sit well with Charlotte's well-ordered view of the world for if there was no order, no hierarchy, where did that leave her, a Countess? Without hierarchy and order, if the nobility was not given the respect it was due, Charlotte Strathsay was little more than an aging woman abandoned by her husband, of little beauty or charm and with no particular talent for witty conversation.

"Oh, come now, Mme la duchesse!" Charlotte scoffed. "Do not pretend you do not know!"

"I do not. Why would I ask if I knew, Charlotte? You are being obtuse for its own sake."

The Countess gave Antonia's hand a perfunctory pat.

"I always maintained the old Duke kept you too sheltered for your own good," she said with a sigh and a glance about for nodding approval from the occupants of the wingchairs and chaise lounges, and was met with only frozen expressions. She was pleased nonetheless that she was the focus of attention. "And now poor Roxton is burdened with carrying on his father's ill-judged legacy. Your son—"

"I did not ask for your opinion of me," Antonia said very quietly. "Your opinions are unimportant and never again will you speak to me of Monseigneur or of my son. I asked that you tell me about the Hôtel. That is what I want to know."

"Know? I only know what everyone else knows, Mme la duchesse."

Antonia scanned the arrangement of sofas to discover faces quickly averted and gazes cast to the Aubusson rug. At that moment, the double doors at the far end of the Gallery opened to admit some of the gentlemen, who had been sitting over the port in the dining room, much to the relief of the ladies who were discomforted by the Countess's very deliberate baiting of the Dowager Duchess of Roxton. Antonia saw Charles Fitzstuart and Tommy Cavendish but her son was not amongst the group; she did spy her daughter-in-law. The Duchess had excused herself after dinner and gone up to the nursery to check on Lord Augustus and to wish her children goodnight. Deborah was now standing at the far end of the Gallery in conversation with someone out of view in the anteroom and Antonia wondered if it was the family physician and hoped Gus was as well as first diagnosed. She closed the sticks of her fan with a snap, determined to quit the tea trolley and her venomous aunt, but curiosity got the better of her and she asked the question.

"So what is it you know I do not that makes you bursting at the laces to tell me, Charlotte?"

The Countess dared to smile triumphantly. She couldn't help herself. She was dizzy with anticipation as to Antonia's response to her news.

"Roxton sold your Parisian Hôtel nine months ago."

Eleven

Charlotte was hoping for theatrics and was bitterly disappointed.

Antonia stood and shook out her silk embroidered petticoats with deliberate slowness. The only sound, the tinkle of her gold and diamond bracelets touching as they slid up and down her wrists. The only sign she was rattled, when she fumbled with her fan but managed to catch it by its gold tassel before it fell with a clatter to the floorboards. A number of ladies, who were holding their collective breath as they furtively watched the Duchess, let out a sigh when the gentlemen came up to the tea trolley oblivious to the air of tension and requested tea and sweetmeats, Tommy Cavendish lifting the mood with the announcement,

"Well my delectable *petit fours*, it's Tommy's guess you've all been discussing the Jonathon prime rib while your rashes of bacon husbands have been out of cauliflower earshot. Am I right? Kitty?"

But Kitty, like the rest of the ladies, had risen off their chairs the moment the Dowager Duchess of Roxton had done so and stood waiting to see what she meant to do. When Antonia turned to go, a nod to her ladies-in-waiting to fall in behind her, the group sank into respectful curtseys then resumed their seats and watched her walk off up the Gallery at what Antonia hoped was the pace of a leisurely stroll.

So everyone knew, thought Antonia. Or thought they knew. She refused to believe Charlotte. She refused to believe common knowledge: that the Roxton Hôtel on the Rue Saint-Honoré, which had been in the family for over a hundred and fifty years, had been sold off by her son to a Parisian merchant. She refused to believe her son could sell his family heritage because selling the Hôtel was akin to selling off a piece of his parents' hearts. The Hôtel was flesh and blood to her. It was part of her. She could no more think of giving up the house in Paris as stop breathing. It was the birthplace of Monseigneur, of his sister Estée, and of Estée and Vallentine's son Evelyn, her own son Julian had also been born there. It was the first place she had called home, the house Monseigneur had brought her to when he had rescued her from Versailles. It was where she and Monseigneur had first made love. There had to be some other explanation. Some other reason Charlotte and the others thought the Hôtel had been sold. She would ask her son and he would tell her it was a ruse. That was all there was to it.

Antonia was determined to seek out the Duke to have his reassurance and then her heart it would quiet and she could return to Crecy Hall. Deborah would know his whereabouts. Perhaps he had gone up to see his children before joining his guests? And then, just as she was half way along the Gallery, Deborah turned and disappeared further into the anteroom and out into the Gallery stepped a stout gentleman whose flowered waistcoat and silk breeches proclaimed the gentleman but whose sausage-like fingers and swollen jowls exposed the glutton.

It was Sir Titus Foley, physician, healer-extraordinaire and confidant to the titled, fawned over and feted by Polite Society as some sort of miracle worker amongst his fraternity; a preeminent physician with a gift for healing fragile minds, particularly the fragile minds of the recalcitrant pretty young wives of noblemen.

Antonia loathed him. She also had much to fear from him.

What Sir Titus Foley had inflicted upon her in the name of *scientific medical treatment* was the stuff of nightmare and Antonia had not told a living soul. The humiliation was just too great. She was still uncertain what was real and what she imagined had happened in those weeks under the dandified physician's care. She had been sedated with laudanum, sometimes so heavily she was left fuzzy-headed and disorientated with no idea if hours or minutes had passed her by. Which was probably just as well.

147

It was a year since Sir Titus had treated her for *melancholia* and yet the mere sight of the man made her shiver with anticipation and dread. She hoped she never recalled in detail the treatments meted out to her in the name of being cured. And here was the physician returned, smiling his fish-lipped smile, with his ferret eyes bright and bowing obsequiously before her as if he was a long-lost family friend.

She did not know what was more laughingly pathetic—that this buffoon of medical quackery had deluded himself into believing he was a learned healer when his perverted methods were a distillation of everything that was loathsome and vile about the medical profession, or that her son had deceived himself into thinking he was doing what was right and proper in trying to have her cured of morbid grief, as if grief could be healed by the bizarre attentions of a lecher-physician and his hocus-pockery.

Coming face to face with her tormentor gave her a frightening jolt. It also saddened her that her son had made good on his threat to send for Sir Titus. Her only hope now was that being out of her black the Duke would decide the presence of the physician was unnecessary. But here he was, bowing and scraping before her and as much as she wanted to snub him it was not in her nature to be cruel or bad-mannered so she kept her features perfectly composed and inclined her head in recognition of his presence and walked on. She would not extend her hand or engage him in conversation. She recoiled from his closeness; the thought of his bloated hands upon her, however briefly, made her nauseous. She stepped aside and continued on up the Gallery in search of her daughter-in-law, leaving Sir Titus with his buttocks in the air and his nose to the ground.

The physician had left the comfort of the dining room, where port and congenial company were plentiful, and then spoken at length with the good Duchess who had apologized that her noble husband was not at liberty to speak with him until he had concluded his meeting in the library, confident he had a place in this world of title and privilege, and was now left standing alone in a long hall blazing with candlelight, the object of ridicule by nose-in-the-air ancestors up on the walls and by the titled and privileged gathered around the tea trolley.

All because *she* did not treat him with the respect he deserved as a learned medical man, unlike those gentlemen who were begging his opinions over the port. He had just concluded a most lucrative contract to provide his superior medical expertise in the treatment of melancholia to Lord Barrow, whose second and much younger wife, a pretty brunette with liquid blue eyes, recoiled from her husband's unusual proclivities in the bedchamber and thus refused to share the marital bed. Lord Barrow believed his wife to be suffering from some sort of nervous disorder and as he wasn't getting any younger and needed an heir—his cousin Henry wasn't getting his hands on the baronetcy or the castle—he appealed to Sir Titus's expertise in such delicate matters to divest his wife of her reluctance.

Sir Titus had confidently boasted to his lordship that under his care he would have the wife cured of her disobedience and back in the marital bed and eager for his attentions within the month. He wouldn't be at all surprised to learn from his lordship that Lady Barrow was with child soon thereafter. He had left Lord Barrow beaming, for this: snubbed and abandoned under the blazing light of a chandelier by the Dowager Duchess of Roxton. He ground his teeth, seething, to be summarily dismissed by the illustrious and definitely the most divinely beautiful woman he had ever had the pleasure to call patient.

Upon receiving the Duke's request he had literally dropped everything and made the arduous twelve-hour journey from his private sanatorium in Northumberland all for the opportunity to have the Duchess under his care again.

Under his care... He couldn't wait. The thought of spending time alone with her... He in control, she to do as she was bid or suffer the consequences... It was the only way... Total submission. It had worked with great success for so many of his delicately bred female patients suffering from nervous disorders. But he had yet to break the Dowager Duchess to his will. This visit he was determined she would submit using his patented Chair of Correction: Strapped ankle and wrist the patient had no option but to surrender to treatment. And he had added a new weapon to his medical armory: Blair's water therapy. To see her in a wet chemise... He felt himself stir and quickly suppressed his desire to scurry after her.

"What a most astonishing and welcome surprise to discover you out of your widow's garb, your Grace! I hardly recognized you in such pretty petticoats, and in a color that compliments your eyes to perfection!"

Antonia made no comment, her ladies-in-waiting following at her back, the physician scrambling to keep up and forced to make a wide arc so that he was at Antonia's side and not following behind.

"This change of raiment is very welcoming, your Grace," Sir Titus continued, one wary eye to his surroundings, careful not to collide with the ribbon back chairs at intervals up against the wall between the undraped French windows. "I am surprised His Grace of Roxton did not mention such momentous news in our most recent exchange of correspondence."

"M'sieur le Duc has better use of his time than report on his maman's wardrobe! But as you see, I am out of my black, so your presence it is unnecessary."

Sir Titus went giddy at the Duchess's heavily accented English. He took a deep breath and cleared his throat of a lustful rasp to say with a light laugh,

"Oh, your Grace, you are so diverting I could almost believe you returned to full health! But I would be failing in my duty to the Duke and most importantly to you, if I did not exert myself to the fullest degree and thoroughly examine your Grace so that I can present my diagnosis to the Duke, and thus settle his Grace's mind as well as my own that you are back to full glorious health in mind and body."

Antonia stopped and turned on the physician and so abruptly that Willis and Spencer almost collided with her and had to stagger back, a hand out to each other to keep upright. She stared the physician up and down and then fixed on his bloated and florid face, a light in her green eyes that thrilled and alarmed him in equal measure.

"M'sieur, if you dare to touch me again I will render you less than a man." She jabbed his genitals with the closed ivory sticks of her fan and smiled when he gave an involuntary yelp. "*Bon*. We understand each other."

At the heavy double doors to the library two liveried footmen stood sentry.

Antonia waited for the doors to be opened for her but when
the footmen did not move and stared straight over her fair hair
she was so taken aback that for one moment she was at a loss
and just stood there waiting. Footmen opening doors for her was
as natural as breathing—done without thinking.

When she took a step forward the footmen moved sideways to
close the gap to the door handles. Again she hesitated. She could
not really believe they were denying her entry to her favorite
room. She had spent more hours in the library than anywhere else
in this house. Even when Monseigneur was at his desk working
on important papers or in meetings she sat curled up in a wingchair by the fire, with the view of the fragrant gardens beyond,
reading. She did not often enter the library through these double
doors. She had used the secret stairwell that connected the private
apartments she had shared with Monseigneur with the library
below. The secret door was behind a bookcase at the base of the
spiral stairs that wound up to the walkways that wrapped around
three walls of the library and gave access to two levels of bookcases that stretched to the domed ceiling.

Nevertheless, when using the main entrance, she never expected
to be denied entry. She regarded the impassive faces of the two
footmen. Neither looked down at her but continued to stare out
over her fair head and above the heads of her ladies-in-waiting to
the opposite wall with its large dark portrait of the forbidding
fourth duke and duchess wearing their bejeweled ducal coronets
and ermine robes.

"Lawrence. Please, you will open the door for me."

The footman on Antonia's right shot a startled look at his
fellow. He did not understand French but he heard his friend's
Christian name clear enough. Lawrence swayed and was no less
astonished to be addressed by the Dowager Duchess of Roxton.
It made him speak without thinking.

"You know my name! How?" then remembered just whom he was talking to and added with an audible gulp and a bow of his head, and in French, "Forgive my outburst, Mme la duchesse."

"Yes, I know your name. And you know mine," Antonia replied with a smile. "I also know that your grandfather he was a most treasured servant of Monseigneur, the butler Duvalier, and that your father he is our head gardener, and that until you broke your arm you had hopes of becoming head groom. So now, you will please open the door, or let me open the door so that I may enter the library to speak with M'sieur le Duc."

Lawrence the footman looked stricken. "I cannot," he replied in a whisper, genuinely apologetic. "I may not, Mme la duchesse. I-I *wish* that I could, *for you*, but I-I cannot."

Antonia was not angry by the footman's refusal but pondered the young man's distress and what she could do about her dilemma without getting either servant in trouble with her son and yet allow her to enter the library. She had to speak to Roxton about the Hôtel for her peace of mind, and tonight.

The footmen's refusal to acquiesce and bow to nobility was too much for Willis. "Step aside at once!" she blurted out. "This is her Grace the Duchess of Roxton, you ignorant oafs!"

"Willis, me they know," Antonia said over her shoulder. "That seems to be their dilemma. Oh! Deborah!" she added, turning away from the door spying her daughter-in-law with the butler at her back. She met her half way across the anteroom. "Deborah, when does Roxton next send post to Paris?"

"Post to Paris, Maman-Duchess?" Deborah repeated. The butler had fetched her the instant he was alerted by a passing upper chambermaid that the Dowager Duchess was headed for the library. She had expected to be met with an imperious demand so the question completely threw her off-balance. "I-I— To where in Paris, Maman-Duchess?"

"To the Hôtel," Antonia replied, as if it was self-evident she would be talking about their house on the Rue Saint-Honoré. "I sent letters to Tante Adelaide yesterday but I want something brought back from the Hôtel with the next post."

"Brought back, Maman-Duchess?"

"Yes. There is a travel journal in our private apartment that I think the boys they will enjoy, particularly Gus who wants so badly to be a pirate."

"A-A travel journal? About-about *pirates*?"

The Duchess wondered where the conversation was headed. But she was willing to entertain the idea of pirates or anything else that took her mother-in-law's fancy but her mention of the Hôtel as if it was as it had always been when the old Duke was alive alerted Deb to what the conversation might really be about. She had warned her husband to tell his mother about the sale of the Parisian mansion months ago but he would not hear of it, believing she was not emotionally capable or ready to accept such news. Now Deborah wondered if he had left it all too late. She glanced at the library double doors and wondered for how much longer the Duke would be in conference with members of the American Colonial War Committee.

"Yes. Yes, Maman-Duchess, I am certain Gus would love a book about pirates."

Antonia saw her daughter-in-law's anxious glance at the double doors and noted she was holding her hands together rather too tightly. She was a little ashamed of herself for being less than transparent with Deborah but she needed to discover if there was a grain of truth to what Charlotte had told her, and Deborah's behavior would tell her better than any outright statement. She did not want her daughter-in-law to be burdened with the guilt of revelation; of knowing she had been the one to tell her the Hôtel had indeed been sold off and thus broken her mother-in-law's heart—that was a burden only her son should bear.

With every halting response Deborah gave, Antonia began to crumble inside.

"Oh, this book is not about pirates, but Gus I am sure will want to be one, or a sailor at the very least," Antonia chatted on, the only sign of her inner turmoil showing itself in the way her left hand hard gripped her right wrist above the gold bangles until her knuckles were white. "If I remember correctly, it is a journal of a certain Captain Cook who commanded His Majesty's ship the *Endeavour*. Monseigneur was presented with a signed copy by a Mr. Banks who was the naturalist who accompanied this Captain Cook about the Pacific seas."

"Captain Cook and Mr. Banks? It sounds most fascinating."

"It is. There are some exceptionally fine engravings of the unusual flora and of the natives on their islands, with tattoos and feathered headdresses..." Antonia met Deborah's worried brown eyes with a sad smile. "I remember this book most particularly because it was one of the last books Monseigneur requested be brought here but sadly, there was no time..."

"Maman-Duchess, I—"

"So you see why it is very special and why I would want the boys to have it. It would greatly sadden me to think it is no longer on the table at the foot of the bed in our bedchamber, along with the other volumes that were Monseigneur's particular favorites—"

Deborah's eyes filled with tears. "Maman-Duchess..."

"—because I am certain he would very much approve of his grandsons having the pleasure of their Papa reading to them about Captain Cook's many adventures and being shown the engravings."

"I know the boys will love Julian to read the journals to them, and cherish it all the more because it once belonged to their *Grandpère*. I am certain we can find it, Maman-Duchess," Deborah assured her, another glance at the doors. "It will just take time..."

"Time? Why, when I have told you where it is? Oh! You mean to send for it from Paris. Of course! How silly of me. But... Won't it take the same amount of time as it does for my letters to reach the Hôtel, yes?"

"Yes. Yes. About the same time," Deborah lied, biting her lower lip.

Now Antonia's eyes were tearing up because she had forced her daughter-in-law to lie and she hated herself for doing so. But she was almost beyond caring. The images in her mind's eye of the intimate rooms she had shared with Monseigneur in their seventeenth century Parisian mansion were so vivid, so eternal, that to think they were now only that—images in her head—was unfathomable.

"But what I do not know... But perhaps you can enlighten me... How much time will it take to locate Captain Cook's journal if it has been packed away in some nameless crate with the hundreds of other nameless crates under covers gathering dust in a nondescript Parisian warehouse?"

"Maman-Duchess! *Please*. You must understand... He did—He did what he thought—what he thought was for—"

Antonia had turned away from Deborah the moment she started trying to justify the Duke's actions and with a swish of her petticoats she swept to the library doors, her ladies-in-waiting forced to scatter in her wake. She glared at the two footmen with her chin up. "Get out of my way! *Immédiatement*."

Both footmen did not hesitate. They instantly parted shoulders and Antonia marched between them and pushed down on the ornate door handles and so hard that the doors flew open and swung wide to bang up against the wood of the bookcases. She advanced up the length of the library, neither looking left or right, until she was standing before the Duke's massive mahogany desk.

She did not see the two gentlemen lounging on upholstered wingchairs or their ancient colleague standing by an undraped window holding up a sheaf of correspondence to the light to better see the print through his corrective lenses. A scatter of paperwork and a rolled parchment littered the low table. A soft-footed footman was collecting used glassware and providing further refreshment while another was collecting up gold and enameled snuffboxes to be refilled.

Antonia saw only her son, buttocks leaning against the rolled edge of his desk, long legs crossed at the ankles, his handsome face in profile because he was addressing the old gentleman by the window.

The gentlemen had heard the bang of the doors and reacted to the noise with a cursory glance up the long book-lined room. But when they saw the small majestic figure in gold and green hooped silks marching up the length of the library they hastily put aside paper and glass and scrambled up as one to bow to her, their astonishment at her angry intrusion masked by mute politeness and diffidence to rank. Five paces behind and looking distressed was the Duchess and all eyes instantly turned on the Duke.

"Is it true?" Antonia demanded. "Julian! Is it true you have sold the Hôtel?"

Twelve

About an hour earlier, when the ladies had retired to the Gallery and the gentlemen remained at the dining table to unbutton their embroidered silk waistcoats after a long meal to talk of horses and politics over the port, three of their number with their noble host excused themselves to their fellows and removed to the Duke's sumptuous library for a meeting of the *Committee for Colonial Correspondence of Interest.* The only topic on the agenda: when, not if, the French would declare their hand and join forces with the American colonial rebels in their war against his Britannic majesty King George the Third.

"Your Grace, we have known for some time now that the French have been secretly funding the rebel cause in the colonies through a bogus Portuguese company *Roderigue Hortalez and Company,*" Sir Kenneth Hibbert-Baker told the Duke of Roxton, a glance at the two other noblemen who constituted the Committee. "Our sources tell us that *Roderigue Hortalez* has the full support of His French Majesty and that it is through Louis' agent, one Pierre-Augustin Caron de Beaumarchais, that all manner of materials are being secured to aid the rebels against us."

"Such as?" asked the Duke, signaling for the gentlemen to sit and with a nod to the footman to set down the silver tray holding port decanter and glasses on the low table between the arrangement of striped silk chaise and wingchairs.

"Gunpowder, cannon balls, mortars, tents, cutlasses, pistols, that sort of thing," Lord Shrewsbury replied with a wave of lace-covered hand, perching on a wingchair.

"And enough apparel to clothe thousands of traitorous black-guards," stuck in Lord Carstairs with disapproval. "French cloth got Washington's rebel army through a damnably awful winter; more's the pity for us! Bloody French!" he spat and snatched up a port glass off the silver tray

"How does this French largesse find its way to American shores?" Roxton asked calmly.

"*Roderigue Hortalez* has its headquarters on the island of St. Eustatius," Sir Kenneth told him.

"Which is where?"

"If your Grace will permit...?" asked Sir Kenneth, picking up off the low table a rolled parchment. When the Duke nodded, Shrewsbury obliged by pushing aside the silver tray and putting to the carpet a stack of papers he had brought into the library to make room for the parchment to be spread wide on the low table. Roxton left his desk to peer down at what was a detailed map.

"This is—"

"—a map of the West Indies," finished the Duke with a nod. "The Antilles Sea is here to the south west, the Atlantic to the east. There are literally thousands of islands claimed by one European power or another in the past three hundred years or so since Columbus claimed everything for Isabella and Ferdinand. Sugar and spices and built on slavery. A veritable stock-pot."

Shrewsbury smiled thinly when Sir Kenneth and Carstairs exchanged a glance of surprise, saying with smug satisfaction, "I did warn you. Roxton has his father's shrewd brain and his divine mother's good-looks."

Roxton gave a bark of embarrassed laughter at the old man's compliment and blushed in spite of himself. "I was rather hoping I had inherited my father's haughty demeanor and my mother's quick thinking, sir. But I'd settle for either parent's brain."

Shrewsbury inclined his powdered head and savored his port. "Just so, my boy. Although I rather think you have too much of your mother's sentiment, which is no bad thing, and that it is Henri-Antoine who inherited the full measure of M'sieur le Duc's sublime arrogance," he said, referring to Roxton's much younger brother. He glanced down at the dark liquid in his glass and sighed. "I miss him and his enlivening conversation..." and then raised his glass and his eyes skyward. "*Repos dans paix, cher ami.*"

There was a moment's respectful silence, for Lord Shrewsbury's heartfelt confession and the fact it was the third anniversary of the old Duke's passing. Shrewsbury had been at Eton with the old Duke of Roxton and was one of his closest confidants; of the same vintage, his own mortality was not far from his thoughts.

The Duke sipped at his port to clear a tightening in his throat and moved the discussion forward. He wanted to visit the nursery to ease his mind Gus was no worse for his ordeal and that his children had settled for the night after the dramas of the regatta. He was also acutely aware that he had left Deborah alone to deal with their guests, and with his mother on this of all days, and there was a recital in the Gallery before he could retire for the evening. As for the absurdly named *Committee for Colonial Correspondence of Interest*, which he reckoned was a thinly veiled title that gave legitimacy to these three noblemen and their select group of Governmental administrators to read and report on other people's correspondence without the author's permission, he was at a loss to know what they wanted of him.

"The headquarters of our fleet in the West Indies is harbored here at Antigua, isn't it?" he asked, long finger on an island in the middle of a chain known as the Leeward Islands.

"Yes, your Grace, that is so," Sir Kenneth agreed, impressed the Duke should know the precise location by the mere glance at a map, justifying Shrewsbury's estimation that here was a nobleman of the highest order who had brain as well as brawn.

The Duke grinned at Sir Kenneth's wide-eyed surprise. "As well as instilling in me a love of languages, my mother is a keen cartographer. There was always a map and grammar before bedtime. But what I don't know is the location of this island of St. Eustatius and its significance to this conversation, which, I might add, I am still mystified as to its direction."

"St. Eustatius is here, between our fleet at Antigua and St. Barthelemy—St. Bart's—which is part of Guadeloupe, here, a possession of our dear friends the French," explained Sir Kenneth, stabbing at various islands in close proximity to one another. "St. Eustatius is part of the Netherlands' possession and—"

"—claims to be neutral! Ha!" stuck in Carstairs. "Neutral my lobcock! The Dutch have always been white-feathered whiddlers. They'd sell their own grandmother for a guilder. Profit is God to those lily-livered curs."

"As his lordship so eloquently put it, St. Eustatius is neutral and as such is used by every privateer, pirate and thief that sails the Atlantic," Sir Kenneth stated calmly. "And because it is neutral our fleet is forced to watch and do nothing while the French under the guise of their Portuguese company *Roderigue Hortalez* load up rebel ships with French supplies vital to the American cause."

"And while this company keeps alive the rebels' bid for independence the French can continue to deny with impunity their involvement in the war on a diplomatic level? How ingenious," the Duke commented. He looked at all three noblemen, a puzzled frown between his brows. "This is all very interesting but I am confident our Foreign Department is doing everything possible to expose the underhandedness of our French friends on the one hand while at the same time making diplomatic overtures at Versailles to ensure his French Majesty does not openly declare his support for the rebels. We certainly do not want war with France and they most definitely cannot afford to go to war with us... So, what has this to do with my good self?"

"Well put, your Grace," Sir Kenneth agreed soberly, an anxious glance exchanged with Lord Shrewsbury. "As you are aware we three make up the *Committee for Colonial Correspondence of Interest* which is part of the larger American Colonial War Committee that deals with all matters related to the war in America. What we, Shrewsbury, Carstairs and myself, have been charged with is investigating the lines of communication between the rebels, the French and persons of interest here in London and Paris, and what is being relayed to and fro. It allows us to make informed judgments and to gather intelligence vital to the war effort."

"You read letters without the author's permission," the Duke stated, unimpressed.

"We do what we have to, my boy, if it means we further our cause and can save English lives," said Lord Shrewsbury.

"It has come to our attention that the rebels are very well informed regarding the deployment of our troops, and the position of our fleet along the eastern seaboard of the colonies," Sir Kenneth continued, allowing the map of the West Indies to curl up in on itself and sitting back on the wingchair as the Duke retreated to lean his buttocks against the rounded edge of his mahogany desk. "This is alarming in itself, but what disturbs us for the future of the English war effort is when, and I say *when* and not *if* because we believe it is only a matter of time before the French enter the war. Thus it is imperative that we put a stop to any treasonous lines of communication at their source. You understand what I am saying, your Grace."

"Yes. And I understand your very real concerns if, as you say, the French openly declare war. But I am still at a loss as to why this committee in particular has sought me out. I have always maintained that what is required is open dialogue with our neighbors across the Channel. However, that is merely my humble opinion and as the Foreign Department prefers skulking backstairs spies and closet double-agents to face to face diplomacy, I bow to their judgment, better or otherwise."

Lord Carstairs scooped up a bundle of letters he had put to the carpet and slapped them down on the low table. He was not as subdued as his colleagues and sighed his annoyance with what he saw as Sir Kenneth's pandering to, and Shrewsbury's esteem for, the ducal house of Roxton.

"Just come out and say it, Kenny!" Carstairs said with exasperation, tugging on the ribbon that kept the bundle of letters in a neat pile. He looked up at the Duke and said without a blink, "Roxton, you're a straight arrow, so I'll just say what my colleagues won't or can't say to your face: We have good reason to believe the Dowager Duchess your mother is working for the French and we want you to put a stop to it."

There was a moment of utter quiet in the library and then the Duke burst into incredulous laughter. No one else laughed.

"My—*mother*? My mother: a-a spy for-for the *French*? My God, are you *insane*?" Roxton grinned, but looking from one solemn face to another suitably sobered his mood. "Are you *all* insane?"

"Is this the Duchess's handwriting?" Carstairs demanded, holding up several sheets of correspondence.

"You have opened and *read* my mother's letters?"

The Duke was astounded.

"It was necessary," Shrewsbury apologized. "If there had been any other way..."

Roxton stared with disbelief at the pile of paper on the low table.

"Do all those sheets belong to my mother? How many letters are there? To whom are they addressed?"

"Is it her handwriting or not, your Grace?" Carstairs continued, still holding up the correspondence.

The Duke's astonishment turned to anger. He snatched up several sheets of paper, green eyes ablaze. "It is beyond my comprehension to think you took it upon yourself to read the personal correspondence of the Dowager Duchess, whose good character is beyond reproach and who could never do a harm to any living thing, least of all cause mischief that would not only call into question her unblemished reputation but bring in to disrepute her family's good name and disgrace to the Roxton dukedom." He slammed the sheets of paper face down on his desk without looking at them, and kept his open palm covering the letters. "I will not read her personal correspondence. Not now. Not *ever*."

Lord Shrewsbury eased himself off the wingchair and scooped up several sheets of paper from the pile on the low table. He took a cursory glance at the elegantly sloping script and then let his arm drop to his side and regarded the handsome nobleman who had averted his face, the thunderous fury evident in his reddened cheeks and the hard set to his strong jaw. "Roxton... Julian... *My boy*... No one other than the four of us here in your library knows what we know and we would prefer it remain that way. We have come to you because we do not mean to take this matter further. We just need your word you will put a stop to your mother corresponding with persons who are known traitors, in the colonies and in France. At the very least, ensure her letters go no further than the tray on the hall table and never leave the estate."

Roxton looked into the light blue eyes of his father's old friend. "She has very little left to her as it is and you expect me to take from her one of her remaining pleasures? No. I won't do it. She can write to whomever she pleases, traitor or no." He looked over the old man's padded velvet shoulder at Carstairs and Hibbert-Baker. There was no warmth in his deep voice. "You've read her letters. You tell me what treasonous utterances she's made and to whom."

"She regularly corresponds with Mr. Benjamin Franklin," offered Sir Kenneth.

"The inventor and publisher?" The Duke was dismissive.

"An American traitor presently in Paris seeking French support for the rebel cause," stated Lord Carstairs.

"She's known Ben Franklin for years! He stayed here at my parents' invitation when I was a boy. And she visited him at his lodgings in Craven Street once or twice, at his invitation. Her correspondence with Mr. Franklin would be full of academic discourse for its own sake." Roxton shrugged a shoulder. "I'll wager neither she nor Mr. Franklin mention the war in the colonies. He is too good mannered and she too respectful of the delicate position in which he now finds himself." When the three men did not dispute this he demanded, "Who else?"

"There's the French Foreign Minister, the Comte de Vergennes," said Sir Kenneth.

"*What?* Vergennes is my mother's second cousin. Her father's mother, her *grandmother* was a Gravier by birth. For God's sake, do I have to state the bloody obvious? My mother is French! She is so French that in all the years she has lived here in England, she has only managed to speak English with a broken accent. What of that? My father spoke exclusively in French with her, he preferred Paris to London and he had a French wife, but that did not make him a traitor to his King and country. He was every bit an Englishman and loyal to the House of Hanover! My mother knew this and respected his wishes." When this was met with silence, the Duke ran his fingers through his black curls and dropped his hand heavily to his side. "Christ! She isn't the only Frenchwoman living in London! Why her?"

"She is the only French *noble*woman with an English Duke for a son, who has mixed in the highest circles at the French Court, indeed is related to more than one French aristocratic family as you so rightly pointed out, who has access to politicians, is friends with politicians and Ministers on both sides of the Atlantic and across the Channel and can speak and write fluently in three or is it four languages? Perhaps she isn't openly committing treason. Perhaps Her Grace is the unwitting pawn in someone else's game. But as we know, and you say yourself, she is something of a bluestocking, so I would be insulting her intelligence if I was to believe she was exchanging information with her French cousins and her American friends unknowingly."

"You're drawing a very long bow, Carstairs, and I don't care for it!" Roxton growled. "Where is your evidence?"

"You have it on your desk, your Grace," Sir Kenneth said quietly. When the Duke snatched up the papers he continued just as calmly, "At first glance there appears nothing amiss with what is written on that page but take a closer look at the recipe for portable soup and you will see the quantities are too great if one was to try and put all the ingredients into a cauldron, however large."

The Duke glared at Sir Kenneth as if he had sprouted a second head. "What are you driveling on about, Kenny? Quantities of *what?*"

"It's not a recipe for portable soup at all. It is a rather ingenious method of relaying numbers. If you remove the names of the ingredients you are left with quantities, but they are not in fact quantities but numbers that perfectly align with our troop deployment numbers around the time the Hessians were defeated at Trenton. And only those in the inner war cabinet knew those figures."

The Duke was still baffled. "And where the hell would my mother get such figures?"

"That is what we need to discover, your Grace."

"To whom was this letter addressed?"

"To a Mlle Anais d'Iese."

"Who the deuce is she?"

"It's not actually a she, your Grace," Sir Kenneth apologized, "but a he. Anais d'Iese is an anagram for Silas Deane."

"And this personage is...?"

"He is an American merchant and secret agent, sent to Paris by the rebels to directly negotiate with the French Government," Sir Kenneth continued when his colleagues remained mute. "He is a particular associate of Mr. Franklin and is presently residing at an apartment at the address that was, until last year, your family's home on the Rue Saint-Honoré. The letters were sent to Mr. Deane under the alias Mlle Anais d'lese. You will see, if you look on the reverse of the second page your are holding, that the direction is indeed written in the Duchess's handwriting."

Roxton turned over the pages, took a cursory glance at the handwriting on the reverse of the second page, and shook his head in disbelief. "Dear God," he muttered more to himself than his audience, "what chance have we of saving the colonies if the Foreign Department expends its time and energies on this wasteful venture."

He shoved the page at Lord Shrewsbury, suddenly weary after a long day that had started at first light when he had made the harrowing visit to the mausoleum to pay his respects to his father on this the third anniversary of his passing, followed up by a day of Regatta activities that had turned into an even more traumatic experience with the dramatic rescue of his youngest son from drowning, and now this *Committee for Colonial Correspondence of Interest* had accused his mother of being a spy for the French or was it the American rebels? Or perhaps it was both? He wasn't quite sure. His patience was threadbare and he wondered if the few remaining hours left in the day could offer up anything further to see the threads unravel and he lose his temper altogether.

He looked from Shrewsbury, who had sidled over to the un-draped window wearing his spectacles to read a page with the aid of the fading afternoon light, to Carstairs and Sir Kenneth who were perched on the edge of the wingchairs as if about to make a dash for the door should their noble host unleash a tirade of abuse upon their powdered heads. The Duke did not have the energy or inclination. He leaned his palms on the edge of his writing desk and summonsed up what little reserves of energy he had left to say derisively,

"Well, gentlemen, I can tell you two things for certain: The hand that wrote out that recipe was not my mother's elegant fist, although the direction on the reverse of the second page was written by my mother, but what of that? When my father was alive he addressed and franked all my mother's letters, as is a common practice. Instead of reading other people's letters without permission all you had to do was ask her to whom these letters belonged and I'm sure she would have obliged you.

"Secondly, while my mother is perfectly at home between the pages of a Latin text by her favorite Roman historian and could point to the location of the island of Tahiti on a map of the Pacific Ocean, even wax lyrical about Mr. Franklin's experimentation with electricity, she is utterly bereft of those feminine abilities usually touted as necessary in a wife. She cannot embroider, paint, play a musical instrument and knows not the first thing about cookery. So regardless of the quantities, she would not know the ingredients in a venison pie or a berries and custard pudding if they were laid out on a table before her, or written up on a scrap of paper in whatever language you care to choose that she can read. You would better expend your energies on hunting down real spies and traitors than misdirecting your efforts on the private scribbles of a widow who has a morbid obsession with the dead. Shrewsbury, I thought you would have shown more sensitivity to my mother's condition."

The old man's smile was sad. "It was because of her obsession I presumed..."

He could not finish the sentence and looked away, out the window. He did not need to, the Duke knew exactly what he meant and was about to make comment when he was accosted.

"Julian! Attend me! Is it true? Is it true you have sold the Hôtel?"

Thirteen

The Duke stepped forward, a glance down at his mother and then over her head at his wife. Antonia's words had not registered but he saw her expression and it was enough to start his heart racing.

"Maman? Deborah? What is it? Not-not Gus?"

When the Duchess shook her head, but bit her lower lip, a warning glance at Antonia before opening wide her brown eyes, the Duke relaxed knowing his son was all right, but only for a moment because his wife's silent gesture alerted him to the fact that something or someone had greatly upset his mother.

"I beg your pardon, Maman?"

"Is it true? Have you sold the Hôtel?"

"The Hôtel? Surely we can talk about this later? I am in a meeting and—"

"So you have sold it."

"Now is not the time to discuss this. If you will just—"

"No! No, I will not just *just* anything, Julian! You will tell me now if our home on the Rue Saint-Honoré it is sold."

Antonia clasped her hands tightly together and continued to look up at her son, waiting his response, forcing herself to remain in control because she still did not believe it was true and she did not want to believe that she would never again be able to set foot in the Hôtel Roxton. When he hesitated she launched into speech, as if by telling him her feelings it could somehow alter the unalterable.

"Monseigneur your father he was born in that house. As was

166

his sister, your aunt and her son your cousin Evelyn, he too was born there. And your grandfather, Monseigneur's father he lived there with your French *grandmere* because he could not bring her to England because she was a Papist. And the Hôtel it was her sanctuary because she had married a Protestant and her family the Salvans and His French Majesty banished her from court."

"I know, Maman," the Duke replied gently. "I know our family's history in that house very well indeed."

"Frederick, your son and heir he too was born in that house. Does that not mean anything to you?"

"It means a great deal. Maman, what is the point of this?"

"It was the home you grew up in. Where you and Evelyn would play hide and seek and we would pretend we did not see you."

"Yes."

"And your little brother... Have you forgotten Henri-Antoine spent many happy years in that house? He and Jack... He and Jack also played hide and seek... And then there were the many, many parties we had there for you and Evelyn and for Henri-Antoine and your friends. Lucian and Estée lived at the Hôtel with us. We were one big family... And there is the bowling green between the chestnut trees..."

"I remember it all, Maman. How could I forget?"

Antonia searched her son's handsome face, hands so tightly gripped now that she no longer had sensation in her fingertips.

"The-the house in Paris it is very important, *very* important to Monseigneur."

"Yes. Yes it was important to *mon père*."

"It was my first home..."

"Yes. I know that, too."

"And so it is very important to me also."

Her voice was little more than a whisper and her eyes had begun to fill with tears. The Duke looked away with a swallow, forcing himself to recall his father's sage advice in those last days of his life; that he had made the right decision in selling off the family home in Paris.

Sell it, Julian. Sell the Hôtel, for her sake and yours. Your mother will never live there again, not without me. There are too many memories... There is a dark cloud hanging over France these days. The thunderstorm, when it breaks, will mean the end of the old order, of the France of my generation. I predict blood in the Parisian streets and in your lifetime... You must protect your sons. No more should there be a M'sieur le Duc d'Roxton. Put your own stamp on the dukedom, as it should be... Your mother you cannot protect...

He had tried to convince his father that he could indeed look after his mother. But his father had disagreed and been almost apologetic in his response: *Julian, you are not the man to make her happy, as she deserves to be happy.*

Those words, the last his father had spoken to him, still smarted and looking down at his mother, at the sorrow in her eyes, he wondered if his father was right. No matter what he did or said, no matter how hard he tried to be understanding, she remained inconsolable and at times such as these, infuriatingly unfathomable.

"You have sold our home in Paris, yes?" Antonia stated.

He did not try to explain himself or his actions. What was the point? It would make little difference to her reaction.

"Yes."

So Charlotte had told the truth. Her home in Paris, the house that held so many wonderful memories for her, had been taken from her and was no more. She wanted to sink to the floor, to curl up in a tight ball and sob. Instead, she remained resolutely upright and asked numbly,

"And our belongings? What has become of them? Of our books? Of Monseigneur's collections of fans and snuffboxes and trinkets in his cabinets? Our backgammon board, where is that? The-the pictures of family members upon the walls, where are they now?"

"An inventory has been taken. The books and pictures and curios have been crated and will be brought here. If there are any pieces of furniture you particularly want, the new owners, I am assured, are only too willing to oblige."

"Our house, who now owns it?"

"Does it matter?"

"Yes. Yes, it matters! Of course it matters! Charlotte, she says you sold it to a Farmer-General. Is that so? Julian? Attend me! Is it?"

"M'sieur Lavoisier is a member of the Farmers-General. Yes. My agent in Paris sold the house to him."

"You have sold your noble French heritage and all that it means to a French merchant?" she asked with deliberate slowness. Numbness and sorrow gave way to incredulous anger. "And of course to show how much he cares for your noble French ancestors M'sieur Farmer-General he has turned three hundred and fifty years of nobility into apartments for rent!" She snapped her fingers. "So that is what you care for your birthright, for your mother's and father's French blood? You besmirch us by allowing tax collectors who care for nothing but profit to make a mockery of your lineage!"

"That is a ridiculous accusation to make. I have done nothing of the sort."

"Have you told your brother? Have you told Henri-Antoine?" Antonia demanded, willing the tears not to flow. "Have you told Henri-Antoine about this wicked thing you have done? That you have sold his childhood home without consultation or a thought for him? That the house his father and his father's ancestors once occupied is now overrun with care-for-nothing tenants beholden to a greedy merchant and who have as much honor and grace about their persons as your father he had in his little pinkie? Well, have you, M'sieur le Duc?"

Roxton baulked at her tone and the use of his title and his voice lost its gentleness. "I answer to no one, Madam. The decision was mine to make and I have made it. It is done. *Fin.*"

Antonia made a noise that was half sob, half laugh. "That is true, *mon-fils*. You answer to no one and thus who is there to tell you it was wicked and criminal of you to sell my memories and your brother's memories in such a heartless fashion?" She glanced over her shoulder at her daughter-in-law, who stood as stone behind her, and behind the Duchess her ladies-in-waiting hovered, and then looked up at her son, a jerk of her fair head in direction of the Duchess. "I would hazard a guess that not even your English wife she offered her whole hearted support for this horrid decision of yours. That—"

"Leave Deborah out of this!"

"—you stubbornly went ahead with the sale despite her objections."

"Enough!"

Roxton took a step forward.

Antonia stood her ground; chin up. "I am not one of your lackeys, Julian, that one harsh word it will silence me!"

Roxton lifted a hand in a gesture of frustrated hopelessness and let it fall heavily on a sigh of exasperation.

"I am not going to argue with you. What is done is done and this is not the time or the place for you to voice your melodramatic outrage."

"Melodramatic? Time and place?" she wondered, voice faltering, tears now on her flushed cheeks. "Does your mother she need to make an appointment with your secretary to do so? *Mon Dieu.* It is *you* who have reduced me to this: barging in on your meetings with Government functionaries to discover for myself what everyone else already knows; what my own son could not bring himself to tell me to my face!"

"I will not discuss this matter further before others. This conversation is at an end for today," he said very quietly, mustering all his self-control and not daring to glance down at her again; hearing the bewildered desolation in her voice was almost too much. And so he stepped past her, exchanged a look of understanding with his wife, whose steady gaze had not left his face for a moment, and then looked across at the two gentlemen still hovering ill at ease by the wingchairs, thankful their French tongue was rudimentary at best. A nod to each and they responded in kind and quietly took their leave. To the two ladies-in-waiting he said, "Her Grace is tired and will be returning to Crecy Hall at once."

"No! Her Grace will *not* be returning to Crecy Hall at once!" Antonia mimicked him in English, swirling about, fingers convulsing in the folds of her silk gown, and quickly reverting to her native French, "Julian! We will discuss this here and now, as is *my* right as your mother! You dare to turn my memories into a great pile of ashes and then dismiss me as if I should see the loss of our Parisian home and all that it means to me as you see it: a financial transaction and nothing more? I do not and never will! How did you expect me to react to such news?"

"With the decorum befitting your rank!" the Duke blurted out and bit down on his tongue to stop himself saying anything further.

Antonia stood very still. No one had ever questioned her ability to carry herself as a duchess, least of all a member of her family. That her eldest son saw fit to criticize her made her suddenly very sad. She wasn't quite sure what was meant by the remark but she understood the underlying premise.

"Whatever my rank, whatever you and others believe I should be, I have always been just myself..."

She glanced around the room, at the downcast eyes of her daughter-in-law and her ladies-in-waiting, and at the elderly nobleman who had quietly left the window embrasure to come stand by a wingchair close to the Duke. Her arched eyebrows contracted in recognition.

"Edward?" she said in bemusement.

Lord Shrewsbury bowed to her with great courteousness. "Mme la duchesse."

Antonia was momentarily diverted, wondering what England's premier spymaster was doing ensconced in her son's library. She knew all about Shrewsbury's covert activities for the English government because Monseigneur had kept nothing from her, not even the fact he was one of the first to be inducted into King Louis of France's personal network of spies, *the Secret du Roi*, undoubtedly a treasonous offence for an English Duke, but Monseigneur had answered to no one, not to his sovereign King George or to his mother's monarch Louis XV. A contemporary of the father and not the son, Antonia wondered at Shrewsbury's business, but then she saw the pile of opened correspondence on the low table and, as always, she was astute and direct.

"You think there is a spy at Treat, Lord Shrewsbury? *Comment ainsi?*"

"As to that, Mme la duchesse, I am not at liberty to say."

"But you are at liberty to confiscate and read my cousin's personal correspondence? *Vous me stupefiez?* Charles Fitzstuart he is a very earnest and idealistic young man."

"Earnest and idealistic young men make the best traitors, Mme la duchesse," Lord Shrewsbury replied with extreme politeness.

"Traitor? Charles? For whom is he a spy?" She looked at her son and back at Shrewsbury. Both men were tight-lipped. "The French? You think Charles he is a spy for Louis? *Mon Dieu. Toupet inconcevable.*" She threw up a hand, the half-dozen gold bangles jingling about her wrist. "Me I do not believe it! I cannot conceive you are party to this nonsense, Julian?"

"It does not matter what you believe, Madam. Nor will I discuss this with you."

"I see. We are not talking as mother and son about our cousin. Me I am but a dependent widow on the Scion of the House of Roxton. Should I curtsey to rank, or are we done with that formality given we are in the middle not the beginning of the argument, M'sieur le Duc?"

"Don't be absurd, Maman!"

"Oh, so I am again your mother? What? When it suits? Make up your mind, Julian, as you have surely made up your mind to divorce yourself from your French heritage," she retorted, a significant glance at Shrewsbury. "Perhaps you think me a spy for King Louis? After all, I am French. Have you read my correspondence too?"

"That is a ridiculous notion! And so I told Shrewsbury."

Antonia baulked. She had been in jest, but her son's retort and ready blush startled her. Her laugh was incredulous. "If it was not so *incroyable* me I would be offended! It is no wonder then why you sold the Hôtel. But do not assume Henri-Antoine he will follow your lead! Though where we are to stay in Paris without a roof over our heads, I know not. As a widow I suppose I should be grateful for any roof, and can always go cap in hand to a French relative."

Roxton sighed his exasperation. "You haven't been to Paris in six years; nor has Henri."

"And now it seems we can never go because there is no house to go to and thus our family we can no longer hold up our heads in French Society."

"Good God, do you not understand? I have no wish to hold up my head in *French* society!" Roxton threw at her, stating in English, "I am an Englishman with an English wife and an English dukedom that descends five centuries through the English line! I would sell a hundred such houses if it would increase the distance between me and a society that is fast falling into the abyss! The French nobility still uphold feudalism where peasants starve on their farms, not because the land is barren but because of indifferent absentee masters who spend their days fornicating behind firescreens in gilded palace rooms while awaiting the opportunity to grovel with abject bows and scrapes to a buffoon of a king! A king who spends more time ruminating about locks and keys than he does good government and who is married to a silly twit of a woman who is running up the French national debt to astronomical levels while people literally starve outside her window! There is no freedom of speech. There is no freedom of the press. It is an *absolute* monarchy. The French idea of diplomacy is to go sneaking behind our backs like naughty school boys offering support to the American rebels in their war against their English cousins, and the absurdity is that the American rebels are fighting for *liberty* while the French have none! Is it any wonder I wish to disassociate myself from our French connections?"

Again Antonia stood very still because again her son had shocked her with his vitriolic attack. She was beginning to wonder if she knew him at all.

"Then it must indeed be a great trial having a French maman," she said quietly. "It all becomes clear to me. I do not wonder now why your children they are not to speak French as naturally as they do the English tongue. Why you have decided not to allow them to visit me. Why I am kept ignorant of your decisions. Me I am an embarrassment to you and your fam—"

"That's not what I meant at all, and you know it!"

"Then say what you mean!"

"If you would only allow yourself to see past your own self—"

"Julian, *no*."

The outburst came from the Duchess as she tugged on the Duke's upturned silk cuff in warning, but he was too caught up in the moment to stop himself saying the rest.

"—*self-centered misery* you would see that it's not about you at all!"

Antonia echoed his words in a whisper.

"Self-centered misery?"

"Well, isn't it?" Roxton stated. "Why should bricks and mortar matter when it is not *objects* but *people* that are important in this life? Dear Christ, Maman, you throw Henri-Antoine in my face when you have not given my little brother two beans-worth of attention since our father died! And Augustus—Gus—*my son* almost drowned this afternoon and here you are agonizing over what happened to a well-worn backgammon board and a few trifles and trinkets, bemoaning the sale of a house whose threshold you've not crossed in six years? What is a house, what is *anything*, when compared to the life of a child?"

Antonia swayed on her two-inch heels. He could have struck her hard about the face such was the deep blush of mortification to her cheeks. He was right of course. Her son was right. What was the sale of a house when weighed against the lives of her children and grandchildren? It was true. In her abstraction she had neglected her youngest son, Henri-Antoine. What sort of mother was she? She should have been thinking of his welfare. She should have been thinking of little Augustus, of his near brush with death and how this had affected his parents, his brothers and sister. Poor Deborah, she looked so tired and distraught and Julian, he had enough worries and here she was making a nuisance of herself over a trifle of a thing. She was being incredibly self-centered. She saw that now. She was thinking only of herself. She had forgotten what truly mattered. What must they think of her? What must everyone think of her selfishness? She was surely an embarrassment to her family. Had she been so selfish, so self-absorbed when Monseigneur had been alive? Surely not... But perhaps, when he finally lay dying...

"You would have been better off with two aging parents, *mon fils*," she said with a sad, shuddering breath, shaking hands to her wet cheeks to wipe away tears. "In that way you would not now have to deal with the one who is left and who walks about as one dead. If I had died with your father..."

"Yes! Perhaps that would've been for the best! At least then he would've had a dignified end!" Roxton snapped before he could stop himself, because only she had the power to make him feel completely helpless, hating to see her so distressed and so unlike herself and loathing himself for having had the thought she had just voiced out loud, and more than once, on occasions such as this when he did not know what to say or do to make her happy. And once he had opened the floodgates on such painful thoughts, there was no stopping. It was as if he needed to say the words out loud to make himself feel better, to make the thoughts finally go away. He not only appalled Antonia but everyone in the room.

"He lingered in this life for *three* years longer than was necessary all because of *you*. He knew what his death would do to you and so he hung on, in pain and distress, *for you*. Not once did he complain or make it known how agonizingly difficult it was for him just to breathe; how much the cancer had taken hold. And you had the selfishness to let him linger because you could not bear to be parted from him! Well, Madam, you can be proud that you-you *added* to his-his *suffering*. He should have been allowed to die with dignity. He didn't want you or me or others to see him in such a wasted state. He was so proud, a prince amongst his peers, who'd never had an illness in his life. To see him thus reduced, a shadow of a man, wasted and unable to get about his own bedchamber without the aid of a cane and, in the last weeks of his life, unable to leave his bed! What a sad indictment—*on you*.

"He should have been permitted to leave this world as he had strutted about its stage, with arrogant self-assurance, and with majesty. You turned his last years into a-a—circus! He thought only of you, *always* of you. He blamed himself for marrying a much younger woman; that it was somehow *his* fault you remained younger than your years; that your beauty did no fade with time. He loved you to-to *distraction* and because of that he allowed himself an ignoble end. And how do you repay his memory? How do you behave? With histrionics and dramatic pronounce-ments of self-pity! He said I could not look after you, and he was bloody-well right! I cannot look after you because I do not know you as you are now!"

There followed a deafening silence in the library. No one moved or knew what to say. Unbeknownst to him, the Duke had been shouting at his mother and with such pent-up emotional rage that everyone was stunned, not least Antonia who went into shock. But her first instinct was to put her arms about her son and cradle him, smooth back his black curls and tell him in soothing accents that nothing was as bad as he imagined because his green eyes were full of tears and his bottom lip quivered and whenever he was upset he forgot his English for the French tongue, his first spoken language; he so reminded her of the little boy he had once been. Yet she just stood there, unable to move and unable to speak.

Finally, Roxton dashed his eyes dry and turned away, distracted by the Duchess who had picked up her petticoats to run as if her life depended upon it towards the black metal spiral staircase that gave access to the narrow walkways that wrapped around the floor to ceiling bookcases, and from where there had burst into the silence a child's piercing fearful wailing. Instantly everyone looked that way and watched the Duke rush to join his wife who was doing her best to pacify their eldest son who was sobbing and struggling to be free of his mother's comforting embrace.

Frederick had snuck into the library via the secret door, as his father and uncle before him had done many times as boys, to sit on the top step of the spiral staircase in his nightshirt and silk banyan with matching nightcap and slippers, hunched over his knees, shivering with excitement to be eavesdropping undetected on the conversations of adults when he should have been abed. He had come to wish his beloved Mema a goodnight because he had not seen her since departing in the *Oudrey* carriage with his mother and siblings. He was bursting to tell her all about the boat race and how he and Mr. Strang had been winning right up until the moment Gus stood up in Papa's boat to wave to some village playfellows, who were shouting out encouragement as they ran along the lake shore, and how Gus just toppled over out of the boat and with a big splash disappeared under the water. And in the next moment Mr. Strang had kicked off his shoes and was out of his shirt and into the water. He had so much wanted to tell Mema and tomorrow would be too late; he was sure he would not remember everything in the morning.

But all was not right in the library, and although he did not understand what was going on between the adults he sensed the tension and that his father was unhappy with Mema. And then his father had started yelling at his beloved Mema. He had never, ever seen Papa in such a temper. He was even angrier than the time Gus and Louis had crept away to a corner of the stables to inspect the gamekeeper's loaded rifle leaning against a bale of hay while their father and the men had their backs turned examining a stallion's injured fetlock, only to be caught out by Papa two seconds later when Gus picked up the rifle and playfully pointed the barrel at his twin.

Mema was crying and his mother was so sad and had tears in her eyes too.

It was too much for Frederick to endure and he finally screamed out for Papa to stop, to stop shouting at Mema! And then his mother scooped him up into her embrace with soothing words of reassurance before he could run to Mema and throw his arms around her to protect her from his father's fury.

Antonia saw and heard none this. Not even when the little boy screamed in fear and distress and called out for her to come back. All she heard were her son's heated accusations reverberating in her head, over and over, and all her self-pity turned to self-loathing. Of course it was her fault. Of course he had a right to be angry with her. How could she have been so uncaring and unseeing? How could she have allowed it to happen? How had she not *seen*? But she knew the answer: She *was* self-centered. She *was* to blame. Not for Monseigneur's death, lung cancer had taken his life, but for the way in which he had departed this life for the next. Yes, that was her fault entirely. She had forced him to live, in pain and indignity, because she could not bear to live without him. She had been so selfish; too selfish to let him die with majesty and in her self-absorption she had forgotten all else, particularly the effect Monseigneur's lingering end would have on his family and friends, most importantly on their sons Julian and Henri-Antoine. She would not have been at all surprised if Monseigneur's drawn-out illness had hastened the end of his sister and her husband who had both died within twelve months of M'sieur le Duc's death.

She walked out of the library, unseeing, unconsciously running her hands up and down her arms as if suddenly very cold. Feeling the bangles under her palms, she stripped off the dozen gold bracelets that dangled about her wrists, letting them drop to bounce one by one to the carpet and clatter and roll along the parquetry in all directions, to disappear under a chair or into a darkened corner. Willis and Spencer chased after them as Antonia crossed the anteroom and passed into the Gallery. Here, she unclipped the diamond and emerald earrings from her lobes and unconsciously let them drop. Up went her hands again, this time to the three diamond clasps arranged in her upswept hair. Unsnapped, they too were consigned to the thick fog that enveloped her. The dozen or so pearl-headed hairpins that held her hair in place were extracted and one by one they went the way of the rest of her jewelry, the great weight of her blonde curls free to bounce to her bare shoulders and cascade down her back in disarray.

She had traversed half the length of the Gallery, not that she knew where she was, when the whist players seated about four tables paused in mid-hand discard and turned their powdered heads in astonished silence to watch her pass. The gentlemen in conversation about the second fireplace half-rose out of comfortable chairs to acknowledge her and stared with mouths agape as she passed them in a trance-like state. At an open French window not far from where a small knot of persons stood under a portrait of her grandmother the legendary titian-haired beauty Augusta, Countess of Strathsay Antonia kicked off her damask shoes and in stockinged feet stepped out into the cold night air, two blank-faced liveried footmen bowing to her as if nothing was amiss with the abstracted and disheveled Dowager Duchess of Roxton.

The cold marble of the terrace under her toes did not register as she hesitated in indecision staring into the twilight out across the rolling lawns to the arched bridge over the now still and quiet lake, and beyond to the oak and beech-lined gravel drive that wound its way to her dower house. A hand to her throat, and awareness registered touching the diamond and emerald choker, Monseigneur's first gift to her. She closed her tear-filled eyes briefly, recalling the moment he had gently placed the heavy choker about her throat on her eighteenth birthday: *To match your eyes, mignonne.* Without him, it was just another object like the rest of her jewelry: a trinket, *worthless.* Decided, she twisted open the clasp with trembling fingers, let the heavy choker slip from around her throat and dropped it into the honeysuckle thicket.

Antonia stepped off the terrace onto the lawn and walked towards the lake.

Fourteen

Jonathon Strang returned to Treat after a sennight spent in London and found an invitation awaiting him. It was from the Countess of Strathsay cordially inviting him to her Buckinghamshire estate for the fortnight to help celebrate her eldest son's twenty-eighth birthday. There was also a letter from Sarah-Jane full of breathless excitement (evident from the ink splotches on the page) telling him what he already knew, given he had broken the seal on the Countess's invitation, and that she had gone on ahead with Lord and Lady Cavendish. She had taken the liberty of having the portmanteaux he had left behind taken up with her, so he was to join her *with all speed* and because she was certain some news of *great importance* would be announced during the week and he just *had* to be there or she would *never* forgive her *dearest* Papa.

Jonathon smiled to himself: Yes, she would forgive him. Sarah-Jane always forgave him. She was, after all, her mother's daughter, with Emily's sweet nature.

There was also a letter from Tommy Cavendish but he did not break the seal because it was a rather fat packet and thus would take awhile to read and digest. So he slipped it into his frockcoat pocket to open at a later date and gave his attention back to the butler who waited in the cavernous entrance vestibule with a liveried footman carrying a silver tray which had upon it the letters Jonathon had now dealt with. One remained, it was a short missive from the Duke, informing him his lawyers in the city would contact

Jonathon regarding the lease of the Hanover Square house and that he would call on him when next in London. That was it. No explanation as to why he was being turned away at the door.

Under the vestibule's domed ceiling painted with clouds atop which sat various Gods and Goddesses surrounded by fat little cherubs, the nose-in-the-air butler took great delight in telling Jonathon the Duke had been called away to Bath unexpectedly, leaving instructions that his young family, who were still in residence in this monolith of a house, were not to be disturbed under any circumstances, Mr. Strang would be supplied with a fresh horse and liquid refreshment, if so desired, to send him on his way.

The butler was certain Mr. Strang would understand.

Jonathon did not understand and he was not about to turn heel and jump on a fresh horse without taking his leave of the Dowager Duchess of Roxton, not when he had spent every night away from her thinking of nothing and no one else but her. He downed the tumbler of ale supplied on another silver tray by a second blank-faced footman, picked up his small brown leather travelling portmanteau and was escorted by a third footman via a series of secondary rooms and narrow passages until he was outside in a wide cobbled courtyard where to the right was the extensive stables and the fresh horse saddled as promised.

Jonathon did not turn right as was expected, and with a wave to the stable hands that awaited him, he went left. He slung the travelling bag over his shoulder and strode off across the lawn to the graveled path that led to a picturesque walk through the Ornamental Gardens being well tended and prepared for summer flowering by a team of gardeners. He nodded to any man who looked up but did not notice the tilled flowerbeds or the sparkling fountains, well-clipped hedgerows or the newly raked walks. At the garden's south stonewall he pushed through the small wooden door cut into the stone work and strode out into the expanse of meadow where sheep, some with newborn lambs, grazed on the other side of a ha-ha.

Here there was a path leading to a stand of willows beside which was an elaborate boathouse that any tenant farmer would be proud to call home, and a long jetty where several skiffs bobbed on the gently rippling surface of the lake. The breeze had picked up, and a glance straight up at the watery blue sky and out across to the eastern horizon where the skies were darker and ominous clouds had gathered, told Jonathon a storm was on its way. If he did not row steadily and fast, there was a good chance the heavens would open up and he would be drenched before he made it to the pretty pavilion on the far side of the lake.

He was determined to spend one last night at Treat before he took himself into Buckinghamshire for more agonizingly dull social engagements on behalf of his daughter's quest to bag a baronet at the very least. And he knew of no better place to spend the night than at the pavilion and with no better person than the Dowager Duchess of Roxton.

He was under the pavilion's domed roof before the first large drops of rain splattered the marble steps. He dropped his portmanteau and shrugged his frockcoat over his waistcoat and white shirt, and was up at the Dower House searching for a way in, travelling cloak over a shoulder, when the Heavens opened to deliver a hard, heavy rain.

The house was in darkness. No candlelight or firelight flickered through a crack in any of the downstairs windows, which were all heavily draped. All doors and windows were bolted, so, too, the outbuildings. It was as if the house had been locked up and its occupants gone away. Jonathon wondered if the Duchess was indeed in residence and he had made a wasted journey, until he finally found signs of life at the front of the house.

He went round to the main entrance, with its circular gravel drive and decorative portico, and ran back to the garden bed, with its central fountain, to better view the entire Elizabethan frontage with its multitude of mullioned windows. A roll of thunder and a flash of lightning and the whole house illuminated, affording Jonathon a spectacular view of the eerily beautiful building with its stacks of decoratively turned brick chimneys. Here he saw smoke curling from two of the chimneys, one in the eastern wing and another, much deeper in the roof line, possibly coming from the kitchen at the very south end of the house where attached was a walled herb and vegetable garden that also contained a spherical icehouse built in Stuart times.

He ran around to the east wing first, and there, in an inner courtyard way up high was the turned red brick chimney with its curls of smoke, and along the row of lower windows being hit hard with rain, light winked from between drapes unevenly pulled across the view.

He stood in the shallow portico of a heavy door that gave servant access to and from the house, the travelling cloak now held up over his head to shelter from the pelting rain, wondering how best to get the attention of the occupants of the only room that had life. And if in answer to his mental ruminations, the door at his back creaked open. From the darkness within a bleak face appeared in the glow of a taper. Wary eyes went wide with recognition. A nod from Jonathon in response and the door opened wider.

It was Michelle, the Dowager Duchess's personal maid.

"M'sieur! You are the one at the pavilion, yes?" she asked loudly in halting English to be heard over the rain, a wary look over her shoulder. "You are a friend to Mme la duchesse, yes?"

"Yes. And I speak French very well."

The woman nodded, opened wide the door to admit him, but was not inclined to say anything further in any language. She merely motioned for Jonathon to follow her down the dark servant passage, and then along another, and finally they traversed a third corridor, having avoided altogether the public and private rooms not frequented by servants unless called upon. Michelle had led him to the kitchen, which was full of light and activity, the enormous deep fireplace filled with an assortment of cooking pots on the boil, trussed fowls being turned on a spit and enough radiant heat to warm the entire room and take the chill from Jonathon's hands.

The chef and two cooks were busy preparing a feast, which was odd given the house was shrouded in darkness, and paused in their preparations when Jonathon entered the room behind Michelle. A nod from Jonathon and the chef, with one well-chosen Gallic expletive to his cooks, who hovered in inactivity staring at the tall, well-built stranger, said nothing further and continued on with his tasks, leaving Michelle to fetch Jonathon a tumbler of warm ale. She took his travelling cloak and placed it over a chair back to dry before the fire and fussed unnecessarily with it, as if by doing the mundane she could steal herself to remain calm, or so it seemed to Jonathon who watched her closely. A puzzled glance at the chef, who was fiddling with the fit of a pie crust, in much in the same manner that Michelle was fussing with his coat, and Jonathon decided that something was not quite right within this household. Before he could beg the question, Michelle turned to him, wringing her hands.

"M'sieur! That monster he is in there waiting his dinner and I say to Pierre to poison him with the pie or the wine! I do not care which but it must be done and if me I am hanged so be it to see him dead!"

The chef grunted. "Michelle! Do not be a little idiot. The fat physician he needs to be kept alive. And you forget, there are the two brutes he has with him, always."

"Poison them all! Me I do not care. Nor should you."

The chef grunted again but said to Jonathon, holding up a finger in a floured fist, "I will gladly poison the fat physician and his attendants, M'sieur, but the time it is not right. First Michelle she must discover the whereabouts of Mme la duchesse; what that fiend he has done with her."

"Mme la duchesse?" Jonathon gave a start. He felt his heart beat quicken. "A physician you say? Is—is she unwell? I do not understand."

The chef started to repeat what he had said in heavily accented English, but then Michelle came to life, flapping her hands at the chef to be quiet.

"This gentleman he understands what you said well enough, Pierre! He is not asking you to say it again. M'sieur," she said to Jonathon, and took the empty tumbler from him and set it aside on the table, "Mme la duchesse she was indeed unwell. It was the night of the regatta... They found her—They found her—" She broke off and took a great shuddering breath. "I do not think I can tell you..."

"Then tell me about this physician," Jonathon said in a measured tone, which calmed the maid.

"He came with Mme la duchesse home from the regatta, he and his two brutes he calls attendants, and now he acts as if this house it is his!"

"That is because he has M'sieur le Duc's authority to do so, Michelle," Pierre the chef stated, a pointed stare at Jonathon. "That is why me I feed him."

"He is still here attending on Her Grace?" Jonathon was surprised. When the maid nodded vigorously, lips pressed together, he added, "Is your mistress that unwell?"

Michelle threw him a cautious glance. "Mme la duchesse she is never ill in body..."

"M'sieur," said Pierre, filling the pie crust with a mixture of vegetables, garlic and cream before adding a generous pinch of nutmeg, "with all due respect to M'sieur le Duc d'Roxton, the fat man sitting in the dining room awaiting his supper, if he is a physician then me I am Louis King of France!"

"He is a monster!" Michelle burst out, a shaking hand to her mouth.

"The physician as he calls himself," said Pierre, a smile spreading across his swarthy florid face as he splashed a dark liquid from a green bottle over the pie filling; Daffy's elixir and the nutmeg and the physician's bowels would surely open of their own accord; he had added a goodly quantity to the potato and cheese soup as well, "he is a *canard.*"

"Pierre! How can you laugh so when—"

"A *quack*? What's this fellow's name?" Jonathon demanded.

"Sir Titus Foley, M'sieur."

"What was Roxton's thinking?" Jonathon muttered to himself and then demanded, "Where is she? Where is Mme la duchesse?"

"We do not know—"

"Do not know?"

"—because he—the physician—he will not allow me or anyone to see her. Imagine Mme la duchesse being denied her personal maid!"

"Michelle, that is the least of Mme la duchesse worries," Pierre murmured, trimming the excess pastry from the pie's lid and crimping the edge between flat thumb and forefinger.

"Surely the gargoyles—Willis and Spencer—Surely they are with her?"

The maid shook her head vigorously.

"Where are they?"

"Mme la duchesse's ladies-in-waiting they have gone away with the Comtesse Strathsay."

"So if they are not with her, and you are not allowed near her, who is attending on Mme la duchesse?"

"The physician he sent all the servants away to the Gatehouse," Michelle explained. "Only Pierre, Guy and Philip are permitted to stay here in the house because—"

"—we fill his belly," Pierre stuck in.

"So she has been left entirely alone with Sir Titus and his attendants?" When the maid nodded bleakly, Jonathon swore and so viciously that even the chef jumped. "When was the last time you saw your mistress?"

When Michelle exchanged a worried glance with Pierre, who with his two cooks had paused in their kitchen duties, floured hands suspended just above a second half-constructed pie, Jonathon's heart missed a beat and he grew impatient.

"Well? Have you seen her this past sennight or not?"

"We have heard her, M'sieur... We heard her the once, shouting abuse at the physician," offered Pierre. He could not help a smile of admiration. "Her swearing it was most excellent and straight from the Parisian gutter, but wasted on the fat *canard*. His French it is pointless."

Before Jonathon could ask, Michelle said quietly, "I have seen her, M'sieur. It was this morning. I followed an attendant—" The maid made a noise, half-sob, half deep breath and then continued under Jonathon's unblinking stare, "I followed the attendant to the cellars."

"Cellars?"

"Yes, M'sieur, that is where there is a second entrance to the icehouse, the one used by servants, and that is where the physician he has his attendants carry Mme la duchesse for her-her treatment."

Jonathon was incredulous and it made his normally pleasing drawl harsh.

"To the *icehouse*? She is *carried* to an *icehouse* for—for *treatment*? Dear God, what sort of treatment are you talking about?"

Michelle jumped. It was not Jonathon's angry astonishment but a great clap of thunder right above their heads that made her shoulders lift of their own accord.

"Michelle. Show him. Take him," the chef ordered with a jerk of his bald head at a doorway that was dark beyond. "M'sieur physician and his brutes will be in the dining room. Me I will serve the soup straight away and that will keep them occupied. *N'est-ce pas?*"

Jonathon was aghast. "He leaves her down there alone?"

The chef shook his head, a worried glance exchanged with the maid. "No, M'sieur. That is the even bigger worry. We do not know where he has her now. That is for you to discover, and you must hurry. One look in that room and you will see why I say time, it is of the very essence."

The icehouse was at the end of a long corridor in the subterranean depths of the Elizabethan cellars, in the coldest, darkest and dampest corner of the dower house: Ideal for the storing and preservation of ice. It was also the room farthest from habitation, with walls two feet thick and thus, with the heavy oak door closed, soundproofed.

Jonathon followed Michelle through the maze of underground passages, she holding a taper aloft to cast light on the dank walls and cobbled flooring, but when they arrived at the door to the icehouse the maid stepped away to allow Jonathon to enter first.

The door was unbolted.

Inside, the room was pitch black, the air arctic and dank, not unexpected given the room's purpose. A cast of candlelight and Jonathon found the wall sconces near the door. More candles lit and the width and depth of the room became apparent. Given the size of the icehouse there were surprisingly few blocks of ice and what there was had been stacked along the one wall, linen sheeting between the blocks to allow ease of separation. A block could be shifted to the great blue stone anvil off center to the room where with hammer and chisel applied to precise points slivers of ice could be chiseled off and put into buckets and taken up to the kitchens for use. If an entire block was required above stairs then it was wrapped in the linen and carted up by two men wearing padded cotton gloves for protection against burns.

High up along one wall was a walkway—a viewing platform—accessed via a spiral staircase from below. A door cut into the brickwork suggested to Jonathon that it opened out into the garden and that this door was used by the noble residents and their guests, to come inside out of the summer heat and for the novelty of having fresh ice for their lemon water and Ratafia.

Summer heat! Jonathon shook his head recalling the blistering sunshine in Hyderabad. The English had no idea what heat was! Gaze returned to floor level and his smile died.

The floor was bricked, like the walls, and sloped toward a central grate where melted ice drained as icy water into an open well. The well's grated cover had been removed to allow access to the water via rope and pulley and bucket. Several empty buckets were stacked beside the well.

What was incongruous to the icehouse was the tall wooden step-ladder beside the anvil, and placed in front of the step-ladder a heavy oak chair, its back up against the ladder's A frame to keep the ladder steady should a man ascend the rungs.

Jonathon took the taper from Michelle to better inspect the arrangement of ladder and chair. He did not need the maid to describe to him what she had witnessed in this room, but she told him anyway, making the discovery of the leather straps with fastening buckles affixed to each ball and claw foot front leg and to the lion-headed arms of the chair, that much more horrific.

"Mme la duchesse had her ankles and wrists bound to the chair with these leather straps so she could not move. Then one man he would be up the ladder and the other would pass him the bucket of water from the well, and when the fat physician he gave the nod and stepped away from the chair where Mme la duchesse she was strapped the man up the ladder he would pour the entire contents of the bucket over Mme la duchesse's head. And then another bucket would be passed up to him and another until the physician he would put up his hand for the pouring to stop, and the men they would swap places on the ladder and the buckets and wait for the physician's signal to begin the treatment all over again. And not once did Mme la duchesse say a word... How could she, gasping for breath? It is icy in here and the water so cold..."

Jonathon put a comforting arm about the sobbing maid's shivering shoulders and led her out of the freezing room, shut the door and bolted it. It was not until they were standing in the passage outside the kitchen that Jonathon was able to speak.

"How often... How often was this-this *treatment* given?"

"I do not know precisely, M'sieur, but Pierre he says the physician he and the attendants went down to the cellars with Mme la duchesse twice in the day each day."

"Twice a day for a week? *Mon Dieu.*" Jonathon wiped a hand over his mouth and looked down at Michelle. "And no one has seen her since when?"

"This morning."

Jonathon's jaw set hard and his eyes went dull. "Right! Time to have a little chat with M'sieur the fat physician!"

Michelle stayed him with a hand on his forearm. She looked up into Jonathon's hard-set features and swallowed. Her voice was very low. "I must tell you something, M'sieur... Something Pierre and the others they do not know and which I do not want them to know, *ever*, but which you should know because I want so very badly for you to punish that monster."

"Be assured, he will be punished and very badly."

"Please, M'sieur, you must listen and promise me that you will not tell Mme la duchesse that I know, or that you know what I am to tell you now."

Jonathon gave her his full attention.

"I give you my word, Michelle."

Michelle was reassured, particularly as the handsome bronzed stranger remembered her name, which, for some unfathomable reason gave her the confidence that he would indeed keep his promise. She took a deep breath and bravely met his unblinking gaze.

"M'sieur, the physician, he does not look on Mme la duchesse as a doctor looks on his patient. He looks at her as a man looks at a woman. You understand me, yes?" When Jonathon slowly nodded she continued, fingers tightening about his sleeve. "That is despicable in itself, yes, because he is supposed to be a respected physician. A man bound by the rules of his profession. But he is not, M'sieur. He is very far from being what he ought to be and says he is. It is worse, *he* is worse, M'sieur. If it was only the way he looked at her... But he—but he has—has *touched* her in a way that is not right; in a way only a husband has a right to touch his wife. It is incredible, is it not? I was as astonished as you, M'sieur, and would not have believed he would dare take such an outrageous liberty with Mme la duchesse. But I tell you *I saw it with these eyes.* The night she was brought home from the regatta and we, the servants had not been sent away to the Gatehouse yet, I went up to her bedchamber to help her undress for the night as I always do and he was there! The physician was in her *bedchamber.* And the two attendants they too were there! Can you believe such outrageous trespass? It is worse than that, M'sieur. For the two attendants they were holding Mme la duchesse by an arm each, so she could not struggle. They were holding her like this," she explained, linking her arm through Jonathon's so that she faced north and he south. She let go and stepped back in front of him. "So you see the attendants with their backs to the physician they could not see what I saw. And I am very sure the physician he meant it that way so they would be as one blind to his real intentions."

"Yes, I believe you are right," agreed Jonathon, not wanting to hear the rest but compelled to do so.

"Mme la duchesse she tried to break free but it was impossible," Michelle continued, fingers gripping Jonathon's forearm. "And the attendants they did not care that she was a duchess and never to be touched! They listened only to their master. And she struggled hard, M'sieur, very hard because he-he, the physician he took *liberties.* He undressed her with his own hands! Imagine! He said he needed to take her pulse to see if her heart it was beating as it should. He unhooked and removed her stomacher, but it is not necessary to remove a stomacher if a physician he wants to take a pulse, is it, M'sieur?"

Jonathon swallowed. "Quite unnecessary."

She held up her wrist. "This is where the pulse it is taken, yes? Or here," she added, two fingers up to her throat.

"Yes."

"But he did not do that. He untied the bows of her stays, saying as he did so that she must not struggle but to let him do his job. But I ask you whose job is it to undress a great lady? It is not the place of a physician, is it, M'sieur? It is the place of her lady's maid. It is *my* place, is it not, M'sieur?"

"You are quite right, Michelle."

The maid nodded, wide-eyed. "He said what he was doing was for her own good and that was why M'sieur le Duc he had summonsed him: To take care of her. Pshaw! That is a great piece of nonsense! For I do not believe for a moment M'sieur le Duc's idea of care meant for the physician to take such liberties, he would not want that man—that *monster*—near her at all!"

"I agree with you, Michelle. Now, you must allow me to—"

"But, M'sieur, I must tell you the rest!" Michelle insisted, oblivious to the suppressed emotional plea in Jonathon's voice. "I saw the look on his face, the way he stared, and it was truly *disgusting*. Mme la duchesse she prefers to wear jumps and so the row of little bows they are at the front—"

"Yes, yes, I know that! There is no need to—"

"—here," she continued as if he had not spoken, drawing an imaginary line between her own breasts, oblivious to the flood of heated embarrassment that not only colored Jonathon's face and neck but invaded his voice. "And he took his time to untie each little bow, I can tell you, M'sieur, that me I wanted to run in there and climb on his back and beat him away! And when he had the bows undone and the jumps gaping open he—"

"I don't need to hear the rest!"

"—made a big show of holding up his pocket watch, and counting the beats out loud as if they were the beats of her heart when all the while he had his hand inside the jumps and was fondling her br—"

"*Enough*," Jonathon growled through his teeth and when the maid cowered quickly regained his composure, saying in a controlled voice that belied an inner turmoil of anger and anguish, "Thank you. It's time I dealt with this-this *quack*."

The maid blinked up at him. "It is true, all of it, M'sieur. I assure you."

"I don't doubt you."

"Thank you, M'sieur. Now you know why I think this physician he is a monster. Why you must do him harm for his treatment of Mme la duchesse. And Pierre, he makes vegetable pie! It is *unbelievable*."

The thought of food, of putting his legs under a table with

190

such a man as Sir Titus Foley who was a disgusting specimen of humanity made Jonathon feel physically ill, yet, to reassure the maid, who looked as ill as he felt, as to the chef's good intentions he smiled crookedly, recalling how Pierre had splashed a dark liquid from a green glass bottle over the pie filling. "Do not worry about the estimable Pierre. He is exacting his own unique form of revenge on behalf of his mistress and if I am not very much mistaken his weapon of choice is Daffy's elixir."

Rain lashed at the glass and wind rattled the mutins of the large mullioned windows in the dining room. The heavy velvet curtains had been drawn across the entire wall of windows with their view of a large internal courtyard, shutting out the noise of the violent storm that raged outside, except for the occasional bright burst of lightning that flashed white where curtains met. Wind whistling high-pitched through fine cracks in the window frames and the intermittent booming of thunder made the three men sitting at one end of the heavy oak table closest the fireplace involuntarily lift in their chairs. But the storm did not quell their appetites.

When Jonathon entered the room unannounced Sir Titus and his attendants were hunched over blue and white patterned porcelain bowls of steaming creamy soup, slurping up the last mouthfuls with heavy silver spoons and licking their lips with satisfaction. A crusty loaf of bread was passed around and torn apart to soak up and savor the last drops. The chef was complimented and fine wine glasses lifted up to toast his culinary skills.

He sized up the two men sitting opposite each other—the physician's henchmen—wondering how best to be rid of them should they prove uncooperative in leaving the room of their own accord. They were big, beefy lads with broad chests and meaty fists, the better to restrain recalcitrant patients. He was confident of being able to go one on one with either of them, but he was not so full of hubris as to be unrealistic. If both decided to tackle him, he would be left bloodied and he wanted to save his strength to punish the physician. First, he had to find out what he had done with Antonia.

"Sit! Sit!" Jonathon demanded casually with an insolent wave of a hand when the two attendants were instantly on their feet, Sir Titus remaining seated and acknowledging him with a curt nod. "Ah! Here is the pie! Please, take your fill. I'm not here to interrupt your splendid dinner." He pulled out a chair, propped his buttocks on the table, put a booted foot on the padded seat and took out the silver case holding his cheroots, an eye on the two cooks as they placed the vegetable pie, garlic-soaked fowls, and an assortment of side-dishes before the three diners. "His Grace charged me with seeing how fares the Dowager Duchess." He looked about the table, as if expecting to see her. "Is Her Grace not joining you?"

Sir Titus spread his fat hands and greedily eyed the dishes on offer. "It is not my practice to allow patient and doctor to dine together. One must keep one's professional distance, Mr...?"

"Distance?" Jonathon pulled a face then grinned. "It's Lord Leven. But a courtesy title I've never used. I'm waiting the bigger prize when great uncle Harold finally drops off the mortal coil. But the dear old fellow lingers on and on." He frowned, thinking a moment, and stuck a cheroot in the side of his mouth, pocketing the silver case. "I don't know why I told you that. Possibly I'm suffering from some sort of delayed shock after what I've just seen and been told, so blathering on about inconsequentialities is perhaps the mind's way of coping with horror." He leaned in to the branch of candles on the table and lit the cheroot, drawing back until the tip glowed red and then sat up again. "You tell me. You're the medical man. That's your expertise, isn't it? Fragile minds. Or is it only *female* fragile minds that you attend upon? Indulge me."

The physician's mouth worked but he really did not know how to reply to such casual and open confidences from a giant of a man seated upon the dining table and puffing on a cheroot as if he was in his club. He was no fool for although the stranger was cavalier in his speech and manner, there was a hard glint to the brown eyes and a tightness in the lean face that set the hairs up on the back of his neck. Before he could put a sentence together, he was waved at.

"Eat up, man! Eat up! The pie'll go cold and you don't want your associates to finish it all. They're onto second helpings and you've not touched a morsel." He smiled at the two men, exhaling a stream of smoke into the air, adding with a laugh, "Restraining a pretty little whirlwind weighing less than a half-drowned cat must be cause for working up a sweat, hey lads?" He stared hard at Sir Titus, but there was no warmth in his eyes or in the accompanying smile. "What say you to that, healer?"

The attendants, who had cleared their plates once and were diving in for seconds paused mid-helping at Jonathon's cryptic comment and looked to Sir Titus for guidance for they had no idea as to the stranger's intent or meaning and wondered what there was to laugh about. Sir Titus was more acute and although he smiled, which was signal enough for his assistants to keep on eating their fill, an uneasy sensation settled in the pit of his stomach and it had nothing to do with the food. Yet, ever the conceit about his medical expertise, he was confident that a reminder as to his pre-eminence in his field of expertise and the fact he had the confidence of the Duke of Roxton would be enough to extinguish this stranger's insolent enquiry.

"My dear sir, you must trust that as a learned physician I know what is best for my patient. His Grace has put his faith in me, not once but twice, to treat the Dowager Duchess in the manner I see fit as her attending physician."

"It's the *manner* that bothers me, but I'll deal with that in a moment. First, tell me how this water *treatment* of yours works."

"I cannot take credit for its invention, sir," Sir Titus confessed haughtily. "That goes to my colleague and good friend Dr. Patrick Blair who has used it to good effect on several occasions treating females suffering nervous distraction and thus unable or unwilling to fulfill their duties as wife and mother. However, I have—"

"Christ, another sadistic misogynist," Jonathon muttered under his breath.

Sir Titus baulked. "I beg your pardon?"

Jonathon was fast losing whatever patience he had brought into the room and he waved a hand at the physician thinking it could not be many minutes before Daffy's elixir took its revenge on the two brutes who had scoffed all but a slice of the vegetable pie which they had charitably left for their master. That Sir Titus had yet to fill his plate pleased Jonathon no end—it meant the physician would be in control of his bowels long enough for him to divulge the whereabouts of the Duchess and receive just punishment.

"However, I have modified the procedure to serve my particular clientele who are more gently bred than the patients attended on by Blair. I for one do not insist on a blindfold, nor do I employ continuous water flow from a pipe, preferring the use of buckets, which are poured upon the patient at intervals and thus is a far gentler approach. So you see my procedure," Sir Titus concluded with smug satisfaction, spooning buttery sauce over the chicken breast on his plate, "is not so much a *treatment* as a *therapy*."

Jonathon hopped down off the table and strolled to the window and lifted a corner of the velvet curtain. Rain was still hitting the window but perhaps a little gentler than before. He spoke to the windowpane; it kept him calm.

"Treatment? Therapy? A splitting of hairs, surely?"

Sir Titus had to turn his body in the chair to address Jonathon because he was standing almost directly behind him. Movement made him wince. Although he did not see the grimace, Jonathon heard the man's sharp intake of breath, as if he was in some pain. It caused Jonathon to look over his shoulder at him and in time to witness the two brutes exchanging silent laughter at their master's expense.

"Treatment implies cure," the physician responded, momentarily distracted by something in his lap. "Therapy is a means of controlling the illness not necessarily curing it."

"I see," stated Jonathon, not seeing at all, hard-gripping the carved high back of the physician's chair. "Treatment does not give you the option to return, whereas therapy allows you multiple visits to your patient, cure not being your intention. Clever."

Sir Titus gave a little nervous jump finding Jonathon so uncomfortably close and a bead of sweat trickled from under his powdered wig into his ear. Suddenly the mouth-watering food set before him was unappetizing and the throbbing pain between his legs more acute. He needed more ice to apply to the swelling, he was sure his cock and balls were black and blue, but he was not about to send his men out of the room, not with a dangerous stranger, title or no title, looming large over him. In the end the choice was taken completely out of his hands.

Without warning, one attendant dropped his spoon to clutch at his stomach, an acute stab of pain opening wide and then shutting tight his eyes as he scraped back his chair to double-over, gripped with agonizing cramps. Fear sparked in his fellow's eyes and seconds later he too was in the same gut-wrenching agony. Moaning loudly and with chairs clattering to the polished floorboards, both men scampered from the room, bent over, arms wrapped around their convulsing stomach, and with no control over their bowels.

"*Pierre, je vous salue!*" Jonathon declared with a laugh and a handclap over his head. "Now, healer, down to business," he said in a wholly different voice, flicking the smoldering cheroot into the fire. He dragged the physician's chair backwards, away from the table, scraped it about to face him and with a hand firmly to each arm of the chair, pinned the physician's fat hands under his. Face stuck in Sir Titus Foley's startled countenance, he had the physician trapped before the door closed on the backs of the two suffering attendants. "Where is she? What have you done with her?"

"Done with her? I don't know what—"

Crack.

The physician convulsed and screamed.

"What have you done with her?"

"I've not done anything with—"

Snap.

Again, the physician convulsed and screamed.

"I repeat: Where is the Duchess of Roxton, you piece of rectal filth?"

"*Stop. Stop,*" the physician pleaded, panting with pain, face a lather of perspiration. "For pity's sake. Are you mad?"

"Well, you'd know all about that," Jonathon snarled. "Should've kept to treating real lunatics. You should *never* have touched her."

"I didn't—"

"*Liar.*"

Crack.

The physician howled piteously.

Jonathon's furious face was so close to the panic-stricken Foley that the sweep of his thick brown hair fell across the physician's sweaty contorted face, tickling the tip of his snub nose. His voice was barely above a whisper but despite being in excruciating pain, Sir Titus heard every word.

"You took something precious and reverential, of the upmost intimacy between husband and wife, and turned it into an utterly disgusting and perverted act, all to slake your depraved lust. No man has a right to touch her. No man, not even her noble husband, a Duke, who worshipped every luminous hair on her head, put a finger to her bare flesh without permission. Roxton set his trust in you to take care of her. You abused that trust and you abused her and for that alone he will see you hang from a gibbet. You imprisoned her; tortured her; debased and defiled her and if I killed you here, right now, no one would give a tester for your life it is worth less than *nothing*."

"No! No! I never meant—I-I lost my head!" the physician pleaded, eyes wide with terror, tears of pain and fear coursing down his reddened cheeks, nose running of its own accord. "I-I couldn't help myself! It's not my fault. She—she—I-I-I'm a-a *man*. For God's sake, you're a man. You've seen her. You can't be immune. I did my utmost to resist... But those magnificent breasts... She'd make a blind eunuch ha—"

"Shut your foul mouth! Where is she?"

"You must believe me! I did nothing more than fondle her breasts. I swear it on my mother's grave! Please! You must believe me."

"Where is she?"

"How would I kn—"

Snap.

"There's the thumb and then I start on the left. Tell me what you've done with her."

The physician was beyond screaming. He stared up into Jonathon's face contorted with rage, face blank and eyes misty. It was as if the whole of his right hand was on fire. And when Jonathon let go of his wrist and stepped aside Sir Titus dared to glance down the length of his arm and he saw the damage he had wrought. There was something odd about his hand. It just didn't look right. The medical man in him pondered why. The fingers. It was his fingers. They were at bizarre angels to each other, so twisted up in fact that he had never seen the like before. How very odd. And then the realization hit him and so hard that an excruciating pain exploded in his hand, shot up his arm and invaded his entire body.

He passed out.

"No, you don't!" Jonathon growled and dashed a glass of wine in the physician's face. He slapped him hard across the left cheek. "Foley! Wake! Where is she? Where is the Duchess?"

The physician gave a start. "My hand! God in Heaven I can't feel my fingers. You've broken them all! You've broken them!"

"That was the point, you bloody bastard! I'll start on the left and then there's your tackle. Where is she?"

Sir Titus let out a squeak of incredulity mixed with absolute panic and dropped his useless right hand between his legs. It was a mistake. Unable to feel his fingers the hand fell heavily and despite the bladder of ice nestled on his groin his cock and balls were so agonizingly tender that he yelped. Jonathon tossed aside the bladder and pressed his knee into the physician's tender groin.

The physician screamed and then began to blubber. "I don't— I don't know... God's honest truth... Disappeared this morning... Last I remember... She had me hard about the ballocks. I thought she'd ripped them off. I passed out. God in Heaven, my hand..."

Jonathon chuckled and, with his jockey boot, pushed away the chair holding the blubbering physician, not wanting the touch or nearness of him. "The ends of the earth won't be far enough away for the Duke not to find you; and if he doesn't, I will. *Disappear.*"

In the kitchens he found the Duchess's servants waiting for him with the light of expectation in their eyes. They had seen the two assistants dash from the room in search of the nearest latrine and heard the physician's screams and pleas for mercy. They had stood huddled in the servant passageway savoring every moment of the pompous physician's agony. Michelle begged the question.

"He is dead, yes?"

"You're a blood-thirsty lot!" Jonathon said with a huff of embarrassment and accepted the tumbler of ale from the cook and downed it in one.

Fury cooled; he was discomforted by the intensity of emotion the physician's reprehensible behavior towards the Duchess had elicited in him. His violent response was uncharacteristic and surprising for one who had eschewed violence at an early age, finding the practices of the Hindus on the subcontinent more to his liking than the fire and brimstone prophecies of the religion into which he had been christened. He did not have the time to ponder what had come over him, but was well aware of the source, because he had had a flash of inspiration while the physician was sniveling on at him about not knowing the Duchess's whereabouts. The more he thought about it the more he was convinced his intuition was right.

Instead of answering the question he made several quiet demands.

"Go fetch a few articles of Mme la duchess's clothing; nothing bulky. No petticoats," he said to Michelle. "Stockings, nightshift, a woolen shawl should suffice. I'll need a waterproof satchel," he added, turning to Pierre. "Throw in a couple of tapers and some food. She hasn't eaten since this morning: Bread, a bottle of wine, cheese and fruit if you have it. And I'll need a hat."

"Do you want Guy to saddle a horse, M'sieur?"

Jonathon shook his head. "And be thrown with the next thunderclap or strike of lightning? No. I'll walk. It's not that far that I'll get completely soaked before I reach cover."

Michelle had bustled to the door but turned and asked before going up to the bedchamber, "You know the whereabouts of Mme la duchesse, yes?"

"Yes. She is with her loved ones."

ifteen

$\mathcal{H}$e found her curled up against the iron gates, trying to stay out of the driving rain. Heavy chain threaded through the black and gold painted wrought iron kept the gates closed. A padlock secured against trespass. An ornate key sat limp in the locking mechanism. Antonia had not the strength in her wrists to turn the key to release the shackle.

Jonathon stripped off his leather gloves to work the lock and remove the chain. He swung the gates wide and opened one of the heavy brass inlaid double doors. With the oiled leather satchel still slung over his left shoulder he scooped up Antonia and carried her inside the mausoleum, kicking shut the oak door on the inclement weather with the heel of his jockey boot.

Beyond the vestibule the interior was pitch black. Jonathon had a sense of expansive space and moved cautiously forward, hoping the family sarcophagi were arranged along the edges of the walls or deeper within the mausoleum.

A series of lightning strikes directly overhead flashed bright light through the glass oculus at the apex of the domed roof conveniently illuminating the center of the vast interior for the few seconds Jonathon needed to find his footing and orientation. Half way along the length of the black and white marbled flooring there was a stone bench directly opposite an ornately carved marble sarcophagus with a suitably grand marble effigy of a seated nobleman.

Jonathon carried Antonia to the bench and sat with her on his lap.

Water from the oiled greatcoat pooled at his booted feet and dripped off the rim of his hat, the satchel hung awkwardly from his shoulder and also dripped water, yet he did not move. He sat still and silent, listening to the sounds of constant rain upon the glass oculus high above their heads and the distant rumble of thunder, staring unseeing into the blackness, needing just to hold her, to feel her in his arms, to know she was alive and out of danger.

He was unsure how long he sat cradling her. They were both so still. He would not have been surprised had she fallen asleep from exhaustion. Yet, when she slowly turned, snuggling in, as if seeking the warmth of him, he came to life. She was shivering and her scant clothing soaked through. He dared not look down for he was very sure she was dressed in nothing more than stockings and a chemise that clung like a second skin to every womanly curve.

He needed to get out of his wet greatcoat and hat to rummage in the satchel for her clothes Michelle had given him. There were also tapers and a small tinderbox and the hamper of food hastily put together by the estimable Pierre. But how best to go about getting her clothed without drawing attention to her nakedness and dishevelment, which would surely underscore the horrendous ordeal endured over the previous week. Being alone with him, a male, and almost a complete stranger, after all she really didn't know him from Adam, would surely only add to her distress. But there was no way round their predicament if he wanted to ensure she did not catch influenza, if she hadn't already, and was to be made comfortable.

So he approached the situation as if it was his daughter Sarah-Jane in the same situation. Which also helped him overcome any reservations he felt at being cast, however tenuously, in the same mold as the lecherous Sir Titus, for while in London surrounded by attorneys, fawning men of business and demanding Scots kinsmen all waiting for an ancient distant relative to breathe his last, he had had plenty of time to ruminate on his future. It was a future that was not the one he had mapped out for himself. That had been taken wholly out of his hands by the misfortune of birth. Others, such as Tommy, saw it as the greatest piece of good luck that every other relative up for the title and estate had died without leaving an heir; Jonathon considered it a burden he could well do without. Not his aging ancestor's debts or the mismanagement of the estates, he would pay those off and turn around the estate with ease, but the responsibility of people and dealing with such intangibles as social position and precedent and the bowing and scraping to *noblesse oblige*—he'd never get used to that. He didn't want that.

One thing he was very sure he did want in his future was this woman in his arms. He desired Antonia Duchess of Roxton with every fiber of his being. He did not try and wonder why he just knew it as fact and that was that. He had felt the same about Emily all those years ago. But what left him startled and shaken this time was that he seemed to have regressed into the nervous callow youth of Oxford days that he had been with his Emily. The realization that as far as his future was concerned no other woman but Antonia Roxton would do scared him witless.

Lightning and thunder brought him out of his reverie and he gently disentangled Antonia from his arms to sit her on the bench, saying tenderly,

"Come on, sweetheart, time to get you out of those wet things and into something dry."

He then immediately turned away to off load the satchel onto the floor and tossed aside the hat. He struggled out of the great-coat and set it aside with the hat and began searching in the satchel for the tapers and small tinderbox. He went about lighting one candle and once lit left it on the marble tile so that there was just enough of a soft glow to see the immediate surroundings, reasoning Antonia would be more comfortable dressing in the relative privacy of a dim orange glow; he would then illuminate the rest of this marble palace for the dead to prepare them something to eat. And then there was the hurdle of bedding down for the night, for there was no expectation in this weather of horse and rider until morning and clear skies.

He found the bundle of clothes wrapped up in a towel with a silver-backed hairbrush and polished tortoise shell comb—*Michelle, you're worth your weight in gold pieces*—and returned to sit beside Antonia. She was staring out into the blackness, knees drawn up to her chin, arms wrapped around her bare legs—*Jesus. The physician had even deprived her of stockings*—The weight of wet honey-blonde hair was a mass of knotted curls falling like fish netting about her shaking shoulders. He put aside the nightshift, stockings with ribbon ties, the brush and comb and showed her the towel.

"Why don't we dry your hair first and then once you're in dry clothes you can untangle it with brush and comb?" he suggested chattily. But when he made a move towards her she shied away, glaring at him in warning, green eyes wary. He offered her the towel but otherwise did not move. "All right, you dry it off. I was only trying to be helpful. Sarah-Jane was the same. Must be a female fixation: precious about your hair. When she was small and I'd take her swimming she wouldn't let me put a hand to her hair. Had to tie it up herself before we went for a swim *and* then dry it off afterwards. *Papa, you always make a muckle of it,*" he said, mimicking his daughter at about seven years of age and smiled at the memory. "I gather she meant muddle, but it didn't matter, it was hands-off with her hair. I don't know why she thought I would be unable to brush it properly when I wore my hair braided *and* it reached to the middle of my back, just like hers. Yes, you can look surprised, Mme la duchesse," he said with a laugh, heart racing because Antonia had inched back up the bench with a frown of enquiring surprise, "but it's the truth." He tugged a lock of his wavy shoulder-length hair. "A more respectable length for good society, so Sarah-Jane tells me. And when combined with my brown skin, Tommy was adamant that if I'd left it long I'd be mistaken for a Sioux Indian chief! What are relatives for if not to be brutally honest?"

He held out the towel again but when Antonia gently pushed it away with a shake of her head he waited, gaze never leaving her face. Through the orange glow he saw her swallow. It took effort and when she put a hand to her throat he understood. It was impossible not to notice the ligature welts encircling her wrist, and he quickly bit down on his tongue to stop an audible intake of breath, hoping his features remained stagnant. When she turned her back to allow him to dry off her hair, only then did he breathe easy. He was anything but calm when it came time for her to change out of the chemise and into the nightshift.

"Let's tackle the knots once you're warmed up and then you can pass judgment on my ability to braid or not. I apologize for only having a nightshift but the satchel wouldn't accommodate petticoats. And given the weather, I was not about to stride up here with a set of panniers over my head. Could've got myself struck by lightning and left charred; an unidentifiable black blob atop Treat Hill; a curiosity for the surrounding villagers to gawp at. A scientific experiment gone wrong and one Mr. Franklin would enjoy writing up in his scientific journal on how *not* to conduct electricity. Not to mention being fodder for the amusement of the local newssheets as "Gentleman wearing panniers found smoking" and I'm not talking about my cheroots! You may giggle at my expense, Mme la duchesse, but think of the shame for poor Sarah-Jane. Not only did her father wear his hair down his back like a woman but upon his miserable end she discovers he looked as if he'd strayed from a Molly house. I suppose that would at least give her an explanation for the long hair..."

There was a short silence punctuated by another series of lightning strikes and flashes of white light through the glass oculus that lit up the interior to eerie effect. Jonathon was shown glimpses of ducal opulence, walls painted with dramatic scenes from the classics, marbled sculptures recumbent atop polished granite plinths under which coffins were secreted, there was even a marble statue of two greyhounds, or were they whippets? No doubt the favorite faithful hounds of a noble master. He was wondering where Monseigneur was to be found within this ostentatious celebration of centuries of noble blood and reasoned his memorial would be the most magnificent of all, his arrogance demanded it, when a thundercrack, so loud they both jumped, interrupted his private reverie. The lightning strike had been very near, Jonathon relieved to be in a substantial stone building, even if surrounded by long dead noblemen and women.

In the ensuing quiet where there was only the sound of steady rain falling on the glass oculus, Antonia spoke over her shoulder,

"I am sorry, but my arms they will not lift above my head, and I am very cold now. So please, I need your assistance..."

"Certainly, Mme la duchesse," Jonathon responded in a neutral tone. Inside he was jumping for joy that she had lowered her defenses sufficiently to seek help. "You won't need to move or turn around. First let's get you out of that sodden cloth before you catch your death. Sorry! That was a very poor choice of words. Blame it on light-headedness. I've not eaten since leaving the city at first light and then only a coffee, a roll and a cut of cheese. If you can cross your arms and gather up the hem I will help you get the chemise up over your head. The thing of it is," he continued in the same light tone as she did as he asked of her and he then took hold of the hem with her from behind and guided her arms up, "there are very few inns that cater for a jolter-headed fellow like me who doesn't eat animal flesh."

"*Pour quoi?* Not eat meat? *Everyone* eats meat."

He laughed at her indignation.

"Not everyone, Mme la duchesse. Not on the subcontinent and not if you lived there for as many years as I did and with a father who eschewed his English heritage to live as a nabob, with his hookah and his harem. I have the chemise now, Mme la duchesse. You may let go. There," he said with satisfaction as he swiftly stripped off the sodden chemise and tossed it aside in the general direction of his greatcoat and hat where it landed with a splat.

"But you went to Harrow and Oxford," she countered, hands crossed over her naked breasts, the thigh-length tangle of hair the only covering to her narrow back and round bottom. "Did you not eat meat at school? Is that why the boys they made fun of you?"

"Ah, so you remember me telling you that about my school days, do you?" he responded, quickly bunching up the white night-shift so he could place the neck opening over her head without fuss, a sudden frown at the flimsy material between his fingers. If this was what she usually wore to bed, cotton woven so fine it was gossamer thin, with pretty lace bordering to the three-quarter sleeves and low neckline, she would need a heavy coverlet or a male bed warmer to keep away the chills. He pulled up his mind where those thoughts were headed and hoped Michelle had indeed put a woolen shawl in the satchel or if he would need to give Antonia his frockcoat to cover the shift and buttoned up to her chin, to keep her decently attired. "No, that was not the reason the boys teased me. What I should have said to be precise is that I do not eat *beef*. Cows are sacred to Hindus. I ate fish and fowl while at school, it was the least I could do to try and fit in. I still eat fish but never the flesh from a warm-blooded animal. Head up and I'll throw this poor excuse for nightwear over your head. You then need only find the arm holes."

"You are a Hindu, too?" Antonia asked when her head appeared from deep within the nightshift. When he did not immediately reply she swiveled, gathering her hair over her left shoulder, and found him on the floor by the bench rummaging in the satchel.

"One must be born Hindu," he replied, getting to his feet having found the woolen shawl. "But I do try to abide by their ethical code: Do not harm another; be truthful; never take what is not yours; be content with life." He shrugged a shoulder thinking of the pain he had inflicted on the physician and had no regrets. "Unfortunately, it is not always possible to be good. Here, this will help keep you warm," he said, fussing with the fall of the shawl about her shoulders. "Wrap it tighter or—"

"I am not ailing, M'sieur! I can take care of myself!" she snapped, pulling away at his touch on her shoulders and hastily crisscrossing the shawl over her breasts. She immediately recanted. "No. That is not true. Forgive me. I am not... I am not—*myself*." She put her face in her hands and after a brief moment sat up to stare straight ahead, quickly dashing the tears from her brimming eyes. She shuddered in a great breath. "I told you I could take care of myself and this you see before you is the result! Julian he thinks me self-pitying and selfish. My neglect of Henri-Antoine it is unspeakable. Deborah... Deborah she must wonder if I am at all fit to be a *grandmere* to her babies. And Frederick... My darling little boy he is most confused about his Mema and her behavior. And now I worry that my babies will be kept from me because Julian he gave me into the care of a sadistic madman. Renard, I tell you he is truly a lunatic and Julian you must not blame. He thought it was for the best because I have not been behaving as a duchess ought and been walking about as one dead for so long... But that madman he is two people—one face he shows to our son, the other he keeps well hidden and only brings out when—when he—when I—It is truly too hideous. I cannot tell you!"

She turned away from addressing the blackness to be gathered up in Jonathon's comforting embrace.

"It's all right, sweetheart, Monseigneur he understands only too well," he murmured, a wary eye on the sarcophagus Antonia had been addressing.

He now knew to whom the massive monument belonged and his gaze travelled up its elaborately carved length. It had all the hallmarks of James "Athenian" Stuart and his master sculptors the Scheemakers, with its Doric columns and classical pediment, sculptured figures of grieving Greek Gods and Goddesses in funerary procession along the lower heavy plinth of red marble. And there, through the darkness he could just make out her Monseigneur, the most noble His Grace the fifth Duke of Roxton, sculptured life size, seated, dressed in his ducal robes and wearing his star and garter diagonally across his waistcoat, one arm with a languid hand resting across the arm of the chair, one foot in a heeled buckled shoe slightly forward, the other turned to show a well-exercised calf muscle, the face with its beak of a nose and penetrating stare looking out and down on the world with thin lipped self assurance—disdainful even in cold white marble.

Such a man would have killed Foley as give him a second glance, Jonathon thought with a wry smile. How fortunate then was the physician to be confronted with a follower of the Hindu path to *Swarga Loka*—Heaven. Undoubtedly Monseigneur was furious with his widow's new friend, and more so that he was comforting her under his very nose. *Well, you had best get used to the idea, your Grace*, he warned as he squared his shoulders, *because I'm not going away!* He blinked his surprise to think he too was now talking to a marble likeness, even if it was in his head. And he didn't even know the man! His movement made Antonia sit up.

"I am sorry. My behavior is not as it should be," Antonia stated, pulling the shawl back over her shoulder, gaze in her lap where her fingers fiddled with the fringe. "It must be because me I am very tired."

In Jonathon's opinion, the whole family from Monseigneur down had cause to answer for Antonia's *tiredness*, if that's what she chose to call the fact that her son was critical she was not living up to her exulted position as a duchess. He wanted to reassure her that all that mattered to him was her happiness and being the carefree woman he had seen glimpses of in the pavilion. Instead, he scooped up the towel and mopped up the rainwater by the bench saying casually,

"We'll eat and then get snug for the night but first you need to put on your stockings." He went down on his haunches before her with the soaked towel. "But before we can do that I need to remove the dirt you collected walking up the hill. Give me your foot." When she hesitated he looked up. She had a hand to her mouth and was shaking her head. "You, well perhaps *you* don't but *I know* there is nothing worse than putting a dirty foot into a perfectly clean stocking. Michelle will not be pleased with you," he added and when this elicited a watery laugh he took the liberty of placing her bare left foot upon his knee. When she tried to withdraw it he held her firm, but not about the ankle for there were ligature welts there too, but cupped his large hand around the bridge of her foot. "Your feet are little blocks of ice and you can't do this yourself, so let me help," he said steadily, swallowing hard at the sight of the red raw flesh caused by her captivity. She must have put up quite a struggle. Why hadn't he broken the bastard's every finger and toe? Her ankles and wrists would need bathing, ointment and bandaging as soon as they returned to the dower house.

"Do you—Do you speak their language, the language of the people on the subcontinent?" she asked, watching him gently clean her toes. "Were you speaking in their tongue with your daughter at the regatta?"

"Yes. Sarah-Jane speaks Hindi fluently. I had her taught, thinking it more practical she learn the language of the people she lived amongst than say French or Portuguese, the other conquerors of the subcontinent. And here we are back in England. Something I had not planned on for her or for me..." He glanced up at her with a smile. "Do you want to know what I said to Sarah-Jane that day at the regatta that I did not want others to know?" he asked rhetorically, tenderly wiping the dirt from her heel. "I told her to make damned sure that if she accepted an offer of marriage from

Dair Fitzstuart she knew she was marrying the man and not the prize of an earl's coronet." He looked up at her again, this time with a frown. "That when all's said and done she'll go to bed with the man, not his coronet. I told her to picture him naked wearing his earl's coronet—"

Antonia gasped and sat forward. "*Cela je ne croit pas!* You said no such thing! You are her *father.*"

"Which is even more reason for me to say it! As she has no mother to tell her such things, it is left to me to advise her." He removed her left foot from his knee and put her right foot in its place. "I told her to consider if such a sight was at all appealing— a naked man in his coronet—or utterly farcical. I hoped such a ludicrous picture would make her see sense."

At this Antonia giggled, so much so that it hurt her sore throat and she took a moment to collect herself. "*Parbleu!* Foolish man. See sense? It is not sense she is seeing. *Naturelment* it appeals. Dair Fitzstuart he is my cousin but I am not blind that even I do not see that he is a very strapping young man. I would hazard a guess that all of him it is strapping, so this coronet upon his head, while ridiculous to you would be the last place her eyes they would be looking."

Jonathon would have smiled to see her laugh at any other time but her response made him frown and pull a face. He tossed aside the dirty towel and put out a hand for one of the white-clocked stockings. She passed it to him without hesitation. He deftly gathered the finely knitted cotton stocking up into itself so she could easily slip her toes into its foot. "Please point your toes and I will be as gentle as I am able... It's still a valid argument," he grumbled, a heighten color to his lean cheeks, not liking her description of Dair Fitzstuart. It annoyed him for all the wrong reasons. "What I was trying to convey to my daughter is the importance of seeing beyond the superficial. What is important is his heart, not his coronet or-or anything else!"

"That is very true," Antonia responded quietly and touched his wrist when he slid the stocking up over her knee and proceeded to tie up the blue riband that kept the stocking in place. "I was flippant. I am sorry. You are right to warn her. Too many girls they marry and only after it is done do they realize it was for the wrong reasons. Who she weds is fundamental to her future happiness..."

He nodded and repeated the task with the second stocking in silence then collected the bundle of tapers lying by the satchel. "Upon reflection, I will amend my previous statement," he said, placing and lighting the tapers at intervals along one end of the lower marble plinth of the Duke's massive tomb, "and say that while Fitzstuart's future coronet is unimportant to me, and my daughter should see it as utterly superfluous to her decision to marry the man, how he chooses to use what he's got between his legs is very important to me."

Antonia picked at the knots in her hair with the polished tortoiseshell comb as he lit the final candle, not at all shocked by his words, and followed him with her eyes when he snatched up the discarded greatcoat and shook it to dislodge the last raindrops, then returned to spread it out, oiled side down, between the bench and the monument.

"You do not like him."

Jonathon dumped the satchel near the makeshift picnic rug and proceeded to empty its contents. He held her gaze. "I like his brother a hundred times better."

Antonia watched him arrange two silver tumblers, a bottle of wine, a loaf of crusty bread, a small wheel of cheese, slices of mushroom terrine, a pottage of pate, a couple of apples and a knife and realized she was famished. She could not remember when she had last eaten. She hopped off the bench and joined him on the upturned greatcoat under the glow of candlelight and waited to be served. He pulled off a chunk of bread from the loaf, cut slices of the terrine and the cheese and using the bread as a plate offered it to her.

"Charles I prefer, too, but Dair he is the one the females want."

"Possessing morals and high ideals just doesn't cut it amongst silly young things," Jonathon replied, an edge to his voice. "It's title and wealth that attracts them in droves."

He offered her a tumbler of wine.

"I do not think it is only your money that interests them. They see you as they do Dair."

She took the tumbler but he did not immediately let it go.

"I was not referring to myself. But if you think me strapping," he added with a grin, and let go of the tumbler and sat back, "then I accept the compliment."

"It is not a compliment," Antonia said dismissively, "to state the obvious. You are fishing, M'sieur!"

"For compliments?" he replied with a laugh and held up his tumbler in a toast. "From you? Always." Then added seriously, "Dair Fitzstuart keeps a mistress and child in Chelsea and he has no intention of giving them up upon marriage. He should do the honorable thing and marry the girl. She's breeding again too."

"You kept a harem on the subcontinent. Is there a difference?"

"No. Not a harem," he said very quietly, wondering where she could have gleaned such misinformation. "A mistress, yes; many years after Emily's passing. Then she, too, died. After that?" He shrugged. "The usual sort of temporary but necessary satisfaction men engage in: nothing important; nothing I would care to repeat; no female that has engaged my finer feelings," he added, holding her gaze, "or caused me to channel my lust into a singular devotion."

Antonia looked away first and said with practiced lightness, "To many females none of that matters. What matters is the coronet. What their husbands do with—as you say—what they have between their legs—is an unimportant detail when weighed against title and social position."

"But not to you..."

"Not to me..." She smiled, the dimple showing itself in her left cheek, adding mischievously over the rim of the tumbler, "What was between Monseigneur's legs was very important to me."

"It goes without saying, but I'll say it anyway," Jonathon added with a huff of embarrassment as he roughly quartered an apple, "and what he did with it!"

"*Mais bien sûr.* Of course. Now please to pass me slices of the apple and then you, too, must eat."

"It's as well then I like nothing better than to rise to a challenge," he muttered as he organized a collation for himself.

But he did not eat immediately, merely took a mouthful of wine then proceeded to shrug out of his dark velvet travelling frockcoat. He could see that despite the shawl and stockings Antonia was shivering with cold though she did her best to suppress the involuntary shudders. He undid the silk covered buttons of his peacock-blue silk waistcoat, removed it and put his frockcoat back on over his white linen shirt.

"Females of my daughter's tender years seem to think it is romantic to marry an arrogant rake who will magically reform his ways upon marriage. Utter twaddle. That rarely happens. And before you say it," he added when Antonia sat up very straight, "you've already set me straight about Monseigneur, but he is the exception to the rule and you wouldn't have married him unless he had reformed himself *before* marriage. Here, let me help you put this on," he said holding open his waistcoat. "You'll be much warmer and can use the shawl across your lap. Now turn about so I can do up the buttons and roll up the cuffs." When she did so without argument he smiled and chuffed her under the chin. "On you it's almost a banyan."

He resumed his place opposite her on their makeshift picnic rug, back up against the cold marble with one long leg stretched out, the other bent and with his hand over his knee. Antonia observed that he looked supremely at ease and not at all disturbed to be spending the night in the family crypt with the wind howling, the rain pouring and lightning flashing outside. The weather was unpleasant to be sure but she had spent so much time here, in this very spot surrounded by her loved ones that it was the most comforting place in the world to her. It was the first and only place she had in mind when fleeing the dower house and that maniac of a physician. What she had been put through in the icehouse all in the name of *medical treatment* no person, not even the criminally insane, should be forced to endure. And when she thought about the times she had been left alone with that perverted weasel... She snatched up the tumbler and drank deeply of the wine, as if it would somehow cleanse her, body and soul.

Jonathon watched her keenly, saw the moment the heat came into her face, her throat constricted and her hands began to shake, and knew her mind was wandering where it should not. He downed his wine and made a fuss of what she had left uneaten.

"Is that how you eat when you're starving? Picking at the crumbs daintily? Leaving the cheese half eaten? My God, woman, we'll never get to sleep at your rate of consumption! And the thunder has taken itself elsewhere so we might even get an unbroken couple of hours if you have a mind to eat up."

Antonia returned to the present with a smile and continued to eat her cold collation but in small bites.

"My son Julian he thinks Charles may be a spy for the American rebels."

Jonathon's eyebrows shot up. "Does he indeed. I'm sure he has his reasons." He dug into his frockcoat pocket and pulled out the letter from Tommy and the pamphlet entitled *Common Sense* he had borrowed from Charles Fitzstuart. He tossed the pamphlet onto the rug and shoved the letter back into his pocket saying,

"This pamphlet makes for interesting reading. A treasonous diatribe is what I guess Roxton would brand it as it attacks all he holds dear in the world: King, country, the English sense of justice to its subjects, or to the writer of this pamphlet's mind *injustice*, and not least the Duke's exulted unquestioning position in society. What I think is, and I am not going to shock you because I believe you have a logical and sharp mind inside that pretty shell of yours, that *Common Sense* has a point and the English have a case to answer. I mean how can you argue against the notion of no taxation without representation?" He glanced up the length of the monument on which he was reclining and then leaned in to Antonia to whisper, "Monseigneur would be none too happy to hear me challenge this well-ordered world of his, now would he?"

"Oh, do not worry, M'sieur," Antonia said sweetly, the dimple reappearing. "Monseigneur he did not care a fig for one side or the other in any argument; there was only his side. That way there was never any disagreements, treasonous or otherwise. It is expedient, yes?"

Jonathon burst out laughing and it reverberated around the cavernous space. "Expedient? Damned insufferable belike! Egad! He and I would have had some interesting discussions!"

"And you, M'sieur, would have had to concede!" Antonia teased him.

Jonathon drank his wine. He smiled into her green eyes, so luminescent and enticing whenever she mentioned Monseigneur, and nodded slowly. He was philosophical. "Yes, I believe I would."

They consumed the rest of their cold collation in companionable silence and when done, Jonathon tidied away the remainders into the satchel and put it aside, making space for them to bed down for the night under the plinth where the soft glow of the candles illuminated part of the marble frieze of grieving Greek Gods. While he fossicked about Antonia sat on the bench and combed her hair free of tangles. She started to braid but her wrists were too weak and she gave up the attempt just as Jonathon sat beside her. He turned her to face away from him and with permission pulled the weight of her curls over her shoulders and proceeded to quickly and deftly plait the thick hair into a long intricate braid. Having no riband he teased out several strands and with these made a very thin braid that he then used to secure the ends. Antonia inspected his handiwork and was so pleased with the result that she smiled up at him with genuine affection and squeezed his hand in thanks. It was all the encouragement he needed to raise her hand to his lips and kiss her fingers. He knew at once he had overstepped the mark when she blushed scarlet and turned away to fuss with the shawl. He cursed himself for dropping his guard.

As if to heavily underscore his impetuosity there was a great crack of thunder followed by a heavy downpour and a blast of icy wind that rattled the iron gates and flung wide one of the entrance doors. Jonathon secured the gates and the doors, thinking with a crooked smile that if he believed in ghosts he would reckon that the sudden display of violent weather, the rattling of gates and the swinging door was not a random weather event but M'sieur le Duc venting his fury in warning not to take liberties with his duchess. He did not believe in ghosts but was willing to respect M'sieur le Duc's wishes here in this his final resting place. Beyond the mausoleum doors, however, he would disregard the Duke's wishes, supernatural or otherwise, for he believed in fate and his fate was inexplicably entwined with this beautiful dainty creature he now coaxed to snuggle up to him or catch pneumonia.

"Here under the coat," he stated placidly, back up against the marble plinth, the left panel of his frockcoat opened wide in invitation. "We will be doing each other a service ensuring the other does not spend the night frozen." When she hesitated he patiently waited, expression neutral. "I am a walking hot brick. Sarah-Jane will tell you so."

This made her smile and she accepted his invitation and tentatively sat beside him. He was not exaggerating. His body radiated warmth and she soon snuggled in, head against his chest, curves pressed to the hard long line of him, a hand clutched to the front of his white shirt as if needing anchorage. He closed the frockcoat over her, drew the woolen shawl across them both and put his arm about her as if it was the most natural and mundane activity in the world. He just prayed his increased heart rate did not give away the glaringly obvious truths that he was acutely aware of the softness of her, that the natural scent of her skin was all consuming, and falling asleep with her in his arms naked was the second most sought-after activity he was utterly determined to share with her.

"Tell me about India," she said sleepily. "Tell me about your life there."

"A bedtime story?"

"Yes. A bedtime story... About you and your long braid and swimming with Sarah-Jane under a hot sun..."

"It would be my very great pleasure, Mme la duchesse."

Sixteen

"Shall we have nuncheon in the pavilion today?"

Antonia did not look up from the sheaf of papers in her lap.

Jonathon let her read on, content to watch. He decided he could watch her all day: how, when she giggled, she put a hand to her mouth; that a tendril of fair hair having escaped from the heavy knot coiled at her nape would, every so often, annoy her and she would brush it from her cheek or absently twirl it round a finger; that when she was greatly amused her shoulders shook with silent mirth; that in her company he felt supremely peaceful. Finally she glanced up, green eyes full of humor, as if his voice if not the question had finally registered and he quickly looked away, feeling the heat in his face for studying her so intently. But she was so caught up in her reading that his preoccupation went unnoticed and as he merely grinned idiotically and chomped into his apple, she returned to reading.

They were at opposite ends of a small rowing boat. A bamboo handled parasol of Chinese painted silk secured to the bow shaded Antonia from the sun. Her knees were drawn up slightly to provide a makeshift lectern for ease of reading, the layers of light Indian cotton petticoats spread about her, hiding her stockinged feet that rested on a tapestry cushion, mules kicked off long ago. Back supported by a scatter of cushions, Jonathon was likewise situated in the stern; left arm behind his head, resting on the cushion at his back, long legs sprawled out down the bowside, shirtsleeves rolled to the elbow. He was decidedly in undress, without cravat, white shirt unbuttoned at the neck, waistcoat removed before the oar blades had touched water. His frockcoat was up at the pavilion.

He was enjoying being idle. He was enjoying more admiring Antonia against the backdrop of a pale blue sky dotted with white fluffy clouds, sunshine sparkling through swaying willow branches and twinkling on the peaks of little ripples made by a family of ducks that paddled between the shore and the boat, the eight ducklings paddling in a higgledy-piggledy line as fast as their tiny feet would go to keep up with their parents. It was a perfect spring day and such a change from the formidable weather of a week ago.

Jonathon had nothing more pressing to do with his time than lie back and admire the view. There was no one to tell him what he should do, or must do, or what was expected of him or what he would be required to do once his ancient relative finally breathed his last. Here, with her, he was Jonathon Strang, East India merchant returned from the subcontinent. A self-made man who didn't give a snap of his fingers for the societal dictates of the class into which he was being thrust. He was so nauseatingly wealthy that despite her father smelling of the shop, Sarah-Jane was accepted in every elegant drawing room and an unwanted consequence was the dowagers who tripped over their pampered pooches in their haste to have their unmarried daughters up before him for inspection. What was more startling, these young misses were more than willing to throw themselves at him in the hopes he would choose one of them to marry.

But with her, with Antonia, he could be himself and, regretfully, there seemed very little chance of her throwing herself at him.

So if you are being yourself, the merchant prince returned, what about the house? his business brain rudely reminded him. *What about your plans to reacquire the Elizabethan house she now occupies?*

He caught glimpses of the second floor mullioned windows and quaintly turned chimneystacks through the swaying willow branches as they drifted on the lake and paused mid-chomp and frowned.

What of your great-grandfather Edmund Strang-Leven who was cheated out of his inheritance by this family? persisted his business brain. *Isn't that why you're here and not in Buckinghamshire? Isn't that the reason you've invested so much time in her? You've managed to retrieve part of your stolen inheritance: the mansion in Hanover Square. You're almost there. Don't lose sight of what's important. What your father dreamed of regaining; remember your prime objective!*

Don't listen to him, what does he know? countered his heart. *He's helped you amass wealth, capitalize on a multitude of business opportunities, taken you all over the subcontinent to some fascinating places and to meet interesting people, but he didn't bring you back here to this cold wet island. You'd not have come if you'd listened to him. You'd have stayed in India where you belong. It's not objectives but family that made you leave your life behind. I brought you here, obligation and doing what's right and good, not what's profitable, that's why you're in England. And if you are truly honest with yourself, you've not listened to me since Emily died. I've been ignored and neglected for so long now that you don't know love when it's staring you between the eyes. And I'm not talking about the love you have for your daughter. That's different. This is different. But you're listening to me now, aren't you, because two minutes in Antonia Roxton's company and it was goodbye Business Brain!*

But it was me who saw her first, argued his most vital organ. *Those two minutes were mine, and every night since then has been sleepless for both of us, me waking him up, stiff as a board, wanting to make love to her, imagining her enjoying me, and then you had to get in the way, Heart. You took away my self-assurance, made me doubt myself, wonder if such a woman would be at all interested in me as a lover when she was married to an arrogant so-and-so who could get it up and keep it up in sub-arctic conditions if that's what it took to satisfy her! And now I can't make good on the promise with Business Brain to seduce her, take the house and move on. I'm the one suffering the most here! When was the last time I had any attention? India! That's when.*

As if you have anything to truly complain about, argued Heart. *It's been fifteen years in the wilderness for me!*

What sentimental clap-trap, Heart! Business Brain said dismissively. *And you, Vital Organ, you're just having a panic attack because it's been awhile since you've been inside a woman. Vital organs have crises of confidence from time to time. It's perfectly natural. It's nothing to do with this woman. There are plenty of beautiful women only too willing to pay you attention, straddle you, invite you in. What you need is a visit to that high-class bordello Tommy told you about; give yourself a good long workout between a pair of luscious thighs and you'll be back to your confident self.*

You just don't grasp what's going on here, do you, Business Brain? Heart and Vital Organ replied in unison. *Listen. It's different this time. She is different. We are different. Everything is different. None of us are ever going to be the same again.*

Well, I don't know about you lot, but I'm hungry, growled Stomach. *You'd think he'd know by now that one apple barely constitutes sustenance! And if we don't eat soon I guarantee that all of us are going to suffer.*

"Oh God," Jonathon uttered, a hand shielding his eyes from the sun, suddenly ill.

He pitched the apple core out across the glassy surface of the still lake and watched it go plonk and disappear, annoyed he had allowed his thoughts, or was it his organs, to take an unexpectedly melancholy and thoroughly introspective turn on such a glorious day and in the company of this most delightful companion. He slumped down in the boat, thinking that perhaps ten minutes shuteye might settle his organs and restore his equilibrium, but in so doing caught his stockinged foot in the layers of Antonia's petticoats and disturbed her reading.

"*Pardonnez-moi, Mme la duchesse,*" he muttered and went to sit up but she stayed him with a hand to his foot tangled in her petticoats.

"I want to read on, but you must be hungry so we will have nuncheon first. In the pavilion, yes?" she said, the laughter still in her eyes, making Jonathon wonder if she had heard his tummy grumble and his thoughts as well. "I want to discuss this play with you very much, but perhaps I will wait until I have read the entire script."

"What scene have you just finished reading?"

"Scene two of act four; it is where Sir Oliver he is chatting with Moses about Charles's extravagance."

"But he would not sell my picture!" quoted Jonathon, dramatically mimicking what he supposed would be a creditable Sir Oliver Surface. "Our young rake has parted with his ancestors like old tapestry, but he would not sell my picture!"

Antonia laughed at his paraphrasing. "And he was so impressed was he not, Sir Oliver, that he means to pay all Charles's debts!" She straightened her legs, wiggled her toes and also slumped against the cushions, arms spread out across the sides of the boat, adding with a smile, "How did you manage to get M'sieur Sheridan to part with his script?"

"I didn't. This is a copy. Had it transcribed while I was up in London. Dick Sheridan wasn't too keen. And I understand his reticence. The play has yet to be performed and he still might make changes to it. But when I told him who I wanted the copy for, he couldn't give his play to my scribe quick enough!"

"You told him it was for *me*?" Antonia was surprised and mystified.

Her puzzlement had Jonathon shaking his head in disbelief. "Now, Mme la duchesse, don't pretend to be so taken aback. There must be hundreds if not many hundreds of would be playwrights, poets and novel hacks seeking the patronage of the Duchess of Roxton. One word from you would sell every copy of a book, all the seats in a theater; make a man's fortune overnight!"

"Yes. But that one word from me could also ruin a hopeful scribbler, *vous comprenez*? Not that I would do such a wicked thing."

Jonathon wiggled her toe playfully. "You could never be wicked..." He smiled crookedly. "Well, not in a bad way... I'm glad you approve of Dick's *School for Scandal*," he continued blandly when she looked away, out across the water, giving him a view of her lovely profile, before looking down at the script in her lap. "The lad has talent, and this play will prove it to the doubters once and for all time. I've not laughed so hard in a long while. I never did see *The Rivals* performed but reading the script and the antics of Sir Lucius O'Trigger and Sir Antony Absolute were enough for me to invest a considerable sum in his venture to manage Drury Lane theater. I've procured a box for opening night..." He wiggled her toe again and this time took hold of her foot, saying when she met his gaze, "He thinks there is only going to be an opening night and no nights to follow. I say that's a great pile of elephant dung. He's being over-modest and to prove him

219

wrong I've given my word to underwrite the entire night's takings should he have a repeat of the disastrous opening night of *The Rivals*. But that's not going to happen. And for two good reasons..."

"Yes? I see that you are bursting to tell me," Antonia playfully taunted him when he hesitated and looked suddenly serious. "What are these two good reasons?"

But he wasn't bursting to tell her, he was unexpectedly nervous because he feared rejection when he revealed what he had promised the playwright. At the time it had been a boast, a moment of hubris, but now sitting across from her in a small boat, her foot comfortably in his hand, she smiling at him enquiringly, he felt a great big fool. God, how did she have the power to reduce him to frumenty? He decided to barge his way through the whole explanation and with as much bravado as possible so she wouldn't be able to say no.

"Firstly, and most obviously, it's a damn good play and, in my humble opinion, better written than *The Rivals*."

"That is a very good first reason," Antonia agreed. "And the second?" she prompted when he hesitated.

"Secondly, I promised Dick Sheridan I'll have a duchess sitting beside me when the curtain goes up on the first performance..."

Antonia waited for further explanation, all polite enquiry, as if he needed to supply her with the name of this duchess who was to sit beside him. He couldn't believe she had no idea he was talking about her. He was dumbfounded and tongue-tied. His organs turned over and his stomach churned. He smiled weakly. And that made her sit up very straight. Her foot slipped from his grasp as she did so and she stared hard at him, a hand to her throat. He not only felt a fool, he knew he was one.

"You promised M'sieur Sheridan that *me* I would attend the opening night of his play with-with *you*?"

He decided to put on a brave face. He sat up in the boat too.

"Well, Mme la duchesse! I don't know what upsets me more, that you will disappoint poor Dick Sheridan, who is so looking forward to you gracing one of his plays with your divine presence—after all you did not attend the opening night of *The Rivals*, despite the very nice invitation he sent you—or that you are amazed at the prospect of attending the theater with yours truly."

"No! No! You are not to be offended in the least!" Antonia assured him. "It's just that I have not attended the theater since... We—Monseigneur and I—of course we often went to the theater during the season. I love the theater, but since he left me, I have not thought about going at all. That is why I did not attend the opening night of *The Rivals*. I could not go without Monseigneur. For me to attend now, without him..." She smiled apologetically. "I do not believe it possible... I cannot attend, M'sieur."

Jonathon nodded sadly, as if in agreement, and sighed. Antonia leaned forward, concerned, a hand out, as if to console him for his disappointment when suddenly he leapt to his feet, rocking the boat violently.

Instantly, Antonia's hands flung out left and right to grip the sides of the boat and she stared up at him, startled.

"Well, if that's your answer, then there is nothing for it. I'll have to drown myself!" he announced, legs splayed to keep himself upright and the boat stable.

"You are being ridiculous! Sit down!"

He crossed his arms.

"Only if you say yes, you'll attend the theater with me."

"No!"

"So you want me to drown myself?"

"Of course not! Why would I want you to do such a thing? Sit down!"

He kicked off his shoes.

"You won't go to the theater with me. Therefore I have no recourse but to drown myself."

"You are a lunatic!"

"Lunatic or not, I will drown myself if you don't agree to see Dick Sheridan's play with me."

"I do not believe you and I will not be coerced in this shameful way! Sit down!"

In one easy movement he pulled the white cotton shirt up over his wide shoulders and flung it in a corner of the boat. He scraped the tussle of thick brown hair out of his eyes to stare down into her upturned face.

"Are you attending the opening night of Dick Sheridan's new play with me or not?"

Antonia did not know where to look with a half-naked Goliath standing over her like a bronzed replica of the Colossus of Rhodes. He was all wide chest, hard stomach and narrow hips, far too masculine for his own good. How dare he keep stripping off in front of her? She would not look at him. She stared out across the lake to the shoreline of reeds and then over her right shoulder, at the jetty, not so far off, but in her present predicament, so far away; anywhere but up at him. She not unreasonably expected a servant, at the very least one of her ladies-in-waiting to appear at her elbow. After all, she had spent most of her life with soft-footed silent servants within earshot if not in line of sight of her. She had no idea what a servant could do that she could not, as they had even less sway over his actions than she did. But of course there were no servants only water all around her and she was alone with this man who was standing up in a rowing boat without his shirt and expecting her to acquiesce to his request and the only thought uppermost in her mind at that moment was what he must look like completely naked. This so shocked and flustered her that she wished with all her being that she knew how to swim. She could then dive into the lake and swim away and be as far from him as possible.

Anger masked desire.

"You will not force my hand, M'sieur! No! I will *not* attend the theater with you! Now you will sit and row me back to shore. I am done with your company for today!"

Jonathon stared down at her with mute obstinacy. Inside he was delighted with her animated intractability after the previous week of listless introspection. Since retuning from the mausoleum he had kept his distance, taking up residence in the pavilion where he wrote letters to Sarah-Jane, Tommy, his man of business in London, and to his dying ancient relative's carers; and kicked his heels in the kitchen, sitting at the table chatting with Pierre and the other servants whom he had released from their banishment to the Gatehouse and who now looked to him for direction. He had also co-opted several of the outdoor servants to help him in a building project by the stand of old oaks, something he hoped would not only delight Antonia but her grandchildren when next they visited.

Michelle was the only one to have contact with the Duchess, who remained in bed with a cold, nursing her wounds, and who, in Michelle's opinion, should not be left alone with her thoughts for much longer or there was a very great chance of her falling back into that pit of despair she had inhabited when the old Duke had died three years ago.

Hence Jonathon's idea for nuncheon in the pavilion and a pleasant idle in a rowboat while the pavilion was being readied. The copy of Sheridan's script *School for Scandal* had been the lure he knew she could not resist. That she was surprised and seemed almost annoyed to find him still at her house when she had emerged from her rooms had bruised his feelings more than he cared to admit. It meant she had not given him a thought since their night together in the mausoleum; whereas he had spent every night since in restless sleep thinking of nothing and no one but her.

And so having her undivided attention, regardless of her anger, and she a captive audience, was an opportunity not to be squandered, even if it meant he would have to sacrifice his newly laundered clothes to the lake gods.

"So you are utterly determined you won't go to the theater on my arm?" he repeated, staring down into her upturned face with a heavy frown. "No chance I can change your mind? That you might accompany me to the theater for the opening night of Dick Sheridan's play all to seal the reputation of my playwright friend and partner. Well, Mme la duchesse?"

"You are being unbelievably dramatic and I do not understand why you threaten to do such a ridiculous thing over a trifle of a circumstance!" she argued, glaring up at him before looking away. "It is absurd. It is silly. And you are being puerile for its own sake!"

And insufferably arrogant and what I really want you to do is hold me as you did in the mausoleum so I can hear the strong regular beat of your heart, feel the hardness and strength in your chest and limbs, and smell the warm musky masculine scent of your bronzed skin so that I may have an unbroken night's sleep, which I have not had in a sennight! It is your fault and I stayed in my rooms hoping you would go away but not really wanting you to go away at all but fearing what might happen if you remained with me here at my house.

Of course she voiced none of these thoughts. Instead she stared up at Jonathon in mutinous fury, more angry with herself than with this half-naked handsome man for allowing him to get under her skin.

"I will *not* be coerced in this way! Drown for all I care."

"Very well. Then it's the bottom of the lake for me!"

It happened within the blink of an eye.

One moment he was standing before her; the next, she was the only occupant of the rowing boat. There was a single splash in the lake, the water rippling and radiating from the point of entry close to the starboard side, and out across the still water. The boat rocked. And then the water was still again. It was as if he had never been in the boat at all and Antonia had woken from a dream to find herself alone. But Richard Brinsley Sheridan's play *School for Scandal* was on her lap and Jonathon's shoes and shirt were discarded in the stern.

She gathered up the pages of script, quickly put them aside and scrambled across the cushions to the edge of the boat to peer into the lake. The water was unbroken and unfathomable. Where had he gone? He could not simply disappear! He could not drown *himself*, he was too good a swimmer. Good swimmers did not drown... Unless... What if in his silliness he had hit his head on some part of the boat as he went over the side and had knocked himself out and was at that very minute taking water into his lungs in some icy depths below the boat? What if he was stuck under the hull? *Foolish. Idiotic. Impossible man.* She pulled her petticoats aside and clambered across to the bowside and peered into the water, hoping not to see a splayed out Jonathon, face down and drifting lifeless in the lake. Perhaps if she leaned over a bit further she might catch a glimpse of the underside and if he was caught there...

A great whoosh of water sprang into the air like the jet of a fountain turned on full and water sprayed across and into the boat. Antonia fell back, her face and the front of her bodice and petticoats instantly soaked. Startled by the cold water, air was sucked down her throat in gasps and such was the force of the water jet that the little rowboat rocked violently. Her wrists buckled and unable to hold firm to the edge of the boat and with her eyes shut tight against further sprays she became disorientated, pitched forward and fell with a splat into the lake.

Terrified, her arms and legs flailed about, splashing wildly and her petticoats twisted up and became heavy with water and she felt herself sinking into the murky depths. Desperate to keep her head above water, she was unaware that the instant fountain that had suddenly sprung up out of the lake and just as quickly died, was in fact Jonathon. He had held his breath underwater for as long as he thought it necessary for her to believe for a sliver of a second that he may have carried out his threat and drowned. His ruse miscarried miserably when he realized Antonia had overbalanced into the water and, as a non-swimmer, was scrambling to stay afloat in the worse possible way—panic stricken and floundering.

He tried to pacify her but she was not listening and when he went to her aid and tried to take her in his arms and calm her, she did not see him. She saw only a possible means of escape out of the water and she scrambled up his torso and tried to sit on his head; not unlike a cat having fallen into a vat of cream and terrified was less interested in the substance than in getting the hell out of there by any means possible, as long as the means was sturdy and would lead to dry land and a dry skin.

When reasoning failed he caught her arms and pinioned her to him, all the while telling her in his deep measured tone to look at him; that she would not drown; that no harm would come to her if she stilled and just looked at him. He repeated his commands over again and on the fifth repeat, when his voice penetrated her subconscious and she quieted, he told her he would let go of her arms and she would not drown. Finally, she looked at him and for the brief moment their eyes met he knew that she was finally aware of him. With utter relief, she clung to him, heaving air into her lungs as her arms tightened about his shoulders and her legs anchored about his waist. He held her with one strong arm to her back while the other, with the help of his legs, sculled the water to keep them both afloat.

In all the commotion they had drifted from the boat, and were half way between the reedy shoreline and the boat in one direction and about the same distance from the jetty where Antonia's two whippets had suddenly appeared bounding along the wooden planks barking to make their presence known. The water was still too deep for Jonathon's feet to feel the bottom of the lake and stand, despite his height, so he drifted with Antonia clinging to him, quiet in the water, not saying a word, wanting her to get her breath back and waiting for the fear to subside; knowing that if they floated a little while longer the feeling of weightlessness that came with being calm in water would stop the rapid beating of her heart and that in his arms she could not drown; she was safe.

Finally, he felt soft earth and washed pebble under his toes and was able to stand. The depth of the water reached just above his navel. He bent his knees to lower his shoulders back into the water, which let Antonia sit on his lap, and with both arms around her they were now at eye level. She still clung to him tightly, fearing that if she let go, even for the smallest of moments, she would plunge into the depths of the lake and never be seen again.

It was only when he pulled back slightly that she finally loosened her vice-like grip about his strong neck, realizing they were no longer drifting in the water; that he had stopped swimming and was now somehow anchored. She kept her fingers entwined at the nape of his neck, but knowing his arms held her safe she was able to breath easy and was no longer afraid. Not since their night together in the mausoleum when she had slept soundlessly in his arms had they been this physically close. Since then, they had gone out of their way to maintain a suitable and respectable distance and neither had spoken about that night or the events that had preceded it.

But here, in the still cool water of the lake, they were so close that she could count each deep line that radiated from the corners of his soft brown eyes, and he, every long dark lash framing her slightly oblique green eyes. She regarded him anew, searching his face hoping to find a flaw, something, anything, in the ruggedly handsome features to give her a reason to look away, a reason to stop drawing nearer, to wanting to put her mouth to his.

He smiled softly into her eyes, as if reading her thoughts, and she felt her face flush with heat despite the coldness of the water. And when he brushed the hair out of his eyes before gently removing a strand of her long hair plastered across her cheek, she did not draw away but smiled back.

They stared at one another for what seemed an eternity of minutes but was in fact no time at all. He desperately wanted to kiss her, for her to kiss him. But he would not initiate that first kiss. He could not. She had to do that. He was paralyzed by the possibility of rejection; that after the trauma she had suffered at the hands of a monster-physician and the ever-present specter of her Monseigneur looming large over them both, any move on his part would somehow be misconstrued. He just hoped all his organs remained on their best behavior and was thankful he was dipped in cold water.

She was obviously blissfully unaware, which was a good thing, but he was acutely conscious that her petticoats floated up around her breasts, leaving her naked from the waist down so that she straddled his lap in nothing but her white stockings that ended just above the knee. Her naked thighs were wide-open, ankles crossed at his lower back, so that she was pressed hard up against his groin. Had the lake not provided a blanket of respect-ability the world would have been presented with an erotically charged scene lifted straight from the Kama Sutra.

He considered it wise to take his thoughts and desires off to lunch, and wondered what delectable dishes the venerable Pierre had contrived to not only excite his tastebuds but also to satisfy his hunger pains. Since he had got rid of Sir Titus and his oafish assistants, Jonathon had become the darling of the household. Chef was his particular champion and no dish, no request was too small for Pierre to fulfill. If M'sieur Strang he wanted for breakfast brioche and his strange hot milky tea infused with cloves, cinna-mon, pepper and anise, which he called Chai tea, it was not for anyone to quibble or question about; he could have it. If M'sieur Strang he only wanted Pierre to serve him dishes containing vegetables and fish and no beef, that was what he Pierre would contrive for M'sieur. Jonathon hoped that for lunch garlic, ginger and pepper were involved, and that there was a rich soup and one of Pierre's mouth-watering flaky pastries...

And then it happened.

She kissed him.

It was feather-light and tentative and lasted but a moment because his mouth was slightly numb from cold and so he was clumsy in his response; not surprising given they were up to their necks in lake water and their lips were turning blue. But she had kissed him and he couldn't have been happier had she jumped on top of him naked and ravished him. She had kissed him. He was giddy. It was the most wonderful kiss he had experienced since his tenth birthday when he had clumsily kissed Digby Spencer's sister Charlotte on the lips under his uncle's library desk. He had been so proud of himself and walked as if on clouds for a week. This kiss like that was so longed for, so thought about and so anticipated that he was left momentarily stunned, as he had been as a ten-year-old, to have his wish fulfilled.

There was no second hesitation to returning her kiss, and when he kissed her, when he brushed his mouth against hers he was just as gentle and diffident as she had been. But Antonia did not draw back as he had and she was not so reticent in her response. It was all the encouragement he needed to press his mouth to hers, to feel the cushion of her mouth, the full lips yield under the pressure of his and finally they gave themselves up to a deeply sensual and utterly pleasurable kiss that was everything hoped for and desired.

So wrapped up in each other and the moment were they that their watery surroundings disappeared. Jonathon rose up out of the water and waded through the reeds toward the bank with Antonia pressed against him, arms about his neck, his large hands splayed across her bare bottom holding her firm against his groin, her stockinged legs wrapped around his torso, sopping wet petticoats bunched up over his arms and pouring water back into the lake; all of it on display to the world. And the world, such as it was in that quiet little corner of Hampshire, was watching.

Seventeen

Somewhere in the deep recesses of his mind, his brain alerted him to the fact they were not alone; they were being observed, not by one person but several and dogs were somehow involved. But his vital organ, having survived the rigors of freezing water and thawing out nicely, thank you very much, ordered his brain to go away. *Was his brain mad?* He had in his arms the most extraordinarily beautiful and bewitching woman he had ever encountered, they were enjoying a heated exploratory kiss, his hands were full of her lovely round derriere and she was pressed against him, warming him up, and his brain was saying stop, all because somewhere far off there were people and dogs about? Not on King George's life was he going to give up this moment. People and dogs could go hang.

The calls from the jetty and the barking of dogs were ignored.

Jonathon's vital organ urged him on, growing stronger and more confident as he approached the bank. Knowing she was naked and her legs wide open to receive him sent him beyond wisdom, and all that mattered was getting out of the water as quickly as possible so he could mount her on solid ground. He had spent too many nights unbearably rigid, throbbing without relief and now was his chance to finally fulfill his most secret desire and nothing and no one was going to stop him. Not if she wanted Nirvana as much as he did, which she did. The sweet responsiveness of her mouth under his, the way she was kissing him, how her tongue played with his, that she was pressed hard up against him, was indication enough that the moist warmth between her thighs was his for the taking if he could just get this last wretched breeches button undone and the drawstring to his drawers untied...

The shouts grew louder, the barking more insistent.

Antonia's whippets had pranced around from the jetty and were pacing back and forth on the bank on the far side of a curtain of willow branches where their mistress had been brought to safe ground. The black whippet bounded into the willow branches, barking at Jonathon only to become tangled and slip off the bank into the water. It retreated with a yelp, tale between its legs, and shook cold water from its coat. Its white and tan companion was not as intrepid and remained on the jetty side of the willow branch curtain but had a louder and longer bark and was determined to get the attention of his mistress, or better still their mistress's maid who had picked up her petticoats and was scurrying along the jetty; one of the men went to follow her but his companion remained at the end of the jetty and called him back.

And then Jonathon's racing heart and the cool business part of his brain combined forces and his vital organ, despite pleading an excruciating need, was overruled.

This is not how I want to spend my first time with her, Heart lectured, appalled, *sodden on a muddy bank engaged in a quick tawdry rut. She deserves the very best of care and every attention. She deserves cool silken sheets and feather pillows and a magnificent four-poster bed. I want to make love to her, slowly and deliberately. I want her to know how I feel.*

And what I want the both of you to do is leave the thinking to me, Business Brain lectured Vital Organ and Heart. *She's a duchess for God's sake and her son is a duke and he'll have your ballocks for buckshot if he even suspects you tried to mount her. Not to mention what she'll think of you after the event! You'll never get a second chance and Heart, don't think she'll believe you when you tell her that you've fallen in love with her! Vital Organ will have ruined that for you. Now pull yourself together before it's too late to resurrect your self-esteem, and hers too. And don't forget about the house and—*

Oh, do shut up about the bloody house, Business Brain! Heart and Vital Organ demanded wearily.

Jonathon lifted his head from kissing the base of Antonia's throat and half-rose, removing his hand from between her thighs; face flushed and short of breath. The color deepened in his lean cheeks realizing just how close he had been to taking her there and then under the willow trees, and because she was looking at him uncomprehendingly and with confusion in her lovely green eyes. He quickly untangled the wet heavy layers of her bunched up petticoats and pulled them roughly over her bare thighs and covered her stockinged legs.

Antonia blinked up at him dazed and disorientated, breath ragged, not wanting him to stop kissing and caressing her; left utterly unsatisfied. She did not understand why he had suddenly and inexplicably pulled away, why he had stopped stroking her, when it was surely evident that she wanted him to make love to her as much as he seemed intent on having her there and then on the bank of the lake. She had finally lowered her defenses and kissed him, which was invitation enough of her desire, and his response was everything she had hoped for and more and then he had inexplicably rejected her...Why?

And then a hundred possible reasons presented themselves and she swallowed, embarrassed. Her green eyes lost their confusion and became wary. She scrambled to sit up, adjusting her bodice, which was outrageously askew, and made motions to wring out her sodden petticoats. She would not look at him and when she went to stand he helped her up but he would not let her go. She tried to turn her head away but he stopped her with a finger under her chin and gently touched his forehead to hers with a small smile of understanding and brown eyes full of apology.

"Sweetheart... It's not that I don't want to... I want to *so very much*. It's—"

"Do not try and explain to me... It is unnecessary for you—"

He caught her face between his hands and halted her words with his mouth. It was a long leisurely kiss and when she yielded, when she leaned into him, a hand up around his neck, he placed her other hand between his legs, saying as he came up for air, "You understand *nothing*," he murmured huskily. "I want you beyond reason. *He* wants you. I've told him to behave, but he has no manners where you are concerned and will not listen."

Antonia stared up at him and her eyes went wide exploring the length and breadth of his rigidity straining against the confinement of fine linen, the drawstring of his undergarment holding him captive. She could not help herself and allowed her gaze to drop between his thighs before looking up into his brown eyes with a twinkle. "He has reason for his arrogance," she replied softly, on tiptoe, kissing his lower lip and playfully tugging on the drawstring. "*Il est magnifique...* I want to unwrap my present now."

"*Mon Dieu, vous me torturez,*" he responded thickly, brain drained of purpose and heart quickening, his vital organ more triumphant than ever and yet there was sufficient reason left, if only in his pinkie, for him to be able to stay her hand, adding in a dry voice, "We have company... Your maid... And others..."

Instantly, Antonia fell away. All the cold, the shivering and discomfort she should have felt at having accidentally tumbled into the lake and being soaked to the skin, dripping wet from the unraveled heavy knot of hair to stockinged toes, now invaded her being and she hugged her arms around her breasts. Her knees went weak and her hands shook, not only from cold but also at the shame of her reckless wantonness. *Dear God, had she lost her senses, she a duchess, and at her age?* She shuddered. *What would Julian say to it? What would M'sieur le Duc...* She mentally pulled herself up from spiraling into the past, gaze sweeping Jonathon's bare wide back as he turned away to adjust his clothing. He was so ruggedly virile, warm and pulsing with life and such a good kisser and the wonderful way his tongue and his fingers knew instinctively where to... *Stop.*

She turned in time to catch her maid also turn her back on her. "Michelle! Why do you stand there as a statue when me I need a shawl at the very least!" she demanded, parting the curtain of willow branches, anger with herself making her sound uncharacteristically harsh. "Scipio! Cornelia! *Talon!*" she commanded when her two whippets poked their wet noses tentatively through the willow curtain then trotted at her heels demanding to be noticed.

Receiving a perfunctory pat, they were satisfied enough to break through the tangle of overhanging branches to trot up to their new-found friend Jonathon, who was standing on the edge of the bank looking out across the lake to the jetty.

"Yes, Mme la duchesse. At once, Mme la duchesse," Michelle replied with a curtsey, eyes remaining fixed on her feet, cheeks apple red; signal she had seen more than she ought. "I will go immediately to fetch a—"

"No. No. I need a warm bath, so me I will come with you," Antonia replied in an even tone. "The boat... It overturned."

"Yes, Mme la duchesse," Michelle replied obediently and dared to glance out across the lake to where the rowboat bobbed gently undisturbed. When she gave a start it was enough to make Antonia look over her shoulder towards the lake.

Jonathon had waded back into the water and was swimming towards the rowboat.

"*Il est complètement fou* and me I am an *imbécile*," she muttered and hurried on ahead of her maid up to the house without looking back.

"Sir Titus?"

A soberly dressed gentleman in brown bobwig standing at the edge of the jetty stared down into the water where Jonathon, whom he had addressed, was standing in the rowboat and had flung a rope up onto the wooden planks.

"Throw that over the bollard," Jonathon commanded. "There's a good fellow."

The soberly dressed gentleman blinked down at Jonathon uncomprehendingly and so it was the older man standing two steps behind at his side, a dapper little gentleman in a scarlet silk waistcoat under his plain black frockcoat, a matching scarlet riband tying his silver hair at his nape, who, despite holding to his chest several small leather-bound and gold stamped books, scurried forward to do Jonathon's bidding.

"Sir Titus?" the soberly dressed gentleman enunciated again in his most patient voice. "Sir Titus Foley?"

Jonathon held up a pile of paper and waved this at the gentleman. "Take this. Bend down! Bend down! I'm tall but not a giant, man!" When the gentleman did his bidding he added, "Take it in both hands. Can't afford for it to fall into the drink. Dick would be sorely disappointed and she would never forgive me. Got it in both hands? Good. Now pass it to your bookish friend before you stand up."

The soberly dressed gentleman did as requested and passed the manuscript to his bookish friend with the scarlet riband, who juggled the manuscript and the books until all were snugly held to his scarlet waistcoat with no fear of them falling into the lake or elsewhere. The soberly dressed gentleman then scrambled to his feet and brushed his breeches free of dirt. His bookish companion smirked at such fastidious efforts; he thought him a pompous prig.

Jonathon climbed out of the rowboat and up onto the jetty with the practiced ease of a man used to physical exercise. He cast a wary eye on the two visitors, who were startled by his height and width, which was not evident while he was standing in the boat, and now craned their necks to look up at him as he slipped on his flat heeled shoes with plain silver buckles. He addressed the old gentleman hugging Sheridan's *School for Scandal* to his chest.

"Mind if you hold on to that a bit longer? I'm too wet for paper and I'd hate to ruin such fine words."

The soberly dressed prig coughed into his hand and said at his most polite, "Sir Titus, I am here at—"

"Who wants to know?"

"I beg your pardon, my lord?"

"Who are you?" Jonathon asked mildly as he turned on a heel, forcing the men to follow him. "Apologies. But I need to change out of these wet garments before I catch my death and Dick Sheridan is forced to write my eulogy."

"Mr. Philip Audley and Mr. Gidley Ffolkes, and your most humble, Sir Titus. We are in the employ of His Grace of Roxton. I am the Duke's secretary and Mr. Ffolkes is librarian here at Treat and keeper of the Roxton *Bibliothèque*."

Jonathon glanced over his shoulder, saw the men had fallen behind and waited. Gidley Ffolkes' bright blue eyes looked vaguely familiar, and he glanced at the books under his arm. "Are those for her Grace?"

"Yes, my lord."

"She'll be pleased to see you then, Ffolkes. And you, Audley?"

Jonathon asked as he continued on up the rise of lawn towards the pavilion. "To what do we owe the pleasure of your company here on this unseasonably warm April day?"

"Your report, Sir Titus," Philip Audley called out, several paces behind Jonathon, unable to match his stride.

"Report?"

"Your report to his Grace."

Jonathon went up into the pavilion two steps at a time.

"Tell me more, Audley."

"As part of the conditions under which you have been engaged by his Grace, my lord, you are to pen a report—"

"About what?"

Philip Audley breathed deeply and made fists of his hands hanging loosely at his sides. He wondered if the physician was as mad as his patients. Gidley Ffolkes grinned; he had taken an instant liking to Jonathon's straight-talking approach. The Duke's secretary coughed and cleared his throat.

"It is a delicate matter... One that I am not qualified to elaborate on."

"You're the Duke's secretary, aren't you?"

"Yes, my lord, but that hardly—"

"You read all his correspondence, draft replies, copy out in your fist documents on this and that and the other. Put the more important bits under his Grace's fine nose and deal with the rest yourself... Isn't that what any secretary worth his salt does for his master?"

"Well, yes, my lord, that is part of my duties for his Grace," Philip Audley blustered, completely out of his depth, "but I fail to see what—"

"Then you know full-well what this delicate matter is all about, so why not just come out and say it?"

The secretary's mouth worked but he was lost for words. He was used to blunt speech from his employer but that was from a nobleman, a Duke, but this loose-limbed Goliath was little more than a purveyor of simples and so he threw a glance at the librarian, expecting the little man to be as horrified as he was, only to discover him not so much holding the books to his chest as hugging them, lips disappeared as if to suppress laughter. Jonathon saw this too and indicated the low table where he noticed, for the first time, covered dishes, cutlery, crockery and a jug of ale and several tumblers. His stomach growled in acknowledgement of Pierre's culinary munificence.

"Off load yourself, Ffolkes, and be good enough to pour each of us a tumbler of ale at the very least."

He looked back at the Duke's secretary. There was something about the man that oozed obsequious efficiency of the worse kind and for this he took him in instant dislike.

"Well?"

"As you are the Dowager Duchess's physician, my lord, it hardly requires that I voice aloud the reason you have been employed by his Grace," Philip Audley said haughtily, the dislike now mutual. "You know it. I know it."

"Ah, now you become interesting, Audley," Jonathon said with a deceptive smile as he picked up off the low wall a towel that was drying nicely in the sun. He had used it earlier that morning, just on dawn, to dry off after shaving and bathing in the lake down by the stand of old oaks. He wiped his face and towel-dried his hair and looked at the secretary with practiced neutrality. "You say I know it, but why should you know it? And what do you indeed know?"

"I beg your pardon, my lord, but you said yourself as his Grace's secretary I have recourse to correspondence, documents and the like, so it is perfectly reasonable that I am well aware of the—um—er—*deterioration* in the Dowager Duchess's—um—*mind*, which has led to this most lamentable state of affairs," the secretary enunciated, waving away the tumbler of ale offered him by the librarian despite a throat parched from frustration. "I was the one who drew up the document which you signed and which requires that you—" He stopped abruptly, realizing his audience was not listening, when Jonathon threw the towel over the balustrade and twirled his index finger for them to turn their backs.

Jonathon quickly stripped out of his wet stockings, breeches and drawers and wiped himself dry then wrapped the towel about his hips and secured it before shrugging into his spare shirt, freshly laundered by the Duchess's very obliging laundresses and brought to him, along with his second pair of breeches, drawers, linen stock and stockings, earlier that morning by Michelle. He would again have to inconvenience the Duchess's household to launder his sparse collection of clothing until his requested wardrobe arrived from London.

"Ffolkes! What is your opinion? Has the Dowager Duchess of Roxton diminished mental capacity?"

The librarian snorted into his ale and gulped but bravely turned to meet Jonathon's gaze and wiped his mouth. "No, no, my lord. She is naturally melancholy, but who can blame her?"

The secretary also turned back to face Jonathon and sighed loudly, throwing up a hand, all pretense of deference vanished.

"Come now, my lord! What's this?" Philip Audley complained. "You are the physician. Ffolkes is merely the family's librarian. What would he know?"

"Merely?" Jonathon pulled a face. "You're not a bookish man, are you, Audley? Your loss. There is nothing *merely* about being in charge of the Roxton *Bibliothèque*. I'd hazard a guess the combined collection of tomes from the various noble residences would rival any university's collection here or on the Continent. And as Mme la duchesse is a voracious reader and likes nothing better than to have her pretty little nose between the pages of a good text, my guess is that Ffolkes sees more of the Duchess than you, your noble employer, and certainly me put together! Ain't that the truth, sir?"

"Yes, my lord," the librarian agreed with a smile. "The library is Mme la duchesse's favorite room in any of their houses." Adding wistfully, "Mme la duchesse and M'sieur le Duc, may God rest his soul, spent many happy hours in the Treat library. She liked nothing better than to read in her favorite chair. It was the same at Hanover Square and of course, in Paris at the library there..." He teared up. "The loss of that house... The magnificent library... Such a great shock..."

"Yes, it must have been," Jonathon sympathized, realizing the dapper little man was referring to his own deep regret as much as he was to the Duchess's feelings. He offered the librarian a seat on the sofa by the low table and refilled the old man's tumbler. He then sat himself in front of the array of dishes, long legs folded up around his ears as he tried to be comfortable before a table meant for the Roxton children. There was a note atop one of the covers, which he read, informing him to partake of nuncheon without the Duchess. "You're welcome to join me, gentlemen. I can wait no longer." He passed the librarian a clean plate then removed the domed silver covers. When the secretary coughed, an annoying trait that made Jonathon want to throw a plate at his head, he looked up from spooning mushrooms smothered in garlic butter onto his plate. "Well? You heard Ffolkes's opinion. The Duchess is sad not mad." He winked at Gidley Ffolkes. "And who can blame her? Try Pierre's fish stew pie, it's excellent," he recommended to the librarian who was bravely partaking of Jonathon's offer to dine with him. When the secretary made a noise resembling a muffled scream, he again took his gaze from Pierre's delectable dishes to say bluntly, "What more do you want, Audley?"

The secretary gaped at him. He was now convinced the physician was as deranged as the morbid females under his care. "*Want?*" he repeated in a thin voice, "*I* do not *want* anything, sir! The Duke *demands* his weekly report which I have come to collect on his behalf!"

Jonathon swallowed a mouthful of fish pie and took a nibble at the sliver of flaky pastry lid in his hand. "A weekly report?"

"Yes! Yes! A weekly report! The report you are required to produce as part of the conditions of your employment."

"A little more pepper and a dash of lemon and the trout would be better for it. What do you think, Ffolkes?" and before the librarian could answer stretched out a hand for one of the asparagus tarts on offer, a glance up at the mule-faced secretary to say with practiced abstraction, "How many weeks did His Grace expect this employment to run for?"

The secretary bit down on his tongue and smiled thinly. He was on the point of demented rage. "If you recall, Sir Titus, you signed a contract for some four weeks of your services."

"*Four* weeks?" The bite of delectable cheese-smothered asparagus tartlet half consumed turned to ash on Jonathon's tongue and he dropped what was left onto his empty plate and swallowed reluctantly. "She was to spend *a month* under that dung beetle's care?" He downed a swig of ale and wiped the frown from his mouth with a napkin before tossing it aside. "Christ! Roxton needs his head read! And why hasn't he been a

Roxton needs his head read! And why hasn't he been a dutiful son and come to see her for himself? Aye, Audley, can you tell me that?"

"It is hardly your business to question—"

The rest of the secretary's sentence went unspoken because the librarian's silver fork clattered to his porcelain plate and the silver knife fell to the tiles as he tried to balance the plate and its contents on his knees. He met Jonathon's gaze with a queer little smile that split his face and when Jonathon smiled back with a wink, the librarian had his suspicions confirmed. He couldn't be happier or more relieved to discover this handsome giant of a man was not Sir Titus Foley. He liked Jonathon's off-hand approach and suspected that beneath the casual distracted demeanor there was a steely determination to get what he wanted. Watching him amuse himself with the haughty secretary was most entertaining.

"Your first report is now overdue," Mr. Audley enunciated into the silence, oblivious to the new understanding between Jonathon and the Roxton Librarian. "If you have the document, sir, then I ask you to hand it over so I may leave you and your patient in peace." And that moment couldn't come soon enough.

"I've got it!" Jonathon announced, sitting forward, a long finger waging at the librarian.

"If you've got it, then pray, sir, hand it over!" demanded the secretary.

"Those bright blue eyes! I knew I'd seen them before," Jonathon continued, proud to have made the connection at last. "There up on the wall in the Hanover Square dining room!"

Philip Audley edged closer to the table and looked from Jonathon, who was grinning at the librarian, and then to the librarian, who was beaming from ear to ear and nodding. The secretary scratched his bobwig, feeling he was the idiot fit for Bedlam, and waited.

"The report is at Hanover Square? Why would you send the report to Hanover Square?"

The secretary was ignored.

"Eyes are a family trait that one cannot hide, however successful we are at concealing other lesser attributes," Gidley Ffolkes said with a twinkle. "I spent the greater part of my life denying all knowledge of my familial connections, head in a book, or should I say books, at the Bodleian until my dear wife passed away... And then I came here, at the invitation of Mme la duchesse, to administer the Roxton *Bibliothèque*... And to live." He took a sip of ale and added with a smile, "If not for the Roxton libraries... If not for the great kindness of Mme la duchesse... Here I have found a second home."

"So who's the dapper relative and his wife up on the dining room wall?"

"My first cousin Lucian Ffolkes, Viscount Vallentine and, in the last four years of his life, Earl of Stretham Ely. Though he remained Vallentine to family and friends. His wife was M'sieur le Duc's sister. Their son Evelyn would be the present Lord Stretham Ely if his whereabouts were known, which they have not been for the better part of five years." The librarian pushed aside his plate and lifted his blue eyes to Jonathon's attentive gaze. "We must assume the boy has no idea both his parents died within weeks of each other and less than a year after M'sieur le Duc's death, leaving Mme la duchesse tragically alone. They were an inseparable four-some: M'sieur le Duc, Mme la duchesse and the Vallentines... And now I must presume I am the last of the Ffolkes and the title will die with me if the boy cannot be found. I say boy, but Evelyn is only a handful of years younger than Roxton."

"You do not use the title."

"No. I do not consider it mine to use. It belongs to Evelyn. I have every faith he will be found one day." The librarian smiled ruefully. "When he wants to be found that is."

All this was news to the secretary and he stared at Gidley Ffolkes as if at an ogre with not one but two ugly heads. "You're the heir to the Stretham Ely earldom? *You*? A *librarian*? *You* are a member of the-the *family*?" He was offended. "My lord, it is most disconcerting of you to let me think, to allow others to think, you are a mere librarian of no social distinction when in fact you are a peer of the realm who should, for the benefit of those beneath you, reveal yourself so that we may know how to conduct ourselves in the proper manner."

"What the deuce are you rabbiting on about, Audley?" Jonathon demanded, tapping the cheroots to the end of the silver case and offering one to the librarian, who declined. He lit his cheroot. "Ffolkes here could be a rat-catcher for all I care about the color of the blood in his veins. So try not to let it bother you; I'm sure it don't bother the family. And Ffolkes won't hold it against you. He hasn't yet." He inhaled as he reclined against the cushions, a hand over the back of the silk striped chaise longue, stretching out his long legs and crossing them at the ankles. The chaise made a much more comfortable bed than it did a place to dine, as he had discovered after sleeping six nights on the said piece of furniture. Though, having slept rough under the stars on innumerable occasions on the sub-continent, a padded chaise longue and an assortment of cushions was luxury. "I hope the coffee arrives pronto. Or would you prefer tea, Ffolkes?"

"Coffee would be most excellent, thank you."

Jonathon looked up at the secretary who was standing as a statue and continuing to stare at them with mute fury. "You still here, Audley? Would you prefer tea?"

"Tea? No! I would *not* prefer tea, sir. What I would prefer is your report. Now, if you please."

Jonathon reluctantly sat up at the sound of footsteps. Two footmen appeared, one carrying the tea things, the other, at Jonathon's signal, to clear away the remnants of nuncheon.

"Ffolkes, you play hostess. Audley?" he said, "Shouldn't you be getting back to sharpen His Grace's quills or decant his ink or whatever it is you do to keep yourself occupied? One sugar, Ffolkes. Oh, and before I forget... Here, you are welcome to cast your eye over this until Mme la duchesse is ready to receive you," he said, a hand flat to the manuscript of *School for Scandal*. "I have every confidence you will find it most amusing."

He picked up his dish of coffee and with the cheroot be-tween his fingers, took a leisurely sip of the bittersweet brew, a smile at the secretary who, as he hoped, was on the point of a demented rage. It was time to put the officious little toad out of his misery. "The report is in here, Audley," he stated, tapping a finger at his temple. "Now run along and make yourself useful. No! No, don't speak. No thanks are necessary. I'll be over the bridge directly to give my report but first I must have a second dish of coffee with my fellow bibliophile."

He turned to the librarian without another look at the secretary who, after a moment to collect himself from launching into a tirade about wasting the time of His Grace of Roxton's secretary, stomped off down the steps and was last seen crossing the lawn towards the stables. "I'd like your advice about the book room at Hanover Square..."

He then spent a leisurely half hour in companionable conversation with the librarian before following in the secretary's footsteps to the stables, leaving Gidley Ffolkes to enjoy Richard Sheridan's comedic genius.

Entering the pavilion, Antonia found the elderly librarian with Sheridan's manuscript upon his lap, tears of laughter streaking his face, the only indication Jonathon had been there, a pile of wet clothes and a towel in a heap beside a travelling portmanteau.

Eighteen

Jonathon was ushered into a sunny morning room with French windows that opened out onto an Elizabethan walled garden. French flowered wallpaper adorned with sprays of pink and white roses and small birds in flight on a sky blue background adorned the walls and matching drapes were pulled back to reveal the view, tied off with heavy tasseled rose gold and pink silk cord. Cotton chintz and tapestry cushions edged in a similar silk cord were scattered on the arrangement of sofas and occasional chairs up against three walls.

A fire blazed in the grate of the white marble fireplace above which hung a heavy gilt-edged framed portrait of the fifth Duchess of Roxton as a young girl, or so she seemed to Jonathon because she was far too young to have on her silken lap a little boy in short skirts, with a mop of unruly black ringlets and in his chubby fist a silver rattle. The artist had situated mother and child in a garden setting, possibly the garden he could see from the open windows, with white roses in bloom and two faithful hounds at her feet, and near the claw and ball foot of the chair, a small stack of books, one with a blue riband protruding to hold a place.

"This is where she wrote her letters," the Duchess said to Jonathon's grin and shake of the head as he peered closer to read the spines of the books; one was Tacitus. "There is a perfect view of the roses from here and she could watch Julian at play, on the carpet or he could run out into the walled garden; years

243

later, Henri-Antoine, Julian's younger brother, also played in here or in the garden. The picture behind you is a family portrait painted when Maman-Duchess and the Duke took Henri-Antoine to visit Julian who was in Constantinople at the time, on the Grand Tour."

Deborah Roxton came away from the lady's French *escritoire-a-toilette*, situated at the sunniest window where she had been reading a letter, and joined Jonathon in front of the large family portrait on the wall opposite the fireplace and waited for him to make the usual remark that all who admired this noble family grouping could not help to make because of their surprise at the age disparity between her husband who, in this portrait, was a young man not quite twenty years of age and his brother who was all of four years of age. But no such remark was forthcoming.

Jonathon stared up at the illustrious family grouping painted against a rich backdrop of mosaic tiled Ottoman interior: the fifth Duchess, still looking absurdly youthful, was seated, the central figure on the canvas, wearing what Jonathon presumed to be Ottoman attire—ankle-length billowy silk trousers, a long-sleeved shift of seersucker gauze that reached down to her bejeweled open backed slippers and over the whole a long-sleeved cardigan in shimmering gold thread, the edges trimmed in ermine. Atop her head was a small silk turban, her fair hair pulled over one shoulder and allowed to cascade to her waist; her youngest son Henri-Antoine, on her left, leaned across her lap with hand out-stretched and looking up adoringly at his elder brother; Julian was on his mother's right, a velvet elbow to the high back of her chair and offering his little brother a multicolored leather ball to play with. Beside him, in profile, a dapper older man with silver hair, in plain wool frockcoat and in his hand a map, possibly of the city of Constantinople. The Duke stood behind his youngest son, a long white hand over the back of his wife's chair, displaying the large square cut emerald ring, the other lay casually across the jeweled hilt of his sword, his head, with its shock of white hair, was tilted down, gaze firmly on the Duchess.

The only one in the portrait looking out on the world was Antonia, and with an enigmatic smile and a twinkle in her emerald-green eyes. Jonathon suspected the painter's secret wish was that she was looking exclusively at him.

"She was certainly the center of their world, wasn't she?" he said, not taking his gaze from the canvas. "The painter's composition and placement of the family conveys this very well. And though they wouldn't own to it, despite the age difference her sons are alike in form. Yet," he added, turning to look at Deborah Roxton for the first time since entering the room, "that may be where the parallel ends. Methinks Lord Henri-Antoine is a far more languorous young man than ever was his brother, or so he would have the world believe. Your nephew on the other hand, can barely sit still for two seconds."

"Oh, so you have met Henri and Jack?"

The Duchess was clearly surprised.

Jonathon bowed. "I had the pleasure of their company in Hanover Square for the sennight I was up in London. But you did not hear that from me, and you do not know that they are now my guests. I made them a solemn vow not to tell the Duke, and I have not done so." When Deborah frowned he added, "Better to have them in familiar surroundings and under a paternal eye, your Grace, than seeking the myriad of entertainments the city has to offer from unknown digs. And," he added with a wry smile, "to be fair to them, they were unaware that the house had been let, and fairly leapt to the ceiling when I made myself known to them."

"If you can tolerate having two fifteen-year-old boys under your roof, Mr. Strang, I cannot thank you enough. They are good boys with good hearts who are intent on the usual mischief their age indulges in. They have been a little neglected of late..."

The scene of Henri and Jack collapsed drunk across ribbon back chairs in the Hanover Square dining room that reeked of tobacco smoke and port, while two boon companions were breeches down, up against the polished mahogany table enjoying the oral talents of two plump prostitutes Jonathon kept to himself.

"But not by you, your Grace," he said with an understanding smile and turned back to the portrait with a questioning frown. "The gentleman in black... He is painted in this family portrait but is not part of the family?"

"Oh, no, Mr. Strang. Martin Ellicott is very much part of this family. He is Roxton's godfather and was valet to his father M'sieur le Duc for almost thirty years. He was the brave soul who accompanied my husband on the Grand Tour. But you did not come to talk to me about portraits, did you, Mr. Strang?" she added, putting out her hand in greeting.

"How remiss of me, your Grace," Jonathon responded, bowing over her hand and seeing her as if for the first time, an eye sweeping her petticoats of green striped muslin, her abundance of shiny auburn hair simply dressed, a weight of ringlets falling over her shoulders where a light woolen shawl was draped, despite the sun streaming through the windows and falling across the deep rugs. She was remarkably beautiful and majestic, with an innate self-assurance well suited to her elevation. Yet, she was rather out of place in these quintessentially feminine surroundings more suited to a butterfly than a lioness. "No, not portraits, but the people in them, certainly." The sound of children at play beyond the French doors made him smile. "Those squeals of delight are not coming from the gardeners, I presume?"

"The twins are determined to catch as many butterflies as their little nets will hold before their afternoon tea, and Julie is most entertained by her big brothers' efforts; hence the squeals."

"How fairs our pirate, your Grace?" he asked, mentally castigating himself; must his head always be full of thoughts of that other duchess?

"Fully recovered from his ordeal and intent on more adventures, Mr. Strang," she answered, and, despite the chairs, did not offer for him to sit, saying with a look about the room, "I agree with you. My surroundings are better suited to the fifth duchess than to me. One day I will do something about it, but for now... The children like it. Shall we walk in the gardens?" she continued smoothly, turning away to the desk to fiddle with the quill in the Standish because at mere mention of her mother-in-law her guest's face had flushed with color. She turned back with the same enigmatic smile, as if nothing untoward had occurred, adding as she picked up the wide-brimmed straw hat off the chair by the open French window, put it on and tied the white silk ribands in a loose bow below her chin, "I have been at that desk for two hours trying to complete all my correspondence because I promised to take the children beyond the wall to picnic by the bluebells which have shown themselves in profusion this year."

"Have they?" Jonathon politely enquired, following her out into the sunshine and along a path bordered with stands of rose bushes. In the distance, Louis dashed out from behind a fountain, net held high, only to disappear again. A shout of Huzzah! and Jonathon presumed a poor butterfly, or some such flying insect, had been captured. "My memory of bluebells blooming is scant at best."

"It is unseasonably warm weather for late April."

"Warm? Is it?"

"Very. Hence, you see the roses are also in bloom."

"Yes. The roses are quite lovely."

"I mean to send bunches to Maman-Duchess. White roses are her favorite."

"She'll like that very much..."

A small head of red curls with a cheeky grin showed itself from behind a statue of Aphrodite and cupid, net turned into a sword and this Gus waved menacingly in the air as his little sister ran past squealing, a nurserymaid hard on her little silk heels. Gus followed in pursuit, makeshift sword pointing toward the Heavens.

Deborah Roxton smiled indulgently at their antics and stopped at an intersection of paths where a team of gardeners were busily refurbishing the brass nozzles of a waterless fountain and cleaning a statue of Apollo atop a plinth. They tipped their hats and continued on with their work, she acknowledging them with a smile before walking on to be out of their way and then turning to Jonathon and lifting up the rim of her hat so he could clearly see her face.

"Mr. Strang, I am not one for small talk and you did not come here to discuss the weather or flowers. I think you also prefer plain speech to dissimulation so please do not spare my feelings. Why are you here and not in Buckinghamshire with your daughter?"

"Ha! Well said. I had hoped to spare your feelings, your Grace. I came to call upon the Duke and was directed to your pretty writing room instead. And I had every intention of joining Sarah-Jane at Lady Strathsay's little get-together but circumstances detained me here. Well, not here, but at Crecy Hall."

"I wonder what circumstances could possibly keep you from your daughter? Who, I may I say, does you great credit. She is a self-possessed young lady who knows her own mind and is wise beyond her years."

"Much like yourself, your Grace."

Deborah Roxton laughed at the compliment and continued on with the walk, turning left into a wide avenue of crushed stone bordered by orange and lemon trees in ornate tubs, Jonathon falling in beside her, hands clasped behind his back.

"Yes! She is, Mr. Strang," Deborah agreed. "I would own it as a Cavendish trait but I do believe she is more like you than she was ever like my cousin Emily. Although, in form she is her mother's daughter and I will own her pretty strawberry coloring to the Cavendish pedigree. She could make a great match if she so desired but..." She tilted her head to look at him. "I sense that is not your ambition for her...?"

"What I wish for Sarah-Jane, your Grace, is for her to marry a man who is deserving of her. A marriage of mind and soul, not title and tether. What is the point of her being Lady Nose-in-the-Air if she is miserable and wretched? I don't want her forever leg-shackled to a spineless sot who is a brute and beats her when he is drunk, or for any reason, because he can, but who can call himself Lord God Almighty because he had ancestors who bowed and scraped and went on crusades for their king. That was the sort of marriage her mother was forced to endure before her lousy lord did her and I a favor and died of a heart seizure in the arms of a whore." When the Duchess remained silent, he shrugged and looked sheepish. "You did ask for plain speech, your Grace."

"I did and I do not disagree with you. But... Sarah-Jane, for all her good sense, is not immune to title, particularly when that title is owned by a devilishly handsome man, Mr. Strang."

"You refer to Alisdair Fitzstuart." Jonathon stared straight ahead, down the long deserted avenue, children, minders and gardeners nowhere in sight, to the old high stone wall and the doorway he had used seven days ago to access the boatshed. Seven days that seemed a lifetime ago now. "I have it on excellent authority he is exceedingly handsome. He flutters the hearts of all women, be they widows, married or unmarried, pretty or no. The man, it seems, is a walking Adonis."

Deborah heard the edge to his voice and did not believe his irritation with Dair Fitzstuart was solely caused by his daughter's interest in her husband's cousin. She may have been caught up in playing hostess while she had guests at Treat, but she like others had not been blind to Jonathon's particular attentions to her mother-in-law. And there was the inevitable gossip that trickled back to her of his uninvited visit to Crecy Hall.

But unlike the Duke, who regarded the East India merchant's behavior toward his mother as predatory and self-serving, Deborah was able to be more dispassionate and, being romantically minded for all her practicality, she was not adverse to opening the door to another possibility for Jonathon's assiduous attentions; one she had not dared to breathe to the Duke for fear he would think her pregnancy had brought on brain fever, because, as a son, he was blind to all possibilities where his mother was concerned. Despite the fifth Duchess being breathtakingly beautiful to everyone with a pair of seeing eyes, the Duke was her son and what child saw their mother in any other role but as a mother? Any thought the fifth Duchess was an attractive female and the object of many a man's lust was naturally dismissed as repugnant and not given a second thought.

Deborah decided to test her intuition.

"You do not approve of Dair Fitzstuart as a fit husband for Sarah-Jane?" she asked lightly.

"I do not."

"Then, pardon my presumption, but as a concerned father, should you be with Sarah-Jane now in Buckinghamshire to ensure she does not accept a proposal of marriage from a man you do not want to see her—as you put it—titled but miserably leg-shackled to for the rest of her life?"

It was Jonathon's turn to stop on the path. He turned to the Duchess, who looked up at him with her customary enigmatic smile, and met her open gaze squarely and without a smile.

"Sarah-Jane departed Buckinghamshire yesterday and is en-route to London with Kitty and Tommy. Her letter informing me of her journey was redirected here. It seems she knows me better than I gave her credit! I can only hope that whatever decision she has made for her future it was taken with careful deliberation and consideration and that the nineteen years she spent with me has had some bearing on her choices."

"I suppose it would be too much for you to expect that she

would write her decision in a letter," Deborah stated. "She would want to tell you, her father, to your face."

Jonathon gave a huff of laughter. "Yes. She tells me that delight awaits me upon my return to Hanover Square. I confess each mile closer to London will test my resolve in my upmost confidence in Sarah-Jane's ability to be discerning."

Deborah bit her lower lip in thought. "I am sure that whatever her decision, she has made it without being overly influenced by Kitty and Tommy."

"Thank you for your candor about your cousins, your Grace," Jonathon replied with a lop-sided grin. "You and I both know that those two would have her married off to a rake twice her age and with one foot in the grave, if it meant she was to become a duchess! If that isn't appalling enough, society would not lift one fine eyebrow to such a circumstance. Indeed many would applaud her good fortune."

"But if she was in love... You would not stop her marrying such a man, surely?"

"No. Not if he reformed himself for her," Jonathon replied quietly. "It does not mean that such a match would make me happy; it would not. I cannot conceive why a man of my years would want to marry a chit from the schoolroom. To be brutally frank," he added, "the very idea fills me with repugnance."

"As we are being brutally frank with one another, I would expect nothing less of you, Mr. Strang, and applaud your feelings. I admit that before I met my parents-in-law, I was skeptical that such an uneven match in age could be a success. And when I met my father-in-law..." She gave an involuntary shudder. "You must believe me when I tell you he could send chills down my spine with one look. No one, and I truly do mean no one, ever crossed him; right up until the end. Even my husband, who for the last two years of M'sieur le Duc's life was Duke in all but name, concerned himself unnecessarily that the decisions he made on his father's behalf were what M'sieur le Duc would want and approve." Impulsively, Deborah placed a hand on his sleeve. "That is between you and me and no other, Mr. Strang."

He covered her hand briefly and then made her a short bow. "Naturally, your Grace."

She nodded and would have turned to continue down the path to the garden wall door but for a sudden memory that made her pause and give an involuntary shudder. "Mr. Strang, we all lived in M'sieur le Duc's shadow until the final breath left his body."

"Except her."

Deborah regarded him with surprise.

"Yes. Yes, you are right. Except her. M'sieur le Duc was utterly devoted to Maman-Duchess." She blinked up at Jonathon, revelation opening wide her damp brown eyes. "Do you know, I do believe Maman-Duchess was oblivious to that ominous shadow? She had no idea of its existence."

"Why would she when she was the ray of sunshine in his life? Now, who have we here?" he said in a loud welcoming voice, stepping past her and going down on his haunches to welcome the twins who were running up the path to greet him. "Fearless Pirate Gus and his fellow salty sea-faring pirate Louis! Oh! And a beautiful damsel in distress?"

Deborah was so startled by his acute observation that words failed her. It was not only what he had said; it was the way in which he had said it, as if it was self-evident and indisputable. *My God*, she thought, turning to greet her children with a bright smile, *the situation is far more problematical than I ever imagined. He's fallen in love with her.*

Trailing behind the twins, their little sister tried desperately to keep up but failed miserably because she did not want to fall into the crushed stone and muddy her pretty lemon-yellow silk petti-coats and matching pantaloons and because she was only three years old and her little legs were no match for the sturdy strides of a pair of five-year olds. She was about to burst into tears of frustration when Jonathon gently off-loaded the boys, who were scampering all over him in exuberant greeting, and in two strides scooped up the Lady Juliana to raise her high in the air, which she found frightening and exhilarating in equal measure and when he set her on his shoulders to look down at her brothers from up on high she giggled her delight and waved to them in triumph.

With the Lady Juliana on his shoulders and the twins holding hands and talking non-stop, Jonathon and the Duchess exited the

Elizabethan rose garden through the stone walled door to enter a field covered in wildflowers. A small contingent of nursery maids and footmen laden with various articles necessary for a successful picnic, followed. Sheep grazed on the far side of the ha-ha and along the path that led to the sizeable boat shed on the shores of the lake. And to the left, a copse, where the floor of ancient fallen leaves and bracken was covered in a purple-blue-green haze litter of bluebells, newly emergent since Jonathon had passed by the previous week.

The twins let go of each other's hands and led the way, running on ahead through the bluebells, nets trailing behind them, to where there was a small clearing and it was here the small contingent of footmen spread out blankets and set down wicker baskets laden with an afternoon tea of cakes, biscuits, fruit, cordial for the children, porcelain plates and cups and a silver tea urn with its very own elaborate silver stand and oil burner to keep the tea warm.

Nursery maids went about feeding the children, ravenous after their play, and footmen waited on the Duchess and Jonathon who took tea side by side on a fallen log fashioned into a make-shift bench. A thick wool blanket draped across the log saved her Grace's embroidered petticoats, and they watched her children joyously munching on orange cake and almond biscuits.

"Where's my rowing companion this fine day, your Grace?" Jonathon asked, sipping at his tea politely, though he found the English way of serving their tea insipid after the spicy Chai tea of the subcontinent. "Surely you have not compelled him to work at his Latin while his brothers enjoy the fresh air and sunshine?"

"Fredrick went with his father to Bath for a short stay with Roxton's godfather."

"Been gone long?" Jonathon asked, hoping his tone was light.

"I sent them away the morning after the regatta. I am expecting them home any day."

Jonathon picked up on Deborah's use of the phrase *I sent them away* and framed his next sentence carefully. He had now read Tommy's letter, left for him while he was away in London, and it gave a vivid, if somewhat unsurprising culinary metaphor-laced, account of the traumatic events of the evening after the regatta. And while Tommy had not been party to what had transpired in the library between mother and son, he was able to tell Jonathon that it was a very heated exchange witnessed by the Duchess and overheard by Frederick. According to Tommy, everyone had witnessed the Dowager Duchess's very public breakdown in the Gallery and that it was more than ten minutes before anyone realized she had not returned indoors but had walked off into the night. Several gentlemen led by Charles Fitzstuart had rushed out into the pitch-blackness with tapers to discover her walking toward the lake and stopped her before she drowned herself. Tommy had used words such as *unsurprising, inevitable* and *suicidal,* all of which Jonathon rejected. Antonia had promised Monseigneur to give Frederick the ducal emerald ring on his twenty-first birthday and that was a promise she would keep with every fiber of her being, however low and disordered her spirits; of that he was convinced.

He was somewhat mollified to learn that the Duke had not been sitting in his palace while on the other side of the lake a lunatic physician had been molesting his mother. Still, that did not negate the Duke's neglect, or his behavior, and so Jonathon intended to tell him when next they met.

"How wise of you to send them away, your Grace," Jonathon commented, replacing the patterned porcelain cup on its saucer. "A few days solely in each other's company will allow the Duke to regain perspective and Frederick to recover from what must have been an exceedingly traumatic ordeal for a little boy not quite seven years of age."

"As you know what occurred in the library—"

"Pardon, your Grace, I know there was an incident in the library," Jonathon interrupted, hearing her disapproval, "but not what occurred or what was said. What I do know about is the aftermath, not because Mme la duchesse confided in me, but because it is on the public record. I have Tommy to thank for the account of the drama that unfolded after she left the library. That is all."

There was a prolonged silence. Had there been crickets, Jonathon would have heard them. And then Deborah Roxton spoke, voice steady, but Jonathon heard the slight tremor and appreciated her internal struggle to take him into her confidence about an episode that clearly still distressed her.

"I love my husband very much, Mr. Strang. But it has not blinded me to his few foibles, one of which is his inability to think clearly and act rationally when dealing with matters that concern his mother. He lived under his father's shadow to be sure, but so do most eldest sons of great and powerful men, and so he accepted that with equanimity. But his mother..." She shrugged. "It is difficult to explain. Perhaps it is because they are close in age, a circumstance with which you can surely sympathize. You were a young father, Mr. Strang... Roxton is closer in age to his mother than she was to his father..."

"I understand only too well, your Grace. There are occasions, more frequent now she is a young lady, when Sarah-Jane acts toward me as if I am her elder brother and she my little sister, and thus, she does not take me as seriously as she ought."

"Precisely! You do understand," Deborah replied with a small sigh and continued, "Mme la duchesse and Roxton are also of a similar temperament, not that he would own to it because it is not considered manly to be sentimental and sensitive, which he is where his family and those he cares about are concerned. I like it. In fact," she said defensively, "I consider it one of his most endearing qualities!"

"And so you should, your Grace," Jonathon replied with a small smile.

"It would be an abuse of trust to confide in you the details of a most painful episode in my husband's youth involving his mother that caused great distress to both his parents, but suffice that what occurred in the library the other day, the unspeakable accusations he hurled at her head were such that he believes he has repeated, in a different way, the imprudence of his youth... For Frederick to bear witness to such unpleasantness... To see his father act in a most uncharacteristic manner... It has left Roxton wondering if it is he and not Maman-Duchess who needs the attentions of a physician who deals with broken minds." Deborah put her empty porcelain cup on its saucer and handed it off to a hovering footman, and sat up straight. "Of course I told him he was talking complete nonsense and that it was overwork and the fact he worries about every little thing, even this new babe I am carrying and my eventual lying in when the babe is not due until the autumn and I have had four healthy children without any trouble at all." She smiled and waved at Juliana when the little girl held up a fistful of bluebells. "Children are very resilient and remarkably forgiving little beings and my eldest son will recover because his father loves him dearly, as he does all his children." She looked at Jonathon. "Roxton is an exceptionally good father, Mr. Strang, and a loving husband. We will pull through this distressing episode, as a family, I believe that unquestioningly."

Jonathon returned her smile. "I believe you will, your Grace. The Duke is fortunate to have you but I am certain he knows that very well and often tells you so." He handed off his teacup on its saucer and waved away the plate of cakes being offered him, gaze remaining very much on the Duchess, who had blushed at his compliment and hung her head for the briefest of moments before again meeting his gaze when he said seriously, "I appreciate your confidence. What you have just told me has decided me that my best course of action is to return your confidence with one of mine own, rather than seek out the Duke, if that is acceptable to you?"

Deborah nodded and briefly held her breath. His lop-sided, almost embarrassed grin made her heart race and yet she managed to remain composed, hands in her lap, and ask evenly, "I presume then that what you wish to tell me concerns Mme la duchesse?" When he nodded she added, "Whatever you tell me, Mr. Strang, will remain between us two, unless you tell me otherwise."

"The Duke will not thank me for confiding in you, particularly in your present condition," Jonathon said seriously. "Yet, I am confident that you are made of sterner stuff than the Duke allows and will be able to deal with it in your own indomitable way, as you did the situation that presented itself in the library."

"May we walk? I promised Gus and Louis a scamper through the woods... But if you would prefer me to remain here, on this log..."

Jonathon glanced over at the twins, who were up off the blankets and running through the bluebells, and then at the immobile footman standing by the log at the Duchess's right shoulder, face front but Jonathon was sure, ears very much wide open. "Send that fellow with the boys to scamper in the woods, and the others, they can return to the house; one nurserymaid can keep your daughter occupied at a distance until I'm done."

Deborah did as he commanded, for it was a command, not a suggestion, the change in him so marked that again her heart raced as to what he could possibly want to tell her. When he stood, absently pulling at a handful of wildflowers growing by the log as he did so, she looked up at him and waited and watched as he collected his thoughts, seemingly concentrating on picking the petals from the tiny flowers. Clearly confiding in her was not going to be easy for him, or was it what he wanted to tell her that was the sticking point?

She was not kept guessing long, and when Jonathon spoke, when he finally gathered the courage and the right words to disclose the true nature of Antonia's care at the hands of the lust-driven lunatic physician Sir Titus Foley, he did so in his inimitable artless way, with no embellishments or hypotheses; his deep, naturally friendly voice stern and unemotional, which was far more effective in conveying the enormity of the unspeakable treatment meted out to her mother-in-law than had Deborah been told in a manner that was emotionally charged and verbose.

"And the—the wounds from the—from the ligatures... Will they—will they heal?"

"Yes; in time. But it is not the physical scars that concern me, your Grace. She has not confided in me the extent of her abuse, and I will never ask her," he added quietly, not at all surprised that the Duchess had turned pale and was doing her best to keep her emotions well in check. She could not, however, stop the tears running down her face. Jonathon handed her his clean linen handkerchief. "What I do know is that for all her outward serenity she does not sleep at night and eats very little. Her maid is naturally very worried for her, and having no one else to confide in, told me. What you can be assured is that Foley will never again practice medicine, not even on a dead dog. What I did to him, short of ending his worthless life, has left him permanently crippled. Nor will he find succor here in England or on the Continent. I have sent agents to track him, to hound him, to make his life a misery. Should he decide to flee to a colony, rest assured, your Grace he will be found and all who come into contact with him will know what sort of creature walks amongst them."

Deborah pulled the woolen shawl up about her shoulders

and hugged herself tightly. She was disbelieving. Not that she thought Jonathon a liar, she believed he was telling her the truth, she just could not believe Antonia had been subjected to such an horrendous ordeal and that Sir Titus Foley, a physician who was well respected within his fraternity and had treated dozens of Polite Society's females, and had come with glowing references, could be one and the same as the sadistic monster now described. She felt sick to her stomach and dry in the mouth and cold, the damp handkerchief squeezed in her fist, and was grateful for the dish of sweet black tea Jonathon pressed into her hand and urged her to drink up. She stared out across the carpet of bluebells gently swaying in the afternoon breeze, listened to her giggling little daughter as she ran around flapping her arms pretending to be a butterfly, and further off, there were the shouts of her sons playing hide and go seek in the wood, taunting William the footman to find them if he could, all life affirming and reassuring, that there was so much good in the world and to this she had to hold firm and be strong, for the sake of her children and her husband, and for Maman-Duchess whom Frederick called *his Mema*.

Most of all she would be forever grateful to whatever higher power had sent this handsome sun-bronzed giant, who was looking down at her with concern, into their lives, for not only had he saved her son from drowning he had now rescued the Dowager Duchess from unspeakable horror; and for confiding in her and not her husband who she was very sure would never forgive himself for offering up his mother into the hands of a sadist.

Jonathon took the teacup from her and Deborah stood. She needed to walk now. Walking made her think clearly. And when Jonathon offered her his crooked arm, she took it saying quietly as they set off into the wood, Lady Juliana quick to grip her mother's outstretched fingers,

"Thank you for not going to the Duke, Mr. Strang. Of course he will have to be given a reason why that monster was so summarily dismissed..."

"A brief description of Foley's water treatment should suffice."

Deborah shuddered. "Yes. It will."

"And may I suggest you advise Roxton never to broach the episode with Mme la duchesse; ever."

"An excellent idea. Although, he does owe her an apology for what was said in the library, and so I told him."

Jonathon's lips twitched. "I am sure you did just that, your Grace."

Deborah laughed and felt better for it. But soon lost her smile, saying seriously, "I know I can never make it up to her, but if there is anything I can do... For her... And for you..."

It was Jonathon's turn to laugh and he swung the Lady Juliana, who was whining for her mother to pick her up, back up onto his shoulders. "There are several things you can do, your Grace. I have a list! All of which I am going to ask of you, for her sake."

Deborah turned to regard him with a slight tilt of her head and a knowing smile.

"I am going to ask you why, Mr. Strang. I believe I know. Yet, to hear you say it would be oddly comforting to this incorrigible romantic."

Jonathon grinned and blushed in spite of himself, yet he did not look away nor did he flinch from giving her the answer she already knew. "Because I love her."

Nineteen

"*M*ichelle, has M'sieur Strang returned from the big house?"

Antonia's personal maid paused in the doorway between the bedchamber and the dressing room, where the Duchess sat before her dressing table looking glass brushing her hair, and met her mistress's steady gaze in the reflection.

"I do not know, Mme la duchesse," she replied levelly and turned to scurry away to turn down the bedcovers but was stopped.

"You do not know because it is common knowledge below stairs or because *you do not know*. Which is it?"

"I—we do not know, Mme la duchesse. No word has come from the big house and none of us have seen him since this afternoon."

"Surely his valet, he must know, *hein*?"

"M'sieur Strang he does not have a valet, Mme la duchesse."

Antonia paused mid-stroke, frowning.

"What do you mean *he does not have a valet*? Of course he must have a valet. All gentlemen have a valet."

"Pardon, Mme la duchesse, but M'sieur Strang he does not."

"You mean he did not bring his valet with him."

"No, Mme la duchesse. He does not have a valet. He had one when he lived in India, but not here since he returned to England."

"But he left the subcontinent almost two years ago and you tell me he does not have a valet? *Incroyable*." She swiveled about on her dressing stool to face her maid. "Then who is it that looks after him?"

"He looks after himself," Michelle stated and elaborated when Antonia put up her brows expecting further explanation. "When he was staying at the big house, he, M'sieur Strang did not have a valet to take care of him and he would not have one. So Oliver told me, and he was told by Lawrence Montbrail the footman up at the big house who is sometimes assigned to wait on gentlemen who do not bring their valets for one reason or another when they stay with M'sieur le Duc and Mme la duchesse for weekend house parties."

"Looks after himself?" Antonia repeated, clearly astonished. "Would not have one? What is his ridiculous objection I wonder? Me I saw his traveling portmanteau in the pavilion and wondered..." She had a sudden thought. "Which bedchamber has he been assigned?"

"Bedchamber, Mme la duchesse?"

Antonia tossed the hairbrush amongst the clutter on her dressing table and stood with a sigh. "Michelle, are you pretending to be dull-witted or are you over tired because me you do not listen to when I tell you to go to bed and instead keep me company who cannot sleep anyway! Tonight, you are to stay under the covers and not make me silly hot drinks which do not help me fall asleep in the least."

"Yes, Mme la duchesse," Michelle answered obediently, yet both knew she would not do as she was told and would be up as soon as she heard her mistress pacing the bedchamber. She helped Antonia shrug a soft-yellow silk banyan over her thin cotton night-shift, placed matching slippers before her, then bobbed a curtsey, saying with a small smile, "If that is all, Mme la duchesse, I will still turn down the covers and see to the fire in the bedchamber in the hopes that tonight we may both sleep through the night."

"*Merci*, Michelle."

Michelle paused in the doorway again and Antonia, who had picked up a book from the small stack brought to her by Gidley Ffolkes and, as was her usual practice, about to curl up in the wingchair by the warmth of the fireplace to read, waited for her to speak.

"In answer to your question, Mme la duchesse, M'sieur Strang he is not in any bedchamber."

"There are fifteen bedchambers in this house of no use to me whatsoever and me you tell M'sieur Strang he is not using any of them?" For a second time in as many minutes Antonia was astonished and she was beginning to wonder if she was acting out a scene from a Sheridan comedic play. "He does not have a valet and he does not sleep in a bedchamber. What does he do then? Sleep under the stars like a native?"

"Yes, Mme la duchesse, that is exactly what he has been doing for the past six nights."

"I cannot believe he is sleeping in my pavilion and that you allowed for this to happen!" Antonia whispered loudly, following behind her butler who was following behind a footman who was holding high a lantern to illuminate the winding stone pathway that led down to the pavilion. Close at Antonia's back was Michelle and behind Michelle, another footman with a second lantern.

"Mme la duchesse, with all due respect, M'sieur Strang he was offered a bedchamber but he would not hear of sleeping inside the house," the butler replied in a similar loud whisper.

"I do not understand at all what is his objection to sleeping inside my house."

"He said it was not fit and proper for him to do so," Michelle explained in a low voice.

"*Shhh*, you'll wake him!" hissed the footman at Michelle's back.

"That is a ridiculous notion," Antonia whispered dismissively at Michelle's explanation. "It is not fit and proper that I have a guest who is uncomfortable and cold! He is being obstinate for some reason known only to himself."

All silently agreed with her about his stubbornness, yet were confident they knew his reasoning, even if their mistress did not.

The small party continued on down the winding path in silence, treading carefully, as if creeping up on a wild animal that, having escaped the gamekeeper's trap, was sleeping peacefully in its lair unaware it was still being pursued and about to be ambushed, and not wanting to wake it. Their progress was aided by a full moon shining brightly across the surface of the still lake, turning the water silver and making silhouettes of trees, jetty and islands against a glass gray night sky, while moonbeams lit up the steps leading into the pavilion, providing a patchwork of light across the darkened interior through the cut outs between the columns.

When Antonia bunched up a handful of her flowing dressing gown and nightshift to alight the steps, the butler stopped her saying with some trepidation,

"Perhaps it would be for the best if I go on ahead, Mme la duchesse?"

It was on the tip of Antonia's tongue to be outright dismissive of her butler's anxiety but she looked at the concerned faces of her assembled group of devoted servants in the orange glow of the two lanterns and smiled kindly.

"I do not think M'sieur Strang he will appreciate a delegation waking him in the middle of the night. And as you all failed to convince him to sleep indoors, it is left to me to order him to do so. That is best done without an audience." She put out a hand for one of the lanterns. "You may return to the house and go to your beds. Our guest can guide me back to the house."

"Mme la duchesse, I will stay with you," Michelle stated, foot on the first step. "You should not be left alone with—"

"It is too late in the day for any of us to worry about the proprieties given the events of the past fortnight," Antonia interrupted quietly. "*Bonne nuit.*"

"*Bonne nuit*, Mme la duchesse," all four servants murmured with downcast eyes, hot in the face and glad of nightfall, Michelle with a curtsey and the men with a bow. It was the first time the Duchess had made reference to her ordeal at the hands of the sadistic physician, and it made them all acutely aware of their failure to come to her rescue and more shamefully for them, how she had not once apportioned blame their way. Without further comment, they departed, though slowly and deliberately, and at the first bend in the path they paused, ears straining to hear any sound out of the ordinary in the still night air, such as the protesting noises of an awakening giant. Hearing only the hoot of an owl, the servants reluctantly returned to the house and their respective beds. It took them many hours to fall asleep.

Jonathon was dreaming. He was back on the subcontinent. Yet, somewhere in the deep recesses of his mind, he knew he was dreaming and that he was most definitely not in India. India was hot and dry; England was cold and damp. Just before he drifted off to sleep on the chaise longue in the pavilion, the coverlet given him by Michelle blanketing his nakedness, there had been a light shower of rain but not enough clouds to hide the brightness of a full moon. He was most definitely in England. Yet, somehow he had been transported across vast oceans to the subcontinent, to the dust and heat of summer, just when the heat became unbearable and then came relief when the heavens opened and the monsoon delivered torrential rains that swelled rivers to overflowing.

It was a sultry night after a particularly heavy downpour and too hot to sleep indoors. He was on the wide veranda of an inner courtyard of his palatial white marble mansion in Hyderabad, sprawled out on the palanquin bed with its brightly colored silken sheets and cluster of soft cushions behind diaphanous silk gauze curtains that rippled gently in the breeze, the damp air heavy with the scent of jasmine.

He had just returned that day from a prolonged absence to the northern provinces and while his daylight hours were spent reunited with Sarah-Jane, his nights belonged very much to his beloved *bibi* Asmita who lived in a house within the gated compound of his mansion, as was custom for all females of a household. But she shared his bed willingly.

But it wasn't Asmita on the palanquin beside him it was an English duchess, French to her pretty toenails, beautiful and beguiling and soon to be his, and so he knew he was not in Hyderabad; it was most definitely a dream, but what a heady intoxicating dream. He did not want to wake up.

She was making love to him. Slowly. Deliberately. Her warm breath on his neck sent a frisson of desire through his heavy limbs and when her lips grazed the hard stubbled line of his strong jaw, a hand to where his heart beat strongly against his ribs, he turned his head, wanting the taste of her mouth. But her kisses progressed down his neck, light, feather-like, barely-there touches until her mouth pressed firmly to his collarbone and she rested her cheek on his chest, to listen to the thudding of his heart.

Fingers lightly caressed taut arm muscles, brushing across bronzed skin as if smoothing out a delicate fabric, before crossing to caress the hard ripple of his stomach; one finger dared to trace the dark line of hair down from navel to groin. His breathing stopped in anticipation of where her exploration would lead but the caress did not venture where he wanted it to and he breathed again, shallowly as the caress continued out along the firm line of his buttock and then down the flair of thigh muscle before finally turning inwards to caress his inner thigh, lightly, slowly, almost tentatively but inexorably upwards, first to cup him and then to explore, fondle, tease and stroke him beyond reason.

He rose up off the cushions onto an elbow, disorientated and half-awake, heat surging through his every vein to ignite between his thighs. And when her mouth finally found his, when she permitted him to kiss her as he had kissed her in the icy waters of the lake, he fell back amongst the cushions, fingers splayed through her waist length hair and one large hand cupping her heavy breast through the thin nightshift as she straddled him.

Earlier, Antonia had stood on the top step of the wide stairs of the pavilion in a pool of orange light, lantern held high, squinting into the blackness beyond. She did not see Jonathon at first. It was a trick of the full moon that streamed light between the columns and across the interior. The chaise longue was in the direct path of the bright moonlight and it was moonbeams that bathed his bronzed flesh in an eerie silver glow so that he appeared as polished marble. And so it was as if Laocoön without his sons slept on her chaise longue.

She had admired the monumental Greek sculpture of Laocoön and his sons in the Vatican's Belvedere Garden, and been so taken with it and the story of Poseidon's Trojan priest who, with his two sons, was crushed to death by giant serpents for Laocoön's attempt to expose the ruse of the Trojan Horse, that Monseigneur had commissioned a replica for the ornamental gardens of their Parisian Hôtel. She admitted to the Duke that it wasn't so much the misery captured in the face of Laocoön that captivated her but the skill in which the artist had sculpted the male physique in all its dynamic muscularity.

Although, in one all-important respect, the statue was a sad disappointment. Teasingly, she advised that when commissioning the replica, Monseigneur was to offer up his own member for replication as a substitute for Laocoön's paltry specimen. After all, she murmured, as she fondled him, such a magnificent physique required a similarly impressive organ. In response, the Duke had caught up her hand, saying with a laugh as he carried her to their bed that it was as well sculptures did not deliver or he might find himself envious of cold marble.

And here in her pavilion was a Laocoön who measured up in every way. He might not have the Trojan priest's full beard or be wrestling a serpent but he possessed Laocoön's wild mane of hair and muscular physique. The coverlet, that at some stage during the night must have covered all of his body, now barely concealed his nakedness, the cloth twisted up between his thighs and up over one brawny shoulder much like the giant serpent wrestled by Laocoön. His face was turned away into his arm, to the striped silk back of the chaise longue, one leg drawn slightly up and his tight torso slightly twisted, revealing a small firm and very white buttock, and at the line she had found so tantalizing, that divided bronzed flesh from white that had not seen the sun, the tattoo at his hip, a circle of three elephants, trunks to tails entwined.

Antonia smiled. The awkward positioning of his body was a glaring indication that her chaise longue was a vastly uncomfortable substitute for a real bed when occupied by a wide-shouldered man six feet four inches in length. And as she set the lantern down, her smile turned into a frown of concern, wondering for the umpteenth time why he chose to sleep out here, in the cold and in discomfort when she had a house full of empty bedchambers.

She found a small space in the small of his bare back to perch on the chaise and put a hand to his shoulder with the intention of giving him a little shake to wake him as gently as possible. But the surprising warmth of his skin under her hand made her pause. And in that small hesitation, as if in answer to her touch, he dropped his shoulder and turned slightly towards her so that she looked upon his face, and what surprised her, and was something she had not thought about or noticed until now, was that with his face in repose he was mesmerizingly handsome.

Ever truthful, she acknowledged she had noticed his virility but it was his ever-present, devil-may-care smile and the mischief, or was it defiance, that sparked his dark brown eyes, that had masked just how handsome he truly was and reminded her in no small way of her beloved friend and brother-in-law Vallentine; that he was supremely indifferent to what others thought of him and trod his own path, she did not have to stray to find to whom those qualities belonged.

That small movement, of dropping his shoulder and turning his head, had the power to draw her down, so close that she caught the essence of him: salty and spicy and thoroughly male. Thoughts of waking him with a shake vanished as she leaned in to lightly kiss his stubbled jaw, and to discover for herself if it was possible to arouse a living Greek statue.

"No. Not-not *here. No.*"

She ignored him.

His sluggish command was firm if muffled as he reluctantly removed his mouth from hers. He so wanted to go on kissing her, to enjoy the moist sweetness and aching arousal of the promises to be had in what her mouth could offer him, of what his tongue yearned to discover between her thighs. His mind raced on to thoughts of them engaging in *auparishtaka* and he moaned aloud the disappointment experienced by his throbbing vital organ when he removed her hand. But he was resolute. This was not the place. He had decided what he wanted, and how he was going to go about getting it; the short-term frustration of denial was a small price to pay if it meant she would share the future with him.

And so he scrambled up amongst the cushions on the chaise, now fully awake, dragged the coverlet up between his thighs to cover his arousal, and raked a splayed hand through tussled hair, gathering his thoughts and formulating an explanation she would understand. Antonia faced him on the chaise, achingly lovely in a nightshift outrageously askew and falling off one shoulder, honey blonde curls a messy tumble about her shoulders, looking thoroughly disconsolate and unsatisfied, to which she had every right.

"I do not understand at all why you say *no* and *not here* when *he* very much wants to make love. Do you not want to make love with me?" she asked wonderingly.

"More than I thought it humanly possible to want anything in this life."

"Then please you will explain to me the difficulty," she continued matter-of-factly, "because me I do not understand at all!"

Jonathon laughed at her petulance.

"I am very sure you don't," he agreed with a smile. "If there is a difficulty, it is making him behave. The mere thought of you and he thinks he is in control, and he is not. I am."

Antonia frowned, unconsciously slipping her nightshift and dressing gown up onto her bare shoulder. "Behave? What is this *behave* and this *control* you speak about?" She had a sudden thought and her green eyes went very wide and she stared at him in disbelief. "*Mon Dieu*, please to tell me you are not one of these young men, like His Majesty and my son, who is a prude about all things of the bedchamber, that they cannot perform unless the door it is locked and the curtains they are drawn about the bed?" She threw up a hand. "And yet it is such men who breed like rabbits! It is unfathomable."

He fell back amongst the cushions, laughing.

"It is not humorous in the least! It must be quite debilitating," she replied indignantly but then she too saw the absurdity and tried hard to fight back a fit of the giggles. "What if the-the mood strikes and the-the bedchamber it is far away? To be so in control... It must affect the health, yes?"

"Yes, but not one's ability to breed. *Mieux baiser comme des lapins que se multiplier comme eux.*" He sat forward and looked into her eyes, all humor extinguished, and put out a hand. "I will readily make love to you here, on this chaise, or out there, in the moonlight, for all the stars to see, and we will, but... Not the first time."

Antonia moved up the chaise and slid under the coverlet, and took hold of the hand he held out, curious. "First time?"

He gently pulled her closer, to kiss her wrist and then the back of her hand, lips pressed to the red scar from the fiendish physician's ligature that had held her fast to the icehouse chair. He looked up into her eyes.

"Do you remember the first time you made love?"

For some unknown reason, Antonia felt her face grow hot. How could she forget? She marveled at her naïve confidence in youth. It was she who had propositioned Monseigneur. She had trespassed into his bedchamber and discovered him naked, just out of his bath. It had been her eighteenth birthday the day before.

"Of course. Everyone remembers their first time," she heard herself say blandly.

He smiled and said gently, pressing her fingers as he sat against the cushions, "And so I want you to remember our first time."

Antonia blinked and brought herself back to the present.

"But it is not our first time so—"

"With you; you with me. It will be *our* first time."

She met his gaze. His sincerity made her uneasy. What had begun as an uncomplicated exercise in satisfying mutual lust was shaping itself into something else entirely and was so unexpected she was uncertain how to proceed or if she was capable of reciprocating. So she made less of it than it was, saying with a shrug,

"Why should that matter? Perhaps because it is the first time you have bedded a duchess? Antonia Roxton has never been with any other man but her husband and now you are to have that privilege." She tugged her hand free and fussed unnecessarily with her hair, pulling the weight over one shoulder and plucking at the long curls. "To bed the Duchess of Roxton it is no small thing and quite a coup, so I am told. I have a page to myself in White's betting book, much to my son's disgust. He tried to have the page torn out. Me, I do not care. But he is very serious about such things, as is his nature. Tommy Cavendish says that not even Julian he could have the page removed. It is too titillating. Too many guineas have been wagered. Oh, on all sorts of ridiculous notions men get into their heads about me."

"Stop it."

"Who will Antonia Roxton bed now she is a widow? When will this *grand événement* occur? Has the Duke my son forbidden me from taking a lover?"

"Stop."

"Did you know he has every right to do that? Imagine! At my age being dictated to by my son."

"Stop."

"But perhaps it is me who is to have the last laugh? After all, no one, most definitely not Julian, in their wildest imaginings will guess that Antonia Roxton lusts after a man not many years older than her son—"

"*That's enough!*" Jonathon growled and so viciously that Antonia was instantly contrite. "You're being self-destructive for its own sake and I won't allow you to ground my honorable intentions to dust under your heel!"

"Will you not, M'sieur?"

"Never again will we speak of age because it is irrelevant. It was irrelevant when you fell in love with Monseigneur, so it is irrelevant now. You don't need me to satisfy your vanity. You and I and the entire fraternity of White's know you are more ravishingly beautiful than most of the women half your age. That is your son's dilemma, and who can blame him for his apprehension? The instant his father breathed his last your virtue became fair game for every man with a pulse! But I am not like them and I won't be seen to be like them." He looked away, out through the columns to the moonlight shimmering across the still lake, and swallowed hard, and she knew her flippancy had hurt him. "As for me and Roxton," he added quietly, turning back to look at her, "there may only be half a dozen years separating us, but in our experiences of life and women, a great yawning ocean divides us, which puts me more on par with his father than it ever will with your son. So when I tell you I want us to remember our first time together it is my sincerest heartfelt wish: *Our* first time. Two people: Antonia and Jonathon, no one else. Understand?"

There was a tight silence between them. Neither looked away from the other. If ever there was a moment for her to retreat from a possible future with him, this was it, Jonathon thought as he awaited her decision, face and body impassive but with the blood pounding in his ears. Finally she spoke, and so softly that through the drumming he had to strain to hear every word.

"It seems you have given this first time of ours a great deal of thought."

"I have."

She held his gaze yet it was impossible not to notice the

tightness in his jaw and neck. Finally, her green eyes sparked and she dimpled with a roguish smile.

"So tell me about this first time," she teased, touching his arm that lay across the top of the gilt wooden frame of the chaise. "Or is to it be a surprise?"

He breathed easy, grinned and pulled her into his embrace and they settled on the chaise, the coverlet over them both, she with her head against his chest.

"A surprise."

She snuggled in.

"*Bon*. I like surprises."

He thought she had fallen asleep, she was quiet so long, and he was content to stare out between two columns at the full moon, fingers absently playing with a long lock of her hair, satisfied one hurdle had been leapt but ruminating on how many more remained before he could be certain that his future with her was secure, not least was the hurdle of how to tell her who he truly was, or more correctly, who he was to become on the imminent death of his ancient distant relative, and how that would signal the first day of the rest of his life by a lake, not unlike this one, but on the far side of Hadrian's wall in remote Scotland; he might as well tell her he was returning to the subcontinent!

"Where is your valet?" she asked drowsily.

"I left him in India. He had a wife and children and could not leave them."

"So who looks after you?"

"I look after myself."

"A gentleman does not look after himself... He must have a valet."

"If you say so."

"I do. I will find you one tomorrow."

"Will you indeed? Do I appear that unkempt?"

"Yes. I like it. But you have suffered long enough. You must have a valet."

He chuckled and hugged her.

She let her hand wander lightly over his chest, across the muscles of his firm stomach and then down to his groin. He caught her wrist before her exploration went further and brought her hand back up to his chest and held it there in his large warm hand.

"Behave yourself."

She giggled into his side.

"But with you, I do not think I can. You are too tempting."

"There is that proverb about all good things coming to those who wait."

"That is a great piece of nonsense! Good things come to those who seize the opportunity."

He gave a bark of laughter and swiftly kissed her hand.

"Now you are thinking like a merchant."

"And you are the one being stubbornly noble!"

He closed his eyes, smiling.

"Sleep, wicked woman."

There was another long silence between them.

"Is *he* the reason you were teased at school?"

"Yes."

"Because he is circumcised. Why?"

"Why was I teased about it or why is he circumcised?"

"Silly. It stands to reason you would be teased because only Jews are circumcised and they cannot attend Harrow."

"Jews and Muslims."

"But you are neither."

"I am neither but I had no say in the matter. My father converted to the faith of Islam and that requires male children to be circumcised. And so in his wisdom he had my elder brother James and I circumcised, as there was little likelihood of us returning to England. He intended for us to live, marry women on the subcontinent, have families and die in India."

"What happened to change that?"

"My brother died; then a distant cousin here in England. I became my uncle's heir and my father, my uncle's younger brother, who had given up all rights to his inheritance upon his conversion to Islam, was persuaded to send me to England to be brought up a proper English gentleman as befitted my new circumstances. I was not much older than your Frederick when plucked from the warmth of the subcontinent and thrown into the depths of an English winter and the bleakness of Harrow."

He felt Antonia shudder and hugged her. "Your daughter-in-law is a wise woman to keep Frederick from Eton until he is old enough to deal with the brutalities of an English boarding school. Being heir to a dukedom is no protection while at school. It only exacerbates the cruelty by boys who will never have another opportunity to meet you on a level playing field." He gave a huff of dismissive laughter. "The tattoo didn't help."

"You had this done as a boy?"

"Right before I boarded the ship for England. Eight years old and full of my own ideas even then. Three elephants in an eternal circle: James, my father and me. It hurt like bloody hell."

There was a long silence between them, so long in fact that he thought she had fallen asleep in his arms, but then she spoke again, this time fighting off sleep yet succumbing to slumber with every sentence uttered.

"Why are you sleeping out here?" she asked drowsily.

"You haven't invited me inside."

"Not invited you inside?"

"A gentleman waits to be asked."

She was incredulous, even as she slipped into slumber. "You... You are the most—the most *frustratingly* and possibly the most— the most *romantically minded* man it has been my misfortune to encounter..."

He grinned in the darkness and fell into blissful sleep.

Twenty

*A*ntonia woke to the sounds of hammering and sawing, and laughing children. If the annoying noise of industry made her wonder if she was suffering her first megrim, the sounds of children at play had her throwing back the coverlet and calling for Michelle. And then she remembered she was in the pavilion— or was she? Half the contents of her bedchamber had found their way to her pretty outdoor sitting room. A Chinoiserie dressing screen, walnut washstand, various articles of clothing and the combs, brushes and silver backed mirror from her dressing table were set out across chairs positioned behind the chaise longue where she had spent a contended night's sleep in the arms of her merchant guest.

Guest? She frowned at the word as she quickly threw the silk dressing gown over her diaphanous nightdress and retied the ribbons. He was her guest, but he had become more than that, and yet they were not lovers, not in the strictest sense of the word; well, not *yet*. She found a pair of silk embroidered mules by the chaise, washed her face with the lavender-scented water, used the toothpowder and peppermint mouthwash then silently returned the towel to Michelle who stood as a statue by the Chinoiserie dressing screen, gaze riveted to the marble tiles.

Antonia wanted to blurt out that nothing had happened the night before so there was no need for Michelle to appear as if she had somehow strayed into a bordello. But as she was very sure something would happen in the near future what was the point of denying now what was surely inevitable? She smiled to herself as she threaded a pale pink ribbon through her messy abundance of curls and was about to ask why it was that for the past sennight she had woken to the discordant sounds of carpentry, when an object amongst the toiletries caught her eye.

She picked up the nondescript glass bottle with its glass ball stopper that had tied about its neck a velvet ribbon with small note attached. She knew what it was and where it had come from. The perfumier M'sieur Floris, or as she had playfully dubbed him *Le Grand Nez*, blended his unique perfumes at his premises in Jermyn Street, and this particular scent he had named *Antonia* in her honor. She had not worn her scent since Monseigneur's internment in the Family mausoleum. She did not need to guess who had left it there but the note intrigued her.

M'sieur Floris assures me the scent is delicate, joyful, unique & divine. In truth: a distillation of all that you are. Thus to wear it is surely superfluous?

"Do you wish for me to break the seal, Mme la duchesse?" Michelle asked, a close eye on her mistress who continued to stare at the note and knowing full well who had left the bottle of perfume.

Antonia shook her head and with a hard swallow thrust the bottle at her maid. "Was-was I dreaming or did I hear the children?"

"Not a dream, Mme la duchesse. They are down at the big oak with M'sieur Strang. They arrived an hour ago but I was told not to disturb you," Michelle explained, scooping up a pair of billowy silk trousers, a long sleeved shift and a pair of jumps. She headed for the dressing screen, expecting her mistress to follow, but when Antonia did not move, she came back to stand before her and the Duchess lifted a leg of the Ottoman trousers with an enquiring scowl, which prompted Michelle to explain, "M'sieur Strang says it is most necessary for you to wear this fancy dress—"

"These are the clothes of a sultan's wife and I have not worn them since the masquerade held to honor Frederick's birth. I do not understand at all how he knew I had such clothes," she muttered to herself, going behind the dressing screen, Michelle on her heels. "Or why he thinks jumps is part of the ensemble. Turkish women do not wear such things."

"The jumps they were my idea!" Michelle announced and rushed on when the Duchess looked at her askance. "It is—it is *scandalous* he has you wear openly such coverings on your legs before children." Adding with a curtsey, "I am sorry, Mme la duchesse, but is the truth."

Antonia pressed her lips together on a retort then said very quietly, "The scandal it is still to come. Now we will not talk. I want very much to see the children."

Dressing was accomplished in silence, Michelle leaving the dressing screen to enquire of a footman standing sentry at the steps as to the whereabouts of the Duchess's breakfast then turning to discover Antonia off across the damp lawn in a flurry of silk pantaloons and undressed hair.

"Mema! Mema! Up here! Mema! Look up! Look *up*. Up *here!*"

Antonia had a hand to her brow to shield her eyes from the morning sun filtering through the tangled branches of the ancient oak tree as she came to stand with a small contingent of nursery maids and servants gathered about its massive trunk. All turned and dropped a curtsey or bowed in acknowledgment of her presence but as she continued to stare up into the tree branches all chins again turned skywards to the heavy armed boughs bursting with bright green leaves and twisting up and out, embracing land, water and sky. A majestic specimen, the ancient oak had grown undisturbed for three hundred years, silent witness to Plantagenet, Tudor, Stuart and Hanoverian Kings, and now its branches were full of people and construction, or so it seemed to Antonia, who was trying to make sense of the activity and noise.

From the exposed gnarled roots close to the base of the enormous trunk a ladder allowed access to the lowest thick bough upon which there was now a platform that had upon it the quarterdeck of a sailing vessel—as if it had been lifted up there in a flood, and now the waters had receded the ship had broken up and only this part remained lodged, forever trapped, held captive by the branches of the old oak. And from the quarterdeck another ladder, nailed to the central trunk led further up into the higher branches to a crow's nest. Two workmen were busy painting this crow's nest while two more of their fellows sat swinging their legs on a lower branch, rigging rope from the crow's nest down to the quarter deck where another workman threaded brass toggles.

And so the old oak, which had minded its own business for three centuries, had been imposed upon, transformed into a most wondrous pirate ship tree house for children.

The twins, who continued to call out until Antonia waved in acknowledgment, beamed down at her from the quarterdeck. They wore requisite tri-corn hats, eye patches and brandished wooden toy swords. With them was the architect of their happiness who waved down to her, Juliana in his arms.

She waved back, smiling, and blew them kisses, feeling suddenly light headed with happiness. And before she could utter a word of welcome there was a great deal of scrambling about as the twins scampered down the ladder, swords tucked into the waistband of their breeches, servants at the base of the steps ready to catch an over eager little lord should he put a foot wrong. But they made it to solid ground with ease and fell into Antonia's outstretched arms to be hugged and kissed and to tell her in a rush of excitement about their new pirate ship in the sky and that Mema must come on a voyage with them when they took on the dastardly Spaniards. Antonia barely managed to say two words to Louis and Gus before Juliana had a fistful of the billowy silk of her Turkish trousers and was demanding to be acknowledged and for Mema to tell her brothers that girls could be pirates if they wanted to be, even if she wished to be a mermaid instead.

"So that's what you look like first thing in the morning," Jonathon stated, smiling down at her with a wink. "Very fetching."

To Antonia's utter disbelief and annoyance she blushed and could not meet his steady gaze. She looked about, at the small knot of servants and then at the workmen who continued on with their multitude of tasks to ready the pirate ship tree house for occupation—paint, soft furnishings, canvas and rope were going up and down the various ladders.

"Now I know the source of the noise over the past sennight," she said with a smile at her grandchildren. "But never would I have expected to find a pirate ship in a tree! What a wonderful surprise for you, yes?" She glanced up at Jonathon. "M'sieur Strang he is full of surprises, is he not?"

The children nodded and giggled, the twins jostling each other with a conspiratorial look at Jonathon, but Antonia was not given the opportunity to question them because one nod from Jonathon and they turned and scampered back up the ladder into the tree house, Juliana running after them but stopped from going after her brothers by her nurse. The little girl immediately called out for Jonathon, who in two strides had her in his arms.

"I see Julie she has you wrapped around her little finger," Antonia quipped with a laugh.

"Only because I want to be wrapped," he responded. "Now up you go and we'll follow."

"Up? Up the ladder?"

"Where else?" When Antonia hesitated he added, "You have no excuse. I've covered the—um—contingencies, as it were. You're wearing Turkish trousers, aren't you? And there's a surprise waiting for you on board ship."

"You have a nice turn of phrase, M'sieur," Antonia muttered, feeling heat in her cheeks at his spreading smile. "Perhaps I should not have mentioned I like surprises," she added, climbing the ladder with ease and without complaint, Jonathon with the little girl clinging to his back as a baby monkey does its mother following close behind. "Particularly if your surprise it has anything to do with the wearing of Turkish trousers!"

"Mema!"

At the sound of a familiar beloved voice, Antonia scrambled onto the ship's deck and to her feet and found all three of her grandsons standing before her in a row saluting her with their swords.

"*Mon Dieu*! Frederick! Oh! My darling boy!"

"Surprise! Surprise, Mema! Surprise!" the twins and Juliana shouted in unison as their eldest brother ran into Antonia's open arms to be gathered up in a tight embrace.

"Mema has her surprise; can we eat now?" Gus asked no one in particular. "My tummy is angry with me!"

Everyone laughed.

Once returned to solid ground and sitting on a scatter of oriental carpets that had been rolled out over the lawn between the oak and the lake and strewn with cushions, Jonathon nodded to the waiting footmen who commenced serving nuncheon from wicker baskets filled with all manner of delectable pastries; the butler arriving with silver service coffee pot and a sealed missive from the big house. It was from the Duke and for the Dowager Duchess. Antonia took the note, put it in a pocket of her Turkish trousers and ignored it until about an hour after the food had been demolished and she was enjoying a leisurely cup of coffee while watching the boys being supervised as they climbed up and down the ladder to access the pirate ship tree house where they practiced their sword fighting skills and Juliana was picking wild-flowers for her hair with the help of her nurse.

She extracted the note from her pocket but did not immediately break the seal, looking across at Jonathon who was comfortably sprawled out across the carpet, propped up on an elbow, and also watching the children, but whose hands were busy deftly braiding multiple strands of fine red cotton twine into what appeared to be a circlet.

"I have had such a wonderful day. Thank you."

"It was my pleasure," he said gently, returning her smile.

She wondered if her smile had the power to quicken his pulse as his did hers and she looked down at the last drop of coffee in her porcelain dish, lest he read her thoughts and see the blush to her cheeks. Inexplicably he had the ability to make her feel unsure and confused and yet also supremely happy. It baffled her. There was a word... Unsettled? Flustered? Yes, that was it! He *unsettled* her. In all her years with Monseigneur she had never felt unsettled, and that also bewildered her.

She turned her son's letter over and with a small sigh broke the seal.

Jonathon continued to braid but with one eye on Antonia's bowed head, and when she quickly folded the single sheet of parchment and thrust it back in her pocket he said as casually as he could muster, "Good news, I trust?"

"He tells me to come to dinner tonight. *Tells me.*"

"Will you go?"

She shook her head. "No. No, I do not think I can face him... yet."

Jonathon sat up. "Then don't. Roxton can wait. Come to London with me."

"London?"

"Yes."

"You are going to London? When?"

Jonathon suppressed a smile at the anxiousness in her voice and said solemnly, "Tomorrow. I must."

Antonia could not meet his brown eyes. She nodded. "Of course you must. Sarah-Jane she will be expecting you and you cannot linger here. She may have some very important news for her papa and you should—"

"Come with me."

Antonia smiled crookedly.

"To see M'sieur Sheridan's play with you?"

Jonathon shrugged.

"If you like. But to see your son Henri-Antoine."

This did make her look at him.

"Henri? He is in London? He is not up at Oxford?"

"He is in London. At the Hanover Square house."

Antonia swallowed and looked towards the lake. "I very much want to see my son but I-I..."

"You've been avoiding him because he has a great look of Monseigneur and that pains you."

Antonia did not deny this. She blinked away sudden tears.

"You have seen him."

"Yes. He resembles his father greatly, more so than Roxton. And from what your daughter-in-law tells me he has his father's arrogant demeanor as well, though he did not try it on with me, but that also makes it all the more difficult for you. But you cannot avoid him forever and the older he gets the more he will become his father's son."

"I do not want to listen to you because you are making perfect sense!" she grumbled which made him laugh.

"Someone had to tell you, sweetheart. It's not the boy's fault he's the image of his pater."

She looked at him through her lashes. "No. It's not his fault.

Me I have been a neglectful mother."

"Roxton has more to answer for neglect. He is his brother's guardian. Not that the lad has been forgotten," he added quickly when Antonia sat up very straight. "Roxton's had a lot on his plate these past three years. But to be perfectly frank, after years of being unnecessarily coddled, I think the lad has enjoyed the respite."

"*Coddled?* Henri said this to you?"

"Of course not. Why would he?"

There was a moment of quiet between them and then Antonia shuddered a breath and shrugged. "I do not know how you know these things but you do and you are in the right. And I do so want to see my little boy."

Jonathon huffed. "Little? If that's what you think you're in for a shock." He set aside the braided circlet, got to his feet and put out a hand. "And your visit will surprise and delight him. Come to London."

She smiled and nodded and allowed him to help her to her feet. He did not let go of her hand. She looked up at him cheekily, a hand on his chest.

"But that does not mean I have decided to go to the theater with you!"

"Will you not?" he threatened and in one easy movement picked her up and slung her over a shoulder, much to the startled horror of footmen, butler and nursery servants alike. "Time to put those Turkish trousers to use again!"

"*Mon Dieu!* Are you insane! Put me down this instant!"

The butler and a footman took a step forward. One dark look from Jonathon and they retreated half a step.

"Be still, woman, and we'll be there in no time. I have one more surprise for you."

He set off at a brisk pace towards the oak with a wriggling and affronted Antonia doing her best to twist out of his hold. He chuckled at her feeble attempts and teasingly let her slip further down his back. It caused her to let out an involuntary squeal and grab hold of the skirts of his frockcoat in fright. And then to add to her mortification he called out to Frederick to round up his brothers and sister and come to the oak.

"*Aliéné mental!* Put me down this instant!"

"A madman, am I? If I am, it is you who have made me so!"

"M'sieur! Put me down! You will upset the children."

"Call me Jonathon!"

"No!"

"By the grins on their faces, I'd say your little darlings think it a great lark. Fifty guineas that by midnight you'll have called me Jonathon."

"I will *give* you fifty guineas to put me down this instant!"

"Ah, Frederick! Good lad. Now the four of you stand well back because when I put Mema down she will likely be a little dizzy."

She was and fell against Jonathon's chest, eyes shut tight and light-headed. He gently brushed the hair from her face and held her, a wink and a smile at Frederick who, unlike his brothers and sister who were laughing at Mema's ride on Jonathon's shoulder, was not at all assured Antonia was unharmed by her ordeal.

"Do you want to see your surprise?" he murmured, lifting her chin. "Reason I had you dress in your captivating Ottoman attire?"

Antonia opened her eyes and he turned with her in the circle of his embrace to face the ancient oak.

They were standing on the opposite side of the massive trunk to where the pirate ship could be accessed via ladder. Here, high up, a very heavy bough twisted out towards the lake shore, and on the ground directly under the bough a great pile of leaves had been raked and stomped into place to form a nice cushion under foot because hanging from this branch was a swing. A padded seat of blue damask set in a gilt wood frame, looking suspiciously like a seat from one of the chairs to be found in the Gallery up at the big house, minus its legs and padded back, was suspended and fixed between two ropes; each rope wrapped with velvet ribbon at the place where the user held firm.

Antonia could not contain her excitement and she gasped, hands to her cheeks, and ran up to the swing to touch the damask seat as if reassuring herself it was indeed real. "Oh it is the most wondrous surprise!" she exclaimed, turning with a bright smile to Jonathon. "Is it not, *mes petits-enfants?* Who will have the first turn?" she asked the children.

"Julie!" Juliana exclaimed and ran up to her grandmother, expecting to be instantly lifted onto the magical floating seat.

All three boys looked to Jonathon and it was Frederick who voiced the earlier understanding the children had come to with him, "Mema is to have the first swing, Julie. Remember?"

The little girl eyed her grandmother speculatively; a finger in her mouth then shook her fair ringlets. "No. It's Julie's turn first."

"Mema first, Julie, or we'll set the wolf on you!" Louis teased.

"Yes! The wolf! Do you want the wolf to eat you up?" Gus stuck in with relish, though he looked a little scared at his twin's mention of such a ferocious beast.

"The wolf! The wolf! We'll get the wolf to gobble you up!" Louis announced in a sing song voice, dancing about on the spot.

Julie burst into tears and Antonia scooped her up and did her best to soothe her fears that there was no wolf; her brothers were only teasing her; of course she could have the first turn on the beautiful swing. The little girl's nurse stepped forward to take her sobbing charge from the Duchess's arms, but Antonia shook her head with a smile and the nurse retreated to stand with the small group of servants who had followed Jonathon under the shade of the oak.

Jonathon rolled his eyes at fate that his surprise for Antonia that should have seen her happy and carefree had been turned upside down by a little girl's fears that a wolf was somewhere prowling about the estate. He did not blame the twins, boys would be boys, but he was intrigued as to where such a nonsensical taunt had originated. He did not have to look far or even ask. Gus volunteered the information with a round-eyed look that told Jonathon he truly believed there was a wolf.

"Gus and Louis, you will please tell your sister there is no wolf," Antonia said firmly, the little girl turning her tear-stained face in the crook of her grandmother's shoulder to regard her brothers with a frown between her fair brows.

The twins looked at each other then at Frederick who at first feigned ignorance by lifting his thin shoulders, bottom lip stuck out. This made Gus angry and he pointed a chubby finger at his elder brother.

"You said there was a wolf! You said it!"

All eyes were on Frederick.

"He did say it, Mema! He did!" Louis added in confirmation of his twin's accusation and looked also at Jonathon, who stood with his hands in his frockcoat pockets patiently waiting for Frederick to own to the claim or not.

The silence continued. Finally it was too much for Frederick who capitulated, his bottom lip now quivering. "I didn't say it!" he countered. "I didn't!"

"Frederick?" Antonia said gently. "Why would Gus and Louis say that you did, *mon chou?*"

Her soft voice was worse than had she been angry with him and Frederick teared up but quickly dashed a sleeve across his eyes, saying with a quaver in his voice, "I didn't say it, Mema. Papa... I heard Papa say it to Grandpère Martin. Papa said there's a wolf at your door and he doesn't know what to do about it."

"There *is* a wolf! There *is* a wolf!" Louis exclaimed triumphantly.

"Hush, Louis," Antonia said quietly, not a look at Jonathon because the Duke's insinuation was evident to both of them and she was angry, that her son should speak of Jonathon in such terms and unnecessarily burden his aging Godfather with such salacious nonsense; as for allowing his little son to overhear his unjustifiable concerns, it was unpardonable.

She was still ruminating about the Duke's audacity while soaking in her hipbath of soapy bubbles later that night, the children gone home happy and exhausted; the dilemma of the swing resolved when Jonathon suggested Juliana sit upon her lap and that they be swung as one; exhilarating giggles from them both at being pushed high into the air, stockinged toes pointing to the white wispy clouds that streaked the blue sky enough of a diversion for Juliana to forget all about a wolf; the boys, once they had each had a turn on the swing, deciding there was more fun to be had clamoring all over the pirate ship tree house pretending to be on the high seas than worrying about a wolf that Jonathon assured them was in truth as ferocious as a kitten and just as cuddly.

Not even the disruptive sounds of Michelle and two upstairs maids bustling about her closet in quiet conversation, pulling open drawers, gathering up various articles of clothing and packing trunks for travel could disturb the serenity of her bath. After all, she could not really blame them for being flustered. She had set her entire household into a flurry of activity, never mind their complete astonishment had dropped their jaws when she announced just before dinner her intention to travel up to London the following day and that several of the servants would be required to travel up with her in the second carriage; the house in Hanover Square was woefully understaffed. And she would be pleased if her travel plans remained within Crecy Hall. The Duke would be informed, not by her servants, by her, when she deemed it appropriate for him to know. She smiled into the bubbles. Her son would know precisely two hours after she had left Crecy Hall and not before, when he received her letter informing him of the fact.

"Mme la duchesse, I am very sorry but there is a difficulty," Michelle apologized with a short curtsey, holding wide the towel as the Duchess stepped out of her bath. "In fact, there are two difficulties," she admitted as she quickly wrapped the towel about her mistress then turned away to pick up Antonia's nightshift.

"Two difficulties? With the travel arrangements?"

Antonia tossed aside the towel and allowed Michelle to help her wriggle into the flimsy nightshift.

"No, Mme la duchesse," Michelle explained, offering the Duchess one stocking and then its twin and requisite garters. "A servant he has arrived from the big house with his trunk claiming to be M'sieur Strang's valet but I know for a fact he is—"

"Yes! Yes! Lawrence Montbrail," Antonia said, shrugging into the silk embroidered dressing gown Michelle held wide. She sat at her dressing table to remove the many pins holding up her curls. "He is here now? He was to be here this morning... No matter. You sent him to M'sieur Strang's rooms?"

"I did."

"And they are now acquainted and pleased with each other?"

Michelle set her mouth in a thin line of disapproval. "Very pleased."

Antonia eyed her maid's reflection in the looking glass as she brushed her hair. "Good. But this it is a difficulty? *Pour quoi?* Or is the valet two difficulties? You will explain this to me, Michelle."

Michelle took the brush from the Duchess and set to brushing her hair. "If Lawrence Montbrail is indeed M'sieur Strang's valet then why, once they were acquainted, did M'sieur Strang send him away again?"

"Send him away? But did you not say he was pleased with Lawrence?"

"Yes, Mme la duchesse. But he, M'sieur Strang, sent Lawrence Montbrail to spend the night upstairs with the footmen, and not to stay in the little room off the Blue bedchamber reserved for a gentleman's valet."

It was on the tip of her tongue to say that there was possibly any number of reasons why Jonathon had sent his new valet to spend the night in the sleeping quarters allocated to the footmen, customs on the subcontinent being one of them, but she kept her thoughts to herself and asked casually, "And this other difficulty?"

"Two of the footmen have been assisting M'sieur Strang rearrange the furniture in his bedchamber."

"And that is a difficulty?"

It was Michelle's turn to look at Antonia's reflection.

"Matthews he says that the furniture in the little room reserved for M'sieur Strang's valet it has all been moved into the Blue bedchamber and that the mattress and coverings on the bed have been removed from the four poster in the Blue bedchamber and moved into the little room."

Antonia blinked. She was disbelieving. "I do not understand. He has stripped his valet's room and is sleeping in there, on a mattress on the floor, in preference to sleeping in the Blue bed-chamber?"

"Yes, Mme la duchesse."

"*Incroyable.*"

"Yes, Mme la duchesse, it is, and Matthews is beside himself as to what can be done about it. It is very irregular for a guest to be sleeping in a servant's room and on the floor! He, M'sieur Strang, also requested many more tapers than is necessary for that room."

"Tapers?" Antonia took the silver backed brush from Michelle and tossed it amongst the clutter on the dressing table. "How many more than is necessary?"

"He asked for twenty—"

"*Twenty* candles!?"

"—but said ten would suffice because he could cut them up himself."

"*Mon Dieu*. What is the impossible man up to? Using the candles for warmth?" Antonia muttered aloud to herself, up off her dressing stool. Slipping her stockinged feet into embroidered damask mules she picked up a taper in its holder and left her rooms, Michelle following, and at the top of the oak staircase in a pool of shared candlelight found her butler in animated conversation with two of the footmen; all three fell silent on Antonia's approach.

"Do you not have arrangements to finalize before tomorrow's journey?" the Duchess asked and waited while Matthews shooed the two footmen away, telling them to return to loading trunks onto the wagon that would be following the two carriages up to London. "Michelle she told me about the candles and—other concerns."

"Mme la duchesse, I am very worried lest M'sieur Strang burn the house down," the butler replied and fell in step behind the Duchess as she went on ahead across the landing and down the passageway to the guest wing; a rather odd name, reflected Matthews, given the house had never had guests in the three years it had been occupied by the Duchess and was not likely to again if the one and only guest set fire to the place with his use of so many tapers in one room. When his mistress stopped at the door to the Blue bedchamber he asked diffidently, "Would Mme la duchesse like me to rouse M'sieur Strang?"

"No. I will. Here," Antonia said and thrust the candlestick at him. "If he has so many tapers alight inside, I will not need this. You may go. And you, Michelle."

"I will wait here for you, Mme la duchesse," her maid said firmly, a glance exchanged with the butler.

Antonia saw the glance and chose to ignore it.

"Both of you go and finish whatever it is needs finishing so me I can leave early tomorrow morning. *Bonne nuit.*"

She slipped into the Blue bedchamber before either servant could protest and found herself in complete darkness. Light, however, was coming from under the door in the far corner of the room, which she reasoned must be the valet's room where

Jonathon had, for reasons only known to him, decided to spend the night.

What she discovered when she opened the door was surprising and she knew that once she crossed the threshold there was no turning back.

Twenty-one

It was as if the stars had fallen from the sky and now littered the floorboards. Twinkling points of light defined the edges of the small rectangular space and two sides of a mattress that had been made up with sheets, coverlet and down pillows, its head pushed up against the wallpaper and the foot facing the door. Small candles also lined the narrow carved mantle of a fireplace where a single burning log radiated warmth. A washbasin and jug on a wooden stand occupied a corner, the only piece of furniture in the room, and directly opposite candles dotted the sill of a mullioned window, their little flames flickering in a tiny draft.

This servant's room was unique because it not only had a window but a window seat, and thus the privilege given the servant proclaimed the high regard in which the occupant of the Blue bedchamber was held by their host. And the occupant of the Blue bedchamber was perched on the window seat, bare legs crossed at the ankles with hands thrust in the pockets of a yellow silk banyan that was loosely tied about his waist and gaped at the throat.

Antonia had an instant of *déjà vu*. But she was not the eighteen-year-old virgin full of naïve optimism and brash self-confidence. Somehow being young and ignorant had made it that much easier to tumble into bed with Monseigneur. She felt anything but confident tumbling into bed with Jonathon Strang. So many reasons why she should not clouded her mind and yet she asked herself what was the harm in making love with this handsome virile man who wanted to make love to her? She enjoyed making love very much. But this was not her husband and she had never made love where her feelings were not confidently engaged. Yet it was almost six years since she had made love—another lifetime. She reminded herself that she no longer had a husband, that she was a widow and that meant she could do as she pleased with no harm done to anyone. So why not just enjoy the experience for what it was: a brief torrid gratification for the body? Men satisfied themselves this way; many women did too. But it was not in her nature; feelings were everything to her, and that scared her most of all.

Jonathon remained seated, watching and waiting. When she finally closed the door over he visibly relaxed but did not move, reasoning she would come to him in her own good time. He followed her with his eyes as she moved about the small space in the orange glow of the myriad of small candles he had carefully positioned to make the room more intimate and welcoming. And when she finally did come over to him he did not stand, he did not remove his hands from the pockets of his banyan; he merely smiled at her and continued to wait. He waited for her to make the first move, reasoning again that if he did he might ruin the experience for both of them because his overwhelming desire was to strip her out of her diaphanous nightclothes and tumble with her on the mattress, giving free reign to his hands, his tongue and his vital organ and wanting, above all else, for her to be enjoying him.

Antonia smiled into his brown eyes. She saw in his eyes his thoughts and what he had no need to voice. She stepped out of her mules and let slip the dressing gown from her shoulders to pool at her stockinged feet. And when he shifted slightly and leaned forward to kiss her, she let him. They were both tentative and gentle with each other and then more insistent as they enjoyed a long lingering kiss. He would have taken her in his arms but she stayed him with a hand to his chest and he let his hands fall away, long fingers hard gripping the edge of the window seat when she tugged at the silk sash of his banyan. The knot undone, the banyan fell open to reveal he was naked and aroused.

She met his gaze with a knowing smile and he smiled back, unselfconscious. He went to kiss her again and again she stayed him with a hand to his bare chest. But this time she moved into him and his long legs uncrossed at the ankles and parted to allow her to draw closer and then folded around her to hold her firm. She pressed her lips to his stubbled jaw, drinking in the masculine scent of him, of freshly scrubbed skin and the tang of lime and sandalwood cologne. She kissed his throat, the kisses light and feathery as they progressed down to his chest to the hard plane of his stomach while her hands slid the silk banyan from his square shoulders and along the contoured muscle of his arms, the silk bunching at his strong wrists and here her fingers held fast, his hands captive in the folds of silk.

When he lifted his buttocks off the window seat, to free his hands from the tangle of silk to allow the banyan to fall to the floor, she would not let go of his covered wrists and so he stilled and settled again, waiting, her warm breath on his naked flesh making his heart race, his breathing short and his arousal unbearable.

She looked at him with a sly smile. "You must wait. I have unwrapped my gift and now I want to enjoy him."

She slid to her knees and he was lost.

Three days later the Dowager Duchess of Roxton arrived at the Roxton mansion in Hanover Square, sending the small staff of servants into a further frenzy of activity. Her Grace had been expected the day before and so covers were whisked off furniture, carpets beaten clean, mattresses overturned and beds made up; sweeps were sent scurrying up and down disused chimneys and fires lit in ornate fireplaces; crystal, wood and silver were polished to a high sheen, and the larder stocked with enough foodstuffs to feed a small army.

All this activity and yet the housekeeper had no clear idea of what was happening for the mansion had sat idle and neglected for years and then the Duke's man of business in the city arrived with a bronzed giant of a gentleman to inspect the house; the housekeeper informed that the stranger was the new leaseholder. No sooner was this visit over with than the Duke's younger brother Lord Henri-Antoine Hesham and his boon companion Sir John (Jack) Cavendish came to stay. And if the carryings on of these two young noblemen wasn't enough to try the patience of the most loyal servant then a wagon of crates belonging to the new leaseholder had arrived and required unloading and storage. And then the Dowager Duchess's note was delivered announcing her imminent arrival.

Michelle, and every servant at Crecy Hall, knew what, or more precisely who, had caused the delay. Twice the carriages and wagon were hitched, the horses of the liveried outriders saddled ready to be off, and twice the horses were returned to the stables, the carriages remaining empty, the wagon with its enormous pile of trunks and boxes secured under tarpaulin and ropes left waiting, and the saddles removed from the horses belonging to the out-riders.

Finally the Duchess and her lover, for what else was Jonathon Strang now he and the Duchess had spent two nights together in the small servant bedroom off the Blue bedchamber, had emerged because another note arrived from the Duke, the servant who brought it saying the matter required an immediate response. Michelle bravely slid the note under the bedchamber door and within the hour the Duchess was reading and then tearing up the Duke's note while in her bath. An hour after that the convoy of carriages and wagons was on its way to London, Michelle not needing to speculate on the contents of the Duke's note to his mother when Antonia said to Jonathon in the carriage,

"I do not see at all what business it is of his who I have to stay at my own house!"

Jonathon squeezed her stockinged foot which was resting on his knee, Antonia reclining on cushions along the length of one velvet padded bench in a froth of fine India cotton striped petti-coats, shoes kicked off and with Jonathon sprawled out in the corner; Michelle, who was drifting in and out of sleep with the movement of the carriage, diagonally opposite, the two whippets curled up beside her. Conscious of the maid, Jonathon said in Italian,

"He is a concerned son. Concerned sons think they know

what is best for their mothers." He smiled and pinched her toe playfully. "When we're married he won't be able to demand my removal, from Crecy Hall or any other place we care to reside."

Antonia chuckled, thinking him in jest and, following his lead, replied in Italian, knowing Michelle, a native French speaker knew enough English, but no Italian so would be unable to follow their private conversation; asleep or no. "We make love five—"

"—six."

"—six times in two days, and you think I will marry you? You do have romantic notions!"

"Is that such a bad thing?"

"What? To be married to you or to have romantic notions?" Antonia teased.

Jonathon shrugged. "Either or both."

Antonia pondered her response with a dimple. "I think we need to make love many more times before I can give you an answer."

"What? Is it my stamina or my technique you consider the aberration?"

She shrugged and pretended to be disconsolate. "How can I tell you if we have only made love six times?"

He gave a shout of laughter at her pout and when he squeezed her stockinged foot a little too hard she scrambled up to playfully rap his velvet sleeve with the closed sticks of her fan. He caught her wrist and pulled her to him. "If the maid wasn't here I'd prove to you that neither my stamina nor my technique are aberrations, divine creature."

Antonia held his gaze, a frisson of desire making her shudder, curiously light headed and wondering at this new sensation. But it wasn't new it was just that she had not felt this way in such a very long time that she had forgotten what it was to be happy.

"And I would let you because I enjoy making love with you very much," she said softly, leaning in to kiss him.

But he pulled back, brown eyes searching her beautiful face, his smile less assured but voice firm with sincerity. "Then marry me and we can make love into our dotage."

Antonia hesitated, and realizing he was in earnest sat up, gaze firmly fixed on his handsome face. She blinked. "But I am married to Monseigneur..."

Jonathon smiled crookedly. "Were married..."

She looked away. "I—I have never given thought to marrying anyone else, ever."

"Sweetheart, you never gave thought to making love with anyone else but Monseigneur either but here we are, you and I, lovers.

"That is different."

"In what way?"

Antonia shrugged and suddenly flushed, flicked open her gold leaf painted fan to cool her throat and breasts, and said quietly, "Marriage is complicated; this is not."

He smiled thinly. "Yes, marriage is complicated and that is why I want to marry you." When Antonia looked up at him, head to one side he provided further explanation. "To say I am delighted our bodily appetites are well matched would not be doing justice to our love making but—and you can call me selfish—I want more from you than mere physical gratification. I love you. I want to go to bed with you openly, via the bedchamber door, as your husband, without any backstairs stealth. I want to make love to you as your husband; to wake up with my wife in my arms, each and every morning. Is that too much to ask?"

To his surprise and delight she shook her head, but her words caused him to swallow hard.

"What you ask is what any man would who is in love but... Me, I do not know how I feel—How my heart feels. I know how my body feels; it wants you very much." She put out her stockinged toes, needing his touch, and when his large hand closed over the bridge of her foot she smiled tremulously. "I have never wanted any other man but Monseigneur until you..."

"And you married M'sieur le Duc d'Roxton."

Antonia held his gaze. "Our marriage it was fated."

Jonathon did not blink. "And if I tell you I believe our marriage it is also fated?"

"I will always be married to Monseigneur."

"Sweetheart, I am fully sensible to the fact there will always be three in a marriage with you, that I will forever share you with Monseigneur, but I am willing to agree to such an arrangement because I love you and want you in my life."

It was Antonia's turn to swallow hard and tears welled up. Her voice was little more than a whisper. She forgot her Italian and said in her native French,

"I do not deserve you."

He laughed at that and stooped to swiftly kiss her toes. "And I don't deserve you! So we are well matched."

Antonia was oddly comforted, and as the carriages had pulled up at the Crown Inn in Alston for a change of horses and to allow the occupants an opportunity to stretch their legs and take refreshment, she rallied, sitting up and saying flippantly in Italian, because Michelle had woken with a yawn,

"I do not see why we cannot just make love and enjoy ourselves and not worry about anything else but that. What is wrong with you? Any other man would be more than satisfied making love to me without the need to declare his love and devotion! I think the sun, it has affected your brain in more ways than you know!"

"You may be right," Jonathon answered good-naturedly and stretched out a hand for the whippets' leads. He waited for the carriage door to be opened and handed the whippets into a waiting servant's care to be walked, relieved and watered, then stepped down and turned to take Antonia's gloved hand, saying as he helped her alight, "I will say no more. But I will ask you again, and soon, because events have conspired against me and when we arrive in London I must bow to duty and obligation."

"Duty and obligation?" She glanced up at him with surprise. "What is this duty and this obligation?"

"I'll tell all when we get to Hanover Square," he replied, slightly distracted, patting his frockcoat pockets as if he had lost or misplaced something of value. "Do you have any money on your person, Mme la duchesse?"

"Money? Why do I need money?" she said with a moment's imperiousness. "The Roxton name is sufficient credit at this inn."

"I am sure it is. It is just that... No, it is of no matter now. You can settle our account later."

"Our account?" Antonia was nonplussed and stopped in the middle of the sunless cobbled courtyard, pulling her fur trimmed velvet cloak closer about her shoulders, her maid at her back.

"What account?"

She was oblivious to the noise and activity that continued on around her, trying to recall a time when she had borrowed even so much as a penny from Jonathon Strang, as stableboys ran to the spent horse's heads, and her contingent of servants from the second carriage, the outriders and drivers from both carriages and wagon were provided refreshment by the eager innkeeper's serving hands come out into the courtyard; it was not every day a carriage emblazoned with the Roxton ducal coat of arms graced the Crown with its presence.

Jonathon, who had kept walking and was now stooped under the lintel of the seventeenth century inn's entrance, waited for her to join him. The puzzlement in her green eyes as she looked up at him with frank enquiry forced him to suppress a grin at his ruse.

"I am sadly disappointed you cannot remember, Mme la duchesse," he said with all the solemnness he could muster, "and to think you have no recollection of the circumstances under which you lost the wager leaves me mortified."

As soon as he said the word *wager* she knew instantly to what he alluded and her face flamed in response. "You are a-a *fiend*," she whispered angrily.

"So you do remember?"

"We will talk of this later. I am thirsty and hungry and your large carcass it is blocking the entrance way!"

Jonathon did not budge.

"So you don't recall calling out—"

Antonia turned swiftly to her maid, startling Michelle, and said before Jonathon could finish the sentence, "Remind me to present M'sieur Strang with fifty guineas immediately we arrive at Hanover Square."

"Fifty guineas? Yes, Mme la duchesse."

"Perhaps you would care to increase the wager to a hundred guineas?" Jonathon whispered at her ear with a grin. "Double or nothing you'll call me Jonathon out from under the covers before the week—*ouch*."

Antonia had brought the two-inch heel of her silk embroidered shoe down hard on the bridge of his booted left foot, mute with fury, but his exclamation was said in jest rather than a response to any feeling of pain, and increased her infuriation. He watched with unconcealed amusement as she swept passed him into the inn, all of her five foot two inches very much a Duchess, and his duchess before summer, if he had anything to say in the matter.

But even the best laid plans, however carefully constructed and thought through, can be unraveled by the interference of others, as Jonathon discovered upon their arrival in London.

"His lordship and Sir John are in the book room, sir," Mrs. Phelps the housekeeper informed Jonathon, and distracted by a commotion at the front door, turned to the entrance vestibule.

At sight of the Dowager Duchess of Roxton the woman's jaw fell open. It was not Antonia's physical presence, but her demeanor that so surprised and delighted the old retainer. The Duchess was as she remembered her when the old Duke was alive, so brimful of vitality, that the housekeeper blinked and wondered if time had somehow wound itself backwards. So much so that she half expected the old Duke to come sauntering in behind his wife.

Antonia came into the black and white checkered marble entrance foyer in a whirlwind of fine cotton petticoats over which was a fur trimmed cloak, the calash hood thrown back to reveal her upswept honey curls, mussed from travel. She allowed Phelps the butler to divest her of this travelling attire, gave him her muff, stripped off her lavender kid gloves, turned to a liveried footman and handed over her two whippets into this startled servant's care, gave her curls a quick prod with her finger tips and then turned back to the butler and asked after his arthritic knee and if he had tried the feverfew decoction prescribed by the apothecary to relieve the pain as she had suggested in her letter at Christmastime? No? She looked over her shoulder at her personal maid and told Michelle to send for the apothecary. Then turned back to Phelps and chided him for not taking better care of himself.

In the next breath she was apologizing to Mrs. Phelps, who had come to stand beside her husband and bobbed a low curtsey, for arriving on the doorstep with very little notice and she hoped that she had not put the household to too much bother, and if it wasn't an extra burden would she please see to it that her dress-maker, shoemaker and milliner were informed of her arrival and that she would see them all on the morrow.

"And what of my son, Mrs. Phelps?" Antonia asked in her thickly accented English as she bustled through the vestibule into the main hall towards the book room, where she saw Jonathon had gone on ahead of her. "Are Lord Henri-Antoine and Sir John behaving themselves? I hope they have not been a burden on the servants?"

"Not at all, your Grace," the housekeeper assured her. "They have been as proper young gentlemen ought, particularly since Mr. Strang has come to stay. May I be so bold as to say how gratifying it is to see you looking so well, your Grace!" Mrs. Phelps exclaimed at the double doors to the book room and bobbed another curtsey, stepping aside to allow her husband to do his duty. "So very, very gratifying, your Grace. I shall have refreshments sent in directly, and your bath drawn."

"Thank you, Mrs. Phelps," Antonia replied with a kind smile, and followed the butler into the book room, wondering what was behind the housekeeper's comment that Jonathon had come to stay yet setting this and all other considerations aside at the prospect of seeing her youngest son for the first time since Christmastime.

Jonathon had gone on ahead to the book room reasoning that if he had learnt anything of Henri-Antoine and Jack Cavendish's habits in the week he had spent coming and going from the Hanover Square mansion to his dying relative's death bed in Upper Brook Street, it was that they spent most of their time laying about the book room smoking cheroots and drinking the old Duke's cellar dry of fine brandy; two vices any mother of a fifteen-year-old boy would not look kindly upon, particularly when the said youth was considered by his mother to be incapable of functioning without a physician as his constant shadow. What Jonathon privately thought of Henri-Antoine's health, ill or otherwise, was unimportant; not upsetting Antonia was very important.

Thus he swooped down on the two youths, who were indeed sprawled out on respective sofas, books and maps scattered about every surface and across the Turkey rug in various stages of being read and thumbed through, brandy decanter and used glasses on a silver tray on the low table between them, and rising above the leather bound volumes each youth had stuck up to his face a thin curl of smoke, clear evidence that they had succumbed to the addictive attractions of the rolled leaf.

To a connoisseur who was intent on eschewing the delights of the tobacco leaf, Jonathon had no hesitation in forcibly removing Jack Cavendish's cheroot from the corner of his mouth and quickly consigning it to the flames in the fireplace. Henri-Antoine's would have gone the same way but Antonia was almost up the length of the room and there being no time to dispose of the cigarillo Jonathon stuck it between his teeth as if it was his and inhaled long and leisurely, keeping the cheroot between two long fingers as if it had been there all the time.

In the uproar of being deprived of such a small pleasure, the youths both sat bolt upright, protesting at the high-handedness of their host until they saw the reason for his actions and were on their feet in an instant; Henri-Antoine pushing a mop of black hair from his forehead and blinking at his mother as if she were an apparition. And then he tossed aside the book in his hand rushed to meet her and twirled her about in his arms.

"Maman!? You've put off your black!" he announced and set her down but did not let her go. "What are you doing here?"

"Do I need a reason to see my son?" Antonia asked, pretending to be affronted, and put out a hand to Jack Cavendish who had scrambled over a stack of books, sending the tomes toppling to the rug, and with a grin, copper curls falling into his eyes. "You are both looking very well, if a little unkempt." She laughed when Jack attempted to brush the deep creases from his rumpled oyster silk waistcoat that was buttoned irregularly, and pulled the youth to her to kiss both his flushed cheeks and brush a copper curl from his eyes. "I have missed you both so very much," she said softly, leaning into her son and trying her best not to tear up. "And by the state of this room and your clothes, it is as well I came to London," she added, a sweeping glance about the disorderly state of the book room, at the empty brandy decanter and glasses and at the two porcelain tea saucers on opposite sides of the low table between the two sofas that were full of cheroot tips and ash, and which she chose to ignore though she did raise her eyebrows at Jonathon who was leaning against the mantle puffing on a cheroot she did not remember him having when they had entered the house.

She stepped away from her son, still holding his hand, to look him up and down, from polished leather shoes with diamond shoe buckles to the neatness of his black silk breeches and waistcoat with short skirts and tight cuffs with silver lacings and plain white linen stock, and fixed finally on his lean handsome face. His dark eyes and strong nose were so reminiscent of his father it brought a lump to her throat and she swallowed hard and forced herself to smile.

"You have grown taller, Henri," she said evenly. "And look very well. But where is Bailey?"

Henri-Antoine kissed her hand and looked into her damp green eyes with an understanding smile. "Bailey was given his freedom more than a year ago, Maman."

"*Pour quoi?*"

"I came to an agreement with Roxton. One year free of seizures and Bailey need not be my shadow. A second year free of seizures and my long suffering physician could be free of me and I of him."

"You have not had a bout of the Falling Sickness in *three* years?"

Antonia was amazed and she glanced at Jack, who was grinning, and then at Jonathon before staring anew at her son. To hide a myriad of emotions at such welcome news, not least of which was remorse at neglecting her youngest son, and to stop the tears from falling onto her cheeks, she said with asperity,

"I am very pleased the Falling Sickness it has left you alone and Bailey he is no longer your shadow, Henri, but it does not give you and Jack leave to drink Monseigneur's brandy like it is water and to take up this silly new habit of smoking tobacco leaves, whatever other foolish young men do, it is not for you to do. Now that I am here," she added, looking significantly not only at her son but at Jack and Jonathon too, "everyone will behave as they ought or me I will become very cross and none of you want to make me cross, *n'est-ce pas?* You understand me?"

"Perfectly," Henri-Antoine and Jack replied obediently, but Jack was unable to contain a laugh when Jonathon rolled his eyes and tossed the cheroot into the fireplace. Before Antonia could turn to see what had amused Jack, Henri-Antoine pulled her into an embrace, saying with suppressed emotion, looking over his mother's shoulder at Jonathon,

"Maman, you have returned to us, and that pleases us so very *very* much."

~~~───◦~~~

They were sitting down to dinner when the messenger arrived. Phelps was reluctant to interrupt. He had not seen the Duchess so animated and full of life in many years and this was the first family meal she had shared with her son in the Hanover Square house since the death of the old Duke. The conversation was unflagging and punctuated with bursts of laughter from the diners; Mr. Strang lounged at the foot of the table in a bright yellow silk embroidered waistcoat, his attire almost as resplendent as the Duchess who sat opposite him in an open robed gown with shell pink silk petticoats embroidered with bud roses on the vine and a matching low-cut bodice, hair upswept, heavy curls falling forward over her left shoulder; the two young gentlemen dressed with all the sartorial splendor they could muster for the occasion, as was the dapper little librarian in his scarlet waistcoat, a large silk bow of the same color holding his shoulder length gray hair to the nape of his neck.

The arrival of Mr. Gidley Ffolkes to dinner was a surprise only to Antonia, who welcomed the librarian with so much enthusiasm that he blushed and when she scolded the others for not informing her that he was a guest in the house he stammered for a suitable response, and it was left to Jonathon to explain that it was he who had engaged Mr. Ffolkes's expertise to make an inventory of the collection in the book room, a task commenced some three days ago. Jonathon conveniently failed to mention that he was in discussions with the librarian to have him travel north of the border to take charge of the library at Leven Castle; the inducement being that Jonathon's ancient relative not only had a vast library that was in total disarray and thus required the much needed services of a bibliothecary, he had one of the best, and possibly the most extensive, collections of illuminated manuscripts in Europe.

Finally, with the dishes cleared away and the Duchess declaring that coffee would be served in the book room, the butler delivered the sealed missive, apologizing in an under-voice that the messenger remained in the withdrawing room awaiting an immediate response. Jonathon read the short note and told Phelps he would need his greatcoat and gloves whereupon the butler informed Mr. Strang that the messenger had arrived in a hackney and that it awaited them both in the square.

Antonia had never seen him so grim faced and she sent the boys and Gidley Ffolkes on ahead to the book room, her first thought with Jonathon's daughter but he shook his head, slipping the note into a waistcoat pocket saying on a sigh,

"Sarah-Jane remains with Kitty and Tommy at their townhouse. I was to send for her to join us tomorrow but now, with this news..." He rubbed his brow as if suddenly tired and tried to be flippant, giving her an affectionate flick under the chin, "Don't wait up for me. I could be away two hours or ten."

Antonia went with him into the entrance foyer and watched as he was shrugged into his greatcoat, a frown between her brows.

"I do not want to add to your burden but there is much you are keeping from me," she stated. "And so I will wait: two hours or ten. Time it is unimportant. What is important is that you tell me."

He looked up from fitting on his gloves and nodded. "Yes. It is time." And was gone out into the night. When he returned three hours later he found Antonia in the book room curled up in a wingchair closest the fireplace reading, and in the wingchair opposite, swirling brandy in a glass and staring broodingly into the fire, Charles Fitzstuart.

Seeing Jonathon, the young man leapt to his feet and said without preamble, "Sir! I've come to ask for your daughter's hand in marriage and I need your answer tonight!"

Twenty-two

Charles Fitzstuart's startling declaration stopped Jonathon advancing to the fireplace. For a full five seconds he stared at the young man wondering if he had misheard him and then he spied the heavy silver tray holding brandy decanter and glasses and poured himself a thumb width full and drank without tasting. The second glass he savored and finally turned to face Charles, a quick look exchanged with Antonia who, by the widening of her green eyes, told him Charles's declaration was as much a surprise to her as to him.

"I must say I applaud your direct approach, Charles. Most young men would at least provide several minutes of inane conversation on all manner of topics designed to bamboozle the girl's father into thinking them a complete paperskull before verbally hitting him over the head with such a declaration. Not you." Jonathon peered keenly at the red-faced young man. "I dare say you're incapable of inane conversation." He looked at Antonia and jerked his head in Charles's direction. "Is your cousin too earnest for drivel, Mme la duchesse?"

Antonia put aside Rousseau's *Du Contrat Social* and rang the small hand bell at her elbow. "It is you who are spouting drivel, M'sieur. Charles he has asked you a perfectly reasonable question which deserves a reasonable response."

Jonathon gave a shout of laughter and set his shoulders against the mantelpiece. "You're right. I am. I've had a very tiring night; that must be it."

But turning to stare Charles up and down over his brandy glass he lost his smile, his brown eyes went dead and there was an uncompromising set to his jaw that made his features suddenly harsh so that he appeared ruthless and unyielding; an altogether different being from the one Antonia knew and she wondered if this was how he conducted business for the Company on the subcontinent.

"So you want to marry my daughter, young man? Why?"

"I love her, sir."

"Love her? Easily said; not easily applied." Jonathon shrugged. "So you love her. You need more than that to sustain a wife. What can you offer her?"

"Offer her?"

"The question is simple enough. What can you, a second son of an earl, who has no prospect of inheriting title, lands or money, who has but one degree, and not a very useful degree at that, languages, and who has no intention of entering the army, the Church or practicing the law, which are the preferred professions of younger sons and provide some semblance of an income to support a wife and children, and you certainly have no skills or experience whatsoever in the mercantile world: What can you offer my daughter?"

"S-Sir, I-I—"

"Sarah-Jane has been raised with every comfort. She has particular expectations, a lifestyle to maintain. She is used to the best of everything and the best of everything costs money, a great deal of money."

"Sarah-Jane does not care about money—"

"Ballocks! Only the wealthy can afford the luxury of not caring about money," Jonathon scoffed. "If she told you that I wonder you want to marry such a simpleton!"

"She isn't—"

"Next you'll be telling me she don't care about title either! Which is also a great piece of nonsense because all I've heard from her for the past twelvemonth is her great desire to marry a Baronet *at the very least*." Jonathon set down his empty glass and peered keenly at the young man. "You have asked her? You did find out the lay of the land before you came here boldly seeking permission from her father? We are not having a pointless discussion, are we?"

"I have spoken to Miss Strang, sir," Charles stated, round chin in the air, meeting Jonathon's hard stare without a blink, "and she has consented to be my wife if you will give us your blessing and consent."

"Didn't it work out with your brother?"

"I beg your pardon?"

"Did your brother not want her—"

"Not want her? It was she who—"

"—so she decided that second best was better than nothing? What a great pile of fartleberries! Sarah-Jane has never settled for second best in her life! So what did you promise her that you can't deliver? You don't have a title, so it must be something mighty substantial to bamboozle a girl like Sarah-Jane. Or have you deliberately put my daughter in a compromising position that she can't now get out of it? Aye? You tell me!"

"*Strang.* That is *enough*," Antonia demanded in an angry whisper, half out of the wingchair.

Yet, when Jonathon looked down at her with an almost imperceptible shake of his head and winked, she understood at once that he was baiting the young man most cruelly and she glared at him in warning, not liking his tactics at all, which almost cracked his hard façade, and she sank back down again and turned to the footman who had appeared at her shoulder to order coffee. She was about to ask the gentlemen if they required anything else but was not given the opportunity. Charles Fitzstuart, who had not seen the exchange between the Duchess and Jonathon because the presence of the footman had distracted him, was livid at Jonathon's accusations and cavalier attitude about his feelings for Sarah-Jane and his sincere wish to marry her and he turned on Jonathon with a rage he had never thought himself capable.

"You are very fortunate, very fortunate indeed, that I came here at all!" he exploded. "Sarah-Jane was all for eloping on the first packet for France! Much you know about your daughter, *sir*. She was willing to live with me in sin, as my mistress, in France, until such time as we could wed on her twenty-first birthday, as stay in this country a moment longer, because she knows that every day I remain on English soil the hangman's noose tightens about my throat! But I said no. I would not consent to her being my mistress. If it came to that, I proposed that she remain with you and that we wait out the two years. That course was not acceptable to her and so she agreed that we do as I first suggested.

"And so here you find me before you, doing the right and honorable thing by her as your daughter and by you, as her father, seeking your permission for us to wed. I want her, *us*, to have your blessing. I want her to always be on good relations with you whatever you may think of me, and what I've done! I considered you a decent and honorable man. A man with a liberal mind prepared to give me a fair hearing; who would realize that his daughter is far better off married to me, who will love and treasure her and be a faithful husband and a good father to our children, traitor or no in your eyes and the eyes of others, than married to my brother who cares for nobody but himself and who would marry your daughter for her dowry with no intention of giving up his mistress! Is that the sort of man you want for your daughter? Well, is it, sir?"

"No, Charles, it is not," Jonathon replied quietly. "It was Sarah-Jane who was determined to marry a title, not I. I have only ever wanted my daughter to be happy."

Charles Fitzstuart stopped his pacing. Not that he realized he had been pacing back and forth before the fireplace, or that he'd had a hand splayed in his hair, and then both hands balled in fists, or that he had been shouting at his prospective father-in-law. He blinked up at the tall man and took a deep breath, suddenly thirsty and embarrassed at his uncharacteristic outburst. He stepped over to where Antonia sat silent, hands in the lap of her silk petticoats, a small smile hovering about her lovely mouth, and bowed solemnly.

"Forgive me, Mme la duchesse. I should never have raised my voice. My feelings—the way I feel about Miss Strang—forgive me."

Antonia put out a hand and when Charles took it with a nervous smile she said softly, "Never apologize for your feelings, Charles." She glanced at Jonathon, who leaned against the mantle, and squeezed her cousin's fingers. When Charles looked down into her eyes she held his gaze and said with a sad smile, "But perhaps there is a matter, a far more serious matter, for which you do need to apologize...?"

Charles nodded. If his face had diffused red with anger at Jonathon it was now puce with embarrassment and mortification at the Duchess and he swallowed and wondered how best to sort his disordered emotions to explain himself. He was given a small reprieve when the butler and two footmen came soft-footed into the book room with the coffee things and although he would have preferred something much stronger, a cup of coffee was welcome and helped steady his nerves and collect his thoughts for the confession he rightly owed not only Antonia, but Jonathon if he hoped to have the merchant's consent to marry Sarah-Jane.

Again, he took the direct approach but he was calmer and found it surprisingly effortless to explain his actions as a traitor to the English crown than he did his love for Sarah-Jane.

"Perhaps when you hear what I have to confess, sir, you will withhold your consent to a union between your daughter and myself," Charles stated evenly, putting aside the porcelain cup and saucer. "Not because I am a second son with few prospects here in England, but because, in the eyes of my countrymen, I am a traitor to His Majesty King George and to my country. I am, and have been since the outset of the declaration of war against our brothers and sisters in the American colonies, been a supporter of those colonists who have taken up arms against us. I find taxation without representation insupportable. The injustices that have been perpetrated by this government against our American cousins are too numerous for me to mention save that I believe the American colonists have every right to govern themselves. It is absurd for this government to think it can rule a colony from this distance, to expect men so far away to petition Parliament and wait a year to receive a response to their request!

"I have always held doubts about the way our society is structured, the fact it is governed by a titled minority who have done nothing to earn their exalted positions than be born from a noble womb; and that birth order determines who is to rule and who must find their own way in the world, regardless of their abilities. In truth, sir, I find the notion of the divine right of kings nonsensical and aristocratic privilege absurd.

"I apologize, Mme la duchesse," Charles added with sincerity, "not for my beliefs but I have no wish to intentionally offend you or M'sieur le Duc de Roxton your son. You are the best of what your class can offer. You are honest and fair and believe the worth of a man is to be found in his deeds, not just in his bloodline, and I believe, sir, your opinions are not dissimilar to those held by Mme la duchesse?" he said to Jonathon who continued to regard him with an expression he found hard to read; an expression that was far more unnerving than his cold demeanor of earlier. "Do you not agree with me that all men are created equal in the sight of God, and thus all men should be given access to opportunity without fear or favor of their birth? That is what the new American nation believes in wholeheartedly and that is the society I wish to be part of, and the one in which I wish to raise a family, with your daughter, with your permission and, it is our deepest wish, with your blessing."

Jonathon remained silent almost too long for Charles to contain himself and then he took his shoulders off the ornate mantle and stood straight and tugged on the points of his bright yellow waistcoat and took a deep breath.

"I don't disagree with most of what you say, Charles," Jonathon replied evenly. "Your sentiments are sincere and it is hard to argue against a society founded on the good deeds of men rather than on the distinction of their birth alone. But what do you propose to do in this new nation, should the American colonies succeed in the war against our King and country?"

"I have employment waiting for me in Paris with Mr. Franklin, sir. I mean to be his secretary and will be his interpreter at the French Court. After that?" Charles shrugged and was sheepish. "It is my earnest desire to enter the political arena in the new nation of the American states. I dare to hope that the colonists will embrace me as one of their own, and that one day I may represent them, should they see fit to elect me to their parliament."

"*Of more worth is one honest man to society and in the sight of God, than all the crowned ruffians that ever lived*," Antonia quoted. She smiled. "I believe you will succeed, Charles."

Charles nodded and grinned that the Duchess chose to quote from the pamphlet *Common Sense* but Jonathon's response wiped the smile from his face.

"That is very noble and worthy of you, Charles, and it pleases me to no end that you are intent on doing something with your life, for men must have occupation and purpose in life or they get themselves into mischief. Can't abide idleness or wastefulness. And like Mme la duchesse I, too, believe you have the brain and determination to succeed at such a venture. But you are yet to explain why it is you think it is that every day you remain on English soil the hangman's noose tightens about your fine neck? We are not at war with the French and so you may cross the Channel with impunity."

Charles coughed into his fist to clear his throat and looked, not at Jonathon, but at Antonia. His remorse was palpable. "I deceived you, and for that I will never forgive myself, Mme la duchesse. I let you believe that the letters I wrote and had you send on to Paris were for a certain young lady."

"Silas Deane, *hein?*"

"Ah, you know. I thought you might by now." For Jonathon's benefit he explained. "I sent coded messages to a representative of the American colonists in Paris with information I deemed of use to them under the guise of writing to a young female. The letters were addressed by Mme la duchesse and sent to the Roxton's Parisian family home. At no time did I tell Mme la duchesse the truth, nor inform her, though I knew well enough, that the Hôtel had been sold and turned into apartments. I make no apologies for my treasonous actions but for deceiving you, Mme la duchesse, I am truly sorry," he added, bowing solemnly to the Duchess.

Antonia looked up at him. "My son he also knows and so does Lord Shrewsbury and the *Committee for Colonial Correspondence of Interest*."

Charles nodded. "His Grace has been most generous. Roxton wrote advising that the Committee had questions for me and I realized then that I had been discovered. His Grace did not have to put himself to the trouble, particularly when he must think me a traitorous dog."

"You are still family, Charles," Antonia interrupted. "And my son, for all his stiff-necked belief in doing what is right, has a deep sense of family."

Charles nodded and cleared his throat.

"Yes, Mme la duchesse. I am forever in his debt for his warning. It gave me the time to put my affairs in order, and to make arrangements for our departure tomorrow—if, sir, you consent to your daughter marrying me."

"The urgency?"

Charles smiled crookedly in spite of himself. "The Duke gained me time but I am still a wanted man. Lord Shrewsbury has requested that I present myself at his offices for an interview. Tomorrow. I am certain that it is only the esteem in which he holds His Grace of Roxton that has forced him to treat me as a gentleman and not as a common criminal. If Shrewsbury had his way I would have been hunted down by now, clapped in irons and be a guest in the Tower. The spymaster's idea of an interview involves the use of torture. I am told by reliable sources that his preferred method of seeking the appropriate response to a question is one often employed by physicians in the treatment of recalcitrants, particularly females, in which the victim is stripped, placed in a straight-backed chair specially fitted out for the purpose with leather restraints and then strapped ankle and wrist and then—"

"Please, Charles, no more," whispered the Duchess, suddenly faint.

"—ice cold water is poured continually over the head until a confession is obtained or the victim—"

"Enough!" Jonathon growled and in two strides was down on bended knee beside Antonia's chair. "Sweetheart, it's all right," he murmured reassuringly, pressing his lips to her hand. He touched his forehead to her hair, saying gently, "I won't let that happen again. Ever. Not to you, not to Charles. Even if I have to break a dozen more fingers and cripple ten fellows. But it won't come to that."

Antonia nodded, took a deep breath and lifted her head to smile into his brown eyes, eyes that searched her pale face with concern. She put a hand to his stubbled cheek. "I know you would. I am being a little foolish but it will pass. *Merci.*"

Jonathon smiled and winked and rose up to his full height, saying as evenly as he could muster given he had just made a public display of his feelings for Antonia and before the young man soon to be his son-in-law,

"I can't just let you run off with my daughter without her reassurances that you are what she wants in a husband and that she is well aware that the life you propose for the two of you means exile; not that she won't be used to that having lived all her life on the subcontinent, but it does mean separation from me, perhaps forever."

"Yes, yes, I realize that, sir," Charles said haltingly, mind still dazed with new knowledge after witnessing the intimate scene between the couple, and he quickly mentally shook himself free, adding, "Sarah-Jane and I mean to call here in the morning, sir."

"With your trunks packed, no doubt."

Charles laughed. "Yes, sir. If we are to make it to Dover on time, we need to depart as early as possible after daybreak."

"She must indeed love you if she is prepared to flee to a country whose language she does not speak with a known spy who is being hunted as a traitor!" Jonathon stuck out his hand and Charles gratefully took it. "God help you both."

Charles grinned. "Thank you, sir. You won't regret it. Thank you, Mme la duchesse," he said when Antonia embraced him and kissed both his cheeks. "I will write from Paris and give Mr. Franklin your best wishes."

"It don't matter a wit if I regret it," Jonathon quipped, walking Charles to the double doors. "Just make certain my daughter never does! And I'll tell you now: Her dowry is—"

"No, sir. I don't want your money."

At that Jonathon laughed so loud the footman clearing away the coffee things almost overset the silver tray he was balancing on one gloved hand.

"You might not, dear boy, but Sarah-Jane certainly will! And these are the conditions under which I'll hand over the twenty-five thousand pounds: Not one penny of her dowry is to be spent on the American cause, not one. I won't have my hard earned fortune used to further a war, regardless of the combatants. Use your brain but not my money. It is for her comfort. If the colonies do win this war and become a free country with free elections then you are welcome to use her inheritance with my blessing and hers as you see fit to better this new society with which you are so enamored, but Sarah-Jane comes first in all things. Always."

"You have had quite an evening of surprises, n'est-ce pas?" Antonia chuckled when Jonathon returned to the book room and sprawled out on the wingchair opposite her and put a hand up to his eyes.

"In the space of one evening I have gone from arranging a funeral to consenting to my daughter's elopement with a wanted traitor. I do not need any more surprises."

When he did not remove his hand she went over and stood before his chair and leaned in to him, hands on the wingchair's padded rolled arms. "Then I shall say good night," she said softly. "It is late and your daughter she will be on the doorstep early."

He splayed his fingers and was presented with the wonderful vista of her deep cleavage visible through the sheer fichu and he sat up, more awake than he had been since returning from Upper Brook Street. He gently pulled her to him and she obliged by gathering up the many layers of her silk petticoats to straddle his legs to sit on his lap.

"You are a good and generous father. You will miss her very much."

"Every day," he agreed, a hand to the small of her back. "But I must content myself that she is well-loved and has chosen her own path. Her letters will be small consolation but perhaps all is not lost? I predict the war will take years to run its course, as all wars do, and if the French become involved, even longer. So Sarah-Jane and her Charles will be settled in Paris for some time. If they cannot come to us, we shall go to them."

"We?"

"We'll take Henri and Jack. You'd like to visit Paris again, wouldn't you?"

"Yes. But I no longer have a house there. Roxton he sold it."

"We'll get ourselves another."

Antonia pinched his chin, laughing. "Another? You think these houses they grow on vines and can be picked like grapes?"

Jonathon frowned, toying with the uppermost pink silk bow of her low cut décolletage, one of a dozen down the front of her bodice. "Sadly, we won't be able to visit for awhile. I've given my word to go north for six months but I suspect we'll be there for nine; there is so much to do."

"Given your word? To whom? How far north?" Antonia was intrigued but also wary of his constant use of the first person plural *we*, as if it was now a forgone conclusion she would fall in with his plans. "What is this *to do* you speak about?"

He stopped fiddling with the bow and looked into her green eyes.

"Tonight my ancient relative finally died. I say finally because he has been near death's door for at least three years. Old fool was on a hunt, attempted to jump a fence, fell off and as a consequence lost the use of both his legs. I was sent for from my sun-soaked sub-continental veranda after the accident because he wasn't expected to live. He did. He was chair-ridden, then bed-ridden, and then dying. I am his only living relative. His son died when I was five, and then my brother died and that left me. Reason I was sent to Harrow and Oxford. I had seen him upon only four occasions in my life, when I was called to his deathbed, so there is no need for anyone to feel sympathy for me, particularly when he has left me nothing but a pile of debts, a crumbling estate and a title I do not in the least want and had every intention of dis-claiming."

"How far north?"

"I've been to the estate. There is a bluestone castle very much in the French manner with circular turrets and mansard roofs of gray slate, and a fanciful drawbridge at the end of a four arch stone bridge because the castle itself is on an island in the middle of a lake—which is called a loch in Scotland; Loch Leven to be precise."

"*Écosse? Scotland?*"

"The aspect is charming and the castle more a chateau, but it needs work," he said conversationally, ignoring her wide-eyed horror. He might as well have said the estate was in Batavia, such was the ends-of-the-earth look on Antonia's face. "To point out fact, it needs a great deal of time and money spent on it. So does the estate. The tenants live in hovels and are half-starved. I shall change all that." He flicked her cheek with a smile. "There's also a splendid townhouse in Edinburgh which also could do with new wallpaper, drapes, furnishings; new everything. The rest is debts, which I can take care of rather quickly now Kinross is dead and soon to be buried. But I see I have given such a glowing picture that you are likely to suffer a nightmare so let's leave the rest of my unwanted inheritance until breakfast, shall we?"

"You did not think to say no to this unwanted inheritance and stay in India?"

"Oh, I thought about it for all of five minutes. But then I remembered the first time I met Kinross. I was Henri-Antoine's age and sent north to spend Christmas with him. He wanted to instill in me how fortunate I was to be his heir and what I could look forward to one day." Jonathon puffed out his cheeks and shook his head. "The degradation suffered by his tenants is staggering. The burden of responsibility on my young shoulders was almost too much to bear. I sailed back to the subcontinent knowing I didn't have a choice; that I had a duty to return when the time came." He smiled at her. "And that time has come. I think nine months should give Sarah-Jane ample time to build her Parisian nest, don't you? Who knows, I could be a grandpapa in the New Year."

"Grandpapa?" Antonia giggled, and was suitably diverted, which was Jonathon's aim. "She and Charles have yet to marry and you instantly have yourself a grandfather? Absurd man! I hope they are able to spend some time together without babies."

"You didn't."

"No. I was instantly pregnant which did not please me at all."

"I'll wager it pleased Monseigneur. It would please me."

Antonia did not know where to look. "I am not—I do not know—I do not know why we are having this meaningless conversation!" she snapped when he grinned at her awkwardness. "If people overheard us talking of babies they would think us fit for bedlam. I have a son who has four children and with another on the way and you talk to me of babies—of *us* having babies? Why are you grinning at me in that idiotic way?"

"But you're not barren, are you? So the conversation isn't meaningless, is it?"

Antonia sat up tall. She was horrified. "How-how do you know this?"

"Your outrage is adorable," he grinned, pulling playfully on the little pink bow. "I didn't interrogate your maid or your servants, if that is your objection. And I don't have an overpowering desire to have children, to have an heir. I never have. It's just that if it happened, if we were to have a child..." He grinned. "Well, we can at least spend the rest of our lives trying!"

She pouted. "It is most inconvenient for a woman of my age to still be cursed in this way! It is not humorous at all, so please, you will put away that ridiculous grin!"

"A curse to you mayhap, but..." he muttered and broke off, distracted when the silk bow unraveled between his fingers; no mere decoration after all, the bows had a purpose: to hold fast the bodice, which now gaped, revealing the little lace edge of her transparent cotton chemise and more of her cleavage. He tugged the chemise away with his chin and breathed in deeply, enjoying the scent of her warm skin mingled with the perfume he had given her, marveling at the glorious weightiness of her full breasts, and silently praising Monseigneur for preferring his wife in jumps to laced back stays. With her hands about his neck, he used his free hand to tug on the second bow. "*Mon Dieu* but you're so damnably *luscious*."

"And you, curse you," she murmured, shrugging off the gossamer fichu from her shoulders, breasts spilling forth from the gaping bodice as he deftly untied the remaining little pink bows then pushed the jumps off her shoulders and down her slim arms, "you are too virile for your own good."

He chuckled. "Shall we go to bed?"

It was her turn to grin.

"Yes," she said, dropping the jumps to the floor. "Later. Much, much later..."

$\mathcal{T}$wenty-three

$\mathcal{C}$harles Fitzstuart was good to his word and he and Sarah-Jane arrived at the Hanover Square mansion as daylight streaked the cold morning sky. The servants were just up and a bleary-eyed footman showed the couple into a downstairs drawing room, where a newly lit fire was doing its best to warm the room, while another woke Jonathon Strang's valet with the news his master had visitors. To Lawrence's surprise his new master had already bathed and dressed himself; not surprising was the fact his bed had not been slept in.

The interview in the drawing room took longer than expected, with tears all round, questions answered and assurances given over endless cups of tea, a startling confession by daughter to father and a not so surprising admission by father to daughter; Charles acting as happy witness. A more surprising witness to this emotional leave taking was Mrs. Spencer and when Sarah-Jane asked to see the Duchess alone for a few moments before setting off on the journey for France, it was Mrs. Spencer she asked to accompany her to the Duchess's boudoir, not Charles and most definitely not her father.

Antonia was seated at her dressing table in dishabille with

barely enough time to splash water on her face and thread a ribbon through her curls when Michelle admitted the two women. She had no idea what to expect from this meeting with Jonathon's daughter but she certainly did not expect to see one of her ladies-in-waiting and her trepidation was so starkly evident that Sally Spencer smiled reassuringly and was the first to go forward and curtsey, saying with a smile,

"I am not here on the orders of His Grace, Mme la duchesse. Nor is my sister with me. I am now companion to Mlle Strang and am accompanying her and Mr. Fitzstuart to Paris."

Antonia glanced at Sarah-Jane with some surprise but said evenly,

"And your sister?"

"Susannah has decided to remain with Lady Strathsay," Sally Spencer informed her. "Particularly," she added in English with a glance at Sarah-Jane, "as this is a most distressing time for the Countess. Susannah has been such a comfort."

"I do not doubt it," Antonia agreed, a picture in her mind's eye of her aunt prostrate on her chaise longue, Willis attentively fanning her with appropriate clucking noises of sympathy that the Countess's youngest son had run off with a merchant's daughter, which would be far more devastating to the Countess's self-consequence than the fact her son had been branded a traitor and was a fugitive.

"Papa is more comfortably resigned to Charles and I fleeing to Paris before we are married knowing Mrs. Spencer is with us," Sarah-Jane confessed in English and when offered sat on the sofa opposite Antonia's dressing stool, Sally Spencer beside her. "Not that Papa could have stopped me going with Charles had Mrs. Spencer not accepted my invitation."

This made Antonia smile and relax.

"You have your father's determination, which is not a bad thing, *cherie*," Antonia complimented her. "You must hold on to this as Charles, he is a very determined young man. So I predict you and he will have some interesting times ahead. And of course I wish you both very happy."

"Thank you, your Grace," Sarah-Jane responded, clasping and unclasping her hands, the only outward sign of her nervousness to be in the presence of the Dowager Duchess of Roxton. "I apologize for not being able to converse with you in your own tongue but Papa assured me your English is very good, and I do hope to learn French. Well, I am resolved to do so given Paris will be our home for the foreseeable future. But I do not wish to talk to you of my future, but my father's future." She bravely met Antonia's gaze and secretly wished the Duchess had been old, gray-haired and plain-faced and not so breathtakingly lovely, and then her father would not have looked twice and this conversation need not have been required. "I do not know if Papa has confided this in you, I dare say not, because he did not confide it in me, Aunt Kitty told me: I am not his daughter."

Antonia sat up, startled, and glanced at Sally Spencer who smiled encouragingly at Sarah-Jane, so knew the story the young woman was about to tell.

"Not his daughter? Why would Lady Cavendish tell you such a thing, even if it were true?"

"In the hopes that I would reconsider Alisdair Fitzstuart's offer and accept it, rather than follow my heart."

"I am sorry, petite, but I do not understand how such a shocking revelation could induce you to accept the one brother if you loved the other? It is incomprehensible."

Sarah-Jane smiled, warming to the Duchess.

"It is, isn't it? But as I had always maintained I wanted to marry a Baronet at the very least, Aunt Kitty assumed that knowing I am my father's natural daughter and not his legal daughter and thus cannot call myself Lady Sarah-Jane, which is the right of a daughter of a peer, I would grab at the chance to be a nobleman's wife; my desire to hide the base circumstances of my birth far outweighing my desire to marry for love."

The Duchess was indignant. "Kitty Cavendish must have cotton between her ears to think such a thing! It is preposterous." She regarded Sarah-Jane with a tender smile. "You are your father's daughter and that is all that matters, yes? And now that you tell me it is not such a surprise because your father he told me once that you were born in South Africa and yet your parents, they did not marry until they arrived in Hyderabad?"

"That is correct, your Grace. When my mother eloped with

my father she was still the wife of her first husband. Mr. Spencer died just weeks after I was born and yet under the law, I am his daughter. Legally I am a Spencer, not a Strang-Leven."

Antonia waved a hand in dismissal. "It is of no consequence. Your father remains your father and Charles, knowing him as I do, would not care an *écu*, for this small detail of your birth; it is unimportant. And of course, all that matters is that your Papa he knows that you love him and is happy."

"Yes, your Grace," Sarah-Jane replied and knowing it was the moment to voice her concerns, took a deep breath and said as confidently as she could muster, "It is my father's happiness that I wish to speak to you about." When the Duchess's pale cheeks flushed with color and yet her smile became fixed, Sarah-Jane had a great desire to grab for Sally Spencer's hand for support. Instead she pressed her fingers together and continued a little less confident than before. "I love Papa very much and it saddens me that we will be separated, despite his assurances that he will visit us in Paris and that if I am happy he will be happy." She looked down at her lap and then directly at the Duchess. "To be frank, your Grace, I was very much against Papa attaching himself to you. You are not young. You were married to a much older husband who was besotted with you and you still mourn for him. Papa is a decade younger than you and yet he, too, is now besotted with you. It is the stuff of cheap melodrama.

"And to be perfectly truthful, it was humiliating to watch Papa pursue you at the Roxton house party. I begged him to leave you alone. He would not. I told him he was making himself and me the object of gossip and ridicule and we argued. I said that if he did not desist I would never speak to him again. He did not heed my threat and we parted on the most acrimonious terms. I went to Lady Strathsay's estate distraught and-and *hating* you."

"*Cherie*, I would never intentionally come between a father and his daughter," Antonia told her gently, "between you and your father, and it pains me that I was the cause of your distress."

"I-I know that now, your Grace," Sarah-Jane confessed and sniffed, taking the handkerchief Sally Spencer pressed into hands and quickly dabbing at her moist eyes. When Sally Spencer offered her gloved hand, she took it in a firm hold and smiled at her before turning to Antonia and saying with a sniff, "Your Grace, I sincerely believed I was acting in the best interests of Papa. Aunt Kitty and Uncle Tommy have been most persistent that my father needs a young wife who can give him many children, an heir. They still believe, and they are not the only ones, his attaching himself to you is not in his best interests and may even harm his chances of contracting a suitable match. But I have since learned from Mrs. Spencer, and also from my dear Charles, that you are not the sort of female who would trifle with my father's affections—"

"Miss Strang, I—"

"And so I ask you—no I *beg* you—if you do have feelings for my father, you must consider his changed circumstances and press upon him that he has a duty to his great-uncle and to those who held the title before him, to contract a suitable match with a woman who can give him a son and heir. I fear you are the only one who can make him see reason. As a duchess and as mother of a duke, you understand that if a man inherits a peerage he has an obligation to have a son."

She smiled nervously, adding with a deep breath, "And if Papa was to contract an arranged marriage he need not—I would not expect him to—give up his mistress..."

Antonia was up off her dressing stool and the two women across from her were instantly on their feet. Coincidentally, there were raised voices on the other side of the boudoir door out in the passageway and all three women looked to the door which provided Antonia a moment's reprieve to collect her thoughts. She did not disagree with the young woman's sentiments and despite Sarah-Jane's olive branch – that she was prepared to accept Antonia as her father's mistress – she was mortified. Yet, what else was she but Jonathon Strang's mistress? And what else could she ever be? If, as Sarah-Jane said, her father had inherited a title of some distinction then yes, he did indeed need to marry and produce an heir, whatever his reassurances that begetting children was unimportant.

Monseigneur had been Jonathon Strang's age when he had finally married and within a year she had provided him with an heir. She had been eighteen years old and so there was every expectation of children. Two sons, half a dozen heartbreaking miscarriages and regular menses did not give her the right to believe she could give Jonathon Strang a child least of all an heir. That she could even allow herself to contemplate such an eventuality startled her. Knowing the exact nature of Jonathon Strang's elevation was unimportant, just knowing he was a peer of the realm, in whatever degree, was enough for her to agree with his daughter's assessment. What solidified her mortification was that this young woman felt compelled to enlist the support of her father's mistress to see that he followed through on his dynastic responsibilities.

She was spared further humiliation when her boudoir door was violently thrown open and Henri-Antoine, Jack Cavendish, Charles Fitzstuart and Jonathon Strang bundled into the room, and by the looks on their faces, chased by a lion escaped from the Tower Zoo and enjoying every minute of the frightening experience.

"The militia are at the door, Maman," Henri-Antoine announced with annoyance.

"They're demanding Charles or they'll break in the door!" Jack threw in, excited at the prospect of the house being overrun with redcoats.

"But Strang has a plan," Henri-Antoine drawled.

"It may be the only way we escape the house and evade capture," Charles apologized to his betrothed, breathing short and heavy from the rapid flight up the grand staircase.

Everyone looked to Jonathon.

"Two of the Duchess's cloaks, Michelle. Pronto!" Jonathon ordered and crossed to Antonia and took hold of her hands. "I need you at your imperious best, sweetheart, for you will confront the militia and demand by what right they have entered your house while Charles, Sarah-Jane and Mrs. Spencer wait here." He turned to include the others in his plans. "Meanwhile, Henri-Antoine and Jack dressed in the duchess's cloaks will pass themselves off as my daughter and Mrs. Spencer while I shall be Charles—"

"But, Papa, Charles is much too short," Sarah-Jane threw at him

"Thank you, my love," said Charles.

"The militia have never seen Charles, so his height is of no importance," Jonathon explained patiently. "We three will exit the house via the front door—"

"The militia will see you!"

"Not if Phelps has herded them into the Blue drawing room," Jonathon added, annoyed to be interrupted again by his daughter. "There are only six of them after all."

"Charles? *Six* militia to cart you away? They must think you very dangerous indeed," Antonia quipped and laughed when Charles straightened his stocky frame to all of its five foot seven inches and dared to smile smugly at his betrothed.

Michelle returned with the cloaks over an arm and Phelps appeared in the open doorway saying with great forbearance,

"I beg your pardon, Mme la duchesse, but there are a group of uniformed *individuals* in the Blue drawing room who are demanding the right to search the house. I have told them that under no circumstances can I allow them access to the house without your permission."

"Good man!" Jonathon exclaimed. "Tell them Mme la duchesse is on her way!" and grinned at Antonia. "Time for your performance, sweetheart." He turned to Charles. "Wait here five minutes then take the servant passage to the kitchen where you'll find your travelling trunks. I've sent for a hackney and Ffolkes will accompany you as far as the George where a coach will be waiting to take you to the coast, Ffolkes returning here by a different route should his movements be followed."

"You have co-opted Gidley into your madcap scheme?" Antonia was impressed.

"He and my valet are littering the staircase with books to impede the progress of our military guests should they make a dash for upstairs. So mind your step on the way down."

"And of course you told Gidley and Lawrence that by their actions in helping a traitor and fugitive they are now implicated?"

"Couldn't stop them if I tried!" Jonathon replied. "If only for lack of space, Lawrence would have gone with Ffolkes. I told him to stay here just in case the militia give you grief. But I am confident you can put in your best performance as indignant Duchess. That you are French will only add to their discomfort. Now go, woman, or my carefully laid plans will be ruined!"

"You are all enjoying yourself hugely!" Antonia accused them all without heat and said as an aside to Jonathon, "You most particularly!"

"Don't tell me you aren't too, Maman?" Henri-Antoine demanded, taking his mother's hand and pulling her to the doorway. "Now go or Strang's plans will be ruined!"

Antonia laughed, blew them all a kiss, but then stopped in the doorway, frowning, and addressed Jonathon.

"Be careful. They are militia after all and will be expecting Charles in the carriage. I want the boys—and you—returned unharmed. Promise."

Jonathon smiled into her eyes. "We'll be home for nuncheon. Promise. But in the unlikely event we are taken into custody, use the hundred guineas you owe me to post bail and—"

"You are a-a *fiend* and a-a *brute*!" Antonia hissed at him and was gone to do verbal battle with the militia, cursing the day a merchant had dared to invade her pretty pavilion by the lake.

<hr />

"I cannot sit here all day waiting!" Antonia announced, up off the window seat of her sunny sitting room. She put aside the copy of *School for Scandal*. It had not diverted her as she had hoped from thoughts of the boys and Jonathon off on their escapade to fool the militia. And there was another matter bothering her. It had been troubling her since leaving her dower house to come to London and she knew it would not be resolved until she had voiced her fears to the one person who knew her almost as well as had her husband.

So she called for her carriage, exchanged her silk embroidered slippers for a pair of heeled brocade mules with diamond buckles and collected up not one but five gouache painted fans from the more than a dozen in a dressing table drawer. Four of these and several bejeweled hair clasps she stuffed into a reticule and pushed on Michelle who obediently followed with reticule, shawl and fur trimmed cloak, should these articles be required, and climbed into the carriage beside the Duchess, with no idea as to their destination. Why the Duchess needed four additional fans and a treasure trove of hair adornments, Michelle was left to speculate. And as if this wasn't enough to fill her mind with worry, her mistress was so wrapped up in her own thoughts that she did not once peer out the window at the view or to wonder why the carriage had slowed almost to a snail's pace. Michelle did, and her concern increased to discover the carriage was trundling along in traffic heading east toward Tower Hill, the narrow streets and congestion of horses, carriages and wagons not to be found in the more salubrious environs of the west end squares and the surrounding streets of the elegant mansions and townhouses of Westminster.

When the horses finally came to a halt outside a double-fronted townhouse in Fournier Street some of Michelle's trepidation subsided, but she was still nonplussed as to why they had come into this part of London and found it almost unfathomable that a Duchess would be on such terms with any person in this neighborhood as to call on them personally.

A crowd had been growing in number as people followed behind the carriage making slow progress through the narrowed streets, and it now closed in, wanting a look at the occupants who travelled in a fine carriage and four with liveried footmen and a noble coat of arms on the black lacquered doors. A liveried footman hopped off the box and pulled down the footrest while another went up the two shallow stone steps to rap on the front door using the brass knocker.

There was a slight delay before the door opened, and then only wide enough for a maid in a frilly cap to poke her head out. She took in the liveried servant and then looked past the servant's powdered wig to the magnificent black carriage and four white horses, and at the second footman waiting silently by the open carriage door, and the girl's eyes went very round and the door was shut in the footman's face. The servant was about to rap the knocker again when the door opened a second time, and so wide that it was possible to see down the length of the passageway where it seemed every adult and child, servant and occupant were spilling out of rooms in a great frenzy of activity.

As three of the townhouse's occupants rushed into the street, the footman barely had the time to retreat to the carriage to where his fellow was assisting the Duchess to firm ground. The crowd closed in, but only as close as the two other footmen would permit, and were not disappointed when a beautiful elfin lady in a fashionable polonaise gown of brocade silk with matching shoes that had diamond buckles stepped from the carriage, upswept hair festooned with tiny bows and diamond clasps and in her gloved hand a painted fan.

There were murmurings of approval that the beautiful lady matched the magnificence of the carriage in which she travelled and discussion opened on whose coat of arms were emblazoned on the doors. One woman ventured to suggest it was Lord Salt Hendon's family shield but an erudite older gent carrying leather tomes under one arm and who had just come from tutoring the spotty-faced son of a brewer confidently proclaimed he would know the Duke of Roxton's coat of arms anywhere—he had once spent a quiet sojourn in the country where his third cousin was curate at the local village church close to the township of Roxton in the county of Hampshire which was part of the ducal seat. Impressed with his brush at the very upper echelon of the aristocracy, however faint the tinge, several in the crowd turned to the older gent to find out what else he could tell them about the ducal family, while a small clutch of women, come out onto the street in response to the commotion, craned to get a closer look at the noblewoman's gown and expensive accouterments.

While Michelle took a quick look about her at the attention the carriage and its occupants were attracting in this part of the city and was overwhelmed, not only by the gathering crowd but also by the commotion coming from within the townhouse, Antonia was oblivious to everything and everyone except the de Crespigny household whom she had come to visit. The two girls and their mother who had rushed out into the street in greeting, brought themselves up short at sight of the Duchess and dropped into low curtseys, as if remembering their manners at the very last moment and just who it was who had come calling, the mother brought to tears to see the Duchess out of her mourning and dressed so very prettily as she remembered her before the old Duke's death.

Antonia brought the stout woman to stand tall and would not let go of her arm when she tried to step away, and with a tremulous smile drew her closer to kiss both her wet cheeks.

This elicited a rumble of approval from the crowd as did the Duchess's greeting of the woman's two oldest daughters who bobbed curtseys and briefly took the gloved hand held out to them, both too tongue-tied and shy to provide anything more than their names and a smile in welcome.

The little party moved inside, Michelle following behind, the Duchess taken upstairs to the warmth of the drawing room where a fire burned in the grate. Coffee and gateaux were ordered from the kitchen which sent the cook and two kitchen maids into a shrieking Gallic panic knowing a duchess had come to call and they rushed about the kitchen grabbing for flour, eggs and sugar and pots to boil water while the housekeeper rattled keys, nervous fingers plying for the right key to open the mahogany hutch that held the best silver coffee pot and porcelain cups and plates.

That the entire household, family and servants alike, spoke exclusively in French only became apparent to Michelle while the various family members were introduced to their illustrious guest. She was so used to speaking in French with her mistress that Michelle sometimes forgot that she now lived in England. She learned that the family's name was de Crespigny and that M'sieur de Crespigny was a prosperous silk merchant with warehouses and weavers in the surrounding streets of Spitalfields; that he had three grown sons from his first marriage who were all married with children of their own: Daniel, Gerrard and Armand were all involved in the family business and thus away from home but would return for nuncheon within the hour, and that his second wife, the woman the Duchess had embraced in the street and who was now sitting beside her on the sofa, had four daughters: Minette who was almost fourteen years of age, Henriette twelve, Louise was ten and then there was the baby of the family Toinette who had turned three just a month ago.

It surprised Michelle that Mme de Crespigny's children were so young because she herself looked much older than the Duchess but Michelle reasoned that Mme must have married late, and she could not be that old because she had a three year old child. It was the three year-old Toinette with her head of gold ringlets that the Duchess took most interest in, voicing her surprise that Mme de Crespigny had not informed her of this latest addition to her family to which Mme replied gently that she had indeed written to Mme la duchesse of her great surprise at being with child at the age of fifty and that she had written again to inform Mme la duchesse at Toinette's arrival but had not expected a reply, after all the Duchess's daughter-in-law had given birth around the same time, to her fourth child, a much longed for daughter. Mme de Crespigny did not need to mention that M'sieur le Duc de Roxton had died within a week of this joyous news.

There followed a moment's awkward silence and then Antonia asked for the reticule. Michelle was slow to respond to the request because she was wondering why all four daughters wore plain gowns when surely if their father was a prosperous silk merchant they could be dressed in any amount of fine embroidered materials. But perhaps this was their at-home wear and the beautiful silks kept for Sunday best and for walks in the parks, if there were such entertainments as parks to promenade in this part of the city.

"Say the word, Mme la duchesse, and I will have Bridgette send you one of her girls," Mme de Crespigny stated primly, gaze firmly fixed on Michelle who had finally woken from her day-dreaming. "I hope you do not spend your hours idle, Michelle Bonnard?"

Michelle colored up and shook her head, startled that Madame knew not only her Christian name but also her family name. She did not have to speculate how because Mme de Crespigny was only too eager to offer her up the information and with a warning.

"Your mother is my second cousin, Michelle Bonnard, as was your predecessor. You would do well to remember the honor done you and your family by the position you occupy in the Roxton household for I have many cousins only too willing to take your place. Good things have been said of you, Michelle Bonnard, but it takes only one bad report for me to see you sent back to St. Germain. Do you understand me, girl?"

Michelle nodded and bobbed a curtsey, Mme de Crespigny appeased, and was surprised when the Duchess squeezed the woman's arm affectionately.

"Gabrielle, will you ever stop looking after me?" Antonia asked with a warm smile which she then directed at the four little girls obediently seated on the sofa opposite, all wide-eyed interest to be in the presence of a real-life duchess who was dressed how they imagined a princess would dress for a ball, such was the richness of embroidery to her gown and the glitter to her shoe-buckles and hair adornments. Antonia placed the contents of the reticule on the low table and said to Gabrielle, "I am sorry I had not counted on Toinette, so I have only four fans and as many hair clasps and pins." She addressed the little girls, "You may choose a fan and a hair ornament each, *mes filles cheries*, and for your Maman I shall send something special tomorrow."

"There is no need, Mme la duchesse," Gabrielle de Crespigny assured her quickly and with a nod to her eldest daughter, signal that Minette was permitted to choose first, she said to Antonia, "You are too generous as always, Mme la duchesse. You never forget a birthday or Christmas and when I think of what you and M'sieur le Duc did for me when I married Bernard, I-I—" She stopped herself and breathed deeply to hold back her tears, turning her attention to her daughters, who contained their immense excitement at receiving such gifts, made all the more special because of who they were from, to remember their manners and curtsey prettily and say thank you sweetly to the Duchess before resuming their seats to inspect their gifts in detail.

It was then that the coffee things arrived and sensing Antonia had not made the journey into Spitalfields merely for a dish of coffee and the pleasure of seeing members of the de Crespigny household, Mme de Crespigny sent the children out with Michelle, to have their morning tea in the downstairs parlor, and with assurances they would be able to see Mme la duchesse off in her carriage.

Alone, the two women sipped their coffee in silence, Gabrielle saying as Antonia put the porcelain cup on its saucer, "How-how is M'sieur le Duc et Mme la duchesse and their—"

"Gabrielle, do you remember when I told you it was fated that Monseigneur and I would spend the rest of our lives together?" Antonia said in a rush.

"Yes, Mme la duchesse. You said—"

"No. Do you remember when—*when* I told you?"

"Why, of course." Gabrielle smiled at the memory. "It was at the Hôtel. I was brushing your hair, readying you for bed, and you told me just like that—as if it was the most natural thing in the world—that you were in love with M'sieur le Duc and that you didn't care in the least who knew it. It was the way you felt and that's all there was to it. You were very determined."

Antonia shrugged a shoulder. "Of course. I was certain of it. So what was there to be hesitant about?"

"To own to a truth: I was never more shocked of anything in my life than when you told me that!"

Antonia laughed and playfully rapt Mme de Crespigny on the knee with her closed fan. "That is a big lie, Gabrielle, because that very night I went to Monseigneur's rooms and gave myself to him and you did not see me for six days!"

This remembrance still had the power to make the older woman blush but she managed to smile and nod. "Well, yes, I will own to being shocked about *that* but at the time my worry for you was far greater than any shock at your actions."

Antonia nodded, saying on a wistful sigh, "All of eighteen and so full of confidence that I was in the right. I never questioned or wavered from that belief ever. I knew I loved him. That was all that mattered."

"It *is* all that matters, Mme la duchesse," Gabrielle de Crespigny assured her.

"I never once felt unsure or worried that perhaps there would not be a happy outcome; even when I was pregnant with Julian before we married. I knew, deep in my heart, that all would work itself out and that Monseigneur and I we would be together forever."

"You had no need to wonder at it, Mme la duchesse."

"I remember that whenever he entered a room my heart it would beat faster." Antonia smiled at her former lady's maid. "It always did that, right up until the end."

Gabrielle nodded and swallowed but could not bring herself to respond.

"I forgot that it did that until very recently..." Antonia frowned. "But I do not remember ever feeling uncomfortable, as if sitting by the fireplace without the screen, so that I blush when it is the last thing in the world I want to do! I cannot help it, Gabrielle. And when he smiles at me from across a room or winks at me... I have the oddest sensation. It is almost as if I am about to faint, but I do not faint. I do not remember having these sensations with Monseigneur. Perhaps there is something the matter with me?"

"You are unwell?" Gabrielle asked hesitantly as Antonia put aside her coffee cup, stood and shook out her petticoats, unsure where the conversation was leading.

"I never once felt unsure or worried and now me I worry all the time!" Antonia replied as if Gabrielle had not spoken. "That cannot be right, can it? I mean, he tells me at every opportunity he loves me so why do I worry?"

Gabrielle watched Antonia pace between the two sofas and unconsciously fan herself. She tried but failed to keep her voice neutral. "He *tells* you, Mme la duchesse?"

"All the time. It is too much! Who is he trying to convince, me or him? No! That is unfair. I believe him. But why does that make me feel uneasy when it should make me so very happy?"

"When-when did he tell you, Mme la duchesse?" Gabrielle asked, reasoning it was better to humor Antonia's delusion that not only could she talk to the dead but the dead replied. Seeing Antonia out of her black had given Gabrielle such hopes that the Duchess was finally putting her mourning aside, but by her conversation it seemed the Duchess was suffering from a deterioration of the mind. It truly frightened Gabrielle and she wondered if the present Duke was aware of his mother's mental decline. For now it was best to keep up the pretense, if only to soothe whatever unfounded fears had taken hold of the Duchess.

"When did he tell me?" Antonia repeated with a frown and felt her face grow hot. "I told you. He tells me all the time. In and out of the bedchamber, which means I cannot dismiss his declarations as mere lust driven ravings." Antonia stopped pacing and leaned over to Gabrielle to say quietly, as if fearing to be overheard, "At least I do not need to worry about the bedchamber anymore. It did worry me but after that first kiss, I knew, and then our first night together..." She straightened and resumed fanning herself. "I cannot describe it but you must believe me when I assure you we are well matched..." She closed her eyes and gave a little shudder. "*Il baise magnifiquement.* He is so virile..." She mentally shook herself from her reverie and giggled, quickly suppressing her mirth behind her fan, but adding with a mischievous smile, "With his clothes on I thought him very handsome, but, Gabrielle, without them he truly is magnificent."

Gabrielle shot up off the sofa, face white as the lace at her elbows. "Mme la duchesse! I do not understand at all what it is you are telling me!"

"I do not know why you are so shocked by my confidences," Antonia grumbled. "Almost twenty years as my maid should have prepared you for any eventuality. Although," she conceded magnanimously, "perhaps not this eventuality." She sat again and spread out her petticoats before holding up her empty cup on its saucer. "I fear I have shocked even myself this time. Another cup of coffee, if you please."

Gabrielle took the cup on its saucer and stood blinking down at the Duchess. "You are not talking about M'sieur le Duc at all, are you, Mme la duchesse?"

"Don't be absurd! Why would I be talking about Monseigneur when he was taken from me three years ago? Where are your wits, Gabrielle? Four daughters and an idle life as a rich man's wife and your mind it has gone counting the sheep!"

"Perhaps I have been counting sheep and fallen asleep, Mme la duchesse, because I feel I am in a dream."

"You not the only one!" Antonia said with asperity and took back her replenished coffee cup and stirred the little silver spoon to dissolve a sugar lump.

"You will please excuse me if I am a little dull-witted, Mme la duchesse, but are you trying to tell me that there is someone— that you and this someone—"

"I have a lover, Gabrielle. There I have said it out loud. It does not make me feel any better about it. To point out fact, I am miserable. He makes me *feel* miserable!"

"Miserable? But did you not say that he told you he loves you? That he only has to smile or wink at you for you to have the oddest feelings? That your heart it beats faster when you see him?"

"So your wits they have not left! Yes, that is what I said, so is it any wonder I am miserable?"

"And as well as these miserable feelings you and he—you and he enjoy making love... And he wants to marry you?" When Antonia nodded bleakly, Gabrielle de Crespigny smiled and squeezed the Duchess's hand. "Oh, Mme la duchesse, have you any idea what this means?"

"If I knew that would I be here bothering you?"

Gabrielle de Crespigny laughed and it was such a carefree laugh that Antonia sat up tall, face ablaze.

"It is not a matter to laugh at, Gabrielle! He is annoying and—and *infuriating* and I will tell you how miserable he has made me because he dares to say to me that he would not think it a bad thing if we were to have a child. Imagine! At my age! And what do I do? I start thinking not how ridiculous that idea is, but that perhaps I would like that very much, when it is not something that will happen. So you see what he has done to me making me have these ludicrous thoughts!"

"You said he was virile."

"Yes."

"And you are still fertile?"

"Yes, but..."

"Bernard was five and sixty and I just turned fifty when we had Toinette. And you are years off that, so it is still possible, yes?"

"But my youngest child is fifteen!"

"Pardon, Mme la duchesse," Gabrielle said quietly. "The last time you were pregnant was only six years ago; it was the strain of Monseigneur's illness that brought on that miscarriage, was it not?"

"Yes. It was very sad. But the birth of Frederick... He means that much more to me because he was born when our child it was due..."

"So it is not within the realms of fantasy to think that a child it is possible, yes?"

"Gabrielle! This is nonsense! We are talking nonsense over our coffee and all because I am being made miserable by a man who is one day a merchant and the next he tells me he has inherited a Scottish title and a castle which he must go and live in because he has responsibilities to his tenants. That is all well and good for him but he cannot expect me to go to Scotland and live in this castle with him. That is the realm of fantasy!"

"But if you loved him you would do just that."

"Loved him? I do not understand why you say *if* I love him?"

"But you do love him."

"That is utter nonsense! I love Monseigneur. I have always loved Monseigneur and always will. No one will ever replace him."

"That does not stop you loving this man."

"His name it is Jonathon—Jonathon Strang."

"You say this Jonathon Strang has made you miserable because you have the oddest feelings for him. Those odd feelings are love, my dearest dear. Don't you see? You are *in love* with this man."

Antonia pouted. "No. I do not see at all!" Yet as soon as she said this she knew it for a lie and when Gabrielle de Crespigny smiled at her in understanding she felt hot tears well up. She was only too willing to be gathered up in the older woman's comforting embrace. "Gabrielle. Oh, Gabrielle, I am so very, very miserable..."

"Of course you are. That is only natural," Gabrielle replied soothingly. "I will tell you about my dearest Bernard. His first wife Elisabeth was the love of his life. They had three sons and when she died he was inconsolable and reconciled himself to being a good father and grandfather, and never remarrying. He said he could never replace Elisabeth, which is true. You will never replace Monseigneur, but you do not want to. And I can never replace Bernard's Elisabeth. I remember the day we met. You were strolling in St. James's Park with Lord and Lady Vallentine and your straw bonnet it blew off and I chased it and Bernard, he caught it and returned it to me. He was at the pond with his sons sailing their little boats... He did not know then that he loved me but he did not forget me from that day. But I knew. Five minutes conversation with him, I knew, Mme la duchesse, that I loved him and would marry him."

She smiled down at Antonia, whose head rested on her shoulder and said with an even broader smile, "I am very sure Bernard never expected to become a father again, and of four girls! He has seven grandchildren by his sons and at sixty-eight he is father to a three year old. *Incroyable.* So unless Jonathon Strang he cannot have children...?"

"He has a nineteen-year-old daughter."

"So! He can breed too. There you are then! You tell me he is more than capable in the bedchamber, so who is not to say that at his age he cannot father another child?"

Antonia sat up at that and dried her eyes with a lace handkerchief. "Gabrielle, there is something I neglected to tell you about M'sieur Strang..."

Antonia's stricken expression caused Gabrielle to go pale. "Yes, Mme la duchesse?" she said softly, silently praying that the Duchess's lover was much younger than Monseigneur who had been old enough to be her father; her Antonia deserved at least that from a second husband.

"You must promise not to be shocked."

Gabrielle nodded. *Mon Dieu*, she thought, *this Jonathon he is just as ancient as M'sieur le Duc.*

Antonia tried to keep her tone neutral, but she could not suppress her dimple or the sparkle in her green eyes. "He... Jonathon... He is just eight years older than Julian."

Gabrielle blinked. Surely she had misheard. But the Duchess just sat there regarding her with an odd little expression, a mixture of embarrassment and smugness hovering about her lovely mouth. And then Gabrielle's eyes went very wide and she exclaimed,

"Mon Dieu! Oh là là! Je suis si étonné, je suis sans mots!"

"Yes, I thought you would be. I hope my priggish son he, too, will be lost for words, which will spare me his thin-nostriled lecture on family morality. Gabrielle, I tell you, it is as well he Julian does not know the half of his mother's wickedness. His nostrils they would never come unstuck!"

And no longer able to suppress her amusement, Antonia giggled and so did Gabrielle, and when a few minutes later the door opened to admit M'sieur de Crespigny come home for nuncheon, it was to find his wife and Mme la Duchesse de Roxton hanging off each other with tears of laughter on their flushed cheeks. He quietly closed over the door again and left them to their moment.

Twenty-four

 $\mathcal{A}$ ntonia arrived home to the news the boys had returned safely and were none the worse for their adventures in evading the militia and that Lady Cavendish awaited her in the Blue drawing room. Antonia went to the book room and had Kitty Cavendish brought to her.

Lady Cavendish took a sweeping look about the room, saw the Duchess warming her hands by the fireplace, and went quickly up to her, her anxiousness making her forget her manners to say without preamble as she rose up from a curtsey, "Tommy and Strang have been taken into custody. Shrewsbury's brutes came back for Tommy once they'd caught up with Strang. Dair Fitzstuart is also answering questions at Shrewsbury's invitation. Something must be done!"

Antonia suppressed her apprehension, picking up on the woman's slip of the tongue. She had never warmed to Kitty Cavendish or her husband. It was nothing to do with the fact they were members of her daughter-in-law's set, indeed Tommy Cavendish was Deborah's cousin which made their predatory natures all the more unacceptable. The couple spent their year, sometimes weeks at a time at the same fine address, hopping from the largesse of one country estate to another, and yet they never reciprocated. And as guests of their extended social network of friends and relations, they ate, drank, gambled and imposed themselves in every way possible on their noble hosts as if they were owed a living.

Antonia may never have voiced her disapproval to her son and daughter-in-law but she had eyes and on too many occasions to mention she had watched Tommy Cavendish gorge himself to the point of bursting and Kitty Cavendish ingratiate herself into the good graces of other guests, as if her husband's next meal and clean bed depended upon it. The couple's championship of Kitty Cavendish's two nieces, the Aubrey twins, as a possible wife for Jonathon had all the hallmarks of their desire to see themselves set up with a permanent address for the season should one of the nieces become Mrs. Strang. Antonia was certain the Cavendishs were well aware Jonathon had inherited an ancient relative's Scottish title and that a remote Scottish castle would not be far enough away for him to escape the avarice of Lord and Lady Cavendish.

Kitty Cavendish glanced about at the vacant wingback chairs and sofa grouped in front of the fireplace expecting to be offered a seat but when Antonia remained standing, she was forced to do likewise, aware that the lack of civility meant the Duchess expected her visit to be of a short duration.

"You say that Lord Shrewsbury's men came back for Lord Cavendish. What do you mean by that, my lady?"

"Your Grace? Came back? Oh! The militia were at our door at dawn demanding to know the whereabouts of Charles Fitzstuart. Naturally we said we did not know."

"Yet your husband he directed them here, for why else would the militia want to search my house?"

Lady Cavendish smiled weakly and Antonia had her answer.

"Tommy thought it best for Strang to deal with them. After all, Charles Fitzstuart is marrying Sarah-Jane and so—"

"Disappointing for you."

"Yes. Yes. It is disappointing. We had such high hopes of Sarah-Jane making a fine match. She could have been Countess of Strathsay one day. Instead she—"

"—followed her heart? Leaving one less house for you and your husband to impose your persons upon. Sarah-Jane, as your niece, would hardly have refused you an invitation to stay as her guest for the entire season, if that was your wish, now would she? But as she and Charles will make their home in Paris and

335

one day the Americas it puts her house, her fortune and her good graces out of your reach."

Kitty Cavendish blinked and baulked and would have offered a weak, almost hesitant and practiced, naïve response, but the hard light in the green eyes that regarded her without sympathy or friendliness was enough for her to realize the Duchess knew her for what she was and could not be duped. She did not like to be outwitted and certainly not by someone she had always regarded as of no more value than a beautiful ornament and wholly resented her for the same reason. She had always believed that the Dowager Duchess of Roxton was who she was precisely because she was a beautiful ornament. She would never have guessed that beneath the beautiful facade there was an acute mind.

"Do you want to know why Strang chose to pursue you, your Grace?" When Antonia continued to stare at her, unmoved, Kitty Cavendish said waspishly, "Because you occupy the house that once belonged to his ancestor Edmund Strang-Leven and which was stolen by the fourth Duke of Roxton when he married Edmund's sister. Not only has the ownership of Crecy Hall been disputed ever since, so has the land on which this house stands. Did you know Roxton has given Strang permission to take over the lease? Strang is also determined to have Crecy Hall returned to him by whatever means necessary."

"And I am that means?" Antonia shrugged a shoulder. "He should have looked into the matter more carefully. I may live in the house but it is not mine to dispose of. Neither is this house. They, like everything else, were left to my eldest son. I am merely his guest. And, if you are correct, I am now M'sieur Strang's guest in this house. You of all people will appreciate the difficult position that puts me in."

"Tommy was at pains to warn Strang that his stratagem would not work, your Grace. Not that he thought you wouldn't be taken in by it, but that the Duke would thwart the outcome."

Antonia smiled thinly. "How fortunate then that I have a son who is always there to watch his mother's back." She shook the little bell that brought a footman. "And while M'sieur Strang was exerting himself to persuade me, your nieces were being sadly neglected by him? It seems your plan was no more successful, my lady." She picked up her neglected Rousseau and sat in her favorite wingchair, not offering Lady Cavendish a seat, indication the interview was at an end. But when the woman did not move, despite the footman at her elbow, Antonia looked up and said with genuine concern, "Do not fret, Lady Cavendish. I am certain Lord Shrewsbury will soon release Lord Cavendish. His part in Charles's treasonous activities must be quite minor indeed, yes?"

Kitty Cavendish bobbed a curtsey. "I wish that were true, your Grace." And would have gone out but in through the book room double doors strode Jonathon Strang and with him was Tommy Cavendish.

"My dearest strawberry dumpling! Here I am unwhipped and unbaked!" Tommy Cavendish announced, taking his wife in his embrace. He whispered a few quick words in her ear and then released her to make the Duchess a sweeping bow. "Mme la duchesse, accept my humble pie thanks for sheltering dear Lady Cavendish while poor Strang and I were being mildly spit-roasted by Lord Shrewsbury. We won't encroach on your hospitality a lozenge longer. Strang tells me you are off to the theater to see a play by that fellow... Sheridan? How delightful. Lady Cavendish and I are already late for a select card party with the lamb and potato Connellys."

"But, Tommy, I thought we were for Dub—"

"Yes, my dear," Tommy Cavendish said through smiling teeth, "to not only cut cards but to cut our losses. The Connellys are indeed in Dublin. Curtsey prettily now and let us be on our way before my beefy brother-in-law changes his mind and turns me into minced meat for pies."

Kitty Cavendish did as she was told, a suspicious glance at Jonathon before being whisked out of the book room by her husband and the double doors closed on their backs by two blank-faced liveried footmen. In the silence, Antonia watched Jonathon who was frowning at the closed doors.

"Did Charles and Sarah-Jane make it safely to their barque?" she asked quietly.

"Yes. Yes," he answered, coming out of his abstraction and smiling down at her. "They'd have sailed by now. The boys here?" When she nodded but did not meet his gaze the frown returned.

"What did Kitty say to upset you?"

"And Dair?" she asked, ignoring his question. "Has Shrewsbury released him too?"

"No. Charles's brother has confessed to his part in the secret correspondence with the American Silas Deane."

"That is a great piece of nonsense!" Antonia said dismissively. "Dair is an officer. He would never betray his regiment least of all his country! I do not believe it and if Shrewsbury does he is not the spymaster he thinks he is. Charles betrayed his country on philosophical grounds, because he is an idealist; that I can stomach. For Dair to do the same would mean betraying his fellow soldiers, and for what? He does not believe in the American cause. He does not share his brother's ideals." She bustled over to ring the little hand bell again. "I will send Julian a note and he will talk sense to Shrewsbury."

Jonathon got to the handbell first and he placed it out of her reach on the carved mantle piece before taking her hand and drawing her to sit with him on the sofa. "Sweetheart, Roxton was there. He was there while we were questioned by Shrewsbury. Uncomfortable and more than a little embarrassing to get a dressing down in front of your son, but better to have him there than as not. Particularly for Dair, who will need all the family support he can get. You see..." Jonathon stopped and swiftly kissed the back of her hand, "My money was on Tommy wanting his slice of the American colonial pie. That he was somehow involved in providing the American patriots with troop numbers and English supply routes, because Tommy would do anything for a guinea if it means a full stomach, soft bedding and a gilded drawing room where he can perch his fat buttocks. But all Tommy's treasonous activities amounted to was blackmailing Charles, and as it turns out, his brother, too."

"But I do not understand why Dair he would do such a thing. Tommy, yes. And Kitty. Those two would rob a grave rather than exert themselves to provide for their own living. But Dair? It is incomprehensible."

"Debts. A great pile of IOUs to the tune of some fifteen thousand pounds."

"He is a gambler? No! This I do not believe! A womanizer.

A risk-taker. But a wastrel?" When Jonathon made no comment she asked with a sniff, "What will happen to him?"

"That's for Shrewsbury and Roxton to sort out with the American Colonial War Committee. I doubt they'll want a fuss because Dair is one of them."

"And the Cavendishs?"

"Ireland and exile. No one will welcome them here. Roxton will see to that."

Antonia looked at her fingers entwined with his and then into his brown eyes. "And has my son also seen to giving you this house we now sit in and Crecy Hall as well? Is that what this is about?"

He shook his head, holding her gaze. "No—I mean, *yes*. Yes, I have leased this house and yes, I had every intention of pressing my ancestor's claim for Crecy Hall but—"

"—but why try to convince my son when you could just marry his mother and as my husband claim the house as yours by right of marriage?" When he hesitated to reply, a flush to his bronzed cheeks, Antonia pulled her hand free and stood, roughly shaking out her petticoats. "If you expect me to believe anything less, you too have grossly underestimated my intellect!"

"No! Yes! It would have been easier, but no, that is not the reason I want to marry you!" Jonathon argued, up off the sofa too and following her down the book lined room to a wrought-iron spiral staircase that mirrored the one in the Roxton library at Treat. "God! You have every right to think me an utter whoreson, but I tell you in all honesty, I gave up the notion of pressing my claim for the dower house the day of the regatta when you came to the pier to see Frederick and me off. You were holding that posy of wild daises given to you by Old Ernest and it was the first time I had seen you out of your black... My God! I just wanted to pick you up and twirl you round and round and shower you with kisses and tell you how much I loved you even then."

He watched her ascend the black iron steps, climb to the first gallery and travel half its length, searching the shelves until she found what she was looking for. He had to step back into the room to watch her fossick amongst the leather tomes of a particular bookcase, pulling a book out here, another there, sliding them back and then finally finding the one she wanted. She opened out a slim, red leather bound journal, flicked through several pages and finding what she wanted, she closed the journal and hugged it to her chest as she descended the black iron steps. She stopped on the third step from the bottom so that she was eye-level with Jonathon who now had a hand to the filigree railing and a booted foot on the bottom step.

She looked into his brown eyes, so troubled and searching and she briefly pressed her lips together, green eyes just as searching. "I do not know whether to believe you or not. My heart it is a very determined organ and it beats too hard when you are near, and it so very much wants to believe what you tell me. And then there is my head, which remembers the promise you made to me in the pavilion."

"I gave you my word I would never do or say anything to intentionally deceive or-or *hurt* you," he said softly, a hand up to her cheek. "And I stand by that, sweetheart. Have-have I hurt you?"

"Perhaps... A little. You should have told me the truth from the beginning instead of me finding out from Kitty Cavendish. I do not know why Julian he did not tell me also!" She opened up the journal at a particular page, removed a folded piece of aged paper and handed it to him. "Here is the fourth Duchess of Roxton's diary for the year 1681. If you read the entry for New Year's you will see she records the death of her brother Edmund. It is very sad because Edmund he had gone skating on the Thames and the ice it broke and he drowned. The ink it is smudged from her tears. What is important for you to read is what she says below this entry."

Jonathon scanned the page of closely scripted female hand-writing and found the Duchess's entry for New Year's Day—25 March 1681 and skimmed what Antonia had just told him and then slowly read the two sentences below this.

"Edmund left Crecy Hall to his sister in his will because he owed the Duke a great deal of money?" Jonathon said in surprise as he closed over the journal.

"And here is Edmund's letter, tucked in the pages of her journal."

Jonathon took the yellowed folded pages but did not open them out because Antonia had put her arms about his neck.

"I have had years to read the books on these shelves. Some are more interesting than others. The fourth Duchess's diaries are the former. As she is your ancestress also, I can direct you to the entries where she talks about her Strang-Leven cousins." She tilted her head to the side, regarding him pensively. "Odd that I did not make the connection earlier. It was the subcontinent and your bronzed skin; much more fascinating, yes?"

She leaned in to kiss him and he let the journal and the letter drop to the steps to take her in his arms. After awhile he asked softly,

"Come to the theater with me?"

"Yes."

He looked into her eyes. "You know what that will mean, don't you?"

"Of course. To be seen in public with you... For us to share a box at the theater... It is very much a declaration. I do not care. It is the truth. We are lovers."

"Roxton will be there. It's opening night."

"Can you think of a better way of opening his eyes?"

"I think his eyes are open wide, sweetheart," Jonathon said with a laugh and from the deep pocket of his frockcoat he removed a flat box covered in worn black velvet. "He said you might want to wear this to Drury Lane."

Antonia did not need to open the box to know what was inside, yet she did, just as a matter of course. Inside nestled on a bed of velvet was the emerald and diamond choker Monseigneur had given her on her eighteenth birthday. Jonathon also handed her a small velvet pouch.

"Bangles, earrings and hair clasps to match."

Antonia merely nodded, too overcome to speak, for surely her son's gesture in returning to her the jewelry she had discarded the night they had argued over the sale of the Hôtel was one of hopeful reconciliation. She pressed the velvet box and pouch back at him, saying quietly,

"Please to put me down. I want to show you something... This is a portrait of my grandmother Augusta, Countess of Strathsay," Antonia told Jonathon when they were standing in the entrance foyer to one side of the broad staircase before a full-length portrait by the painter Allan Ramsay. "She was a great beauty and when she was fifteen she married my grandfather who was a Scottish General and a bastard son of King Charles. It was not a happy marriage and she fell in love with her sister's husband, Lord Ely who was the great love of her life."

"You inherited her eyes and breasts and Charles her coloring. She is most decidedly a beauty," Jonathon agreed and smiled down at Antonia, "but you are far more beautiful."

Antonia stared up at her grandmother with her mane of flame red hair, oblique green eyes and who was draped provocatively in oyster silk dishabille that showed her deep décolletage to best advantage. She nodded with a sigh. "Yes. I did not please her at all," and when Jonathon gave a bark of laughter squeezed his arm, saying, "I am not exaggerating. She did not like me at all. I was very shocked by her immorality. But now that I am older I better understand what her life was like: To be in love with someone she could never marry; to not be able to live openly with that person because it would cause one big scandal. She had scores of lovers when Lord Ely was away at his estate. He wanted her to live with him but she would not leave the city. They were both very stubborn. But I will not take other lovers while you are in Scotland," she added. "I am not like her in that way. And when you return to London for the sitting of Parliament, we can be together here in this house." She turned away from the portrait to stand before him, chin tilted up, a hand to the silky smooth front of his embroidered waistcoat and said resolutely, "I do not care what anyone says and-and I will not enquire about your life in Scotland if you do not wish to tell me. But if you wish to tell me about your wife and your children then I would be pleased to listen—"

"Stop! Stop there!" he demanded. "Have you not been listening to me? Don't you believe me when I tell you I love you? Are you mad, woman?" He pulled her to the broad stairs and then down to sit beside him and took her face between his large hands. "Listen to me, Antonia. If you do not marry me I will not marry anyone. If you want to live in sin with me, then so be it. But we will live in sin together." He kissed her gently and then let her go to hold her hands. "My Scottish peerage demands that I live at my estate for six months of the year. And to do justice to my elevation and my tenants I could not do anything less. I want you to come north with me. I cannot conceive of living there without you. The other six months we will live here, in this house, and yes, I will attend Parliament. But in what capacity, that depends on you. If you do not marry me, I will disclaim my peerage and enter Parliament as the Member for Leven. If you marry me, then I will keep my title and all the pomp and grandeur that goes with it, for you."

"But I do not want you to be anything but Jonathon Strang!" Antonia argued. "Why must you keep this title because of me? If you keep your title then you must marry and have children, an heir, to carry on after you. That is the natural order of things. That is what will be expected of you."

"Sweetheart, my actions have never been dictated to by what others expect of me. Until I fell in love with you I had every expectation of disclaiming my title. Keep the estates, meet my obligations, sit in Parliament, but wear a coronet? I cannot think of a more awkward hat for my merchant head! And I certainly had no intention of remarrying because of it. But I cannot envisage spending my life with anyone but you and you as anything less than a duchess, *my* duchess, and so I will reluctantly don the ermine and accept my ancient relative's elevation."

Antonia blinked at him and before she could ask the question he took from his waistcoat pocket a thin red bracelet of finely plaited cotton threads that was open at both ends. Antonia recognized it as the circlet he had been platting the day the pirate ship tree house and swing had been unveiled and, instinctively, she held out her left wrist. He deftly platted together the open ends so the circlet closed around her wrist and then kissed it saying with a smile,

"It's not diamonds or emeralds but if you want those too, I can easily supply them. But this has far more value to me, and I hope it will for you too. This bracelet is a kavala, a scared Hindu thread that once complete cannot be broken. Nor can the bracelet be removed. The cotton must naturally deteriorate. You are now mine and I am yours." He smiled into her eyes. "Marry me?"

She touched the bracelet. It was far more precious to her than had he given her jewels, and she drew his fingers up to kiss the back of his hand.

"I love you."

"And I you. So marry me. Tomorrow."

"Tomorrow? Why tomorrow?"

"Tomorrow I must travel north."

"You are leaving me *tomorrow*?"

The disbelief in her voice and bleak, astonished expression were oddly comforting.

"I must accompany my ancient relative's coffin north. He will be buried in the family chapel at Leven Castle with all the pomp and circumstance his title demands; though I doubt he will be missed, certainly not by his neglected retainers and tenants. As it so happens, I've been banished to my ancestral pile in Scotland on Shrewsbury's order—the condition for my release for helping Charles evade capture." He flicked her cheek and tried to sound cheerful. "It has turned out rather neatly, all things considered."

"Neatly? But I do not want you to go at all! It is too soon!"

"I must but let me go a happy man. Marry me, tomorrow."

"But there are such things as banns, and arrangements and— Oh! A hundred other ridiculous formalities that my son he will insist upon all in the name of family honor! That is, if he was to give his consent and we don't—"

Jonathon held up a document affixed with the Archbishop of Canterbury's seal. "A gift from your son."

Antonia's green eyes went very wide. "*Parbleu*! No? A-a special license? From *Julian*?"

Jonathon's lean cheeks flushed. "I can only presume it suits his sensibilities to have his mother married to a Scottish nobleman than she the mistress of a merchant. So, marry me tomorrow?"

"But... Even if I were to marry you tomorrow, I could not leave my sons, Frederick, my babies... It is too soon! And I must— I must tell Monseigneur..."

He helped her to stand with a sigh of understanding. "Yes. That is true. I had not thought of that. Yes, you must tell Monseigneur... Then I shall travel north tomorrow after we are married and leave you here with every expectation of returning in the autumn to claim—to claim my autumn duchess."

Antonia pouted. "I shall miss you dreadfully."

"And I shall miss you, sweetheart."

"Maman! Strang! If we don't leave in the next hour we'll miss curtains up!" Henri-Antoine announced from the first landing and came down to meet them. "Roxton's got a box and he and Deb have brought *Grand-père* Martin up from Bath." He looked at Jonathon. "I can't wait for you to meet him. You'll like Martin. He's a good ol' stick, isn't he, Maman?"

"It is not right of you to call your brother's godfather a-a stick, Henri," Antonia admonished her son, suppressing a smile.

"But will Martin like me, Henri?" Jonathon asked with an eyebrow cocked at Antonia.

Lord Henri-Antoine stuck out his bottom lip in thought. "That's hard to say. He was *mon père's* valet for thirty years so that makes him practically a duke."

Jonathon rolled his eyes. "Just what I need," he murmured to himself as he went to change into raiment befitting an opening night, "the living embodiment of Monseigneur to ruin my evening." But he was to be pleasantly surprised when Martin Ellicott made himself known to him at Drury Lane theater.

———⌒∽—⌒∽———

"Isn't this what you predicted, Julian?" Deb Roxton asked her husband as she fanned herself in the ducal box at Drury Lane theater, fixed smile directed out across the crush of theater goers in the stalls to the private boxes that hugged the walls in a semi-circle where powdered and bewigged heads had turned in direction of one box in particular closer the stage and whose occupants were just settling in for the performance.

"A scene? Yes. It can't be helped," replied the Duke, slipping his snuffbox into a pocket of his blue damask and silver thread frockcoat and pretending an interest in a speck of powder on the knee of his black silk breeches. "Let us pray the curtain rises before they fully realize she is here."

"Too late," said Martin Ellicott. "They have not only noticed, but she has obliged them by coming to stand at the railing." The old man smiled and sighed. "How gratifying to finally see her out of her black."

Roxton looked up and straight at a box that was near the stage and there was his mother, resplendent in embroidered gold silk, the emerald and diamond choker about her slim throat, her hair left unpowdered and thus the same luminous color as her petticoats. She had a long gloved hand to the polished brass railing, and was languidly fanning herself and talking over a bare shoulder to a bronzed colossus in a magnificently embroidered emerald-green frockcoat, with matching breeches and an oyster silk waistcoat of which the pockets and buttons had emerald-green and red embroidery. He was stooped to hear her words over the din of loud conversations and laughter echoing off the walls. At Jonathon Strang's shoulder and looking more narrow shouldered than usual because of who he was standing beside, Mr. Gidley Ffolkes in habitual red waistcoat and riband. And on the Dowager Duchess's left, Henri-Antoine, elegant in black velvet, was peering out across the crowd through his quizzing glass, a miniature version of their father and with practice he would also, in time, have his elegance and arrogance in equal measure; and beside him his wife's nephew Jack, beaming from ear to ear and unable to keep his head still at so much color and light. This did bring a smile to the Duke's mouth and he turned away to smile at his wife and grab her gloved hand.

"We shall get through this, Deb. I am determined."

"You must, Julian, for her sake," the Duchess replied with a smile, squeezing his fingers in response.

"For all our sakes," was Martin Ellicott's response and when the Duke looked at him, rather surprised, he added, "He isn't going to go away, is he, my boy? He looks a decent sort of fellow. Has shades of Lucian Vallentine about him, so Deborah tells me."

"Uncle Lucian?" Roxton was horrified to think the man his mother was to marry was being compared to his eccentric muddle-headed uncle. He stared at the Duchess. "Surely not Uncle Lucian?"

"Oh, I surely think so, Julian; all the best bits of him. He is also swooningly handsome."

"*Swooningly* handsome?"

The Duchess and the old man laughed at the rise in the Duke's voice.

"Frederick looks upon him as his best friend and the twins adore him."

"And so does Mme la duchesse," said Martin Ellicott and was surprised when the Duke winced. "Well, she must or she would not be over there in that box seated beside him for all the world to see. At interval I am going over there and if you wish relations between the two of you to mend, you will accompany me."

"I have done my best to start the healing process, *mon parrain*. They will be married by special license tomorrow morning before he heads north to bury the Duke of Kinross. But when I think I put her into the care of that monster Foley... Father must be cursing me from Heaven..."

"You told me Strang dealt out fit punishment."

"He did. But I couldn't leave it there. My mother wasn't the only gently bred female subjected to that cur's terrifying methods. Crippled he may be, but I had to make certain Foley would never reoffend."

"On which remote tussock have you put him, Julian?"

The Duke gave a satisfied huff. "I remember Maman reading to Father from Captain Cook's journal; contains wonderful etchings and charts. I found a chart of the Pacific Ocean, took a stab at a chain of islands and there Foley will rot. One can only hope the natives prefer the taste of their Englishmen excessively fatty."

"Monseigneur would approve."

"Yes, that's what I thought, too." The Duke glanced at his Duchess and then turned to face his godfather, saying with some difficulty, "But I can't help wondering if he will approve of this outcome for her... Martin. The last words he ever spoke to me were about her; that I could not make Maman happy the way she deserves to be happy."

"You can't."

The old man could have punched the Duke in the nose such was his astonishment. He smiled in understanding at his godson, pale eyes full of humor though he kept his face remarkably relaxed.

"You would not have noticed; you're her son. But I am confident Deborah is only too well aware. Mme la duchesse is not only extraordinarily beautiful she is a very sensual creature; she deserves to be loved as a woman. In his inimitable way Monseigneur was letting you know that she had his blessing, and thus your permission, to find someone worthy of satisfying her in every way and with whom she could spend the rest of her long life."

Roxton resettled on his chair, the old man's words making him embarrassingly uncomfortable; nonetheless he accepted the truth in them. He took out his snuffbox, staring out across the light and color of the theater without seeing any of it.

"He's asked permission to have her personal effects from Paris shipped to Leven Castle."

"Naturally, you gave your permission."

There was a pause before the Duke replied to his godfather's statement due in part to a roar that went up amongst the theater goers in the stalls. Roxton thought it in response to the curtain beginning to rise but a large section of the audience had got to its feet and was making elaborate gestures of acknowledgement by bowing and waving their hats up at the row of boxes filling up with England's first families and their relations, one box in particular.

"A brazen fellow has thrown a bunch of flowers up to your mother!" Deb Roxton exclaimed with a laugh, sitting forward on her chair like everyone else. "And Strang caught it. Well done!" She chuckled behind her fan. "How like her to blow kisses to the fellow in thanks!"

The Duke groaned and wiped a hand across his face.

"But will she want reminders of Father strewn about?" he asked in response to his godfather's statement. "I'm surprised he would."

"They won't be reminders to him, will they? He just wants to make her happy. And it will make her happy to have mementoes of your father and of their shared life. It's a very generous and commendable gesture on his part, you must admit."

"Yes. Yes... Martin, I told her they were just things... I said they didn't matter. I was wrong. I've been wrong about so much where she is concerned."

"Yes, you were wrong but it does not mean she won't forgive you. She is your mother. Objects hold powerful, usually happy memories and they are a comfort." Martin Ellicott rummaged in a deep pocket of his velvet frockcoat and produced a small, very shiny from wear, leather ball. "I carry this everywhere, and have

348

done for thirty years. For the past ten years it's been useful to relieve the arthritic pain in my thumbs. But I don't carry it for that reason. I acquired it when your mother first came to stay at the Hôtel, before she married your father. She asked me to play at fetch with her and M'sieur le Duc's dogs. To be truthful, I was horrified at the prospect. But who can deny your mother anything when she smiles? I played at fetch with her and it was such a-a liberating experience for one such as I so bound by ritual and formality. So the ball reminds me that when life offers up a surprise it is best to see it as an opportunity not as an obstacle. It is also there to remind me of what a wonderfully fulfilling life I have had as part of your family. First with your father, mostly because of your mother, and unquestionably as your godfather."

"*Mon parrain*, if not for you..." The Duke's voice trailed, the elaborately tied stock about his throat suddenly uncomfortably tight.

"At interval I will need your arm to lean upon to go visiting, " Martin Ellicott said, dropping the ball back into his pocket.

"I will stay here and hold the keep," the Duchess said cheerfully, sitting back in her chair, a smile across the Duke's square shoulders at the old man. "I will signal my approval with a wave of my fan which will set tongues wagging all along the row, and be vastly entertaining to watch. I also predict visitors very soon after and will shoo them away before you return."

"Deb! This is no laughing matter!" Roxton grumbled. "You know what it means if we go over there."

Behind her fan, the Duchess kissed Roxton's cheek. "Of course, my darling. None better. You're approval means everyone will approve. But I don't care about anyone else. I only care what it will mean to your mother and to you, for both of you to be happy. And I for one couldn't be happier for them. They'll make a wonderful Duke and Duchess of Kinross." She leaned back to look at her husband. "That at least should please you?"

"It does. Very much. She deserves nothing less."

Deb Roxton and Martin Ellicott turned their attention to the stage, for the curtain was rising and the Duke's words were lost in the crescendo of deafening cheers.

No one enjoyed the comedic genius of John Palmer as Joseph Surface and the incomparable performance of William Smith as

Charles Surface more than the Dowager Duchess of Roxton, whose lips, those in the boxes closest hers were astounded to witness, moved in silent synchronicity with the actors, as if reciting the words along with the actors. Sheridan's *School for Scandal* was such an astonishing comedy of manners and so well-received that by the end of the third act, there were few dry eyes in the house from continuous laughter and amazement as to what the characters would say and do next.

Antonia was on the edge of her seat the entire performance and on more than one occasion she turned to share a smile with Jonathon at a particular part in the play they had discussed earlier, in the boat on the lake or in the book room at Hanover Square when Henri-Antoine, Jack and even Gidley Ffolkes had been coerced to act out a scene or two after dinner. The audience was left in no doubts as to the relationship between the two when the India shawl draped across her shoulders slipped and Jonathon was quick to reinstate it, Antonia's hand over his at her shoulder, the smile of thanks up at him and his comment close to her ear looking very much like an illicit kiss, sending necks craning and tongues wagging in direction of the Duke of Roxton's box, the gossips disappointed that the Duke and his godfather were absent, leaving the Duchess in conversation with Lady Hibbert-Baker who came bearing wine and a surfeit of gossip.

"I have heard the most astonishing piece of news," Lady Hibbert-Baker was rattling on, her fan of ostrich plumes waving much too fast across her décolletage. "You will simply die laughing when I tell you! It concerns the Dowager Duchess your mother-in-law and Jonathon Strang—"

"Then it is in all likelihood true," replied Deb Roxton with a sweet smile and looked past Hettie Hibbert-Baker's shoulder, down the length of boxes, to one box in particular. She waved her fan in acknowledgement of her husband's bow in her direction and then inclined her head also.

Stunned, Lady Hibbert-Baker paused in mid wave of her fan, mouth half-cock, then realizing Deb Roxton's attention was elsewhere, and because of something else, a hush, yes, there was a general hush in the theater that was most uncharacteristic, she turned in her chair and followed the Duchess's gaze to where all powdered heads were focused.

The mouche at the corner of her ladyship's mouth began to twitch of its own volition.

The Duke of Roxton was bowing over his mother's outstretched hand. The Duke's elderly godfather came forward and bowed his gray head to the Duchess who, no surprise to anyone, pulled him to her and kissed both his cheeks. She turned a shoulder to introduce him to Jonathon Strang who came to stand beside her. Lord Henri-Antoine and Jack Cavendish scrambled forward to join in the conversation, the Duke inclining his ear to a request from his younger brother and obscuring Lady Hibbert-Baker's view just at the moment Martin Ellicott and Jonathon Strang shook hands. The two youths then moved on to the back of the box in time for her ladyship and everyone else in the theater to bear witness to the most extraordinary sight. The Duke shook Jonathon Strang's hand then gripped his upper arm before kissing his mother on each cheek, and then she—Lady Hibbert-Baker's fan stopped in mid wave—she, the Dowager Duchess of Roxton, tilted her head up to Jonathon Strang who did the most natural thing in the world: he kissed her on the mouth.

"Kiss me again, Jonathon," Antonia murmured, up on tiptoe. "I want everyone to see."

Jonathon's eyes creased with mischief. "That's two hundred guineas you now owe me, Antonia," and before she could protest, took her in his arms and crushed her mouth under his.

Three thunderous cheers and a hip-hip-hooray! shook the theater.

$\mathscr{A}$uthor note

$\mathscr{S}$ir Titus Foley is based in part on the real Eighteenth Century physician Patrick Blair. Blair specialized in treating married women who had mild hysteria and had opted out of their "marital duties". He used the "water treatment" to sadistic effect (see Porter, D. & Porter, R. *Patient's Progress, Doctors and Doctoring in Eighteenth Century England*, 1989, Stanford University Press, California).

Roderigue Hortalez and Company was indeed a Portuguese registered company with its headquarters on the Dutch island of St. Eustatius that smuggled French supplies such as armaments, clothing and other items to the American Colonial Army to aid the revolutionary cause. Pierre-Augustin Caron de Beaumarchais, Silas Deane, Ben Franklin and the Comte de Vergennes all played their parts in helping the Colonial Americans win the War of Independence, France openly entering the war early in 1778.

To be continued

The Roxton Series continues in Book 4, DAIR DEVIL, about Lord Alisdair (Dair) Fitzstuart, heir to the Earldom of Strathsay and Miss Aurora (Rory) Talbot, granddaughter of England's Spymaster General, Edward, Lord Shrewsbury.

CPSIA information can be obtained at www.ICGtesting.com
Printed in the USA
LVOW112105180412

278142LV00001B/233/P